Praise for J.T. Ellison

'Scintillating...

Pub

KT-445-701

'Mystery fiction has a new name to watch.'
John Connolly, *New York Times* bestselling author

'Tennessee has a new dark poet.'
—Julia Spencer-Fleming

'J.T. Ellison's debut novel rocks.'
**Allison Brennann, *New York Times* bestselling author
of *Fear No Evil***

'Creepy thrills from start to finish'
James O. Born, author of *Burn Zone*

'Fast-paced and creepily believable...gritty,
grisly and a great read'
**M.J. Rose, internationally bestselling author of
*The Reincarnationist***

'A turbo-charged thrill ride of a debut'
**Julia Spencer-Fleming, Edgar Award finalist and
author of *All Mortal Flesh***

'Fans of Sandford, Cornwell and Reichs will relish every page.'
J.A. Konrath, author of *Dirty Martini*

'Shocking suspense, compelling characters and fascinating
forensic details'
**—Lisa Gardner, *New York Times* bestselling author of
*Catch Me***

'*A Deeper Darkness* has everything I love in a thriller: stunning
twists and shocks, fascinating forensics and heroines I deeply
cared about. J.T. Ellison is one of the best writers in the game.'
**—Tess Gerritsen, *New York Times* bestselling author of
*The Silent Girl***

J.T. Ellison is a bestselling author based in Nashville, Tennessee. She writes the Taylor Jackson and Samantha Owens series, which have been published in more than twenty countries. Visit her website, www.JTEllison.com, for more information or follow her on Twitter @Thrillerchick.

jt Ellison

EDGE OF BLACK

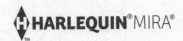
HARLEQUIN®MIRA®

First published in Great Britain 2013
Harlequin MIRA, an imprint of Harlequin (UK) Limited,
Eton House, 18-24 Paradise Road,
Richmond, Surrey, TW9 1SR

© J.T. Ellison 2012

ISBN 978 1 848 45262 6

59-1213

Harlequin's policy is to use papers that are natural, renewable and recyclable products and made from wood grown in sustainable forests. The logging and manufacturing processes conform to the legal environmental regulations of the country of origin.

Printed and bound by
CPI Group (UK) Ltd, Croydon, CR0 4YY

TUESDAY

CHAPTER ONE

Washington, D.C.

A single beam of light illuminated the path ahead, hovering and bobbing against the concrete walls. The tunnel was narrowing, growing tighter across his shoulder, forcing the joints to compress, pushing on his lungs. His breath came fast. He reminded himself to calm down, inhale through his nose. The mask was making it difficult to see, to smell, anything that might give him a sense of where he was. He paused, counted the number of times his limbs had moved forward. Once, twice, three times, twenty. Roger that. Five more evolutions and he'd be in place.

He squeezed forward, slithering like a snake along on his belly, his legs bunching up behind him, his arms forward, the Maglite in his left hand, his right feeling for the way. Slowly. Slowly.

There. He felt the hinge. Turned it gently, sensed the cooler air blowing up into the vent from below. Reached down into his shirt and pulled out the canister. The gloves made his hands clumsy, but he couldn't risk contact. He'd die stuck in this shaft, wedged in above the vent, stinking and rotting until someone finally sought the source of the smell.

No one would think to look for him if he were to go missing.

He had no one. He was alone.

He double-checked his mask, made sure he was breathing clean. All systems go.

The clock in his head ticked away, closing down to the final moments.

Five. Four. Three. Two. One.

Time.

With sure hands, he opened the cylinder and depressed the button. The can discharged, spraying silently into the vent.

One. Two. Three. Four. Five.

Empty.

He shook it lightly, but there was nothing else to release. It was done.

He tucked the cylinder back into his shirt and started to move away. He needed to get out of the shaft and back onto the platform, all while avoiding the cameras.

He could do it. He had faith. He'd done three dry runs, and all went according to plan.

He moved out, reversing the slither, arms bunching, forcing his body backward until the resistance ended and he could move his shoulders and hips without constriction. The pipe grew larger, big enough that he crawled onto his knees, turned and faced the exit. He fed a mirror mount down the shaft. No one was around.

Clear.

He dropped lightly to the ground, took three steps to the right to make sure he didn't accidentally get caught on film, found the metal ladder and began to climb. Higher and higher, his heart lighter and lighter. Success was his.

Below, he felt the first blast of air that indicated a train was coming. The rumbling grew louder, the ladder began to shake. He could have sworn he heard a cough. He paused his climb, held on and breathed into his mask.

This was a better high than you could pay for.

The train passed below him, streaking silver in the dark, rushing the air from the vent toward the platform. He let the rumbling shake his body for a few moments, counting off again, then continued to climb. The exit would be deserted, he'd made sure of that. He had a two-minute window during the shift change to get out.

He set the stopwatch in his head. Two minutes. Mark.

He opened the hatch and climbed onto the deserted platform. Three steps to the right, two steps forward. He'd left his backpack in the trash receptacle. He worked quickly. The mask, canister and gloves went into a sealable plastic bag. His clothes were next: he exchanged the black running suit for jeans and a white cotton T-shirt, pulled on yellow Timberlands. He used hand sanitizer on his arms to eliminate any traces that might have been left behind.

He zippered the bag, tossed it on his shoulder and started walking.

One minute.

The giant disposal catchall was nearly full. As he passed it, he tossed the bag into the depths. He knew they'd be around to empty it in two hours, and all tangible evidence of the crime would disappear into the vast chaos that was the dump.

Now unencumbered, he made better time.

Thirty seconds.

He could hear voices, ahead in the gloom.

Twenty seconds.

He stretched his stride, long legs eating up the pathway.

The elongated shaft of the tunnel appeared before him. His

senses were overloaded—orange and blue and white lights, people milling about, yellow hard hats obscuring peripheral vision, getting ready to go back into the tunnels and hammer for the next several hours. He ducked around a column, reversing direction, and slid into the last of the line with the rest of the workers.

Ten seconds.

The first shift ended with a shrieking whistle, and a subway train arrived, rumbling to a stop on the platform. He followed the crowd into the metal tube, took a seat. The rest of the workers filed in behind him, exhausted after their long overnight.

Time.

The train pulled away, building speed, taking him farther and farther from the scene, away, in the other direction, from the canister's contents.

He was safe.

He risked a small smile. Around him, men's heads nodded in time as the train rushed along the tracks. He started counting forward, and at ninety-eight, the train began to lurch to a stop.

At exactly one hundred, the doors opened, and he stepped out into the brilliant early-morning sunshine.

Only one thing left to do, then he could depart. Leave this cesspool of a city behind.

Glory was his. Glory be. Glory be.

CHAPTER TWO

Washington, D.C.
Dr. Samantha Owens

Dr. Samantha Owens walked into her lecture hall at exactly 7:00 a.m. The students were already arranged in the chairs, some sitting upright, some obviously wilting. Sam placed her notes on the lectern and turned to the class.

"Perk up, buckaroos. I know it's early, and I realize the ice-cream social last night involved more ethanol than frozen coagulants, but we have work to do. Who can tell me what Locard's Exchange Principle is?"

There was quiet laughter, the rustling of paper and laptops opening. Despite the obvious hangovers of many of the students, hands shot up all over the room. Sam called on the closest.

"First row, blue shirt. Go."

The boy didn't hesitate. "Any time you come in contact with an object or a space, you take something away and leave something behind."

"Very good. So when you're thinking in terms of a crime scene?"

The class chanted together, "There are no clean crime scenes."

"Exactly." Sam turned to the whiteboard and wrote Locard's Theory at the top.

Sam was two weeks into her first teaching gig, and loving every minute of it. She missed the hands-on work that came with being a medical examiner, sure, but this was almost like vacation. Eager, happy, excited, sometimes—okay, often—hungover kids, all dying to learn the tricks of the trade so they could rush out and become the latest and greatest forensic investigators. Once the fall semester began, she'd be teaching at Georgetown University, heading up their new forensic pathology program, but in the meantime, her boss, Hilary Stag, the Georgetown University Head of Pathology, had volunteered Sam for the summer science continuing education program, which included a week of guest lecturing at their rival medical school, George Washington.

She'd been back in D.C. for just a month now. The move had gone smoothly, almost too smoothly. Her house in Nashville had sold quickly despite the depressed market, so instead of rushing into another mortgage, she'd decided to rent on N Street in Georgetown, a beautiful three-story Federalist townhouse that had been gutted inside and completely redone in nearly severe modernism, all glass and stainless and open stairwells, with an infinity lap pool in the backyard. It was as opposite from her snug home in Nashville as she could find, and she quickly realized the minimalist aesthetics pleased her. The only pricks of color were from the flowers she brought in and a few Pollock-like paintings on the walls. Everything else was black and white. She'd sold the vast majority of her furniture anyway, keeping just a few things she couldn't bear to part with, including a supple white leather couch and her rolltop writing desk—it had been her grandmother's. She purchased a bed, a small glass table and Eames chairs for the eat-in, and left the rest to chance.

Once the house was set up to her liking, she'd ventured west, into the mountains, to another aesthetically pleasing home nestled in the Savage River State Forest. Alexander Whitfield—Xander—a former first sergeant in the Army Rangers, held a similar outlook: less is most definitely more.

She'd spent a month on the mountain with him, fishing, hiking, sitting in companionable silence in front of his huge fire pit, listening to him play the piano, scratching his gorgeous German shepherd Thor's ears in languorous time with the music. He wrote songs for her, and with each new note, she could feel the pieces of her soul slowly knitting back together. She treaded gingerly but purposefully into the new relationship, finding surprising compatibilities in many areas, intellectually and physically.

Running away from Nashville had been the smartest move she'd ever made.

D.C. greeted her with warm, sunny days, white marble-columned buildings, grassy expanses and gray-blue waters flowing quickly under the majestic bridges. Xander greeted her with himself. The city paled in comparison.

She realized heads were cocked, awaiting her next bit of wisdom. Anytime Xander got into her thoughts, she got distracted. She figured that was a good thing.

With a smile, she apologized, then ran the class through a typical homicide crime scene, from the job of the death investigator to investigation and collection of the body to the postmortem. A few faces pinched when she started with the autopsy slides, but most hung on her every word.

She was nearly to the last slide when a low murmur began in the back of the room.

She turned to see what the issue was. No one was looking

her way. Instead, they were staring at one of the students, a slight blonde who was clearly not paying attention.

"Are my slides boring you?" Sam asked.

The girl didn't look Sam's way. She was slumped in her chair. Sam could immediately see something was wrong, though her first thought was, *Wow, she's completely hungover. Hope she doesn't puke.*

A brunette four rows back raised her hand. "Um, Dr. Owens? I think she's really sick."

The room began to titter. Sam glanced at her teacher's assistant. "Reggie, hit the lights."

The room brightened immediately, and she could see concern written on the students' faces.

She walked up the stairs to the student and started to take inventory.

Her eyes were glassy. She was shivering, a fine tremor that moved on a loop through her body. Her breathing was shallow and labored, and a sheen of sweat glistened across her face. Her lips were even tinged blue.

Respiratory distress. Hypoxia. Fever.

Shit.

"What's your name, sweetie?"

Sam felt terrible that she didn't already know the answer to the question; she'd only learned a few names so far. The students had a month of different classes, and this group had only rotated in a couple of days before. The girl didn't answer, just stared at the floor and coughed a bit.

"Her name is Brooke Wasserstrom. She's in my dorm." The brunette who'd alerted Sam was standing over her friend, worry etched on her face.

Sam put her fingers on the girl's pulse, which was weak and thready. Her skin was terribly warm.

"Was she drinking last night?"

"Yeah, maybe a little bit. She left early—she was going home to spend the night and the Metro closes at midnight. She came back this morning, I saw her come out of Foggy Bottom when I went for coffee."

"Do you know if she has any preexisting conditions? Is she diabetic?"

"Not that I know of. I've never seen her take anything other than, like, Advil. I don't know her that well, she lives on my hall is all."

Brooke's breathing was getting worse. She needed medical attention immediately. And thankfully, there was a hospital less than half a block away. It would be faster to take her there than call EMS to come to the school.

Decision made, Sam stood up and announced, "I need someone to carry her."

Reggie came to her side. "I'll carry her. What's wrong? Do we need to alert the school?"

"We need to get her over to the emergency room. She needs oxygen. We can worry about the school after she's stabilized. Let's go. Kids, class is dismissed."

The students poured forth from the room, quiet and somber. A few were crying, including Brooke's dorm mate, who stood frozen on the steps. Sam reached back and touched her arm.

"You need to come with us. Sorry, what's your name?"

"Elizabeth."

"Elizabeth. I know you're concerned. But we need your information about Brooke's activities over the past few days. So tag along, okay?"

"Yes, Dr. Owens."

Reggie lifted Brooke into his arms. She folded into him, lethargic and coughing, and Sam grew even more concerned. Elizabeth grabbed the girl's backpack.

Sam led the way, out the doors, down the hallway and out

onto the street. The thin wail of sirens rose in the background, and she felt a chill crawl down her spine. Premonition. Déjà vu. Something.

They exited the building on 22nd and crossed the street to the GW Medical Center. Sam walked them directly into the emergency room entrance, and right up to the triage window. There was a lot of activity behind the glass. Sam glanced around and realized the emergency room was full. Strange for this time of day—they usually filled up at night, when people were ill and couldn't see their primary doctor, or got themselves involved in a brawl or had too much to drink or took too many drugs. Ten on a Tuesday morning wasn't exactly peak time.

She pounded on the glass until she got the attention of the harried triage nurse, who flung the glass window open and said, "Have a seat, we'll be with you in a minute."

"I have a hypoxic teenager here in acute respiratory distress. She needs oxygen immediately."

"Jesus, another one?" The nurse slammed the window closed and came around the desk to open the door. "Bring her in."

Another one? What the hell?

They brought Brooke into the triage station. The nurse took one look at her, opened the door to the back and yelled, "Stretcher, oxygen, STAT."

Two seconds later a gurney rolled up to the door. Reggie deposited Brooke on the white sheet. She was looking even worse, her eyes closed, her breath coming in little pants. Sam could hear the laboring breath, wheezing in and out, knew the girl was most likely developing rales, the first steps to pulmonary edema. But without a stethoscope, she couldn't be sure.

This was maddening.

"You may need to intubate her. What do you mean, another one?"

"You're a doctor?"

"Yes."

"We're getting slammed with people with breathing issues this morning. From all over town." The nurse glanced furtively at Reggie and Elizabeth, whose faces were strained with shock. "We don't know the cause yet. You two wait out here. You, Doc, come with me."

Sam narrowed her eyes at the nurse. She turned to Reggie and Elizabeth. "I'll take it from here. You guys don't leave without me, okay?"

"Yes, Dr. Owens," they chimed.

Sam followed the nurse as she pushed Brooke's stretcher back into the bowels of the emergency room. Obviously she was trying to keep from alarming everyone, but it was clear something major was happening. This was an emergency room in crisis.

The nurse slammed an oxygen mask on Brooke's face and shouted, "Dr. Evans, we have another one."

A doctor, bald on top, with a tonsure of curly gray hair circling his skull, approached the stretcher as they pushed.

The nurse ran through the symptom list quickly as the doctor examined Brooke. Brooke's breathing was declining, and as they pulled the stretcher into an open bay, he called for an intubation tray. A team of doctors and nurses leaped into action, swarming the girl, cutting off her clothes, putting the breathing tube down her throat, getting IVs started in both arms, taking blood. Brooke didn't even whimper, or fight. She was just lying there, almost comatose.

Sam stepped back out of the way and let them do their work, but couldn't help noticing that Brooke's clothes were being handled with extreme care, and all the people working on her were in level-two special protective clothing.

Not good.

The doctor, who Sam surmised was a supervisor, turned to her.

"Are you exhibiting symptoms, too?"

"No."

"Name?"

"Dr. Samantha Owens."

"I'm just going to have a quick look." He shone a light in her eyes, felt her pulse. "Ph.D.?"

"Forensic Pathology, thank you very much."

He met her eyes then, a lopsided smile on his face. "Southern girl, too."

"Nashville."

"I've been there. Good barbecue. Any shortness of breath?"

"No. I've got no symptoms. I'm her professor, we were in class at GW when she decompensated."

"Okay. Fever? Cough? Tightness in the chest?"

"No. Nothing. I'm fine. As far as I know, so is everyone in my class except for Brooke. What is going on?"

"We don't know. We're seeing people from across the city who are all presenting in respiratory distress. You stick around, okay? Just in case, here's a mask. We'll do everything we can for her. Might want to get her parents in, if you can."

He turned away, dismissing her. He wasn't telling her everything. Despite his attempt at good humor, she could see the tight lines around the edges of his mouth and eyes. She put on the mask, then allowed the triage nurse to lead her back to the waiting room.

Reggie and Elizabeth had found a corner oasis free of coughing people. Sam took two masks from the nurse and went to the students.

"Put these on."

They both slipped into the masks, eyes wide with fear.

"What's happening, Dr. Owens?"

Long low beeps began, different tones and beats. All of the phones in the room were chiming, including hers. She reached for it, but Reggie beat her. He turned his phone in her direction so she could read the text. It was from Alert DC.

Washington D.C. Metro System is temporarily closed. Tune to your local emergency channels for updates.

Sam felt a massive ripple of unease.

Reggie got another text. "It's up on GW Alert, too. What do you think's happening, Dr. Owens?"

"I don't know. You know how emergency services can be, though. They tend to overreact."

They both knew she was lying.

Sam wanted to comfort them. Reggie was handling himself, but Elizabeth looked like she was about to fall apart. "Okay, kids. Hopefully this is just a false alarm, a mistake, even a drill. We do need to get in touch with Brooke's parents. Reggie, can you call the chancellor's office and let them know what's happening? Elizabeth, how about you get in touch with your RA. Let's see if we can approach from two sides."

Reggie received another text. Then another. With every new ding Sam's heart beat harder.

"It's official. They're sending people with symptoms here, to GW."

Reggie finally started to look worried.

"Why?" Elizabeth asked.

Sam met her eyes. "Because they have the largest mass decontamination unit in D.C."

Decontamination. That was not the word she wanted to

speak right now. Decontamination implied a biological or chemical attack. Which meant only one thing.

Terrorism.

Reggie nodded. "It gets worse. It's happening right below us."

"Below us?"

He looked at her in horror. "They think it started at the Foggy Bottom Metro."

CHAPTER THREE

Foggy Bottom was the Metro stop that fed George Washington University, as well as Georgetown. It was the last D.C. stop on the Blue Line west before it slipped under the Potomac and headed into Virginia. Just a stone's throw away from the Watergate and the Kennedy Center, six blocks from the White House, it was one of the deepest Metro stops in the system, with an escalator that defied gravity and was constantly under repair. You could cut half an hour off your gym workout if you climbed those stairs.

Sam's mind was a blur, but she processed the information quickly. She had training for these types of situations—in the post 9/11 world, all law enforcement in Nashville had been given extensive briefings and training sessions, and as head of the medical examiner's office, she'd been a part of that. Her first inclination was to figure out how to help.

"Stay here," she said to Reggie and Elizabeth.

"Where are you going?"

"To see what I can do to help."

"Dr. Owens, it's not safe."

She turned back to Reggie and Elizabeth. "I'll be very careful. I promise. You follow the instructions you're given by the doctors and nurses here."

She booked it to the exit. The scene had changed dramatically in the fifteen minutes they'd been inside the hospital. Blue and white lights flashed, and she could hear shouting. The street was littered with fire engines, HAZMAT trucks, cops, ambulances and first responders rushing purposefully toward the Metro. Crime scene tape had already gone up around the park and the roads were closed, traffic being diverted away from the scene. Techs in Tyvek suits with SCBA—self-contained breathing apparatuses—streamed down the frozen escalator. A uniform shouted at Sam, gesticulating wildly toward the medical center. The message was clear. Get the hell out of the way.

The only comfort Sam took from the scene was that it was still intact. A suitcase bomb would have eliminated the area.

So not nuclear. Biological or chemical. It could be anything, really. Her mind started into overdrive, and she could swear she was starting to itch. She hoped it was a psychosomatic response.

A first receiver, bundled in Tyvek and nearly unrecognizable as a male aside from his size, stopped her. People dressed similarly were streaming past them into the bowels of the Metro.

"Ma'am, were you in the Metro?"

"No. What's happening? I'm a doctor, with disaster training. Can I help?"

"Not until we can be sure you're okay. Get inside the hospital. You'll be decontaminated and asked to stay for observation."

"I just came from the hospital. I'm fine. I want to help."

The receiver shook his head and pointed toward the doors.

"Too bad. You've exposed yourself. You have to go though the process. Get inside."

Oh, son of a bitch. She shouldn't have gone back out until the scene had cleared. Now she was going to be stuck.

Sam was tempted to disregard him, to surge forward, but the thought was fleeting. She'd just be in the way.

She turned and went back into the hospital. A line was forming on the right side of the emergency room, snaking down the hall. Sam knew immediately what they were doing: triage for the people who were in the Metro, and triage for those who weren't. So whatever substance this was, they were taking precautionary measures for the people who were close to the attack, and a whole different set for those actually exposed to the contaminant.

Another receiver met her, this time a no-nonsense nurse with steel-gray hair and a sharp chin. Sam tried again. "I'm a doctor. What are we dealing with? What kind of toxin?"

The woman shook her head. "We don't know anything just yet, sugar. Now shut up and get in line, you're holding things up."

Nurses. The same everywhere. All dedicated to helping, and no time for bullshit.

Maybe this was just a massive false alarm. She prayed fervently that was the case, but the precautions now being taken—those that she could see, anyway—precluded that.

Sam was passed from hand to hand, interviewed briefly, and when it was clear she hadn't been in the Metro proper, nor was exhibiting any symptoms, was sent to yet another line. People formed in behind her, more excited than scared.

What the hell was going on? Sam wasn't used to being incapacitated like this. She felt just fine. Obviously the exposure was in the Metro. She could see people coming in on stretchers, their clothes rapidly being cut off and disposed of, oxygen applied. One man was intubated, the rest were just moaning. Sam watched the first receivers bathe his body with a solution of soapy water, getting whatever he had been exposed to off his skin.

Words were starting to float around now, from the people coming in off the street.

Respiratory distress. Coughing. Burning eyes. White powder.

Sam's trained mind went to a different place.

Anthrax. Ricin. Sarin.

D.C. was always on extra high alert, just like New York, and all the major cities, really, for any hint of terrorist activity. There was one plus to the situation—they were prepared for nearly anything. But the fallout from any of those kinds of attacks could last for days. She combed her memory—what was today? An anniversary of some sort, with meaning only to those involved?

Her line, the double-check line, she'd dubbed it, took only ten minutes, but it felt like hours. Sam was finally in front of Dr. Evans again.

"Name?"

"Dr. Samantha Owens. We met an hour ago."

He was taken aback for a moment, then nodded. "I remember. Nashville. What are you doing here?"

"I went outside to see if I could help."

"Brilliant, Doctor. We'll need you on the back end of this, not in the middle. Any new symptoms?"

"No. I'm fine."

"Since you've been in the contamination zone you have to stay isolated for the time being. Maybe you could keep an eye on the folks here, let us know if any of them start showing symptoms. The reports are coming in that the people who are sick took the Metro this morning. So we're just being extra cautious with people who were in the area. Can you do that for me? Keep yourself out of any more trouble?"

"Of course. But what should I be looking for outside of respiratory distress? What are we dealing with?"

"We don't know yet. They're in the tunnels doing air-quality tests. HAZMAT is getting positives for an unidentified neurotoxin. Might be a false alarm, but I've seen too many people who aren't looking good to think it's just a mistake. Good news is, while we've got a few critical, none are dead yet. Hang in there. It's going to be a while before we can release you."

"I have HAZMAT training. I can help."

"We're fine right now. We're the best in the country at response. Thanks, though."

She was shuffled off to the right again, taken down a long hallway, then asked to sit on the floor and wait.

This was insane. She should be helping, not sitting in a hallway with a bunch of scared people waiting to see if any of them started coughing.

They couldn't stop her from thinking about the situation, though. She knew exactly what the HAZMAT teams were doing, the tests they'd be running. If there was powder, they'd be able to analyze it on-site. If it was airborne, that was a whole different kind of response.

The logic of the situation started to eat at her. If Foggy Bottom was ground zero, why stage a biological or chemical attack at the Metro station closest to the best decontamination unit in the area? Remorse? Desire to allow innocents to live? Terrorists wouldn't be kind, or allow for convenience. They'd stage as far away from help as they could to maximize the dead, then hit the first responders as they came in, as well.

Come on, Sam. You are really jumping to conclusions now. You don't even know what's happening—it could just as easily be a chem-

ical fire as it could a terrorist attack. The Metro was constantly under repair, and steady work was being made on the new Silver Line to the airport. This was most likely just a local issue that needed extra precautions.

That made her feel better. It wasn't like her to assume: she was a scientist, after all, logic and evidence her closest friends. But it felt different to be involved, not on the outside trying to figure out what was happening. Without a cadaver, a set of sharpened Henckel knives and a dissection tray, she was sometimes lost.

But she'd been involved in plenty of investigations in the past. She couldn't help herself. She let her thoughts distract her. How many victims would there be? If it was a biological or chemical hazard, it could take hours until they knew what they were dealing with. If it was airborne, it could be ten times worse. So many of the airborne toxins took hours to manifest symptoms, and were practically impossible to contain. With this many people already down, perhaps it was something else. Chemical, most likely.

It was rather cruel and unusual punishment that there wasn't a TV in the hallway they could tune to. She figured the media was going absolutely stark raving mad by now.

Her iPad was first generation wireless only, damn it, or else she could be researching exactly what was going on right now. Her phone was just that, a phone, with the ability to dial in and out, and receive texts. She wished she could text Reggie, let him and Elizabeth know she was stuck back here, but she didn't have his number in her phone.

She wished she could call Xander. But he was fishing today, off in the wilderness. She'd never be able to reach him. One of the things that they were both happy about in the relationship was the freedom. Sam wasn't a hoverer, and Xander needed his space. He liked being able to come and go without letting her know his every move, and so did Sam. It was becoming the bedrock of their relationship. But right now, all Sam wanted was to hear his voice, to know that he was okay. To feel his arms around her.

The people near her started talking among themselves, and she listened to the rumors fly.

"It's all over Twitter. They don't know what's going on but they're saying fifteen dead."

"I just heard two dead."

"Twenty-nine bodies."

"No one knows what the deal is."

"Holy shit. They're ordering extra body bags."

Sam felt the blow to her gut. Any casualty would be too many. Two, fifteen, twenty-nine—she hoped to God those numbers weren't just climbing as more cases were reported. If that number was even close to the truth…and with many airborne toxins, instant death was rare. Obviously people had made it out of the Metro; the triage nurse wouldn't have asked her if they hadn't.

Jesus. She just wanted to know what they were dealing with.

Fletcher.

Ah. Why hadn't she thought of it before? Detective Darren Fletcher, her buddy in D.C. homicide. He'd tell her what was going on, if he knew, at least.

She went through her phone until she found his cell number. She hadn't talked to him since she got back to town and started teaching, irrationally hoping he wouldn't be upset with her. She'd worked a case with him before she moved back to D.C., the death of her ex-boyfriend, and the two of them had formed a bond. Fletcher would have liked that bond to go further, but he'd respected the fact that she was with Xander now. Sort of. She hadn't been willing to test that theory yet.

The phone rang and rang and rang, finally going to voice mail. Well, that wasn't good. That meant he was either avoiding her call or too busy to take it. She decided to try one more contact—Dr. Amado Nocek, one of the city's medical examiners. Nocek had offered her a position with the M.E.'s office when she told him she wanted to move to D.C. She appreciated that offer so much, but being an M.E. wasn't what she needed to be doing right now. She was still recovering, still trying to make sense of her life. Her job in Nashville had become an albatross around her neck instead of a joy. She needed to do something that didn't involve day-to-day contact with the dead.

That's why teaching appealed to her. She could talk about her field in a theoretical way, and not be hands-on again until she was ready.

Nocek answered on the first ring. His strangely lilting voice, the result of a European upbringing that drew on both Italian and French, combined with several years in the polyglot accent that made up D.C., calmed her immediately. "Samantha. It is very fine to hear from you this morning. I suppose you are calling to ask the nature of the emergency we find ourselves in, and not developing plans for a small, intimate gathering for dinner at your new house?"

Nocek always did have a way of cutting to the chase.

"You know me too well, Amado. I'm actually sitting outside the decontamination unit at GW. No one's been forthcoming with information."

"I will give you what I myself know. We have been getting reports of a biological contaminant that was released in the Metro. Multiple reports of people being taken ill, all over the city."

"Any idea what the contaminant is?"

"No. People are presenting with respiratory distress, fever and coughing. It could be most anything."

"Casualties?"

"None that are related to this that we are aware of yet, but that will most likely change as the day wears on. We are in an uncertain time at the moment, Samantha. I am well pleased to hear that you are safe."

A stern-looking nurse tapped Sam on the shoulder. "Ma'am. Please turn off your cell phone."

"And you, Amado. I'm sorry, but I'm going to have to go. Will you call me if you can once you find out more?"

"Of course. Be well, my dear."

Sam hung up the phone. The nurse nodded at her, satisfied that the breach was under control, and strode away.

There was a young man sitting next to her. He raised an eyebrow and said, "Well?"

"Nothing concrete," Sam said. She wasn't about to tell a stranger what Nocek had just disclosed. That was just enough information to cause a wild panic.

"Are they going to let us out of here?"

"I hope so. My friend said there have been no confirmed casualties. So that's good news. This may be a false alarm after all. Sometimes in an emergency situation, people who are already sick have issues."

She turned away from him and stared at the floor.

This wasn't how her new life was supposed to begin.

Is it possible to ever really start over? To find yourself after a tragedy? How do you measure the pain you've experienced, and know what is appropriate and what isn't? Sam had lost her husband and her twins in the Nashville floods two and a half years ago. And lost part of herself, too. She'd come to D.C. the shell of a person, one going through the motions of a daily life, a breathing ghost. More loss had led her to Xander, and her path back to the land of the living.

She had to admit she felt a little snake-bit. Nashville, and her life there, had been decimated. She'd run to D.C., and now it, too, was under attack.

She could only hope that the damage would be minimal. To all of them.

CHAPTER FOUR

Another hour passed. Sam was just about to start stamping her feet and demanding answers when the nurse who'd run the initial triage came down the hall.

"Is everyone feeling all right?"

There was a chorus of affirmations.

"You've been cleared to leave. Please come back immediately if you have any unusual symptoms. Use your masks until you get home."

Sam couldn't wait to get out of there. If she'd been stuck much longer, fretting and worrying, she might not be able to control her anxiety. And losing it in a group of strangers wasn't exactly her cup of tea.

They broke off into packs and left the hospital through the emergency room doors. A corridor had been created for their exit, and they were able to leave unmolested. Sam tried to look for the kids but didn't see them. Hopefully, they'd been released much earlier.

The scene had calmed considerably since her preliminary foray outside. The bright summer sun beat down on the asphalt, making waves of heat shimmer in the foreground. News trucks had replaced the first responders, though there were still a few HAZMAT trucks parked at the curb.

Sam turned her phone on the second she was clear of the doors. She had two messages—both from Fletcher.

She played them in order.

"Saw you called, I assume you're wondering about what's going down. Call me back when you get this."

The second was more abrupt. "Where the hell are you, Owens?"

Ah, that was sweet. He was actually worried about her. Fletcher was a good man. A good man, but not her type. They were destined for friendship only.

Sam hiked up to 23rd Street, found a bench and called Fletcher back. He answered on the first ring, obviously annoyed.

"Where have you been?"

"At the hospital, Mom. One of my students got extremely ill and I took her to GW, then got caught in the decontamination fuss. I've been sitting in a hallway for two hours. They made me turn off my phone."

"Are you okay?"

"I'm fine. What's going on? I talked to Amado and he told me—" she glanced around then covered her mouth with her hand "—it's a biological attack."

"We don't know yet. Total clusterfuck. People sick from all corners of town, we can't trace it down, and the entire city is on alert. Homeland Security raised the threat level. They are in a dither."

"That's to be expected. What can I do to help?"

"Nothing." Fletcher sounded horrified at the idea, which hurt Sam's feelings a little.

"I can't just sit here, Fletch."

"You most certainly can. Better yet, get home and stay

there. I have to go, but I'll call you later. Don't interfere, Sam. Just let us do our jobs. It's our town, we know how to handle things."

He hung up, and she felt stung all over again. Dismissed like a civilian. It was her town now, too.

She stowed the phone in her pocket and started the walk home. It would only take fifteen minutes or so on a normal day, but the sidewalks were crowded with people, and the traffic was a snarled nightmare.

As pissed and upset as she was, she reminded herself again that she was no longer involved in the day-to-day operations of law enforcement. And that had been her choice. A choice that until this very moment she thought she was content with. Instead, here she was, a victim again. Caught in an attack, unable to do anything to alter her course. She started itching for some hot water, satisfied the urge with a dollop of antibacterial gel.

At Washington Circle she turned left on Pennsylvania Avenue and followed the throngs of people trying to get out of the city on foot. She'd worn sandals today, thank goodness. Hiking all the way home in heels would have been brutal. It was bright and sunny, warm, but without the summer humidity that usually choked D.C.'s air from May until September. All around her people were talking, worrying, panicking, preening, many on cell phones relaying their close call with... something. They didn't know for sure what. A fever of excitement and nervousness permeated the crowds, overlaid with an overwhelming sense of fear.

Fear of the unknown. Of what could be happening. Of getting home and finding out that someone you know, someone you love, was involved. Was hurt. Or worse.

Sam remembered that awful feeling from 9/11, the hours of uncertainty, the unanswered phone calls, the nightmarish quality of the news reports, almost as if Hollywood had decided to drop a CGI green screen against the Manhattan and D.C. backdrops and shoot a heart-wrenching action sequence. She'd lost several friends that day: two who were in the towers when they fell, one on the plane that crashed into the Pentagon.

Even one casualty was too much.

When she arrived at her house on N Street, it was just after 2:00 p.m. Four hours had passed since Brooke's swan dive in class. Four interminably long hours. She was exhausted. She just wanted to take a long, hot shower, and wait for Xander to get back within cell range.

Sam took the steps to her front door, inserted her key. The door was unlocked.

She thought back, trying to remember if she'd locked it this morning when she left for class. Of course she had. She always locked her doors.

She heard her best friend's voice mentally admonish, "Back out, and call the police."

Sam shook homicide lieutenant Taylor Jackson out of her head. There was a perfectly legitimate reason for her front door to be open. The only problem was the timing. She turned the knob and pushed the door open with her foot.

"Xander?" she called out.

"Sam!" Xander came barreling out of the kitchen. She was struck by how handsome he was, even with worry lines creasing his forehead. His dark eyes locked on hers. He reached her in two long strides and pulled her to his chest.

"Jesus, I've been worried sick. You weren't answering your phone."

She let him hold her, just reveling in the normalcy of it, how warm his skin was beneath his T-shirt, how she could just reach all the way across his tightly muscled back, his scent, woodsy and clean. He'd showered recently; the edges of his dark hair were still damp.

She pulled back.

"What are you doing here?"

He didn't answer, instead kissed her, long and soft, so sweetly that she nearly forgot everything that had happened this morning. Nearly everything.

When he released her, she smiled up at him. He topped her by several inches. He made her feel downright dainty.

"Trying again. Why are you here, Xander? Not that I'm not thrilled to see you, but I thought you were fishing."

He draped an arm across her shoulders, walked her into the kitchen.

"There's tea. It should still be warm. And I did go fishing. My guy never showed, and nothing was biting so I decided to head back to civilization and check my email. I heard about the attack and started down here immediately. I called as soon as I got here. Why didn't you answer your phone?"

Sam reached into her pocket. She opened the phone and saw a blank screen. It must have run out of battery on her walk home.

"Whoops. It's dead."

"That's a seriously cheap-ass phone, lady."

"It's a seriously old phone, and I should probably get a new battery for it. Otherwise, it does its job."

His playful tone changed.

"How bad is it?" He didn't need to say more.

"I don't know yet. Fletcher blew me off and Nocek said there were no casualties yet. It's a biological agent of some kind. What's the news saying?"

"Multiple contradictory accounts. I'm so glad you're home. I was worried about you. Are you…okay?"

Sam knew what he was talking about. Since the flood,

since she lost her family, these kinds of events had a tendency to shake her. Natural disasters—tornadoes, hurricanes, wildfires, floods—fed her anxiety and caused her to relapse into obsessive hand washing. She tried not to sit up nights watching the Weather Channel, but sometimes succumbed. She felt that the only way she could ever move past the fear was through immersion. If you're afraid of spiders, you spend time letting tarantulas crawl on your arm. If you're afraid to fly, you get on airplanes as often as possible.

If you're worried a terrible flood might sweep your life away…

It wasn't necessarily a healthy choice, but it worked for her.

Xander, on the other hand, spent his time avoiding all things that could remind him of his own stormy past. He didn't understand her need to watch, to experience, to relive. To punish herself through others' pain. He'd served multiple tours in Iraq and Afghanistan, seen things she could only imagine in her worst nightmares. He'd lost friends. He'd spent nights under fire, days in armored carriers driving IED-laden roads, weeks on foot in the desert, not knowing if each breath was his last. When he got out of the Army, he went to ground, alone in the woods, cut off from everyone and everything. Until Sam.

They were a perfect fit. Each damaged, each desperate. Each so very alone.

She considered his question. Was she okay? Strangely, she'd only had a few moments today where she wanted to wash. Instead, she'd been slightly jazzed by it all. She took that as an encouraging sign.

"I'm good. I promise. I was worried about you, too. I'm really glad you're here, Xander."

She poured a cup of tea, and they settled in the living room where Xander already had the television on. Every channel was in full-on breaking-news alert. Sam had enough experience with emergency situations to know that half of the information was wrong, and the other half would change fifty times before the end of the day. What they could glean so far wasn't much more than what Sam already knew.

She flipped channels while Xander used her computer to surf the internet, searching for anything he could find. As a former Ranger, he had a different set of contacts than Sam. When the news broke another piece of the story, Xander would confirm or deny based on what his military brethren were saying across their message boards and chat rooms.

By 5:00 p.m. things had boiled down to a set of certainties no one could deny. Someone had released an airborne toxin in the Washington, D.C., Metro. It caused a progressive pulmonary distress. And two people were confirmed dead.

Everything else at this point was just speculation. The tests were being done on the toxin; so far they'd ruled out some of the obvious—the ones that would have created different symptoms. Sarin, ricin. Anthrax was still high on the list of possibles. The words made chills slip through her system.

The problem was, testing took time.

Just the idea of that made her skin crawl.

Sam decided she'd had enough. She went to the kitchen and began making dinner. She'd just unwrapped a head of butter lettuce when her phone rang. She glanced at the caller ID, saw Fletcher's number. She pretended not to notice the uptick in her pulse as she answered.

"Fletch? Everything okay?"

"No. I need you, Sam. I'll be there in five minutes. Meet me out front, we don't have much time."

"Need me for what?" she asked, but he'd already hung up the phone.

She replaced the receiver and put the lettuce back in the refrigerator.

Xander was on the laptop in her office. "Hey," she said. "Anything new?"

"No. Same old shit—speculation and fear mongering. No one has a clue what's going down."

"I have to go. Fletcher just called. He's picking me up in a few minutes."

He rolled back in the chair. "Go where?"

"I don't know. He just said he needed me and to meet him outside."

"Why don't I come with you?"

"I get the sense I may be a while. He sounded totally stressed-out. They might just need some extra hands."

"But there's only two dead."

"Xander, I have no idea what he needs. I would assume it's my services with the sharp end of a scalpel. Come out to the street with me, let's see what's happening. I'm sure he'll tell us when he gets here."

She grabbed her bag and her phone, tossed a light sweater over her shoulders just in case. Xander held her hand as they walked down her front steps to wait for Fletcher. She appreciated that he didn't nag her about running off with another man. He was special, he knew it, and he was comfortable with his place in her world.

They didn't have to wait long, Fletcher arrived with a squeal of tires a moment later. He put the passenger window down.

"Get in, Doc. We gotta go."

She stuck her head in the window. "What's up?"

He shot a glance at Xander, who was leaning in as well, over her shoulder. His face tightened imperceptibly.

"Classified."

"Come on, Fletcher. He has the right to know."

"Sorry. This one comes from above. You can call him later. Now, Sam. I'm not kidding."

She turned back to Xander, who had a frown on his face. "I'll call you as soon as I know anything. Don't worry, okay?" She kissed him lightly, then got in the car before he could protest.

Fletcher slammed the gas and the car leaped from the curb. Sam grabbed the seat belt and jammed it into the lock.

"Jesus, Fletch. What the hell?"

He didn't move his eyes from the road, spoke grimly.

"Congressman Leighton is dead."

CHAPTER FIVE

Sam recognized the congressman's name, but that was all. She told Fletcher that. He glanced over at her and barked a small, humorless laugh.

"You're probably the only one in D.C. who doesn't know everything about him. Peter Leighton is the head of the Armed Services Subcommittee. Four-term congressman from Indiana, Democrat, big-time dove. He's been shooting down the military for years, authoring bills to cut spending, shutting down VA hospitals, the works. But lately, he's had a change of heart. He authored an appropriations bill that will give more funding to the military. It's a massive reversal. He's been under fire."

"Now I've got him. Xander isn't a fan."

"I can't imagine why not," he said drily.

"So what's the story?"

"He collapsed in his office on the Hill about two hours ago. They said he was having trouble breathing. He was dead on the scene but they transported him anyway. Called it at GW half an hour ago."

"And I'm racing with you where, why?"

"Morgue. Nocek wants you to help post him."

"Why me?"

He glanced at her again. "I may have asked if he'd be cool with having you come in."

"I'm flattered. Again, why me?"

"Because something isn't right with the congressman's death. I want to move fast, and I trust you to take an unbiased look. That's all I'm going to say."

"Cloak-and-dagger doesn't suit you, Fletch."

"Just trust me, okay?"

"Was he on the Metro this morning?"

"Undetermined."

"God, you sound just like Xander when he doesn't want to give up information. One word grunts. Come on, Fletch. I can't do my job if you don't give me the facts."

He sighed. "They're still running air-quality tests in the Metro. Nothing is registering. It's not ricin, sarin or anthrax. It made over two hundred people really sick, but only two are confirmed dead. They were on the Metro early this morning, so the thinking is they were exposed directly, soon after the toxin was released. More could die—there are a few in medically induced comas and a couple in critical. We need to find out what the cause was, and fast, so the injured can get proper treatment."

"Shouldn't I be posting the two who died then?"

"Nocek is on it. He and his team finished the two from earlier and have run all the samples to the labs. But Leighton is different."

"Different how?"

"Just...trust me."

They were screaming up Constitution now, heading toward the Capitol. Even in a disaster, the view was stunning. The lights of the city shone brightly on the eerily empty sidewalks. The corners were manned by police in full armor, weapons at the ready. No one was on the streets, an unnerving sight.

She'd never been able to travel so quickly through the city before—Fletcher had his mounted light going, was blowing through the stoplights like they didn't exist. Sam was getting the sense that something much, much bigger was going on than just the death of a congressman.

The morgue was as depressingly bland and old as it had been the last time she'd been forced to visit—to do a secondary autopsy on her former boyfriend, Edward Donovan. Donovan's murder had led her directly to Xander, who had been, at the moment she met him, the police's prime suspect. Things worked out for the best, but she hadn't held a scalpel over dead flesh for three months.

Would she be rusty? Would she be compelled to wash? Would the stillness overwhelm her and make her run away?

She didn't like not knowing how she was going to react. It made her anxious. And her anxiety triggered all kinds of demoralizing, embarrassing tics.

She hadn't been like this before the flood. She had never considered herself a strong woman, that was Taylor's job. But Sam was steady. Reliable. Rational. She saw herself as a skilled forensic pathologist, nothing less, nothing more. She wasn't a people person to start with, had few friends she truly trusted, but now she got to add in a dead husband and a lost family. She'd been systematically pushing people away for two years, and at the moment, their invisible absence stung.

Jesus, Sam. Way to go, feeling sorry for yourself in the middle of someone else's crisis.

She shook her head slightly to dispel the melancholy, and followed Fletcher into the morgue.

A small, young woman with lively green eyes was waiting for them.

"Detective Fletcher? Dr. Owens? I'm Leslie Murphy, death

investigator. Dr. Nocek is waiting for you. The press hasn't arrived yet, but it's only a matter of time."

Sam turned to Fletcher in surprise. "You've managed to keep this quiet?"

He gave her a smug grimace. "I told you it was classified."

Sam shook Leslie's hand. "Let's get me suited up then."

"Right away, ma'am. Follow me."

"Please don't call me ma'am. Sam is fine."

The girl looked back over her shoulder. "I'm Murphy then. My mom's the only one who calls me Leslie."

"Gotcha," Sam said.

The doors opened into the antechamber that led to the autopsy suite, and Sam was pleased by her reaction. She felt relaxed, comfortable. The tension bled from her shoulders.

Home. You're home.

Moments later, gloved and prepped, she entered the nave of her own personal church.

The smells were right. The air, cold and dead, whispering from the vents. The warm musk of blood, the slight meaty scent of open bodies. Metallic notes from the stainless tables and scales, overlaid with the squeaky markers used on the whiteboards. Thin scents of bleach and formalin, worn linoleum, and sweat.

The normal aromas of the autopsy suite, as comforting and natural to her as fresh roses in a vase.

Sam heard Fletcher curse softly under his breath. She caught his gaze and understood immediately.

A small boy lay in full rigor on a table off to the side, against the far wall. Out of the way. Eight, maybe nine years old. A quiet hush went through her, perhaps a prayer, maybe less than that. Her own son hadn't gotten out of his second year; she had no way to compare the real with the might-have-been—the length of bone in the femur, or the shock of dark hair, only slightly mussed. The marble pale flesh of his body, unmarred for the moment.

Nocek caught them staring. "Such a saddening case. He was hit by a car while on his bicycle. He was not wearing the helmet, and as such suffered a traumatic brain injury. They took him off life support last night. We will do a partial autopsy, there is no doubt as to his cause of death."

A partial autopsy—an exterior examination, X-rays, a vitreous fluid sample and blood draw. No cutting. Small mercies.

Sam felt a flash of anger—such a perfect boy, his brain damaged but his organs intact and usable, yet his family had not chosen to allow him to help others through donation. She chided herself for the thought. *Who are you to judge, Sam?*

She turned away from the child, touched Fletcher once on the shoulder in comfort. He had a son, a live one.

"I'm ready. Where is the congressman?"

"He is separated from the rest. Please, follow me."

Nocek led them to a door to the right of the main room. "Let us take a few extra precautions. I would request that you double your masks and wear them at all times. We have set up special ventilation for the room. We are still unsure as to what the situation may be."

Sam washed her hands again, thoroughly, even though she could hardly give the dead man her germs. There were levels of prevention based on the situation at hand. Because of the nature of the investigation, she wanted to be as sterile as possible to ward off any hint of cross-contamination and potential problems down the road. She had to wear special protective gear as well, also just in case. Which was fine, but it got in her way.

Once she was finished and they were all gloved and prepped, they entered what Sam knew to be a decomp suite: every decent-size morgue has a separate room for the decomposed bodies that come in to be posted. For the most part, the natural effluvia of fresh bodies wasn't terribly offensive to the olfactory system, especially once you grew accustomed to the smells. But decomps were a different story. By isolating them, several things occurred: chain of custody remained intact; special precautions could be taken; evidence collected could be kept separate from the rest of the suite. Blowflies could be isolated; they had a pesky tendency to colonize decomposing bodies. Ashes to ashes, dust to dust. But before that could happen, the biological chain of command kicked into high gear. Blowflies and maggots and larvae, oh my. Sam knew several forensic entomologists who lived for decomps.

Sam noticed several desiccated fly husks near the drain, under the table. Hatchlings, with no food to sustain them. Not unusual.

More interesting was the man lying on top of the stainless tray. Mid-fifties, silvery-gray hair, probably five-ten or so, naked, which was where it got interesting: he was as smooth and hairless as the eight-year-old boy on the other side of the door.

Sam circled the body, absorbing details. There were classic marks on his chest where someone had tried to revive him. His flesh seemed doughy and dented easily, which led her right to excessive edema. The cavities of his mouth and nose were red and irritated, his throat slightly ulcerated. Petechial hemorrhaging in his blank, bluish eyes gave her even more bits of the story.

It hadn't been an easy death, that was for sure.

She looked closer at his legs, groin and chest, ran her fingers along his calf. The stubble there was no more perceptible than Sam's was at the end of the day, several hours after she shaved her legs during her morning shower.

The congressman shaved his legs. And everything else, besides. This took manscaping to a whole new level.

"He shaved. His whole body. Thoroughly. Regularly. And practiced. Why?"

Neither man responded, and she started to get a glimmer of why she'd been asked to come in and do the post on the congressman. Discretion was needed. Real discretion.

"What was he into?" she asked.

"We don't know for sure," Fletcher answered. "There's been scuttlebutt about him for years, but really subtle stuff. A couple of the girls in town might have mentioned in passing that he enjoyed trying on their clothes. Primarily their underclothes."

"Seems harmless enough. He wouldn't be the first cross-dresser in the government."

"And a couple of the boys might have mentioned he liked to have a few cameras around while they did their thing."

Sam met Fletcher's eyes. "A bisexual cross-dresser with film? Anyone ever gotten their hands on it?"

"I haven't seen it. And a few of them have said he's gone a bit too far before."

"Too far how?"

"Choke and revive. People being asked to play dead. That sort of thing."

"Sounds like you have more than rumors to go on," Sam said.

"Listen, Doc. This guy is a really big deal. Former dove, now an outspoken proponent for the military, looking for funding from every quarter. Served for years, a decorated veteran. He has a kid in Afghanistan. He had a presidential run in mind. His proclivities get out, it's embarrassing for a whole bunch of people, you know?"

"He's just a study in contradictions."

"Sam…"

"That's fine, I understand. But why all the secrecy around his autopsy?"

"Because of this. A text that came to the congressman's phone. His office reported it about an hour ago."

Fletcher pulled his notebook from his pocket and read the text verbatim.

Dear Congressman Pervert,
You messed with the wrong people.
Today's attack is on you, shithead.

CHAPTER SIX

Washington, D.C.
Alexander Whitfield

Xander didn't like waiting, even though it was something he was accustomed to doing. In the three years since he'd left the service, he'd been marching to the beat of his own drummer. His background made that an easy choice—his parents had been hippies who lived on a commune, and originally named him, in the trippy-dippy fashion of all their friends, Alexander Moonbeam. He'd taken the necessary steps to reclaim a normal name and was now legally Alexander Roth Whitfield. The Third.

And instead of Moonbeam, which his parents still preferred, he went by Xander.

Xander's grandfather was a hearty son of a bitch who ran a television enterprise. Xander's dad had told his father to take the money and shove it, and as such, married Xander's mom, Sunshine, and had two children in quick succession, Xander and his sister Yellow. They moved their burgeoning little family from San Francisco to a mountain farm in Dillon, Colorado, when Xander was a baby. He'd grown up in the woods, homeschooled, self-motivated and a prodigy. His parents were furious when he enlisted instead of attending Julliard. Dedicated pacifists, they didn't know where they'd gone wrong. They wanted a life of pleasure for him, a life without hatred or fear. Instead, he ran headlong in the other direction.

When he was eighteen, he didn't know how to make them understand his point of view. He didn't want to smoke dope and drop acid and find the universal meanings of life in the shiny swirls of colorful trips. He didn't want to grow organically or manufacture hemp linens. He wanted to see the world. He wanted to give back to the land who'd given him the freedom to make that choice. Yellow had been a dutiful daughter, opened a metaphysical shop in Modesto, California, carried her parents' all-natural products. Xander played with guns.

There was something as soothing about disassembling an assault weapon blindfolded as there was in mastering Chopin for him. He knew he was different. Smart, yes, but there was something more. Something he couldn't put his finger on. His commanding officers called it courage, intelligence, instinct. The school psychiatrists called it genius. His parents called him gifted.

He just saw it as a way to distinguish right from wrong, to use his gifts to milk the world of its incredible beauty. Under his fingers, the piano could render 8400 chords, each of which, when combined with another, told a story with infinite possibilities. Bullets did the same thing, if used properly.

He ended up in infantry on purpose. He could have been a pilot, he just didn't feel like dealing with all the extra training. It was more enjoyable to be on the ground than in the air, anyway. More chance for a little one-on-one action, instead of floating above it all. He'd actually started the Apache training once, but pulled out to go to sniper school when a candidate had to drop and a slot unexpectedly opened. He was nineteen at the time with a raging hard-on for the Army. Anything they wanted to teach him, he wanted to learn.

Age tempered his enthusiasm a bit, but only just. Ranger School, Airborne, Sniper, Demolition—anything they could throw at him, he jumped at the chance. It was so different from the world he grew up in, so structured, so formal. There were regulations that he was expected to follow, and he thrived in the environment. Of course, he was a rising star, which meant he was getting respect and extra attention along the way, and that helped things a great deal. If he'd been a grunt and been treated like a grunt, dismissed out of hand by his superiors, he may have felt differently. He recognized that, tried to keep his star from burning too brightly so he could at least maintain some friendships along the way. If he hadn't been an enlisted man, he could have gone pretty damn far.

But he mustered out at First Sergeant and was happy as hell to go. The Army had changed in the years he'd been suckling at her teat, marveling at his toys. A war that he felt was mismanaged, an officer he respected committing the ultimate sin, the constant day-to-day grind that became his life in the desert, fighting for every little thing he could gather up for his men—it turned him sour on the whole enterprise. After the shooting of his friend Perry Fisher, who they'd jokingly called King, it was all over for him. He knew the military would never again have that shine, the excitement that it first held, so he took his gear and his medals and his still-living ass and hurried on home.

Part of him was ashamed, and the other part knew it was for the best. The Army was an ever-evolving beast, and in the intervening years, as he grew from boy to man to warrior under their direction, it had become a different place, a political football. He didn't feel his skills were being put to proper use, nor those of any of his brethren.

Of course, they were all dead now, too. He was the only one left from his tight-knit unit, and he felt the absence of his comrades keenly. When he mustered out, he found a quiet place in the mountains, away from everyone, his family, his friends. He led a monastic life on the land—something his parents could finally get behind.

The Savage River forest was kind to him. He fished and hunted when he needed meat. He brought vegetables and herbs from the ground when he needed flavors. He picked fruit from the trees when he needed something sweet. He watched the breeze wind sinuously through the trees when he needed a distraction, and used the sun and the moon as his guide when he needed to establish time. He was happy alone, felt safer that way. Since he'd been trained to kill, to be able to take a life without a second thought, he felt the need to repent.

The joke among his brethren, what do you feel when you kill a terrorist? Recoil.

And not the kind that meant your stomach was turned.

Repent wasn't the right word. *Recalibrate* was more like it. He was a dangerous man, and he knew it. His mind needed to adjust back to the world where threats didn't linger in the shadows, where he could sleep without his hand on the trigger.

He wasn't quite there yet.

And then Samantha paraded into his life, and turned his world on its ear.

Samantha was more than his lover; she was his savior. He hated the circumstances that brought them together, but he'd fallen in love with her almost immediately, though he hadn't shared that information with her. He hadn't needed to— she'd felt the same pull. A connection, however faint, however strong, had been made in their first meeting. Pheromones, maybe, or their beings acknowledging kindred spirits. Regardless, something about her made his soul sing. He'd had other women—not many, sex was still a sacred act for him, another anomaly he'd developed in spite of his exceptionally liberal upbringing, where sex and nudity were as natural as the sun rising in the east—but enough to know the difference between lust and love. But Sam, beautiful, smart, *good* Sam, was different. He finally understood how his father could abandon his entire life and legacy for a woman.

And with that understanding came another—he'd been on the path to becoming an empty soul, devoid of feeling, of being unable to find the splendor in the world anymore. Sam was more than just the aesthetics. She'd brought him back from the near-dead. He would do anything for her.

Which was the reason, while watching the top of the hourly news update and waiting for Sam to confirm why she'd been rushed away by Fletcher, he felt compelled to reach out to a group of people he was familiar with.

The answers were out there.

And Xander might be able to help find them.

CHAPTER SEVEN

Washington, D.C.
Dr. Samantha Owens

Sam read the text again, then looked up. "Did the congressman see this before he died?"

Fletcher shook his head. "This came in to his official cell number, so an aide holds the phone. There's a ton of incoming calls we have to trace, and texts. The number was blocked, though, so it was probably a burner phone. We can get the details on it, but you know how long that can take."

She did. Paperwork on disposable phones was akin to wandering through the seven circles of hell—doable, but no one in their right mind would choose that path.

"Good luck with that."

"Thanks." Fletcher got quiet for a moment. "In case the text was sent by the suspect, we need to look at this situation with a fresh eye. That the congressman was the real target. So call me if there's anything weird here, okay? You can't imagine the pressure I'm under right now."

"I can imagine, and of course, I'll call as soon as I have something."

With a grateful smile, Fletcher left to start his investigation into the congressman's last hours. Nocek asked if she needed help. She demurred, so he went to deal with the other insanities, and she and Murphy got to work.

Leighton was the third death of the day, that was indisputable. But without more information, doing the post, seeing the other victims, Sam couldn't say conclusively that he was a part of the attack.

So she focused on the task at hand. After her initial examination of the body's exterior, which showed exceptional edema of the head, neck, eyelids, upper and lower extremities, frothy blood coming from the mouth and nose, and a bluish cast to the skin, Murphy did the preliminary dissection, opening Leighton's chest with her scalpel, a wide-legged Y incision. She fed the flesh away from the breastplate and used the shears to snap the ribs, one crunch at a time, until the breastplate came clear and Sam could look into the chest cavity unhindered.

What she saw was unusual, to say the least. More frothy blood, plus all of Leighton's organs swollen beyond proportion, especially his heart, bulging in its pericardial sac, and his lungs, so distended they engulfed the chest cavity and touched at the midpoint. She poked around a bit, trying to get the lay of the land. His spleen was visibly bloated, the liver fatty, and more edema present. She began the dissection. His enlarged heart was otherwise healthy for a man his age, with little cholesterol plaque built up in the arteries, so cardiac arrest wasn't the culprit. She started to work on the block of lungs and quickly realized Leighton was suffering from an underlying disease. His lungs were distended and the air pockets diffusely enlarged, ravaged most certainly from a lifetime of asthma. Bronchiectasis. Which made her wonder—why hadn't he used his inhaler? In a case of fulminant pneumonia, surely the congressman would have been sucking hard on his albuterol. And if that didn't work…

"Hey, Murphy, you have his clothes?"

"Sure." She pulled out the plastic bag and held it up. "What do you need?"

"Look through his pockets for an inhaler. He's asthmatic. Just curious what he was using."

Murphy dug in, but came up empty.

"That's weird. I guess he could have dropped it at his office, right?"

"Sure. In the heat of the moment, absolutely. It's not something we would grab to bring in, either. What are you thinking, Doc?"

"He's had asthma for a long time. He definitely had an attack quite recent to his death. The airways are reddened and swollen inside. His inhaler would have started to make at least a little dent in the swelling in his bronchial tree, but I'm not seeing any evidence of that. Honestly, I'm not seeing anything that indicated he tried to arrest the attack at all."

She went back to the body and looked him over carefully. On a man who had a normal spread of hair on his body, a needle mark could be concealed and missed on the initial examination. On skin as smooth as the congressman's, though, an injection site should show itself easily. She couldn't find one. He was in shape, no extra folds of fat to hide the marks. His thighs were clear, as were his buttocks, arms and stomach.

Interesting.

She thought about how the situation must have gone down. The attack would have started small. Staying calm and not hyperventilating is the key to keeping a mild asthma attack from becoming a major event. The congressman might have breathed into a paper bag, or something equally calming. But that didn't work, so he brought out the defenses—his inhaler, maybe a nebulizer. Perhaps even popped a bit of prednisone, knowing the anti-inflammatory would help. Toxicology would tell what medications he'd taken. A witness would be of help, too, especially since the tox screen wouldn't show the corticosteroid.

When none of the usual treatments worked, he should have called 911 and broken out his EpiPen. Jammed the lifesaving medicine into his thigh and gotten his ass to the hospital.

But he didn't have a mark on him.

But he did have massive pulmonary edema. His lungs were yellowish and heavy, and the fluid in the chest cavity was bloody. Significant airway wall thickening showed evidence of a hyperacute pulmonary attack and fulminant pneumonia.

All signs pointed to a massive asthma attack, of that Sam was sure.

But what had triggered it? Without knowing Leighton's schedule, without knowing if he'd been exposed this morning, she couldn't say for sure that his death was related to the others.

Tracking down Leighton's every move was Fletcher's job. For the meantime, all Sam could do was send the samples to the lab and have them tested, and begin the long wait. But there was something more present in the congressman's system. An irritant, something that caused the blood to froth.

She'd never seen a ricin poisoning up close and personal, but this certainly looked like what she'd read about. But the tests so far had been negative for ricin. That was very strange.

Sam made quick work of the rest of Leighton's organs, dictated her findings to Murphy, then stripped off her gloves and mask and tossed them in the trash. She desperately wanted to wash her hands, and it wasn't just the OCD talking. Posting the congressman had solidified her feeling that there was more than met the eye about the attacks this morning.

She left Murphy behind to close the body and sought out

Dr. Nocek. He was in his office, writing up his findings from the earlier autopsies.

She took a seat across from him and smiled. "Good thing you talked me into getting licensed here in D.C. This is becoming a regular event for us."

"My dear Samantha, I wish that it would be a daily occurrence. Your talents are not wasted teaching our young doctors the skills they need to succeed in pathology, but they could certainly be put to advantageous use with us. It was kind of you to indulge the detective's wish for a completely unbiased postmortem. Perhaps you'd like to rethink your current path and join us?"

Nocek smiled at her. He was an odd man, cadaverously thin, with thick glasses and a long beak of a nose. He was called Lurch behind his back, or The Fly. He did bear an uncanny resemblance to a winged insect. But he was unfailingly kind, intelligent, intuitive and unafraid to ask for help when he felt it was needed. Sam liked him a great deal.

"I'll think about it. How many are ill?"

"At this point, reported illnesses have topped two hundred. But still only the three deaths. If this is a biological agent, it could be several days before we are in the clear on mortality rates. It is entirely possible people have been exposed and are simply not showing symptoms yet."

"I was thinking it could be ricin despite the negative field finding. But it's not textbook, that's for sure. What were your findings on the two dead?"

"Internal bleeding, pulmonary edema and hemorrhage. Perhaps anthrax. Do you recall the case in 2001? Five died, seventeen survived. I worked on two of the victims. The findings had some similarities."

"Similarities, but not exact, right?"

"Yes. I did not witness the external pustules that were apparent in the 2001 cases."

"We won't know until the toxicology comes back, so there's no sense in speculating. But just between us, it looked very much like ricin poisoning to me."

"Detective Fletcher is not going to want to hear you say that."

Sam played with the stress ball Nocek kept on his desk. Squish, roll, squish, roll. "Fletch will live. I will tell you this. The congressman had a massive, acute asthma attack, and that was what killed him. He had pneumonia, too, which didn't look like it was being treated. Until the tests are back on the tissue and blood, I won't know if he inhaled what everyone else did. But it is feasible his death is unrelated to the attack. Just a matter of bad timing."

Nocek steepled his considerably long fingers in front of him.

"Do you believe this is the case?"

"I don't know. Something isn't right. If he was in acute respiratory distress, there were steps he would have taken. He'd been asthmatic for a very long time, surely this wouldn't have been his first pulmonary event. I didn't find any evidence he used an EpiPen. So either things progressed normally and he stupidly forgot his pen today, or..."

"Or?"

She shifted in her seat. "The possibilities are endless. Let's see what Fletch has to say first. Now, why don't you show me the bodies of the other two DOAs."

CHAPTER EIGHT

Washington, D.C.
Detective Darren Fletcher

Detective Darren Fletcher was getting incredibly frustrated. He had been left sitting in the antechamber of Congressman Leighton's stuffy office for over half an hour now. He was about to start banging on the door to the great man's inner sanctum and demand to be seen.

To kill just a bit more time, he checked his phone and saw the new message from the head of his division, Captain Armstrong, who had some semi-interesting news. Fletcher was being assigned to the Joint Terrorism Task Force that was investigating the subway attack. And three different Middle Eastern terror groups had stepped forward to claim responsibility. Fletcher was to report to the JTTF offices as soon as possible to get briefed.

He knew he should be honored, but all he could think about was the other cases he'd been working on that would have to be reassigned. And damn his partner, Lonnie Hart, who was on an island somewhere in the Pacific taking his first vacation in five years. He was still on disability after the shooting three months earlier, and honestly, Fletcher was wondering if he'd ever come back from it.

He didn't like working alone, true, but the JTTF? All of their open cases would be given away. Fletcher wondered if he could fight to keep on one or two of them but knew that was probably wishful thinking.

His phone began to vibrate. Sam. Finally.

"What's up?"

"Leighton's official COD is an asthma attack."

"I didn't know he had asthma."

"You do now. He didn't have his inhaler on him, so if you could ask around and see if they know what he was taking, it would be a help. Save us the time while we wait for a subpoena of his medical records. Have you found out whether he rode the Metro this morning?"

"I don't know yet. They've kept me waiting."

"Well, this is just between us then. All signs are pointing to a ricin-like toxin. It looks and acts like it, but it's not exactly right. It could be some sort of hybrid. I've given the samples to Amado for him to run through their lab, so we won't know anything conclusive until those come back. I'm going to keep hunting to see if I can narrow it down even further. But if you can get a picture of his day, that would help."

"I'm trying. Thanks, Sam. I'll pick you up and get you home in just a bit."

"No hurry. I only had a peek at the other bodies, I'd like to go over them more thoroughly."

She hung up. *Okay. No more Mr. Nice Guy.*

He went back to the intern sitting at the front desk. She was a timorous thing, eyes wide and staring, probably wondering what she was going to do next. Most likely be sent back home to Indiana, if she'd been from Leighton's district. If she were local, she might be reassigned, or be out of luck entirely. When he said, "Excuse me," she jumped a mile.

"Yes, sir?"

"I'm going to have to insist on seeing the chief of staff immediately."

"I'm sorry, sir. They're in a meeting, and they said they weren't to be disturbed. For anyone. He told me that you need to wait outside."

Fletcher gave her his most charming smile. "You go in there and let him know he has one minute to open the doors or I'll kick them in."

Her rabbit eyes grew wide and she made a beeline for the doors. Fletcher didn't wait, he followed right behind her, and when she opened the door, he touched her on the shoulder.

"Thanks. I'll take it from here."

"But, but…" Fletcher left her stammering in the doorway and stepped through into the congressman's office. He didn't make a habit of interrupting meetings—he had no right to do so—but there were exigent circumstances at play.

A thin man with precisely cut brown hair and a pristine gray pin-striped suit was sitting behind the desk, with three people, less well dressed, facing him—two men and a woman. If Fletcher hadn't known the congressman was dead, he would have assumed the man behind the desk held the power. Which, in many ways, he did.

All four were staring at him now, but it was Pinstripe that Fletcher locked on to. His coolly appraising eyes swiveled to Fletcher, to the open door and the desperate intern, then back to Fletcher. Without moving, he said, "That's fine, Becky. We don't need you anymore today. Why don't you head home. Someone will be in touch about tomorrow."

"Yes, sir," she whispered, and beat a hasty retreat, pulling the door closed behind her.

Silence. Fletcher cleared his throat and opened his badge case, flashed them his gold. "Sorry to bother you, but I've been waiting quite a while, and I have other places to be. Detective Darren Fletcher, Metro homicide."

Pinstripe didn't move. "Glenn Temple. I'm the congressman's chief of staff. It is an unfortunate day."

"I'm sorry for your loss," Fletcher said automatically, a phrase he'd uttered too many times.

"Thank you. What can I do for you, Detective?"

"I'm investigating your boss's death. I need to know everything that happened today."

Temple flicked his hand at the three staffers. "Sperry, get the datebook for the detective. Allison, you and David are dismissed. I'll be in touch later."

Fletcher needed to get the upper hand here, and fast. "I'd actually appreciate all of you sticking around. I'm going to have to interview each of you individually."

Three sets of eyes looked to Temple for approval. There was no question who was running this little fiefdom. All of Fletcher's nerves were singing; something was wrong with this picture. It wouldn't have been the first time a group met to practice their stories, making sure they had all the details straight.

"Why don't we start with you, Mr. Temple?"

A pause, just a few breaths, and Temple nodded. "That's fine."

The three underlings stood and melted away, out the door, silent as the grave.

Fletcher helped himself to a seat.

"Mr. Temple, can you give me an idea of what's happening here?"

Temple got up and went to the small wet bar in the corner of the spacious office, dropped a few ice cubes in a glass, poured in a clear amber liquid from a crystal decanter.

"Just some damage control. The congressman has enemies. Drink?"

"Scotch, if you have it." A disarming answer. A by-the-book cop would never drink on duty. It was meant to show Temple Fletcher was a good sport. That this talk was man-to-man. Trust could be built in the strangest ways. And it had been a seriously shit day. He needed a drink.

Fletcher accepted the crystal lowball and took a sip. "Mmm. Macallan 25?"

Temple gave the first hint of a smile. "You know your Scotch."

"Occupational hazard. You say the congressman has enemies. Any of them crazy enough to want to kill him?"

Temple resumed his spot behind his boss's desk. "You think he was murdered?"

"You don't?"

"I don't know what to think. One minute he was fine. The next, he was down on the floor, choking to death."

"You witnessed his collapse?"

"The end of it, yes. He arrived this morning at eight, like he always does. We had the morning staff meeting. He was upbeat, cheery. The vote on the new appropriations bill is tomorrow, and he felt like it was a done deal. The last vote before recess, and trust me, these guys have earned a rest. Without him, without the promises he's made, the deals he's guaranteed, that bill has no chance of passing. I've spent the day trying to shore up our votes, but it's not going to happen. Months of work, down the drain. We're fucked."

Temple tossed back half of his glass.

Fletcher was again reminded of why he hated politics and politicians. Cold-blooded bastards, the lot of them.

"So after staff, we watched the news about the attacks for about ten minutes, then had a few meet and greets, the usual stuff, people in from Indiana who want to bend his ear, get their picture taken. He had five minutes with each of them, then a coffee down in the dining room with Windsor Mann, the head of Ways and Means. He came back to the office a little ruffled, but Mann always pisses him off. They have to pretend to be friends in front of the cameras, but they don't like each other much. He came back to the office, had just hung up his jacket and shut the door for some quiet time when Becky heard a commotion and knocked. He didn't answer so she came and found me. It couldn't have been more than a couple of minutes, but when I got the door open, he was down. He has asthma, I don't know if that's part of the record yet. It looked like he was having a really bad asthma attack. He didn't like to let people know, thought it made him look weak."

"How'd he make it into the service?"

"Oh, this was something he picked up in the first Gulf War. Bunch of them came home with lung damage. His manifested as asthma. Pretty severe, too, and stress didn't help things."

"So you entered the office, saw he was down, and then what?"

"I searched his jacket pocket, thinking I'd get his inhaler, but it wasn't there. Then I saw it on the floor next to him. I picked it up and handed it to him. He could barely hold on to it. We got it in his mouth and I pressed the trigger, but it didn't seem to help. His eyes were rolling into the back of his head, and he was turning blue. He kept an EpiPen in his briefcase, but his briefcase wasn't in the office. I looked everywhere. He'd stopped breathing by that point, so I started CPR and yelled for someone to call nine-one-one."

"Where's the inhaler?"

"I have no idea. The EMTs probably took it." He looked to the ceiling and shut his eyes. "I should have called earlier. If I had…"

"If it makes you feel better, I don't think that would have made a difference. The autopsy has been completed, and the attack was quite severe."

Temple didn't say anything, just maintained his position with his face aimed at the ceiling, like he was trying to hold back tears from spilling down his cheeks.

"Did the congressman take the Metro this morning?"

Temple sniffed once, hard, then faced Fletcher again. "He takes it every morning. Part of his job, he says, to be with the people, be a part of the populace. Of course, he has security on him, and he only rides it one stop, from Eastern Market to Capitol South. You know. Kisses his wife goodbye, hops on the subway. It makes him feel normal, like a regular guy. Joe six-pack, he liked to say. So yes, he was on the subway today."

"Where's his wife now?"

"Gretchen? Flying in from Terre Haute. She'd gone home to get one of their…charities settled. She is devastated."

"I'll need to speak to her as soon as she arrives. And I need to speak to his detail. I'll also need the names of all the supporters who were here this morning."

"I will have the detail get in touch immediately, and the list of people sent to you."

"The detail weren't here, in the office?"

"Not at his time of death. In the building, yes. More than likely. They were scheduled to go out with him at two. The congressman had a meeting this afternoon at the University Club. He was scheduled to speak to the Daughters of the American Revolution, of all things."

Fletcher appreciated the irony—speaking to a group whose membership could trace their lineage to the first attempts of the country to gain their freedom on the day the most important city in the world was attacked by terrorists was rich.

Temple tapped a pencil on the clean desktop. "Do they know what the attack was comprised of? What the agent was?"

"We don't know yet," Fletcher replied. "What about the rest of it?"

Temple glanced at him.

"I don't know what you're talking about."

"I think you do."

He gave Fletcher a pointed look. "Trust me. I don't know."

"Mr. Temple. We're both grown-ups here. I have no intention of using the information to demean or embarrass the congressman's legacy. You saw the text. The language seemed… purposefully inflammatory. Has the congressman been harassed lately?"

He shook his head, finally showing some interest in the situation. No, that wasn't fair. He hadn't been disinterested before. He was under control. Very much under control.

"Peter Leighton is an American patriot. He served his country honorably in the service, came home and decided to continue his selflessness in this thankless job. He is the greatest man I know."

Fletcher sat back in his chair and took a sip of his Scotch. "You know, I've been a cop in D.C. for eighteen years. I've seen a lot of shit. It is not my job to be judge or jury. Your boss had a reputation in the very quiet corners of this town, and you can't expect me to believe that, as his number-one guy, you aren't aware of that."

There it is. Right over the plate.

"No idea what you're talking about."

"Come on. You want to tell me what this is all about? Who might have sent something like this? Who did the congressman piss off?"

Temple swiveled the computer screen around to face Fletcher.

"Who hasn't he pissed off? My God, we get five thousand emails a day, and I'd say a solid ninety percent are upset about something. Take, take, take, blame, blame, blame. That's all these people know."

"Mr. Temple. Please. I'm talking about something a little more private than constituents with a burning desire for a new road."

Temple shook his head but wouldn't meet Fletcher's eye.

"Truly, don't know what you're talking about."

"There are rumors…"

Temple laughed. "This is D.C., Detective. If there isn't a rumor about you, you're doing something wrong."

It was a good story, as far as stories went. Temple looked like a hero, he'd done everything he could think of to save his boss. The interviews with the three other staffers corroborated his story. Either they were all telling the truth, or they had decided on the story before Fletcher got there.

Not a single one was willing to breathe a bad word against their boss.

This was going nowhere, fast.

Fletcher got a crime scene tech to come to the office and take exclusionary fingerprint samples. That took fifteen minutes, and while it was going on, Temple arranged for the service detail who'd been with the congressman this morning to meet them in the office. Fletcher dismissed Temple and talked to them—a man and a woman, Mac and Sally—grizzled old hats who'd been assigned to the congressman for several months. Nothing in the routine this morning was different from any other day. They didn't know where his briefcase was.

Neither were feeling ill. Both were going for stoic, but Fletcher could see they were genuinely distressed over the news.

He pushed them on the rumors, too, but they clammed up. He took their statements, assured them he'd let them know what was happening, and let them leave, feeling vaguely uneasy.

They gave him a list of the people who'd been in the office over the past few days, and this morning. The official congressional photographer would send over the photos from the morning's meet and greet. Otherwise, it seemed there was nothing here.

Someone was lying to him. He just didn't know who. Or why.

CHAPTER NINE

Washington, D.C.
Dr. Samantha Owens

Sam waited for Fletcher in Nocek's office, watching the late-breaking news story that had finally leaked its way into the media. The anchors looked shaken; even though they'd known for at least an hour, the media had kindly waited for the wife to land in D.C. and get to her husband's side before they broke the news.

Congressman Peter Leighton, Democrat from Indiana, was dead, a suspected victim of the morning's attack.

Sam was always amazed at how thorough the media could be when they wanted. Granted, Leighton was a public figure, and as such, packages were built in the event of an untimely death. But considering he was just one of four hundred and thirty-five serving members, there was quite a bit of material that had been collected on him.

The minute the news was out, the attack itself became secondary. Every station was giving their own eulogies of the congressman.

Leighton had been a classic dove for most of his career, using his own service record as an example of why the United States should stay out of foreign domains. He'd flip-flopped about a year prior, started fighting for the troops, for them to get more money, better equipment and better services when they mustered out, damaged and broken. A seismic shift, brought about by the death of his son, Peter Leighton, Junior, a battalion commander in the Army who'd gone to Afghanistan and been decimated by a roadside IED.

Grief changes you. Sam understood that. It mutates your soul, your emotions, your thoughts. Green becomes yellow, the sun disappears from the sky, and your lifelong convictions no longer seem to matter. As she watched the multitude of clips of the congressman defending his change of heart, she understood completely. He hadn't done enough to keep his own child secure and protected, so he'd launched a campaign to keep the remainder of the soldiers on the ground and in the air safe. Too bad he hadn't been fighting for them earlier. It might have meant a different outcome for his own son, not to mention countless others.

At least the media didn't have the text message yet. Once that slipped out, the wolves would circle and all bets would be off. The congressman would stop being lauded and start being blamed.

And maybe he should. If the text was real, authored by the perpetrator behind the attacks, there was something to be discovered in the congressman's very publicly private world.

Sam muted the television. The message was unmistakably clear. What she was trying to ascertain was why, if the attack was directed at him, had so many others been included.

Two hundred sick, some clinging to life. Two other deaths, random, people wholly unrelated to the congressman. She felt bad that their deaths were being overshadowed by the demise of someone more famous.

Even one death is too much.

Planes were flying overhead, the high-pitched roaring whine of the F/A-18s unmistakable. Helicopters chattered. There was talk of shutting down the bridges. There was a curfew in place, yet there were still news stories about chaos and absolute fear reigning in some neighborhoods. There'd even been a couple of reports of looting, down near Anacostia. But the congressman's face was taking up ninety percent of the airtime.

And they still didn't know what had caused the turmoil.

There were hundreds of people working on figuring out what the substance was. She knew that. But it was disturbing that nearly twelve hours after the event, they still had nothing more than speculations to go on.

That told her something unique was happening.

Sam shut the television off and went over her notes again. Fletcher had called to tell her that, yes, the congressman had been on the Metro this morning. But in looking at the maps, he was on the Blue Line, and it had been confirmed that the other two casualties had taken the Orange Line right through Foggy Bottom early this morning.

It made sense that people who were immunosuppressed would have a more severe reaction. The congressman was an asthmatic, so any irritant could trigger an attack. Without the proper medication to arrest the attack, he could very easily die, as he had.

The other two deaths weren't as cut-and-dried. She had notes on them from the initial investigation Fletcher and his team had done when they'd come into the morgue. The only thing they had in common was the fact that they were smokers.

Different parts of the city, different ages, different worlds, all affected by a single event. D.C. was a giant ecosystem, with thousands of moving parts, and each world was unique unto itself. Like species that couldn't intermingle and breed, the people of D.C. found their comfort zones and rarely, if ever, deviated from course. Debutantes hung out with debutantes, jocks with jocks, politicos with politicos, lawyers with lawyers, lobbyists with lobbyists, teachers with teachers. There might be a Sadie Hawkins Day every once in a while, and a debutante would get it on with a politico, but that generally ended up in *The Washingtonian,* disguised as a society wedding, and the aftermath was full of fireworks and lawyers and mistresses and front-page news.

Sam pulled the charts of the two other victims and flipped through the pages. She had nothing better to do.

The first was a forty-year-old woman named Loa Ledbetter. She owned a market research firm on L Street, lived in the Watergate. She rarely used the Metro to go to work—she made off-site calls to clients, so she normally drove—but her car was in the shop.

The second was a nineteen-year-old junior from American University, Marc Conlon. He lived in Falls Church, and took the Metro into town for school daily. He'd switch from the Orange Line to the Red at Metro Center and scoot out to the Tenleytown/AU stop, then take the shuttle bus onto the AU campus. On Tuesdays, he had an 8:00 a.m. history class, so he made sure to get into town extra early, to have a coffee and beat the crowds.

Sam said a little prayer for her own student, Brooke Wasserstrom, who at last check was holding steady in the intensive care unit. Sam hoped that her quick actions meant Brooke had a decent chance of survival, but without knowledge of what they were dealing with, all they could do was treat, and pray.

A congressman, a student and a market researcher.

Three strangers, brought together at the hand of a madman. What had they done to deserve death as a punishment?

Now, Sam, you know that this isn't a healthy line of thinking. Random things happened. There aren't always answers as to why people have to die. Why their number has suddenly come up. They were obviously in the wrong place at the wrong time. She could fully comprehend that. She knew that they weren't connected in any way law enforcement could use their deaths to track their killer. A terrorist attack is a random event.

Random. Chosen without method or conscious decision.

She hadn't chosen for her family to die. That had been random, too.

She shook them away, the voices of her dead, and refocused.

A random act.

Then why did someone send a text to Congressman Leighton blaming the morning's events on him?

The only real evidence they had was the text. It could be the key. Leighton could be the key.

Not Dr. Loa Ledbetter, a small brilliant redheaded beauty with a gaping slit in her chest, nor Marc Conlon, too young to even have grown fully into his bones, his sagittal suture not entirely fused.

Quit personalizing, Sam.

What Sam was interested in was why those three, out of all the people exposed and the two hundred exhibiting symptoms, were the only ones who died.

Ledbetter was dead on arrival at GW, after being found collapsed on the floor of the ladies' room at her office by one of her staffers.

Conlon died in an ambulance on the way to the hospital. He'd gone into cardiac arrest at the top of the stairs of the Tenleytown Metro.

Neither had a history of lung disease; that was reserved for the congressman. Neither exhibited signs of illness, their initial blood work had been normal, and neither had a history of ill health.

Their families could give more information. Sam was itching to talk to them.

But this wasn't her investigation. She'd been brought in to do a task, used for her discretion and talent, not to run off trying to explain the unexplainable.

Except she knew every puzzle had a solution.

Someone wanted Leighton to feel responsible, yes, but dead? Perhaps that was just chance. Perhaps that was a fluke. And there was absolutely nothing that said the text-sender was the same person who'd indiscriminately put a foreign substance into the air ducts at the Foggy Bottom Metro and made so many people ill. It could just be a pissed-off constituent who wrongly blamed the congressman for a completely random event.

There she was, back to the arbitrary again.

Fletcher had brought her into this investigation when he asked her to post Leighton. He wasn't dumb; he knew she'd press for more information, for a chance to help. She wasn't constricted by the rule of law here. She was a private citizen. She'd sworn a different kind of oath, one that she believed in, one that bound her to care for the sick, to have special obligations to the public she served. She could do whatever she chose, so long as she worked within the bounds of her ethics and didn't break the law.

She was starting to feel a bit tingly.

She debated for exactly ten seconds before writing down the addresses of the other victims, folding the paper into halves, then quarters, and stashing it in the pocket of her trousers.

It was damn good timing, too, because she'd barely raised

her palm from the linen when Dr. Nocek came into the room, followed by Fletcher.

"You ready, Doc?" Fletcher asked. He looked worried and rumpled and tired. His beard was just starting to make its appearance, and lent him a vaguely menacing air. Next to the taller, more collected Nocek, he looked a bit like a brawl just waiting to happen.

Sam gathered her bag and sweater. "I'm ready. How are things on the Hill?"

"Fucked."

That's all she got. Nocek raised an eyebrow in her direction, and she responded by giving him a warm hug. "I'll see you soon. We'll have dinner."

"I would like that very much," he said, and she sensed the sadness in him. Nocek was a widower, not fully used to going home alone in the evenings. On a day like today, after all the hoopla, the fear and adrenaline, having only ghosts to talk to could be hard.

She squeezed his arm and said, "Call me if you need anything," then followed a glowering Fletcher from the room.

The longest day she'd had since she left Nashville was finally drawing to a close.

CHAPTER TEN

The streets were still eerily deserted, the dark skies inter-rupted by the scream of jets. Fletcher was silent until they hit M Street. Sam knew better than to try and drag information out of him; he'd share when he was ready. They got stuck at the light at Wisconsin, and he finally started talking.

"Leighton's chief of staff is giving me the runaround," he grumbled.

Sam smiled. "Isn't that his job?"

Fletcher glanced at her, saw the amusement etched on her face. It provoked a smile of his own, and he relaxed a bit.

"Yeah, I suppose it is. Fingerprints on the inhaler belong to him. That matches his statement that when he came into the office and saw the congressman down, he retrieved the inhaler and gave it to his boss."

"Okay. So where's the issue?"

He drummed his fingers on the steering wheel, then ran his hands through his hair. "I don't know. I'm tired as hell. I'm getting put on the Joint Terrorism Task Force."

"That's good, right? You'll be able to see this through to the end."

"Maybe. We'll see. They might have me running around town with my dick in my hand."

She cleared her throat, trying to hide the laugh.

"Sorry, Sam. That was crude of me."

"You're fine, Fletch. The image was priceless."

He laughed with her then, and the light turned. He took a right, then a left, and she was at her door a moment later. There was a pause, awkward and three beats too long. He looked like he wanted to say something important, but refrained. Instead, he shook it off and said, "Get some sleep. You did good today."

"Thanks, Fletch. You, too. Call me if you need anything else, okay? And if they get the results back on the toxin, let me know."

"Will do. Last round of calls got it down to two or three, with ricin still leading the pack."

"If that's true, we're damn lucky there are only three people dead."

"You said it, sister."

He watched her go up the stairs, waited until the door was unlocked to drive away.

She caught the blue glow of the clock on the microwave. It was nearly two in the morning.

Exhaustion suddenly paraded through her body, and she sagged a bit. She wanted a shower and bed. She took the stairs carefully, quietly.

She found Xander crashed out cold on top of the covers. Just the sight of him caused a little thrum in her stomach. She stopped in the doorway and watched him, marveling at the fact that he belonged to her.

With a soldier's unerring ability to sense a threat, he opened his eyes, and she saw he already had one hand tucked under his pillow, where she knew he kept a loaded weapon. Only one of many stashed throughout the house.

"It's me," she whispered. "Go back to sleep."

He rolled up in one smooth motion, both hands free.

"I'm glad you're home. We need to talk."

He gave her fifteen minutes to S-cubed—military jargon for shit, shower and shave—and met her in the kitchen with a fresh pot of coffee and her laptop glowing on the table. She took one look at him and went to the liquor cabinet, fetched a bottle of Lagavulin. She splashed some in both their cups, then tucked her damp hair behind her ears and settled in, recognizing Xander in full operational mode. He might as well have had his uniform on and a rifle strapped to his chest.

Loaded for bear.

He sat across from her, took a deep drink from his cup. Xander made seriously good tea, but he was a first-class coffee maker. A connoisseur. Sam was amused when the first thing he did was buy her a Bunn, claiming it was one of the finest coffeemakers in the world. She found that ironic, considering he often made his coffee by throwing the grounds in a pan of water and heating it over the fire. He took personal affront at Starbucks and the like, instead preferred to grind his own beans, which he imported from a friend in Colombia. She wasn't entirely sure that was legal, but she could hardly complain—the coffee it made was out of this world.

"There's a message from GW on the answering machine. I heard them leave it. School's closed for the rest of the week."

"Not surprising. I assume they are going to have people combing that Metro stop and the surrounds for a few days to make sure things are safe."

They sipped their coffee. Finally, Xander set down his cup.

"Aren't you going to ask?"

She stared into his eyes, best described as a deep chocolate-espresso—eyes that were so like the dark, intense brews he favored—and sighed.

"Fine. You were here in D.C. at least an hour before you should have been if you'd heard about the attacks on the news. Which means you fibbed to me this morning about your fishing date gone wrong."

He smirked. "I didn't fib. My guy didn't show, and I did go to the café to check things out."

She knew the café he mentioned was the Mountain City Coffeehouse in Frostburg, Maryland—the closest internet café to Xander's cabin that had decent food and coffee. She had to admit, it was a quaint, charming place, perfect for him to stay under the radar. He liked the window by the fireplace; he was able to see the rest of the room, the entrance and exits. Once a soldier, always a soldier. The cabin didn't have internet access, so Xander made it a routine to head to Frostburg a couple of times a month to check his mail, set up his appointments as a fishing guide, and generally check up on the world. She was tempted to buy him an iPad so he could save himself the trip, but she knew it was more than that. He shed his humanity in the woods—like his daily piano practice, the bimonthly sojourns were his way of keeping himself engaged. He didn't want more than that, and his psyche couldn't stand less. Without some sort of socialization, he might truly get lost.

Then he dropped his bomb.

"But that was all yesterday."

All sorts of words rushed to mind, but all she managed was, "What?"

He flipped the laptop around so it was facing her.

"See this?"

She looked at the screen. It was a message board of some kind. "What's this?"

"One of the groups I sometimes look in on. It's comprised of people…like me."

He rose to fill his cup again, leaving her to wonder exactly what that meant. She wasn't able to focus properly.

"Soldiers?"

"Some. Some want to be. Some could have been, but chose a different path."

Sam felt the edge begin, the panic, like an annoying little mosquito buzzing around her head. She pulled her hair back into a chignon, stuck a chopstick through the knot to hold it in place. She closed her eyes for a moment and took a deep breath. In four counts, hold four, out four, wait four. Then, the urge to wash her hands dispatched, she addressed her lover.

"Xander, honey. It's late. I've been up for twenty hours, been in the middle of a terrorist attack, did an autopsy on a congressman, and have my own little anxiety disorder brewing. Would you mind cutting to the chase?"

"Survivalists, Sam. I don't think this was a terror attack. I think it was one of our own."

CHAPTER ELEVEN

Sam's expression moved from confusion to incredulity in a matter of seconds.

"You've got to be kidding. Are you talking like…what, a militia?"

"No. Well, sure, some of them. It's like any group of people, there're bad seeds mixed in with the good and innocent. There are militias spread all across the country, homegrown groups who like to think they're the law, parade around in uniforms, ragtag batches of locals who spew nonsense and are basically harmless. But there are groups who are dead serious, people you wouldn't want to cross. The government keeps a damn close eye on them. And some of them are idiots, people who are just wrong in the head and can't be fixed. Skinheads, those kinds of yahoos."

"Ruby Ridge?"

"Right. But the people I'm talking about—no, they're not militia. Just concerned private citizens who have shared their knowledge of survival to help like-minded individuals prepare in case there's a catastrophic event. Anything from a nuclear bomb to economic collapse to a tornado."

She noticed he didn't say flood, though that would certainly qualify.

"They're good people, just trying to figure out where we're headed, and what to do in case something awful happens."

Sam raised an eyebrow. Sometimes she forgot that they came from very, very different worlds. She was a debutante from Nashville, a good little Southern girl, raised on manners and money and all things genteel, and he was a soldier who'd been raised by hippies, seen too much and had a healthy mistrust of the government.

He must have caught her thought, because he continued. "Okay, this isn't something that you and I have talked a lot about. It's hard to understand, but there are people out there who think things are going to hell in a handbasket, and are trying to make preparations in case it does. They're harmless, and smart. They're like pioneers, able to grow food and build shelter and live off the land and, most importantly, defend themselves if it's needed."

"Like you."

He smiled.

"Like me. Many of them are ex-military, of all generations. You know many of us don't fit back into the world anymore, Sam. What we've seen, what we've done, civilians can't necessarily comprehend. It's only natural that some of us fall back on our training, and want to be prepared. Just in case, you know? When, or if, the shit hits the fan, you're going to want us on your side, if you get my drift."

"I follow."

"Okay. So this one group that I check in on from time to time lit up last night. Like they knew something was about to go down. Chatter."

"And the feds didn't see it?"

"Trust me, there are no feds in this group. It is very private."

"There's no privacy online. You've told me that a million times."

"And that's true. But even if they do know about it, they can't get in."

"My God, Xander, if these friends of yours were talking about an imminent attack, why didn't you do anything? Say anything?"

She'd said the wrong thing. He closed up tight as a drum. Slammed the laptop closed and stalked from the room. He went to the bedroom, started gathering his things.

She followed. "Xander, I'm sorry. I didn't mean it like that. This isn't your fault. None of it is your fault."

He kept his back turned. "You don't get it. I'm not mad at you, I'm mad at myself. I *should* have said something. Maybe if I had, it wouldn't have happened. Instead, I couldn't sleep, and finally ended up leaving Thor with Bryan at the Forest Ranger station and heading down to the city. I must have just missed you this morning, but by then it was too late. The attack had already occurred."

She took the bag and his semi-folded shirt from his hands and set them gently on the bed.

"Hey. I'm sorry. I'm exhausted, and that came out wrong."

He was silent for a moment, then shrugged. "Accepted. There was nothing specific anyway, just a couple of guys talking about this dude they knew who had recently joined up, and was flapping his gums. It just felt…wrong to me."

"All right. So let's call Fletcher and let him know."

"It's too late."

"It's not. He can get a subpoena, go after their records—"

"Seriously, it's too late. The site's dark."

"Dark?"

"Gone. The owners took it down. It's like it never existed."

Sam wasn't a computer expert, but she knew that it was

virtually impossible to get rid of every footprint on the internet. Caches existed of material. It could be accessed. Someone talented enough could get in there and find it. She told Xander that. He shook his head.

"You don't understand. The group doesn't exist. The site *doesn't exist*. It was a closed portal on another site's network, accessible only to certain people who knew certain ways to get into it, and then had the proper passwords. They've erased everything."

He sat on the edge of the bed, looking despondent.

"You know who they are, though, don't you?"

He was quiet for a moment.

"I know their internet handles. I've been looking for them since you left. I've trolled every site I can think of, and a few that I had no idea existed. They've gone gray."

"What's that mean?"

"They're hiding in plain sight, where no one will be able to find them until this thing is over. They'll lay low and wait until the time is right to resurface. They can't take the chance that they'll be strung up in this mess."

Sam's pulse increased. "Until this is over…you mean he's not through? Whoever did the Metro attack?"

"Not by a long shot."

"Xander. There's no choice here. We have to tell Fletcher. Right now. He's been added to the Joint Terrorism Task Force. He'll know what to do."

His answer was very pointed. "*I* know what to do."

"You just said you've been searching for them all afternoon with no luck. Let Fletch and the JTTF take it from here. This is too much for just you. You're brilliant and talented and, given the right amount of time, I have no doubt you could find them. But, Xander, people are dead. More may die. It's bigger than you, or me, or a group of like-minded individuals on the internet. We need every available resource on this. If they know who this is, or what he might do next, they must be found."

"Fletcher won't find them. He has no idea what he's up against."

Sam knelt before him, took his face in her hands.

"We have to let him try. Okay?"

Xander hesitated a minute, then nodded. "Okay. But you better get a guarantee out of him first."

"A guarantee of what?"

"That he doesn't come roaring in here and arrest my lily-white ass."

"He wouldn't."

"Fletcher might not. But the feds? They don't exactly stop to ask questions. Shoot first, that's what they're taught."

"You mean that metaphorically, don't you?"

He gave her an exceptionally oblique look that again reminded her just how different they really were.

"If that lets you sleep at night, darlin', have at it."

CHAPTER TWELVE

Washington, D.C.
Detective Darren Fletcher

Fletcher needed sleep. He needed it in the worst way. He wasn't young anymore, couldn't pull these forty-hour-on shifts like he could when he was a rookie. At some point, his brain just plain shut down, and there was nothing that could be done for it until he closed his eyes and recharged.

But the JTTF was expecting him, and his city was under siege. Sleep wasn't an option.

He fueled up at the 7-Eleven on the corner of 24th and New Hampshire Avenue, an extra-large black coffee, and headed to the address he'd been given.

He rolled up on the JTTF at just past one in the morning. Nineteen hours post-attack, and the investigation was in high gear.

The people inside the offices weren't dragging, that was for sure. They were chipper and rushing about and calling out factoids over their impressively toned shoulders. He hoped that somewhere in here was someone his age. Someone who didn't get their information from Twitter and could speak in complete sentences without using "like" or "really" every three words.

Now, Fletch. You're being unkind. If the kids are part of the JTTF it's because they're damn good at their jobs, and nothing else should matter.

He was getting old. Old at forty-two. Old and broken down and lacking faith in humanity.

A young woman in bulky glasses, with blond hair clipped high in a ponytail and a trim black-skirted suit paired with fantastically high heels, met him at the front desk. She didn't smile, but her face lit up when she saw him come in the door.

"You must be Detective Fletcher. I'm Inez Crow. I'll be your assistant while you're on the JTTF." She started him walking toward a steel door. "As you can see, we've got a lot going on. There's too much paper for you to handle by yourself, so I'll be dealing with as much as I can for you. Anything you need, you call me." She handed him a slim mobile phone. "All my numbers are already programmed. I hope you'll take advantage, I'm pretty good at this."

She'd managed the whole speech without a breath.

Fletcher followed her through the door, which she unlocked with a thumb on a fingerprint scanner, then a series of numbers and letters on the keypad. Decent security, but he would expect nothing less.

"So what's your story, Inez? How'd you get to be an assistant to a scrub like me? Punishment?"

She gave him a look of sheer incredulity. "Hardly. B.A. in criminal justice from Princeton, graduate school in Bern, Switzerland, in International Affairs, two years at Interpol, went through the FBI Academy last year and I'm just finishing my Ph.D. in forensic psychology at Harvard. I asked to be assigned to you so I could make sure you could get up to speed quickly and make sure you don't step on your own feet, which you've already managed to do and you haven't been here for five minutes, which isn't a record, but damn close to it, and that tells me I made the right call. In a few months you'd have to call me Dr. Crow. In the meantime, I'll settle for Inez, and a bit of respect."

She stepped off again, back straight, walking briskly, and he took a deep breath and slurped back some coffee and followed. He didn't know whether to laugh or cry. Inez Crow had more qualifications than he did to be on the JTTF, yet she was working for him.

When he caught up to her, he said, "No offense meant, Inez. Just trying to get to know you."

"I understand, sir. These things happen. This is your desk. And that is mine."

There was a bit of privacy to the setup—they were in a corner, and not in the main flight path through the room. The desks were in a U, there was a window overlooking the lights of the Capitol, and the coatrack hid them from the main foot traffic area.

"You pick this spot?" he asked.

"I did."

"Well done."

"I know. We'll want some privacy, and it's quieter here." She smiled, a thousand watts of bright white teeth, the front two slightly crooked, and he forced himself to check his libido. She was young enough to be his daughter, assuming she was as gifted as she sounded and had been conferred her degrees a bit earlier than was the norm, and that wasn't right. But man, the girl was a looker. She had that sexy librarian thing going on.

"So what's first?"

The smile disappeared, replaced by Inez's usual rapid-fire demeanor.

"Agent Bianco would like to meet with you."

"And who, pray tell, is he?"

"Bianco is a she, and she's your boss for the foreseeable future. Special Agent in Charge Andrea Bianco, former head of the Futures Working Group, graduate of University of Virginia, summa cum laude, four years with the FBI in counterterrorism, two years at Interpol, a return to the FBI for three years in the BSU. Got her Ph.D. in behavioral psychology, steadily moved up the ladder since. In her latest role, she was tasked with figuring out what's coming down the pike at us, and she was handpicked this morning to head up the Metro investigation. She'd like a briefing on your information in five."

Inez was big on the qualifications and short on the personal. All he managed to glean from that recitation was the chick he'd be answering to was smart. Really smart.

"All right. I'm ready to go. Let's do it."

Inez hesitated for a moment. "Don't you want to prepare? Bianco is a stickler for details."

Fletched held back a laugh. "How old are you, Inez?"

"Twenty-four next Tuesday, sir. Assuming we have a next Tuesday."

"How many briefings have you done?"

"Plenty, but remember, I'm just the assistant here."

"I've been doing this awhile. Almost as long as you've been alive. I think I can handle it. Let's go."

More offices, more hallways, more glamorously intense young people rushing about. Children, really. The clatter of keyboards complemented the ringing of phones and the occasional shout. This section of the JTTF held twenty people total, but they were generating enough energy to power a small city grid.

The whole place felt…alive. Fletcher couldn't help but catch a bit of the buzz.

He followed Inez into the big cheese's domain. There was a conference room set up, and she led him there.

"Do you have any multimedia you'd like to use?"

Fletcher raised an eyebrow. "No, I guess not."

She got him seated with a fresh pad of paper and a steaming hot cup of coffee, stood by his side for a moment, then whispered, "Don't worry about notes, I'll transcribe everything," and slipped back against the wall.

He could get used to this.

Ten seconds later the door to the conference room opened, and in came Bianco's team. Fletcher didn't need to be introduced to see who was in charge.

Andrea Bianco was dressed in dark jeans and a black jacket, with a Glock on her hip in a tooled leather holster. She had green eyes and hair the color of a burnished sunset, and skin as white and flawless as a bowl of milk. God, was every chick at the JTTF pretty?

She shook his hand warmly, not at all what he expected from Inez's prep. He figured Bianco would be hard and calculating. Instead, she seemed incredibly calm and approachable, like someone he would like to share some boiled shrimp and beer with on a rainy Sunday afternoon. Just a couple of cops, talking about the injustices of the world, the patter of drops on the roof making them slide inexorably toward a more comfortable position…

He rolled his eyes inwardly. Beautiful women always jarred his poetic side loose. He had a line out the door of them. Some even deigned to still speak to him.

"Detective Fletcher, I'm Andrea Bianco. I'm so glad to have you on board. Welcome to the JTTF."

"Thank you, ma'am."

"No ma'am necessary, you can call me Andi." She went around the table to the other five people, four men, one woman, all serious and capable looking. "I don't expect you to get everyone's names immediately, but this is Nick Cusack, Ron Halder, Tom Hasty, Eduardo Mancha and Hyatt Sutton. I'll let you get to know each other later."

Fletcher shook hands with everyone, intentionally not lingering on Sutton, who was so severe looking and tightly contained he was afraid she might leap up and bite him on the neck.

"I understand you've been working the Peter Leighton angle for us today. I know you must be tired, we all are. But would you mind giving us your briefing now?"

"Of course. I don't have much."

He ran them through his day concisely, only presenting the facts, skipping over his suspicions, the rumors about the congressman's private life, the weird feeling he got from Temple, the chief of staff who knew everything and nothing. He talked for about ten minutes, outlining the case. Bianco listened with her head cocked slightly to one side, nodding occasionally. When he finished, he glanced at Inez. She gave him a little wink, which he took to mean he'd done a decent enough job.

Been at this party a few times, kid.

Bianco twirled a pen around on her blank notepad for a moment. With a small smile that belied her words, she said, "That's all great information, Detective. Now, would you mind filling in the blanks? You left a few things out."

"Ma'am?"

"Andi. You left a few things out. We need to hear it all. We don't operate like some of the folks you may have worked with. We must investigate all the angles, all the issues, all the rumors and innuendoes. We are life detectives, in a sense. Nothing is safe, absolutely nothing. Nothing is sacred if it means stopping these bastards from hurting another person. So give it to us, and give it straight this time."

Fletcher ignored the small, humor-filled cough that emanated from behind and to the right of his shoulder. Perhaps Andrea Bianco was more of a force to be contended with than she first appeared. The friendly welcome was a guise, he saw. Inside, she was hard and unforgiving as a chalky cliff.

He took a breath and started again. At the top. He detailed what he'd left out, which was precious little. Bianco sat in her bird pose and watched him, listening, again, and when he stopped she gave him a curt smile, then stood. The room's focus moved to her, and she began to speak. Her voice was infused with passion.

"Thank you. I appreciate that you were uncomfortable gossiping about the congressman. But everything matters right now. We have an interesting situation on our hands. The attack this morning caught everyone by surprise. That, in and of itself, is somewhat miraculous, considering how well plugged in we are to all the terrorist networks. There have been claims of responsibility from groups we've had under close scrutiny, which leads me to doubt the veracity of their claims.

"There is more than meets the eye in our attack this morning. The head of the Armed Services Subcommittee is dead, along with two others. Many people are sick, but none are dying. The tests that have been run have narrowed the toxin to something biologically similar to ricin. We have a thousand people working this case, and it's going nowhere. There are two groups forming, one to investigate what happened, one to make sure it doesn't happen again. Prevention is the biggest tool the JTTF has, and we failed this morning. I won't let us fail again.

"Ladies and gentlemen, this attack is a stain on our character. I don't believe that it's a terrorist cell. I think it's a lone renegade cell, independent, self-actualized, and far from finished. My bosses don't agree with me, so it is our mandate to prove them wrong. With their approval, we are going to work separately from the rest of the JTTF, go at this from a different angle. Nick, Ron and Hyatt, you are on the Metro. Figure out how the toxin was delivered. I want a step-by-step, moment-by-moment breakdown. Eduardo, I want you to compile a list of possible threats that focuses on the United States. Tom, you're our scientist. I want you to assess what the toxin is, where it came from, everything." She turned to Fletcher. "Darren, you're with me. Any questions?"

Silence.

"Good. Brief me at ten. Go to it."

The others gathered their things and scooted out of the room. Bianco watched them go. When they were the only ones left in the room, she excused Inez, who shot Fletcher a meaningful look and shut the conference room door behind her.

"So." Bianco sat at the table and pulled out a red file folder. She placed it carefully in front of her, squared the edges with the table. "What do you think of my theory?"

"It's as sound as anything else I've heard today."

"Why did you bring in an outside medical examiner to do the autopsy on the congressman?"

"Like I said, she's the best at what she does. That's not a knock on our medical examiners, she's just gifted. She thought it was a ricin hybrid, something new, something developed specifically for the attack."

"You didn't mention that."

"She asked me not to. She didn't want to speculate. Ricin-like was all she'd commit to officially, that ricin mimics the findings from the autopsies, but doesn't match exactly."

"All right. First things first. This is eyes-only." She slid the file to him. "Read it. I'll wait. You want some more coffee?"

He glanced at his empty cup and then at the wall clock. 3:15 a.m. "Yes, ma'am."

"Andi," she said, then left him to read.

He waited until the door shut, opened the file. The first line of the report made him suck in his breath.

Holy shit.

CHAPTER THIRTEEN

Fletcher couldn't believe what he was reading.

There was a DNA profile, a confirmed match between two identical sources. He read the name on the bottom of the page, and his suspicions began to grow.

The DNA profile belonged to Congressman Peter Dumfries Leighton.

Fletcher's mind immediately raised all sorts of questions—why do they have a file on Leighton, where did they get the DNA, why do they have DNA, what the hell is this?—but he flipped the page and started to digest.

The top sheet was a summary police file from 2004, a cold-case murder from Indianapolis, Indiana. Christine Hornby, age sixteen, found beaten and raped in a ditch off the side of a state road leading into town. No one was ever caught, despite a solid DNA profile put into the system.

Fletcher flipped further. There was another cold-case murder, this time from 2006. Diana Frank, seventeen, also from Indianapolis, Indiana. Another beating and rape. In 2008 there was one more, Brandy Thornberg, seventeen, from Terre Haute. Three in all. Christine Hornby, Diana Frank and Brandy Thornberg, all brunette teenagers murdered by the same person. DNA matched all three of their cases, and no killer had ever been identified.

A deep knot began building in his stomach. He turned back to the front sheet, the DNA profile.

Tried to fit the pieces together.

Peter Leighton—congressman, soldier, father—a serial killer?

He sat back in his chair and rubbed his face with his hands. What in the hell had he gotten himself into?

Bianco was back. She handed him a steaming cup of coffee, sat at the table next to him.

"Now you know why I wanted the gossip along with the facts. It started when he was making his first congressional run back in 2004."

"This is hard to believe."

"Trust me, I know. I received the report this evening, after the DNA profile matched."

"Why was Leighton's DNA run? And how did you get it?"

"He tossed out a soda with a straw last week. McDonald's. It was retrieved. They extracted the DNA and sent it in to run through CODIS."

"He was being investigated for the murders?"

"I don't have all the details. Indiana Bureau of Investigation was handling this until three hours ago. I haven't been fully briefed yet. All I know is it was brought to my attention the moment word got out that he was dead. We have to take into consideration that he knew about the investigation and used the attack this morning as a cover to commit suicide."

"Suicide by asthma attack? Isn't that a bit hard to manage?"

"You stated very clearly that the chief of staff had to find his inhaler and give it to him, and the autopsy found no evidence of use of an EpiPen. The briefcase where he normally carried these items is still missing. It's not impossible to get yourself into respiratory distress if you're already compromised."

"Or that someone knew about this and decided to kill him."

"Yes."

"Or that this is just a wildly crazy coincidence."

"That, too. What do you think?"

Fletcher closed the file and slid it back to her. "Too early to draw any sort of conclusion. If the samples from the three autopsies match, then we know it was a coincidence. If they don't, then you can look at the other scenarios. But I'd make sure I crossed every T and dotted every I before I went forward with allegations like this."

"I'd like you to look into this for me."

Fletcher didn't answer right away. He sat back in his chair and sipped his coffee. JTTF did a better job with their brew than his homicide office did, that was for sure. More funding, better coffee. He'd always thought that was hearsay, but here he was, in the exalted offices of the best of the best, finding out firsthand that the rumors were true.

And now he was starting to understand why they wanted him on the JTTF.

"What about the text message he received this morning? How does that fit into this?"

"Again, Darren, that's under your purview. You have free rein to do whatever you feel is necessary to uncover the truth here. You will have all the resources you need to do a thorough investigation into the congressman's every move for the past eighteen years. All we ask is that you keep your inquiries discreet, and not share your task with anyone. Even your bosses."

Bianco was leaning forward, and the top of her blouse was gaping just the tiniest bit. He caught a hint of lace and cream, dutifully looked away and went back to his coffee.

"Well?" Bianco asked.

He sighed. "This could be a suicide mission, *Andi*. Can you imagine the headlines if we fuck up?"

"Can you imagine the headlines if you don't? You'll be a hero. Some would say this was a gift."

He saw what she'd done. *We* to *you*. This is your problem now, Fletcher. We're going to wash our hands of it and let you take the heat, keeping the JTTF's nose clean in case somewhere along the way, someone else screwed up. *Some would say this was a gift.* He caught her meaning—who was he, a lowly homicide dick, to look a gift horse in the mouth? A huge story, earth-shattering news, at least a couple of weeks in the news cycle, Fletcher's name and fingerprints all over the bloody mess.

It was a setup. He felt it immediately. There were stakes he wasn't aware of.

Worse, what had he done to deserve this? He'd pissed someone off. Two years from his twenty, a decent career under his belt, and he was being thrown to the wolves on a case that looked damn close to a foregone conclusion.

Something else was up. Something big.

"I have to think about it."

Bianco actually sat back in her chair and smiled. She had a nice smile, her parents had sprung for some orthodontics and her teeth were even and white. She ran her bottom lip up over the edge of her top teeth. The effect made her lips fuller, a move that he associated with prolonged use of a headgear. His son, Tad, had the same habit.

Stop thinking about her lips, Fletch.

He looked down at the file before him. What a mess.

"Of course you do. Go on home and get some rest. I always find a good night's sleep helps me think clearly." She stood then, stretching her back a little, almost as if to say, *See, I'm tired, too. I'm working hard. I'm all kinked up and I know, I under-*

stand, what you're going through, and shook his hand, effectively but kindly dismissing him.

He found Inez back at their respective desks. She had her nose deep in her laptop.

"Anything new?" he asked.

"No. Everything cool with you?"

"Sure," he replied. "I'm going to go home and catch some z's. You should, too. Meet me back here at nine, okay? We have a big project to tackle."

"Yes, sir."

"Inez?"

"Sir?"

"You can call me Fletch."

Fletcher left the JTTF office buzzing with adrenaline. Hand chosen to handle a fuck-all dog of a case that could wind up being his death sentence with Homicide. He wanted out, sure, but not like this. Not on a case that smelled to high heaven.

He lived in a row house on a quiet Capitol Hill street, catty-corner to the Longworth House Office Building, the very place he'd spent the better part of his afternoon trying to glean enough detail from the monosyllabic answers of Leighton's staff to figure out what the hell was going on.

He kept a light on in the foyer so it looked like someone was around, though the neighborhood itself was very safe, and most of his neighbors knew he was a cop and kept an eye on his place in addition to their own. But tonight it was off. He had to think back—had he turned the switch off when he left God knows how many hours earlier? No, that was impossible, he never did. Maybe the light was out...but he had one of the new long-lasting compact fluorescent bulbs in there that was supposed to burn for five years or more. He couldn't remember the last time he'd changed it, but it certainly wasn't five years ago.

Curious.

He put his hand on the butt of his Glock and slid his key in the lock. The bolt was thrown, the bottom lock engaged, just like he left it. He twisted the knob and entered his foyer at an angle, sliding against the wall. He listened carefully, heard nothing but the normal night sounds of his house, the refrigerator rumbling quietly in the kitchen, the barometer clock on the wall by the door ticking the seconds away.

He moved quickly, clearing the house room by room, then returned to the foyer.

The switch had been turned off.

He holstered his weapon and flipped it back on. Sloppy of them. Whoever *them* was.

Shit. At least his instincts were right on the money. Something else was going on with the congressman's case.

He searched the house again, more thoroughly this time, but saw nothing out of place. If it weren't for the faux pas with the light, he wouldn't have had any idea that someone had tossed him. A stupid environmentally conscious crook who couldn't leave the light on had just left behind his markers.

It had to be someone from the JTTF, checking up on him. Making sure he wasn't going to embarrass them. That he didn't have a blow-up doll girlfriend or a drawer full of latex and whips.

Jesus, whatever happened to asking a man about his sensitive proclivities?

Then again, perhaps that was the mistake they had made with the congressman in the first place.

Sleep was dragging at him. He'd deal with this in the morning. He didn't bother with his bed, just stretched out on the couch, his usual resting spot, kicked off his shoes and shut his eyes. He'd be able to figure all of this out later, after his batteries recharged.

Darkness enveloped the room, and he didn't see the tiny glowing light secreted on the back edge of his television, a dusty Bermuda triangle that never got cleaned, or noticed.

Fletcher slept without dreams for four hours, then woke to the clamor of his cell phone. Cursing, he reached for the offending object, managed to open it and grunted, "What?"

"Fletch, thank God. I was starting to worry. I've been calling you for hours."

Sam.

Fletcher groaned and rolled onto his side.

"Time is it?"

"Almost 7:30. Are you okay? You sound horrible."

"Up late." He struggled into a seated position, hand shielding his eyes from the sun spilling in through his blinds.

"I need to talk to you. It's an emergency."

"Okay. What's up?"

"In person, Fletch. This isn't a conversation for the phone. Can you come to the house? We have something to show you."

We. He hated that term where she was concerned. Hated it even more that he actually liked Xander Whitfield. It would be easier if the man were a tool, but he wasn't, not in the least. He was rugged and outdoorsy and smart and decent looking, if you liked the tall, dark and handsome set, which most women did.

He looked at his watch. He needed to be at the JTTF to embark on his suicide mission at 9:00 a.m. "Yeah. Give me fifteen. Make some breakfast, will ya? I haven't eaten a proper meal in two days."

Sam laughed under her breath. "Anything for you, Fletch. Now hurry."

WEDNESDAY

CHAPTER FOURTEEN

Washington, D.C.
Dr. Samantha Owens

Sam had used a couple of belts of Scotch to get back to sleep after Xander's bombshell, and was feeling frachetty. She'd only managed two hours of sleep, had gotten up as soon as she woke to try and reach Fletcher again. Her mission finally accomplished, she was happy to fulfill Fletcher's demand—a hot breakfast to soothe his tired bones. It might help give her and Xander some energy to make it through what was certainly going to be a long day.

She grabbed a quick shower, threw on a pair of gray summer-weight wool trousers and a cream short-sleeved cashmere T-shirt, and put her dark, wet hair in a bun. It was getting longer, her bangs growing out so they swept to the side and tucked behind her ears. She liked the new look, thought she'd go ahead with it for a while. When she was working back in Nashville, she kept her haircut appointments with military discipline; the shoulder-length bob she'd worn for years served her well, accentuating her heart-shaped face and staying out of her way while looking both chic and practical. Now that she wasn't going to be spending her days bent over a dissection table, she could let things go a little, be freer. The professors she'd met thus far had long hair. They wore loose-fitting clothes, comfortable and roomy, sometimes even scrubs, and smelled faintly of patchouli. She wouldn't go that far—she was too attached to her sumptuous fabrics and Chanel No. 5—but a bit of leeway wouldn't hurt.

"Xander?" she called as she went down the stairs.

There was no answer.

She assumed he had gone for a run; he did that often when he was here in the city. Her house was close to the canal, which was his favorite path to follow. She'd gone with him a few times, but she knew she held him back. Years of daily PT made him strong, streamlined and seemingly unstoppable. He had reserves she couldn't come close to emulating.

A canal run up the Potomac meant he'd come home starving, so she decided to make blueberry pancakes and eggs and bacon. That should sufficiently feed her men.

Her men.

She had a pang of inconsolable grief at the thought. She'd moved from daily, all-consuming sorrow to the sneak attacks, images and smells and memories that came at her out of the blue like snipers' bullets. As much as she wanted to, Sam couldn't replace Simon with Xander and Fletcher, couldn't use the new people in her life to erase the ones who were gone.

Matthew and Madeleine, her twins, had adored blueberry pancakes. It was a Sunday morning ritual: after church, they would go to Le Peep in Belle Meade, just a mile from the huge house she'd grown up in, and have a family breakfast. Sometimes her friends Taylor and Baldwin would meet them, sometimes Simon's parents. It was a tradition, built purposely so the kids would have a memory, a habit, to cling to as they got older. So they'd understand the value of a treat. Of family. Of togetherness.

Church. Sam hadn't been back since they found their bodies. She couldn't believe in a God who'd strip a woman of her family. She was surprisingly comfortable with the decision, considering she'd been a devout Catholic before the accident. It was freeing, not having to share all her little venial sins. Not taking the comfort she'd always found in communion, that feeling of magic watching the transubstantiation. She had believed in all of it. Believed down to her bones. Until she didn't. She'd never known faith could be like a switch on a lamp, on one minute, off the next. When they died, she hadn't even bothered trying to turn the switch on again. She never would. That ship had sailed while she scattered their ashes, the winds at the top of Xander's mountain whipping their beings away into the ether, taking the part of her that believed in magic and mystery and faith along with them.

She put the pancake mix back in the pantry and retrieved two baking potatoes instead. Hash browns would fill them up just fine.

Fletcher arrived on her doorstep just as she was sliding the bacon from the pan. She dumped the shredded potatoes into the skillet to let them cook in the rendered grease, and went to the door, wiping her hands on a towel.

He looked like something the cat dragged in. He'd showered, but barely. Stubble bristled from his jaw, and his blue eyes were shadowed with deep pockets of dark skin. He had on a suit that was rumpled, and mismatched socks. Fletch on a case was a sight to behold.

"You want to use my bathroom, try again?" she asked.

He just shot her a look and came into the house. She looked to the northwest for a second, down N Street toward Georgetown University, wondering how long Xander would be, then decided feeding and watering Fletcher took precedence. Her stove had a warming setting; she'd put Xander's plate in there and he could eat when he returned. She shut the door and went to the kitchen, where Fletcher had already grabbed a mug and was filling it from the coffeepot.

She flipped the hash browns and started to assemble their plates. Fletcher sat at the table with his coffee, sipping and groaning in the kind of earthy delight only men who can appreciate decent coffee and women's backsides could pull off.

She slid a plate of food under his nose, then joined him with her own. He dug in immediately, shoveled three forkfuls in before taking a breath.

"God, this is good. Thank you. What do you need?"

"We should wait for Xander. It's his story."

"Where is he?"

"I think he went for a run. He was gone when I got up. So he should be back shortly. What's happening with the investigation? The TV said there were no more deaths overnight, and a few of the victims would be released this morning. That's good news, right?"

He crunched his bacon. "You know as much as I do right now."

"But you're working with the JTTF, right? I figured they'd have all the scoop."

"They do. I don't. I am tasked with something else. A smaller part of the investigation."

She heard the annoyance in his voice. "Want to tell me about it?"

"I can't. Not yet. Suffice it to say, one misstep and I'm toast." He ran his forefinger along his throat in a slash.

"Really? I can't imagine Armstrong letting you get into trouble."

"He doesn't know about this. I've been asked to keep the 'nature of my investigation' to myself. And trust me, it's something I want some cover on. A single fuckup, and I'll be on the first train out of town with pitchforks and brands thrown at me."

"Are you in trouble?"

He ate some more, took a big drink of his coffee. "I don't know yet. But I have to make some decisions pretty damn quick. So let's get a move on. You can tell me what's up, and when Xander gets back, he can fill in the blanks."

She glanced at the clock. He should have been back by now.

"Let me just call him. He usually takes his phone with him when he's in the city."

She grabbed her cell. Xander's phone rang once, twice, then he picked up without a greeting.

"I wondered when you were going to call."

"Where are you? Fletcher and I are about to eat your breakfast."

His voice changed. "Fletcher's there?"

"Yes. Remember, we were trying to touch base so we could tell him your theory?"

"I do. And so you may."

"Where are you, Xander?"

She heard the noises in the background then, a familiar squelch, and realized exactly where he was.

"Oh, come on. That is so not fair. Where are you going?"

She could almost hear the smile in his voice. "You're good, Dr. Owens. Don't worry about me. I'll call you when I get there."

"Xander, we need you here. You need to show Fletch what's going on."

"He has enough to deal with. Just let me figure this out, and see if I can't track them down, then I'll tell him exactly where they are, and he can swoop in and scoop them up with all the fanfare he wants."

"Xander—"

"Samantha, honey, I don't want to jam up these people if they have nothing to do with the attack."

"And if they do?"

"They don't. I know it. I just need to have enough proof so they won't be arrested."

Fletcher was watching her closely now, as if he knew already the situation at hand.

"You kept something from me. You do know who they are, and where they are," Sam said flatly.

"I have a sneaking suspicion."

"This isn't your fight, Xander. Come home. Let's deal with this together."

His voice deepened. "It most certainly is my fight. They're calling for me to turn off my cell, sweetheart. I'll be in touch."

The phone went dead. Sam didn't know whether to curse or throw her cell across the room. In the end, she chose a few deep breaths and set the phone gently on the glass kitchen table.

Fletcher set his fork down on his totally clean plate. He watched her expression, then sighed and said, "If he's not coming, can I have his breakfast, too?"

CHAPTER FIFTEEN

While Fletcher continued to eat, Sam explained what was going on.

"Xander's being a cowboy."

"You like that sort of thing? I could strap on some chaps and spurs and little else if it would do it for you." He smiled wickedly and Sam just shook her head.

"Fat chance, bubba. I'm allergic to horses."

"Alas."

"Alas. No, Xander thinks he has an idea of who committed the attack on the Metro yesterday, and he's running off half-cocked to try and prove his theory."

That got Fletcher's attention. He pushed his plate and cup away, crossed his arms on his chest, and said, *"What?"*

Sam sat in the chair across from him. "He was on a survivalist website he frequents, and the owners of the site made mention of a new member who was apparently spouting off. Before he could dig deeper, the site went dark. He thinks he might know who runs it, though. We were supposed to sit down with you this morning and lay all this out, but it seems the man has different ideas. Which means he's in deep shit and doesn't want it coming back on us."

Fletcher stared at her, not at all amused. "Where the hell is he?"

"On a plane. He was banking on being in the air before I called."

"Did he tell you where said airplane was heading?"

"No."

"Jesus, Sam. What computer was he using?"

"My laptop."

"Get it."

Sam got up from the table and went to fetch her laptop. She heard Fletcher on the phone. Shit. This wasn't going as planned. Now instead of helping Xander look for the perpetrator, the law was going to be looking for him instead.

She found her laptop on the coffee table in her living room, the only object on the smoky tempered glass. There was a Post-it note stuck to the top. "Don't bother. I erased the history. Love, X."

Sam gritted her teeth. Damn that man. He knew exactly what they were up to here in the townhouse, trying to piece together his meager clues, and was probably laughing his ass off at the idea of them searching for him.

He, the man who knew more about going to ground than the entire D.C. Metro police force combined.

She brought the computer and the note to the kitchen table, handed both to Fletcher, who glanced at the note and promptly blew his top.

"Does he not realize this is national security we're talking about? If the JTTF finds out about this, he's going to go to jail for hindering the investigation."

Sam looked at him squarely in the eye. "Then I trust you won't be sharing how you got this information with the JTTF, will you."

Fletcher's look was incredulous, and her heart sank. Oh boy. Now she'd stepped in it.

"Sam. You're kidding, right? You think I can hold back how I received the information? You know I can't do that."

"You can, and you will, or else I won't cooperate, and you'll have to arrest me, too."

"Don't think I won't. I'm not fucking around here."

"Then do it. Arrest me. I won't help you arrest Xander, too."

They were nose to nose now, shouting at each other.

"Such loyalty for a man you barely know."

"What the hell is that supposed to mean?"

"It means that you ran off with him without thinking about the consequences. Left your practice, your city, your life, to live in the woods and shit in an outhouse because you've got the hots for soldier boy."

"So? Why do you care what I do or don't do with my life? We hardly know each other, and we're barely friends as it is."

"And why is that, do you think?"

"You're jealous," Sam spit.

"Damn right I am. You deserve better. You deserve a man who's emotionally available and capable of taking care of you properly, not someone so caught up in his own demons he's going to rush off at a moment's notice to save the day."

"And that's you, Fletch? You can take care of me properly? What would Felicia say about that? And your son?"

"Don't bring them into this. You have no *idea* about the situation with my family."

Sam was about to bite back when the doorbell rang.

Neither of them moved for a moment, both still ruffled and arched like furious cats. Then Sam broke his gaze and started for the door. He grabbed her shoulder, squeezed hard enough to hurt.

"Don't even think about it, *Dr. Owens*. This is a crime scene now. Go sit your perfect little ass back down at the kitchen table, and don't touch a damn thing."

"Fletcher. Who is at my door?"

"Sit. Down." His voice was dangerously smooth; his face red and blank with anger.

Because she recognized she may have pushed him too far, and he was the one with the gun on his hip, she decided to capitulate.

She suddenly understood why Xander had run off unannounced. He knew Fletcher would call in reinforcements, that he wouldn't stop to see sense, that he'd just react instead of strategize. She wanted to be mad at him for leaving her to deal with the fallout, but she couldn't. She saw the sense in his plan now, and had to admit, he'd probably done the right thing. Fletcher could be lacking in imagination when it came to law and order.

Sam heard an abbreviated wail, like someone cut off a siren, and car doors slamming. Oh, Jesus, he wasn't joking. He'd actually called in the Cavalry.

She didn't want this to be adversarial. She rubbed her hands together absently, a small comfort, strained to hear the conversation happening in her foyer. She couldn't, the voices were pitched low.

A moment later, two women came into the kitchen with Fletcher. The younger of the two had blond hair in a ponytail and dark glasses; the older was a striking redhead who Sam could immediately tell was running the show.

Fletcher did the introductions. "Dr. Samantha Owens, this is Special Agent in Charge Andrea Bianco, with the JTTF, and Inez Cruz, my assistant. Now, speak."

Sam was reminded of the first time she spoke to Fletcher, just a few months before, when he'd answered his phone in the same gruff way, and she'd immediately barked to loosen the tension. That wasn't going to work this time, she could tell.

The Bianco woman shot Fletcher a look, then stuck out her hand and approached Sam civilly.

"Forgive my colleague, Dr. Owens. He needs some more sleep. It's nice to meet you. Would you mind if we shared your coffee? It smells delicious."

Disarming, charming, collected. Everything Fletcher currently wasn't.

Sam shook the woman's hand. "Of course. I'll make a fresh pot, there's only a cup left."

"Excellent. While you do that, would you mind giving me the lay of the land?"

The woman was as sweet as pie. She sat down primly at the kitchen table, motioned for her subordinates to do the same. Sam could tell Fletcher was still steamed, but he sat as well, glowering at her.

Sam explained Xander's thoughts while she made a fresh pot of coffee. Bianco didn't interrupt, just listened with her head slightly cocked to one side. The younger girl, Inez, took copious notes.

When she was finished, Bianco nodded. "Any reason you didn't share this with us last night?"

Sam was half tempted to say, *I tried, but Fletcher didn't answer his phone until seven o'clock this morning,* but she recognized a chance to perhaps calm his rage, so she just filled the woman's coffee cup and said, "I called Fletch as soon as I got up this morning."

She tried to catch his eye, but he wasn't looking at her. She did notice his shoulders drop, though, some tension dissipating and thought, *See, I'm your friend, even if you aren't mine.*

"I understand. Can you tell me when your gentlemen friend—you said his name is Alexander Whitfield, correct?"

"That's right. He's called Xander. With an *X*."

"Excellent. Do you have any idea where Xander with an *X* might have gone?"

"Ma'am, I don't. I swear it." She showed her the note. "I wouldn't hold back on this if I knew. I understand just how important this information could be. I also know that Xander is a highly trained operative who wouldn't want the government's time wasted on a wild-goose chase. That's why he's gone to do the legwork himself."

Bianco smiled. She had a nice smile, seemingly friendly and open. Like a pit viper. Sam immediately distrusted the woman.

"I can appreciate that sentiment, Dr. Owens. But unfortunately, now we must try to find your Xander so he doesn't get himself hurt. So I'm afraid we're going to have to take you into custody while we start our search. Just…informally."

Sam glared at Fletcher, who was staring hard at his right shoe. "Is that really necessary?"

"Yes, I believe it is. All of my resources are at the JTTF, not here in this townhouse. It's more convenient for me, you see, if you join us there, rather than us trying to set up shop here, waiting for word. As a medical examiner, you've been involved in investigations before. I daresay you understand. We'll have your phone rerouted to your cell, too, just in case."

"Are you arresting me?"

Bianco stood, motioned to her team. She gave Sam another one of her beatific smiles. "There's no need for that now, is there? You'll come with us and cooperate because it's the right thing to do, because you're a patriot who wants to see the bad people punished, correct? We wouldn't want to have to put cuffs on you and let you sit in a cell while we tear apart your life and tap your phones and freeze all of your accounts indefinitely. That's so messy, and such a load of mind-numbing paperwork. Then again, that's why we have assistants, isn't it? Inez, are you up for a challenge today?"

"Yes, ma'am," the girl said smartly.

Sam's bluff had officially been called. She sighed.

"Let me get my bag."

CHAPTER SIXTEEN

For many years, he eschewed all forms of technology in his personal life, basking in his Luddism. He didn't have a television or a computer. He built his bombs and cooked his juice by perfect recall of books he'd read in the library. They were wrong, those amoral creatures who spent their time staring at computer screens, rewiring their brains into hyperinflated mush. To waste your mind was a sin, one of the many he saw committed day in and day out, carelessness and selfishness and greed stamped on their foreheads like so much chattel as they shopped and chatted and commented and simpered and swooned.

What a waste his society had become.

He got his news the old-fashioned way, in letters, and from the shortwave radio he kept in the barn, away from the girl, so she wouldn't be tainted. He needed to keep her clean, to keep her unsullied. Her mother was a perfect example of what the slow march of technology could do to a person. Once unsullied herself, pure and clean and beautiful in her homespun, she was a beauty to behold. And she'd chosen him. *Him*.

They'd been married in the custom of their people, with the full and complete will of each individual bound in a col-

lective spirit, no license needed, no priest, just the acknowl-
edgment of their love and the dispersion of property from one
parent to a spouse. Like it was supposed to be. And after, she'd
lain with him, and he'd found the true glory of life. He found
himself hurrying through his chores so he could return to the
house and blow out the candle, take her to his bed. Shirking
his duties, never, but finding ways to make them go faster,
to be more efficient. Then he began coming home for lunch,
and filling himself both with her food and her body.

It must be a sin, the pleasure, because he was not single-
minded in his objective. The delights of procreation perhaps
outstripped his beliefs. But his faith said to be fruitful and
multiply, and he obeyed with tireless drive. Since he enjoyed
it so much, more the better.

When she had fallen with child he had never been so proud.
He'd created *life*. More than cultivating vegetables, and hus-
bandry with the animals, and the high, wide stalks of corn
in the fields—he had created a different kind of life, through
his love and his joy and his gratification.

They were at last content.

And then it all went to hell.

She was a small woman, and begged to have the child in
a hospital, where it would be safe, fearing the wilds and the
vagaries of chance. He dismissed that notion out of hand; he
knew plenty about birth, he'd been shepherding his flock into
existence his entire life. There was no need for strangers to
handle the delivery, he could do it himself. He studied the
books and relayed the information to her at night. She was
resistant to the idea. She actually fought back, told him no.
She would not allow it.

As her husband, he was her lord and creator. She had no
right to disagree, to disobey.

She did not obey.

When she was six months pregnant, she disappeared.

Six months after that he found her. She was living in the most wretched city in the world, and the child was not with her. He watched her for days, trying to discern what she'd done with his babe, the rage and fear and anger building in him to the point where he thought he would burst.

He began to despair, fearing the child had been lost after all. So he went to her and knocked on her door, and when she opened it she screamed in fear and tried to slam it shut, but he stuck his heavy shoe in the crack, and pushed with his fists, and the door opened wide before him, and she cowered on the couch while he asked her where their child was.

When she revealed their daughter was with strangers, he beat her senseless, and then started his most important journey. The mother was of no consequence to him anymore. It was his progeny he wanted.

Adoption.

That word shrank his soul.

He was a big man, strong, intimidating. It took little time to establish the child's new home, in West Virginia, a small mining town, with small people. Took less time to release the child from her bonds, and return her to her proper place.

He named her Ruth, for his mother. The obedient one.

Whither thou goest, I will go.

They'd left the group when she was three, because he felt it was time for them to be on their own. He built their camp by hand: the cabin, the stable, the work shed, the fields. And they lived happily in the mountains, eating the food he caught and grew, being entertained by books from the library in the town forty miles away. He educated her himself.

And Ruth grew older, and began to look exactly like her mother.

And hatred grew in his soul. He fought it—the commandments were clear on this, love thy neighbor as thyself—but he couldn't stem the tide. It built until it flowed over and he felt he had no choice, no recourse, other than to fulfill its destiny.

The release he felt at this decision made him realize that this was the path he was supposed to follow, and if he were successful, the hatred would dim, and the child's mother would join him, and they could raise their child in peace.

In peace.

But to create that peace, he must first remove the impediments, and there would be death to those who wronged him.

So he prayed for forgiveness from his God, bought a small, third-hand laptop computer, enrolled in a community college class and embraced technology, for it would mean he could fulfill his plan while staying home to educate his daughter. The one piece of him that mattered.

Now, he watched the fallout of his actions online, and reveled in his power. He hadn't planned to do more than scare the people, and eliminate the ones in his way, but the pleasure of seeing his actions discussed everywhere he turned was more than he could have hoped. The plan had been executed perfectly, the diversion laid in, and no one had a clue where to look for answers. It was a masterful performance.

He knew his compatriots would be discussing it. The people he'd left had a website now, openly discussing their lifestyle. Idiots. He went to the site and sure enough, there they were, talking about him.

He cruised through the other sites he frequented, before trying to get in to the one he really enjoyed, the supersecret quiet site. He'd been given the password, emailed to him on an anonymous Yahoo.com address he used when he needed a log-in and password.

It was his favorite place. He knew he was among like-minded individuals. He sometimes felt like they were talking to him directly. Giving him ideas. Allowing his already rampant imagination to flow. He could do anything, be anyone, when he was within its confines. It made giving up his hatred of technology worth it. They were his friends.

The site was embedded within another, an ingenious hack that the website owner had no idea was there. You had to know where to click on the picture to open the portal to the private site. He clicked the eye of the smiling woman and waited for the log-in box to pop up, but nothing happened.

He tried again, switching eyes, trying the nostril, the mouth. Nothing.

The site must have gone down.

The first edges of worry started to gnaw at him. Why did they disappear? What had driven them away? Unless…the government jackboots had figured it out and gotten into the site. That could be problematic; he had perhaps made one slight little mention of his plan there, not looking for accolades, but to share in their fervor. To fit in. He was getting lonely, just he and the girl in the woods. He'd thought about returning to his group, but they'd been rather adamant when he left that he was not welcome back. Ruth they'd be happy to take in, but not him.

He closed the laptop. Worry fled, and anger took its place.

They were keeping him out on purpose. The site wasn't down, they'd moved, and made sure he couldn't track them.

Anger was a sin. He fought it, pushed it down in his gut where it wouldn't assail him, turning him black with rot, but it was no use. The blackness consumed him.

There was only one thing left to do then. Reach out in person, with a message especially for them. And he knew exactly how to get their attention. They wanted something to talk about? He'd give it to them.

CHAPTER SEVENTEEN

Denver, Colorado
Alexander Whitfield

The plane's wheels touched down with a juddering impact, and the engines wailed in protest at their violent juxtaposition, reversed to help the screaming bird land and stop before running out of runway and plunging into the prairie land below. Xander had always liked landing. He liked takeoffs, too, but the feeling of 400,000 pounds of metal being slung at the flattened earth and stopping on a dime was especially fun.

They taxied for a few minutes, and he looked out the window toward the mountains of his childhood and felt a great peace stealing through his system. It was good to be home.

He grabbed his bag from the overhead bin and exited the plane, back ramrod straight. Some things he couldn't let go of, his posture and physical fitness only two of many pieces of him the Army still owned.

Sam must be beside herself with fury at him. He didn't particularly want to call, but he'd be in much worse trouble if he waited.

In the terminal, he spied a Blue Mountain coffee shop. He

would take his chances. A steaming cup of coffee, a banana, a bag of trail mix and a bottle of water refueled him, and he tossed his trash and started out of the terminal. Once he got into the open air, then he'd call her. Not before. Too many eyes and ears around at airports. Too many opportunities for his words to be overheard, misinterpreted, misconstrued.

The air outside the terminal was thin and warm, but he could feel the promise of coolness underneath the easterly thermal flow, the slipstream over the mountains whisking the breeze off the tops of the highest still snow-covered peaks. They'd had a late spring here, with a walloping storm that dumped six feet on the fifteenth of May. Those late-spring storms made him nostalgic; born on the last day of April, he couldn't remember a birthday that didn't see the bluebells and larkspurs in the pasture shivering under a thick coating of white.

He got on the rental car bus, went through the indignities expected of him, signed his life away in triplicate, retrieved his vehicle, a Ford Explorer, and once inside the vehicle and out of the garage, flipped open his phone.

A relieved-sounding Sam answered on the first ring. His initial assessment was correct, she was hopping mad.

"Where in the name of hell are you? You've been MIA for hours."

"Hi, honey."

"No, no, no, no, no, don't 'Hi, honey' me, Xander. You left me in deep shit here. Where are you?"

"What kind of deep shit?"

He heard her swallow, then her tactic changed. Her voice calmed. "I need to know where you are. Things didn't exactly go as planned this morning."

"Fletcher wasn't pleased with you, I take it?"

"He's fine with me, it's you he's furious at. Come on, Xander, no more games. They hauled me down to the JTTF. They aren't messing around."

Shit. He was hoping for more time.

"Is that where you are right now?"

"Yes. Now, please. Will you just play ball so I can go home?"

Damn it.

"I'll call you later, sweetheart. I'm sorry." He flipped off the phone, quickly disassembled it. They couldn't have traced it that quickly, but all they had to do was get paper from his cell company to see where the call came from. He was going to have to work fast. Without the battery they wouldn't be able to nail it down better than that last call. So they'd see he was in Colorado, but nothing more.

He pointed the car toward the mountains, and drove. If his hunch played out, he'd be golden. If not, then he'd face the music. He felt like hell lying to Sam, but it was only to keep her safe, nothing more, nothing less. He just needed a few more hours.

That fool Fletcher must have strong-armed her into telling him everything, playing on their friendship to get more than their planned statements out of her.

Well, no matter. Another couple of hours and he'd be where he was heading, and start stalking his prey. Then together they'd be able to quietly and quickly nail the son of a bitch who thought he could terrorize the nation.

CHAPTER EIGHTEEN

Washington, D.C.
Dr. Samantha Owens

The JTTF was surprising, to say the least. Having been in multiple law enforcement headquarters, Sam was impressed with their setup. Technologically advanced, for sure. A wide cross section of people from all walks of law enforcement, young and determined, old and grizzled. And they had decent coffee, though she'd had so much caffeine by this point that her hands were starting to shake.

She was loosely under watch at Fletcher's desk. He was sitting next to her, and vibrating with anger still. She hung up the phone and glanced at him.

"He won't tell me where he is."

Fletcher snarled at her. "That's some man you've got there, Sam. Willing to let his woman stay in custody rather than share his whereabouts and whatever idiotic plan he has in mind."

Sam let her hair down; the pins holding her bun were starting to give her a headache. She shook it out and it spilled over her shoulders. That was better.

"Fletcher, lay off it. I get that you're pissed. But I don't control Xander. I trust him. If he thinks this is the right thing to do, then it probably is. Why don't you let me help you while we're waiting?"

"Help me? You're in custody."

"And whose fault is that?"

"Jeez, would you two give it a rest? None of us can get our homework done when mommy and daddy are fighting."

They both turned to see Inez, her glasses pushed up high on her nose, holding her hand up in a universal stop sign.

"Sorry," Fletcher mumbled.

"Yes, I'm sorry, Inez. This must be terribly disruptive to your workday."

Inez scowled at Sam. "Don't try to suck up. You deserve to be behind bars, not sitting here. I don't approve of your methods."

Fletcher smiled at his assistant, then turned to Sam. "What she said."

"Okay, okay. Fine. You've got to give me something to do, though. I'm going stir-crazy."

"Why don't you type up your autopsy report?"

"I already did that."

"Then here. Take my laptop and surf the Net. Facebook. Twitter. Write a blog. Shop for some shoes. I don't care. Just leave me alone so I can get some work done."

He shoved the laptop across the desk to her, and she demurely said, "Thanks."

She resisted cheering; it wouldn't be seemly.

Inez looked at Fletcher. "Are you sure you should let her do that?"

Fletcher shrugged. "If it shuts her up, I'm all for it."

Sam tapped away at the keyboard. As it happened, she did have a Facebook account, purely for business. She'd joined about a year earlier, ostensibly to get in touch with some friends from her high school, Father Ryan, but in reality to keep an eye on one of her employees whom she suspected was stealing illegal drugs from the evidence lockers at Forensic Medical. One of her former death investigators, a girl named Keri McGee, had set up the account for her and "friended," as she called it, several of the staffers. Sam wasn't fond of the site, it felt too much like spying on people to go to their pages and look at their pictures and hear the intimate details of their lives, but the sting worked. The staffer was caught, summarily dismissed, and Sam had biometric locks installed on the door to the evidence room so it wouldn't happen again.

She hadn't been back on the site, had meant to close her account, but was now grateful for the oversight. She could do a little investigating of her own without anyone being the wiser.

She typed a name into the search box, careful to get the spelling correct. Loa Ledbetter.

Boom. Up popped the woman's page.

Sam looked at the profile picture and couldn't stop the lump from forming in her throat. Ledbetter was a beautiful woman, very natural, with a self-assured smile. She was standing in the midst of a group of Maasi tribesmen, staring right into the camera. Sam read her information; she was a Harvard girl, with a B.Sc. in cultural anthropology, an M.A. in sociology and a Ph.D. in sociocultural and medical anthropology. She owned a market research firm that specialized in ethnographic research. In other words, a very intelligent woman who'd made a good life for herself studying other people's behavior for a living.

What would she have made of the attack?

Sam clicked through a few of the pictures; not being a friend of the deceased, she was limited as to what she could see. But when she went back to the front page, the "Wall," as it was called, there was a new status update. From Loa Ledbetter herself. An update from the grave. Sam shook off the chill at the coincidence.

Dear all: I am so sad to have to share that my mother was a victim of the heinous attacks in D.C. yesterday. We are devastated, and appreciate your prayers during this difficult time. When arrangements have been made we will update this page. For now, I will leave you with my mother's favorite quote: "We must dare to be ourselves, however frightening or strange that self may prove to be."—May Sarton

Even one death is too many.

Sam took a deep breath to steady herself. This was how it was meant to be. Children were supposed to mourn their parents, not the other way around.

She looked at Ledbetter's "friends" page and saw there was one person labeled as family. A daughter, also named Loa. She clicked on the profile, but unlike her mother, Loa the younger's site was closed off to even the most cursory of investigation.

Sam didn't waste any time. She sent the girl a friend request and a note that read, Please accept my deepest condolences. I am one of the medical examiners on your mother's case. I would like to talk to you if you have a moment. She left her cell number and email address.

Marc Conlon's page was very different from Loa's. It was unrestricted, open for all to see. His friends had been actively posting, there were hundreds of wall entries sending the boy and his family prayers and good wishes, recounting good times had, and numerous tear-jerking replies. Sam was amazed, as she always was, at the openness with which the younger generation lived their lives. Everything they did or said was on display, with no thought to the consequences. The concept of privacy was lost on them.

Sam scrolled through the post until she found his latest entry. What she saw shocked her.

The night before the attack, at one in the morning, he had posted: Operation TEOTWAWKI entering final stage. Will report back on its success or failure. Wish me luck.

"Fletcher?"

He looked up from his desktop. "Yeah? What is it?"

"How much do you know about Marc Conlon?"

"Not my part of the investigation. Why?"

"Look at this." She spun the laptop around so the screen was facing him. "What does TEOTWAWKI stand for?"

He read the status update. He paled, then turned to Inez. "Get me Bianco, right now."

She didn't hesitate, shot up from her chair and marched off in search of their boss.

"Fletch, what? What is it?"

"It's an acronym for the end of the world as we know it."

CHAPTER NINETEEN

Washington, D.C.
Detective Darren Fletcher

Fletcher cursed himself for letting Sam anywhere near his laptop. Of course she'd be digging into the lives of the dead, that was her job. He had enough respect for her instincts not to throttle her on the spot, though now he really was going to catch hell.

Could a nineteen-year-old boy manage to stage a biological attack of this scale on the Metro? Not without help, which meant there were more of them out there.

He couldn't help himself, the REM song jumped into his head.

If the end of the world as we know it had Lenny Bruce involved, surely a suburban student could be, too.

The edges of a plan started to form in the back of his mind. It was risky, but what else could he do? He was being hamstrung here, and that wasn't acceptable. He couldn't just quit the JTTF, either; he was invested enough in the outcome of the Leighton case to want to see what the truth was, and now his fingerprints were all over it, literally and figuratively, so walking away wasn't an option.

But someone else might be able to walk away.

"Listen, Sam. When Bianco gets here, let me talk. I'd rather neither of us go to jail today, all right?"

Sam crossed her arms and sat back in her chair. It wasn't like her to gloat, so she must still be pissed at him. Great. How could she blame him? He was just doing his job. Covering his own ass. He was a bit miffed at her, as well.

Inez came back, looking harried.

"Bianco wants you to pass the information to Cusack. She said to stay on Leighton."

Of course she does.

Sam finally spoke. "Well, that's not fair. You found the info, you should be able to investigate it."

Fletcher shrugged. "Technically, you found the info. But Bianco is all-powerful here. Inez, you didn't hear that."

"Of course not, sir."

Crap. He didn't want to do it like this, but it was unavoidable.

"Would you do me a favor, Inez? I'm starving. Sam must be, too. Think I could bribe you to grab us a couple of pastrami and Swiss sandwiches from the Au Bon Pain down the street?"

Inez was no dummy, but she stood automatically and held out her hand for money. He handed her thirty bucks and said, "Get one for yourself, too."

"Thanks, Fletch."

She disappeared down the corridor, and he turned to Sam. He spoke low so they wouldn't be overheard.

"Here's the deal. What you did was wrong. Nothing matters right now more than capturing the person who orchestrated the attack. Not our friendship, or your relationship. Can we agree on that?"

She was silent for a moment. "Agreed."

"I trust you, Sam. I know that you'd never purposefully do something to hurt me, personally or professionally. We are friends, even though you feel we might not be close. You could have told Bianco that you'd been calling me all night and I didn't answer, but you didn't."

Sam nodded. "I didn't see the point."

"I appreciate that. Because that would have made things even worse. I'm being railroaded here. The case on Leighton isn't what it seems. There are some pretty intense accusations being laid on him, and if this investigation isn't handled just right, it's going to be me that goes down. You with me?"

"Fletch, what is it? What do they have on the congressman?"

With a quick glance over his shoulder, he slid the file to her. She opened it and, after a few seconds, looked appropriately shocked. She read through the reports swiftly, then closed it and pushed the file back to him.

"Oh. I see."

"Yes. Something in my gut tells me we aren't being given all the pieces of the puzzle. So I want your help. I really do. But I'm stuck here, dealing with this portion of the investigation. But you...you aren't. You have the freedom to do what you want."

She gave him a wary glance. "I thought I was in protective custody."

"You are. But sometimes the greater good must be served. The door is over there."

"What do you want me to do?"

She was quick, he'd give her that.

"Get the hell out of here, go dig up everything you can on Conlon and Ledbetter, find your fool of a boyfriend, and get back to me as fast as you can. Be careful, though. Don't get picked up. Lay low. If something bad happens, and you can't get back here, go to Captain Armstrong. He likes you, he'll take care of you."

"What are you going to do?"

"Try to figure out what the hell is going on here with Leighton. Now go, Sam. Before I change my mind."

She was up and out of the chair before his lips closed. She walked with purpose away from his desk, neither looking right nor left, just focused on the door. Fletcher glanced around the bullpen, saw Bianco walking toward the conference room, her view of the door to the hall obscured. Providence.

Sam was gone, out the door, and when no alarm bells went off, Fletcher knew he'd just made the right decision. He could cover for at least an hour before Bianco figured things out, and that might just give Sam enough time to get some of the answers he needed to set his mind at ease.

He sent a note to Armstrong, a heads-up, just in case. And then he pulled the file to him and looked at the DNA again. Such a coincidence, the congressman managing to get himself dead just as the FBI found out he was a serial killer.

Something wasn't right here. And he was going to figure out what that was, no matter what it cost him.

CHAPTER TWENTY

Washington, D.C.
Dr. Samantha Owens

Sam was a city block away from the JTTF before she let herself take a full breath. She'd been careful to go in the opposite direction from the Au Bon Pain so she wouldn't stumble into Inez. Every step she took she expected an arm to land on her shoulder, grabbing and pulling her back to the JTTF offices, where she'd be stuck in a cell this time—they didn't take kindly to suspects, or witnesses, or whatever role she was supposed to be playing for them, walking out of their custody unmolested.

But she didn't perceive any immediate threats to her freedom, so she kept walking.

D.C. had recovered from the attack the day before. People streamed through the streets; the Metro was still closed, so they were forced to drive and taxi and walk to their destinations. There was still a large law enforcement presence, but the overwhelming mood was one of cautious optimism. They'd been attacked, and only three had died. It wasn't cause for celebration, but it was a testament to the American way—

you might be able to punch us, but you rarely knock us down, and never knock us out.

Summer in D.C. was a kaleidoscope of colors: flowers and trees thick with blooms, dresses in bold pinks and purples and yellows and greens, men in lightweight linen suits, even some seersucker. Nothing screamed hot weather to Sam like seersucker. She tucked herself behind a particularly portly man who not only wore a lightweight suit, but sported a hat and cane besides, and headed directly four blocks west to K Street, where she found Ledbetter's office building with no difficulty.

She ducked inside the revolving doors, waiting a minute by the wall to see if anyone was following her. She felt rather ridiculous; she wasn't used to not being able to use the power of her office to gain information. Sneaking around like this was insane. When she was growing up, and she'd ask her mother for advice about something she thought was questionable, her mom always told her, "Well, Sam, if you have to ask, then it's probably the wrong thing to do." That's how she felt right now. Sneaking around like she had something to hide, when all she was doing was trying to help.

She tried to make sense of everything that was happening while she caught her breath.

A terrorist attack with an unknown substance. Xander running off to track down the owners of a survivalist website. Fletcher being asked to investigate the congressman as a serial killer. A teenage boy who talked publicly of an apocalyptic event. She couldn't see what an anthropologist market researcher had to do with any of that.

But that's why she was here, to try and pull the pieces together for Fletcher. To help him out from under the thumb of this Bianco character. Sam didn't know if the woman was trustworthy, or out to cover her own ass. Whether the sweet-

ness was an act belying a bitchy cream center, or her real dispo-
sition. She leaned toward the former, but only time would tell.

She glanced at the board that listed which office was where,
and saw Ledbetter was on the sixth floor. Sam picked another
office on the sixth, that of an OB/GYN, and went to the front
desk, got in the line to move through the building's security.
She watched the three people in front of her as they signed in:
the security guard didn't ask any of them for ID. When Sam's
turn came, she altered her name, wrote Sarah Jackson on the
sheet, and the doctor's name. The guard didn't blink an eye,
just issued her a pass and motioned her through the turnstile.

Obviously no one at the JTTF thought Loa Ledbetter's
death was anything but a horrible accident, or they had already
checked her out and didn't find anything of consequence; otherwise, they might have had a tighter lock on the security in
her building. That was lucky.

The elevator was inlaid marble and dark walnut, very elegant, and Sam got the impression that perhaps Ledbetter had
been doing all right in the business department.

The OB/GYN offices were the first thing she saw when
the doors of the elevator opened. Ledbetter's suite was 640,
around the corner, away from the main thoroughfare, without
the constant parade of patients in and out. Smart. Sam didn't
hesitate, went to the double glass doors and entered the offices of Ledbetter Market Strategies.

The doors closed behind her with a whispered rush, and
Sam realized her initial assessment about Ledbetter's level of
success was correct. The offices were gorgeous. The walls
on either side housed floor-to-ceiling mahogany and glass
shelves that held all sorts of artifacts, masks and jars and shields
and art in a variety of textures and colors. It was an impres-
sive display. Sam was reminded of a childhood trip to see the
Egyptian mummies, and all the finery that accompanied their

kings and queens to the graves. She'd been in awe of the fact that it was all so very old, and that so many ghosts still floated around the scene. She felt that here as well, the presence of the people to whom the materials had belonged. Watching over their treasures.

"May I help you?"

A man in his mid-thirties with dirty blond hair and a dimple in his chin sat at the reception desk. She hadn't even noticed him when she walked in.

"Yes. Good afternoon. My name is Dr. Samantha Owens. I'm a medical examiner, and I am working on Dr. Ledbetter's case. I am so sorry for your loss."

His face crumpled. "You're kind to say that. We aren't quite sure what to do now. Dr. Ledbetter has two partners, but they're both out of the country at the moment, unreachable, so we're all just gathered here trying to move forward and get through the day. Her loss is inestimable. I'm George Capra, her assistant. She was like a mother to me, I've worked with her for years. Since she taught me in graduate school, actually."

Good. She'd walked right into the firm's institutional knowledge. That was going to make things easier.

"I know how hard it is to lose the ones you love." *Oh boy, do I know.*

"Yes. It's terrible. What can I help you with, Dr. Owens?"

Sam set her Birkin bag on the frosted glass bar that separated her from the assistant, and said, with a tone of confidentiality, "Honestly, George, I'm not quite sure. The details of the investigation haven't given me a great deal to go on, and I find it helps my work to have a complete picture of who my... guests are. I'd just like to know more about her, if you've got a few minutes to share."

He cracked a weak smile. "You're an ethnographic researcher, just like her. You need all the components of her life to make sense of her death."

"Yes. That's it exactly."

"See, if the police would just look at their crimes in those terms, they'd solve so many more cases. I'm happy to help. Why don't you come into her office, that's the best place to start. Can I get you some coffee, or tea?"

"Tea would be lovely, thank you. Light and sweet."

"Of course. Follow me, please."

The hallways of Ledbetter's offices were adorned with photographs of the company's namesake. Sam stopped to look at a few of them. There was the shot of Ledbetter with the Maasi tribesmen she'd seen online, and another of her bundled up in snow gear with a six-pack of Inuit and frolicking huskies.

"She did the Iditarod three years ago. That was taken after the race. She didn't win, not by a long shot, but she finished, which was more than the majority of the nonprofessionals who entered."

"She sounds like an extraordinary woman."

"Oh, she was. Traveled all over the world, never saw a challenge she didn't want to tackle. For the past year, she's been training for alpine climbs, wanted to do the seven summits before she got too old. Of course, that meant she needed to stop smoking, and she'd tried so many times, and failed every attempt. It was the one thing I've ever seen that she wanted to do but had trouble with. But she'd pretty much licked it. She hadn't had a cigarette in six months. She finally gave up doing it on her own and tried hypnosis, and it seemed to work."

"Nicotine is worse than heroin."

George laughed a bit, sadly. "That's what Loa used to say."

The pictures continued on, a parade of events that led down the hall into her office. It was just what Sam expected, neat as a pin, organized, well laid out. On the wall were more pictures, one of which Sam recognized from trips as a girl, the volcanoes of Hawaii. Ledbetter knelt with a huge grin on her face and her arm flung out to the right, framing the mountain behind her, as if to say, *Wow, look at this!*

Sam looked closer at the shot. Her heart started to beat harder.

"George, do you have a magnifying glass?"

He shook his head. "No. But that shot is on her computer. She was one hell of a photographer, as you can imagine, and has every trip she's ever taken digitized. You need a closer look?"

Sam tapped the photograph. "I need to blow up this area right here. Just to the left of where she's kneeling."

"Sure. You want me to do it now?"

"Please. Thank you."

Sam took the picture off the wall and stared at it, her mind whirling while George tapped away at the computer and pulled up the original.

"Here we are."

Sam could understand why George held his position; for an exacting professional like Ledbetter, she needed someone who was as driven and talented as she was to be her eyes and ears and an extra set of hands. A second brain.

Sam went around to the back of the desk and looked at the area in question that George had blown up.

Son of a bitch.

"Were the cops here, George?"

"Oh, yeah. They took a bunch of files and asked us all questions last night."

But they hadn't seen the picture.

"Excuse me for just one second."

"Sure. I'll go get that tea."

The minute he was out of earshot she got on her cell phone and called Fletcher.

He answered on the first ring but didn't say her name, just said, "Fletcher."

"I know what the toxin was."

"That's my girl. What is it?"

"Abrin. From the rosary pea plant. One of the deadliest, most poisonous plants in the world. They use the seeds in jewelry all over the tropics. It's actually naturalized in Florida and Georgia, grows primarily in warm places. The labs would never know to look for it, because it's never been successfully weaponized, like ricin and anthrax. The tox screen and air-quality tests will come back inconclusive unless we test for abrin specifically. But if it's inhaled, it can absolutely cause hemorrhagic pneumonia like we saw in all three victims. It would mimic ricin, but the effects can be slower. The people who are still sick can get sicker if they've been exposed to enough of it."

"How did you figure it out?"

"I'm at Loa Ledbetter's office. There's a picture of her in a pasture in Hawaii surrounded by the plants. When I saw it, everything clicked. I remember it from school, just a basic from the list of poisonous plants you're supposed to stay away from."

"Are we looking at her as a suspect instead of a victim?"

"I don't know yet. I'll call Nocek and tell him to change the tox screens, see if I'm right."

Fletcher hesitated. "Will you do me another favor when you do that?"

"Of course."

"Ask him to get a DNA sample from the congressman."

"I thought you already had it confirmed."

"Before I go off half-cocked into this investigation, I want to make sure the previous investigators have it right."

"Good call, Fletch. I'm going to go. You need to get with your people and have them spread the word of what the toxin is so they can treat the remaining victims as quickly as possible. I don't think there's an antidote, but there may be things they can do to help flush it from their systems faster."

"Are you off to Conlon next?"

"I'm going to be here for a bit, look deeper into her life. The cops took a bunch of her files and such, but her assistant knows everything."

"All right. Be careful. Bianco hasn't figured out you're gone yet. I've managed to distract Inez, but she's going to catch on any second."

"See ya, Fletch."

She hung up the phone, feeling triumphant. Knowing what the toxin was would go a long way toward figuring out who was behind the attacks.

CHAPTER TWENTY-ONE

Dillon, Colorado
Alexander Whitfield

Dillon, Colorado, was a small town nestled in a valley ten miles east of the Continental Divide, with a pristine lake that accepted the runoff from the surrounding mountains and provided a perfect place for ski season lodging and summer sports. Xander had grown up skiing the nearby slopes of Keystone and Breckenridge and Vail and Beaver Creek in the winter, boating on Lake Dillon in the summers, fishing its tributaries for trout that his father would fillet and his mother would cook for dinner. It was an idyllic spot, the perfect place to raise children when you wanted to stay off the beaten path. Xander's parents had set down roots there, falling in love with the stunning setting, the sense of privacy and the fertile land.

His parents still lived in the house on Bootlegger Ridge Road. He laid bets with himself as he took the exit off the highway—Sunshine would be in the garden, Roth would be in the smokehouse.

He was right. When he rolled up in the driveway, he could see flashes of the cheerful yellow sundress his mother was wearing, one of her own making, from design to fabric to dye, and smoke rising from the chimney of the small shed to the right of the alpine house.

His parents' dogs, Star and Day Lily, came rushing out to the car. Star was a German shepherd, sister to his own dog, Thor. Day Lily was a black spaniel, happy and giddy and sweet and silly. Sunshine was right behind them, a huge grin on her face.

"Moonbeam! What a wonderful surprise! You didn't send word that you were coming." Xander grimaced at the name choice, but he knew from many battles long and short that his mother would never of her own free will call him Alexander.

She enveloped him in a hug, and the scents of his childhood overwhelmed him: earth, sun, sweat, the sharp tang of herbs, the milky scent that she'd never fully lost after Yellow was weaned, the clingy odor of fresh cannabis, overlaid with a healthy dose of patchouli. It made him happy, and he hugged her back, tight.

The dogs danced around them, caught up in their joy.

Xander finally stepped back and looked at his mother. She was still beautiful, her face relatively unlined, but her cornflower-blue eyes were crinkled around the edges and her gold nose ring sparkled in the sun. Sixty, and still slim as a girl. It was all the homegrown, pesticide-free vegetables she ate, she swore up and down. He thought it was more to do with the strain of pot they'd perfected that didn't make them hungry, but he stayed as far away from that business as he could.

Another scent rose up, this one tantalizing.

"Roth getting ready to smoke a deer?"

"Lord, Moon, your nose is as sensitive as a truffle pig. He's going to be thrilled to see you. Let's go scare him."

His mother would forever be a child.

But he humored her, because sometimes he was just a bit too much of an adult.

They snuck around the back of the shed, and at her cue, flung open the door and screamed like Indians. Alexander Roth Whitfield II jumped and screamed in turn, whirling on them with a skinning knife in his hand. When he realized the joke was on him, he set it down and laughed.

"You're going to give me a heart attack one of these days, Sunshine. Moonbeam, good to see you, son."

Xander accepted his father's embrace gladly. Though his parents hadn't supported his decision to join the Army, they still loved him, and stood by him, especially when he came home from the war and disappeared into the woods. The desire for solitude to come to grips with an unjust world, that they understood. They'd made their life on the sentiment.

"Give me a minute more here, son, I'm nearly finished."

His mother chimed in, "Moon, you just missed lunch, but I can put together a plate for you. Fresh kale and edamame and toasted sesame dressing suit you? I can cut up some tofu if you want protein, we just finished the last of the chicken. The venison isn't cured yet, obviously. The rest is put aside for stew tomorrow. What timing you have!"

"That sounds good, Sunshine. Thank you. I'll be in in just a minute. I need to ask Roth something."

"All right, sweetheart. Oh, it's so good to have you home."

She left the shed, the dogs following her as if she was the pied piper of the canine set.

He watched her go, smiling at her glee. When he turned back to his father, he saw the look echoed on the older man's face. Nice to still be madly in love after forty years together.

He hoped for that with Samantha.

The thought brought him up short. He hadn't wanted to admit to himself that after just three lovely months, all he wanted was to put a ring on her finger and call her wife. He didn't think she'd want that, not yet, not so soon. He didn't doubt her love, quite the opposite. She wouldn't have gotten nearly as angry with him if she didn't care. But he wasn't sure if she was ready, and so he didn't want to push the issue. Better to let it arise organically. He wanted a life of bliss with her, that he couldn't deny. Maybe even children, if she could bear the thought of trying again. But he had a mission to execute right now, so he put thoughts of love and romance aside to speak man-to-man with his father.

"Help me, will you? This last bit is always a pain."

Xander took his designated spot at the rear of the deer, helped guide his father's knife. It was a stag, maybe eight point, a big fellow.

"Took him with your bow?"

Roth felt hunting with a rifle was unsportsmanlike, instead used a crossbow. He thought it evened the odds a bit.

"Yes. We're out of season, but it was a mercy kill. His leg was broken. We saw him limping around in the forest two days ago, and I couldn't let him suffer. And the wolves didn't deserve an easy snack—they took three of the chickens last week." He patted the skinned rump of the deer. "He led me on a chase, too. A fine beast. He died with honor."

He said this with the gravest respect. Roth and Sunshine had taught Xander reverence for their fellow beings, regardless of their sentience, especially the ones that fed and clothed them.

"You in trouble?" Roth asked, finishing the skinning with three short, quick, practiced cuts.

"Not me. Not yet, anyway. Have you heard what's been going on?"

"No. I've been in the woods for the past day and night, and you know how Sun is."

He did. Growing up, his mother forbade television and radio, insisting instead on books and self-made music and imagination to entertain her children. There was a small portable television set they kept in the garage in case of emergency, but the fears of Washington hadn't permeated the open land of Colorado yet.

"There was a supposed terrorist attack on the subway in D.C. Have you seen Stuart Crawford lately?"

"I have. You think he was behind it?"

"Why do you say that?"

"You know Stu. He still thinks everyone west of the Divide should secede."

Xander laughed. "If I remember, you weren't entirely against that idea."

"No, I wasn't, but it was too political for me to worry about. I'm a farmer, not a fighter." There was a catch to his voice, not disapproval, per se, just a statement of fact. It was not lost on him that he was a pacifist who'd somehow raised a warrior.

"Stu's son, William? Remember him? He's the computer genius. That's who I'm looking for."

Roth took a break, leaned his hip against the table.

"Little Will Crawford. Think he lives somewhere west of here, might be as far as Grand Junction. But Stu's always around. We can go see him after you humor your mother and eat some lunch, if you'd like."

"I'd like. Thank you, Roth. I wouldn't ask if it weren't important."

His father nodded once, still formal in his movements after all these years. "Of course. Now, let me get finished here, and you go see Sunshine."

He'd never loved kale, but he ate it anyway, knowing how many vitamins and nutrients it had. Dark leafy greens warded off illness, as his mother liked to remind him. She was right, and her influence meant he generally ate exceptionally well, getting all of his nutrition from a balanced diet of vegetable, fruit and protein matter, with very little carbs that weren't whole grains. Sam had been shocked at his culinary skills when she first moved in, not expecting him to be able to cook so well, but Xander was a bit of a gourmet, albeit an all-natural one. She'd joked that he should write a cookbook, *The Warrior's Guide to Clean Living*. Her sherry-drenched eyes would laugh as she teased, her mouth quirked in a grin. The mouth he loved to settle his own upon, just because he could.

God, he'd only been away from her for six hours and he was already pining. If that wasn't love, he didn't know what was. He did know he'd never felt like this about another woman.

Sunshine cleared her son's plate when he was finished, and, as if on cue, his father came to the door, washed and combed and neat after the slaughter, ready to escort his son into the lion's den. Stu Crawford was an excitable sort; it would be best to have a friendly face along on their excursion. Sunshine kissed them both and told them to hurry back.

The drive to Crawford's ranch would take twenty minutes or so. Xander and his father settled on a safe topic of conversation, Bach's Sonata in A Major for Violin and Piano. After agreeing that it was among their favorites, they evolved on to a slightly touchier subject. The *Chaconne* was Roth's particular passion, and Xander had sent him a CD he'd recently acquired with Juliette Kang performing on the violin. Xander thought it masterful, Roth agreed, the young prodigy was excellent. But she wasn't Xander.

Xander had chosen piano over violin when he was only ten, though he could play both exceptionally well. Sunshine favored the piano, while Roth favored the violin; it was the first conscious decision Xander made that went against his father's wishes. He'd nearly mastered the *Chaconne,* considered one of the most difficult pieces of music to play in the world, but the piano held more of a challenge for him. He didn't feel the strings in his soul the way he did the ivory.

They were past Avon now, the exit for Crawford's Ranch coming up quickly.

"If he comes out with that Remington pointed anywhere but at the sky, let me talk."

Xander glanced at his father, saw he wasn't joking. Roth shrugged. "He's gotten crotchety in his dotage. Perhaps has a touch of dementia."

"He's younger than you, isn't he?"

"By the calendar, perhaps. But hate ages a man."

Roth said nothing else, and Xander took the hint. He took the exit for the ranch, wound up the mountain, through the deep, undisturbed forest until the gate showed itself. Xander drove across the metal cowcatcher over the gully into the turnoff. He rolled down the window and killed the engine, kept his hand visible. The gate had a small box where visitors could announce themselves. Xander did a moment of recon, saw two cameras, assumed there were two more that weren't as easily spotted. His father wasn't kidding, Crawford had gotten paranoid.

A voice crackled in the box.

"By all that's holy, is that Roth Whitfield? And Xander Moon?"

"That's right, sir. May we come up?"

"Sure. Drive slow. The dogs are out."

"Roger that." The gate swung open with a hiss, and Xander drove the Explorer through, careful to put up his window. The "dogs" were an attack squad of Dobermans, highly trained and battle ready. Beautiful animals, well maintained—they had a roomy doghouse that was heated and had running water, and they dined on raw steak, oats and vegetables. They lived better than some soldiers, and were twice as mean.

The drive was a mile long, dirt and gravel, which meant the vehicle had to go slow or risk sliding off the edges into the ditches on either side. Well defensible. It took five minutes to make the trek up to the house, a two-story A-frame similar to Xander's parents' place. Crawford was waiting in the turnabout with the advertised Remington on his shoulder and one of the Dobermans, a red bitch, quivering at his side.

"Good grief. Man looks like he's ready to go to war. This is Colorado, not Afghanistan."

"Once a soldier," Xander said. "You want to talk first?"

"That might be best."

They exited the vehicle slowly, so as not to excite either the dog or Crawford too much.

"Stu. Moonbeam was in town, wanted to pay you a visit. You mind putting the gun away?"

Crawford regarded them shrewdly, head cocked to the side. Once he'd assessed the situation, confirmed that his visitors were who they said they were, were unaccompanied and unarmed, he welcomed them with open arms.

"Come on in. *Mi casa,* and all that."

CHAPTER TWENTY-TWO

They settled at the kitchen table with coffee, and shot the shit for a few minutes before Xander felt it was time to get down to business.

"Sir, I was wondering if you'd seen your son Will lately."

"Well, that's a strange as hell coincidence. He's here for a visit. Out hunting right now, turkey. Should be back before dark. Why do you need him?"

"It's about a website I think he may run. We had a situation down near where I live and the site went dark right after. I wanted to ask him about it."

"A situation? You're talking about that damn fool who attacked the subway in the viper's den? Not sure that's a bad thing, that son of a bitch Leighton got caught up in it. Glad to see him go."

Xander left that alone. "Yes, that's what it's about. I just need to chat with Will about someone who'd been on the site. I assume he took it down because he and I are both thinking the same thing."

"Now, you don't be dragging my boy into any messes, Moon. I remember the trouble the two of you used to get in."

"Goodness, no, sir. I'm a grown-up now. The only trouble I get into is all good clean fun."

The dogs started to bark, and a moment later the door opened from the deck and William Crawford stalked into the room. He was taller and heavier than Xander remembered, but muscled, his shoulders straining against his hunting camo. He was still towheaded, the hair on his scalp thinned to show the pinkness underneath. He saw Xander and Roth and did a double take. Xander caught the alarm on his face, knew at once his theory was correct. Will did know something.

The younger Crawford collected himself quickly, started in with a swagger.

"Well, well, well. Why are you here, Xander Moon?"

"Now, Will, is that any way to greet an old friend?" his father chided.

Xander showed Will his palms, happy that at least someone was using a part of his preferred name. When he'd declared he wanted to be called Xander, the girls in his circle seized upon the nickname Xander Moon, and that stuck.

"I come in peace. The site went down, I was worried about you."

Will's florid face stayed carefully neutral. "So worried that you flew two thousand miles to check up on me? That's awful sweet of you. And not necessary, as you can see. I'm just fine."

"Can we speak in private, Will?"

He shrugged and sat on the couch next to his father. Helped himself to some coffee.

"Nothing you have to say needs hid. What bee got in your bonnet?"

"All right. Before you went dark, there was chatter that a stranger was talking about cooking something to release in the subway."

"That's true. We sussed him out and deactivated his account immediately."

"Did you keep his information?"

Will sat back and regarded Xander for a minute before answering. "Moon, this ain't your fight. Why are you really here?"

"I'm just looking out for a friend," he said lightly.

"That's mighty kind of you. But you don't need to worry about little ol' me. I'm taking care of things. That's why I came down here for a visit, just to be extra cautious. We'll get the site up again in a day or two. Different host, that sort of thing. Just in case people who aren't our friends go talking to the wrong sort. Know what I mean?"

The sentence was pointed, and Xander received the message loud and clear.

"I do. I'd also really like it if you would share this character's last knowns with me. It would go a long way toward smoothing out the situation for us both. I can go to my people with the information and leave you out of it entirely."

He didn't flinch when Will shot up out of his seat and took three steps toward him. He was expecting it. Intimidation was one of the things Will had always been good at. When they were kids, Xander may have succumbed to the peer pressure a time or three. But he was a man now, battle tested, and Will Crawford didn't scare him a lick. Xander knew four ways to kill him without moving from his seat or breaking a sweat.

But he found the move incredibly interesting. Will was covering for someone.

"I thought you left the Army, Xander Moon."

"I did. But the Army will never leave me. I'm just trying to do the right thing here, Will. A lot of people got hurt. He tries again, maybe a lot of people get dead. I'd like to help make sure that doesn't happen."

Silence again. The tension in the room had ratcheted up a notch. Xander had no idea why Will was protecting a stranger, which told him more than he wanted to know.

"Fine," Will finally said. "I don't have much. It's gonna take some serious talent to do anything with it. I hit a dead end, myself, and I'm pretty seriously talented." He laughed then, and they all joined in, Xander and Roth not quite as heartily as Will and Stu. Five minutes later, their goodbyes said, they left.

Xander had the information he wanted.

Most of it.

The drive back was quiet. His father stared out the window, but Xander could tell he wanted to talk. With a sigh, Xander said, "What?"

The invitation extended, Roth didn't hesitate. "You should have let the police handle this, Moonbeam."

"I'm not in the habit of uncovering problems and handing them over to others to handle. That's not what I was trained to do."

"But, Moon, Will had a point. You aren't in the Army anymore. This isn't your responsibility."

Xander took three breaths so he wouldn't say anything he'd regret later.

"I know you don't understand, Roth, nor would I expect you to. We are very different men, you and I, and I respect your beliefs, and love you for them. But I am compelled to serve my country, whether they're paying me to do so or not. Just because I'm not under command doesn't mean I shouldn't do the right thing when I can. If I'd told the police about this, or the FBI, instead of handling it myself, they'd have come in here guns blazing, and you saw how twitchy Crawford was. He'd have managed to get into a standoff, and people would have died. I wasn't about to let that happen. My responsibility is to both this country and the people who share my convictions, as well as yours. Now I can get the appropriate information to the appropriate people with little to no danger to my friends. Surely that makes sense to you."

It was a good speech, one of his better arguments, actually. But Roth didn't say a word.

Well, he'd tried.

The sun was setting behind them, casting a lovely light on the lake. When they reached the turnoff to Dillon, Xander was shocked to feel his father's hand on his shoulder. Patting the muscle, then squeezing.

"Well said, son. Well said."

CHAPTER TWENTY-THREE

Washington, D.C.
Dr. Samantha Owens

Sam called Nocek the moment she hung up with Fletcher. She had to wait a minute—he was in the middle of an autopsy—but he came on soon enough.

"Amado, I've found something. I think the toxin is abrin."

He was quiet for a moment, and Sam could practically hear him thinking.

"*Abrus precatorius.* Samantha, that makes perfect sense, and fits all of the findings we've discovered. It would have to be inhaled to cause the exact damage to the organs we witnessed."

"I agree. Ledbetter, Conlon and Leighton all inhaled it. The question is, why did these three people die almost immediately after they were exposed? From what I remember, abrin poisoning can take hours to manifest, even days. Which also means the people who are still sick aren't out of the woods, and more could begin to exhibit symptoms. I've told Fletcher, he's warning the CDC and Homeland Security. The hospitals will need to treat specifically for this toxin to save their lives, and a public warning needs to go out so people who might have been exposed can look for symptoms."

It wasn't lost on her that she was also still within the window of showing symptoms; hell, during the attack she was on top of ground zero. She could have been exposed and didn't know it yet. The thought made her pulse pick up, and she immediately lifted a hand to her forehead. If she was going to manifest symptoms, they'd be similar to what Brooke showed yesterday in Sam's classroom: lethargy, fever, cough, respiratory distress.

Her forehead was cool to the touch, and she felt a bit of relief. Since there was no documentation that she was aware of about the toxin being used in an attack of this nature, it was quite possible that the only way to be fully exposed was to be in the Metro at the moment it was released.

She heard Nocek tapping on a computer keyboard, most likely pulling up the information on the plant.

"You are correct in all of your assumptions. I am very impressed, Samantha."

She flushed with pleasure. It was nice to have an *attagirl* from a man she respected.

So one part of the mystery solved. Now she had to move on to parts two through six, and find out where Xander had rushed off to.

"Amado, I need to ask you one more favor, and I need you to not ask me why."

"It would be my pleasure. Anything for you."

"Can you grab a blood sample from the congressman and send it for DNA typing? With an emergency return?"

"Of course. Would you like me to disguise the name so there are no red flags raised?"

Sam smiled. "Yes, I would. And thank you."

"You will be interested to learn, perhaps, that you are not

the first person to request something private from the congressman today."

"Really? Who else wants DNA?"

Nocek cleared his throat. "Not DNA in particular, though that would certainly be a by-product. No, the request was for fluids of a more…personal nature."

Sam immediately knew what he was talking about. "Please tell me it was the wife asking."

"Yes. That is correct."

"Did you give it to her?"

"I did. She was in possession of a judicial order. I warned her there were no guarantees of strength or vitality, though it most likely was in time."

"Now that is one of the most interesting things I've heard all day. Do you think the semen could have been tainted by the abrin, assuming he tests positive?"

"I do not know how quickly it moves through a body. That will be something for a geneticist to examine. As I understand it, the *matériel* was needed for an in vitro harvest procedure expected to take place two days hence."

"Wow. Quick thinking in the middle of the kind of grief she must be feeling."

"She was quite calm, actually. Upset, but determined."

God. Sam felt sorry for Mrs. Leighton. Not only losing your husband, but your chance of having his child, especially in the midst of the horror that was preparation for in vitro fertilization. It *was* quick thinking to gather his semen for the procedure. Generally, sperm had a window of about twelve to thirty-six hours where it could successfully be harvested postmortem unless special precautions were taken. Sam had never been faced with the situation Nocek was describing, but she'd certainly heard other medical examiners talk of it. It didn't often work, but there had been cases where successful live births had been reported. It was normally a very gray ethical area that resulted in court orders and the like, which took so much time it damaged the chances of getting usable sperm.

But there was a science for everything these days.

Sam made a mental note to share that tidbit with Fletcher. Talk about something that would extend the news cycle on Leighton's death for yet another week. The man's life grew more complex by the hour. Pervert, serial killer, about to be a father again, dead in a terrorist attack.

Too many facets, too many coincidences.

"Amado, I need to run. Thank you for everything."

"I will let you know what I am able to discern. Be well, Samantha."

"And you." She hung up just as George returned to his boss's office with her tea.

"Thank you."

"You're welcome. Is there anything else I can do to help?"

"Two things. I'd like to get to know Dr. Ledbetter. Would you mind if we looked through her photographs, and you can share some of her stories with me?"

George gave her a wistful smile. "Of course. That might actually be helpful for me, to say goodbye. Let me get you set up in the conference room. It will be easier to project them onto the screen instead of both of us hunched over her laptop. What's the second?"

"I'd like to talk to her daughter."

At that, George pulled up short. "Um, that might be harder to manage. They were estranged."

"Oh. I saw her post on Facebook earlier about her mother's death. I didn't get the sense that she was anything but a grieving daughter."

George coughed out a dry, sarcastic laugh. "Grieving, no. Celebrating is more like it."

"Why?"

He waved his hand around. "All of this? Everything Loa had, her money, her holdings, her business? All of it goes to Loa the younger."

"Really. How much are we talking?" Sam asked.

He raised an eyebrow. "In the neighborhood of twenty million, give or take. Which is criminal considering how much she hates her mother."

"Whoa."

"Yes. So now you understand. That's about twenty-million reasons to want your mother dead."

CHAPTER TWENTY-FOUR

Sam made another quick call to Fletcher while George hooked up the laptop to the projector.

He answered, a little more wary this time.

"Where are you, Sam? You need to get back here right now."

"Ah. Bianco knows I'm gone?"

"You better believe it, sister. You are under orders to return here immediately."

"Is anyone listening to this?"

"No."

"Standing nearby?"

"Yes."

"All right. I'll be quick. Go check out Gretchen Leighton. She retrieved her husband's sperm about an hour ago. They were about to do in vitro. DNA will be run for you. And Ledbetter was worth $20 million, her sole heir is her estranged daughter, also named Loa. Nothing on Conlon, I'm still here."

Fletcher's voice got a little lighter, like he held the phone away from his face. "Shit. She hung up. She didn't say where she was, only that she was planning to head back to her house.

You should probably send a couple of agents there to pick her up. I'm sorry, Andi. I thought I could keep her on longer."

Damn, he was good. She'd never seen the deceitful side of Fletcher. She didn't have much time, that was for sure. At least the agents would be heading to her house. She'd avoid home like the plague.

She listened as Bianco ordered a couple of people to go find Sam and bring her back in, then listened to Bianco dress Fletcher down.

"I still can't believe you let a suspect go to the bathroom by herself, Detective. Sloppy work."

"Yeah, well. I thought I could trust her."

"You obviously are not thinking with the head resting on top of your shoulders."

There she was, the bitchy Bianco Sam suspected resided behind the sweet, polite veneer.

"I said I was sorry. You'll snatch her up in a few minutes and we'll all move on with our day. Any more news about her boyfriend, Whitfield? Did you find him past Denver?"

"No. The call traced to the cellular tower closest to the Denver International Airport. The authorities are looking for him now. You stay focused on your task, Detective. You're all Leighton, all the time. Report in to me as soon as you have something."

Denver. Now his flight made sense to her. Xander had gone home. That was hugely valuable information. *Thank you, Fletcher.*

With any luck, he'd stay ahead of the JTTF until he had the information he wanted. She couldn't call him and warn him off, either, though she assumed he knew he was working on borrowed time.

Fletcher came back on the line. "She's gone. You get that?"

"Yes."

"You know where he's headed?"

"Yes."

"Finish up there as quick as you can. I'll get you on a flight."

"You want me to go track him down?"

"Yeah. I think his theory is right. JTTF found the remnants of the website he was looking for, they're going to go hot to look for the owners soon. You might be able to save Xander from getting wrapped up in this. Good job on the abrin, by the way. The ones who are still sick are being treated for it. You saved a lot of lives, Sam."

"With your help, Fletch. Thanks for everything. I'll call you from Denver."

She hung up and something else in her brain clicked. She went into the conference room where George was patiently waiting.

"George. You said you met Dr. Ledbetter when she taught your graduate class. Where was she teaching then?"

"Harvard."

"Does she still teach?"

"Yes. At American University. She's on the anthropology/sociology staff there."

CHAPTER TWENTY-FIVE

Time was getting short. Sam had no real way of knowing how close to placing Marc Conlon and Loa Ledbetter together the police might be, and she knew she needed to get a move on to get to the airport and fly out to Denver before everyone started looking for her. God, Fletcher was going to be summarily fired, and probably prosecuted, if Bianco caught on to his scheme. And so would Sam.

"George, there's no chance she teaches during the summer session, is there?"

"No. Too busy. She does most of her excursions during the warmer months. But she teaches a class in the spring. Sociology 102."

"Do you happen to have that class list? From this last spring semester's class?"

"Sure. Hold on a second."

The screen went blank. George tapped a few words into the computer and then excused himself. He was back in just a second with a sheet of paper, a printout of the Sociology 102 class in hand. He gave it to her, and it only took Sam a moment to find the name Marc Conlon.

"Damn it, she taught one of the other victims." Another

thought hit her. "George, she wasn't friends with Congressman Leighton, was she?"

"Not that I know of, no. But she had a wide circle of acquaintances, people who met her once and just loved her. It was a gift."

"I can see that. Hold on one second."

Sam grabbed her phone and tapped out a text to Fletcher, not wanting to risk calling him again in case Bianco was back to ride him.

MC was LDB's student @ AU. SOC 102

She needed to get out of there, but she felt the photographs could tell her something. They had led her to the toxin, which was already one coincidence too many for her liking.

She decided, in order to narrow things down and make the search go faster, she'd focus only on the excursions that featured prominently in Ledbetter's mythology: the framed photos on display in her office hallway. Those were obviously the moments she was most proud of, the ones she wanted to be remembered for. Every client who entered her business would be led past the pictures, and if they wanted to make a good impression, or she did, the photos were on display to be remarked upon.

She told this to George, who assessed her with a shrewd look.

"You should be a detective. Thirty minutes here, you've discovered more than the entire team of police did last night."

"Well, being a medical examiner is more than just cutting open bodies. You sometimes need to look deeper, and know what kinds of questions to ask."

That wasn't a completely bald-faced lie, but close to it; she wasn't an investigator, legally or otherwise. Her job was to

lay bare the secrets of the dead using the evidence she collected from their bodies, nothing more. The relationship she
had with the police in Nashville was a special one; not all
medical examiners were utilized in the way she had been, as
a congruent mind in their trickier investigations.

It was nice to be needed this way again.

Her text chimed. It was Fletcher, also in code. She had to
think about it for a second before she realized he'd sent her
flight information. Her plane left in exactly ninety minutes.
She wasn't going to have time to do the photos after all.

"George, this is unfortunate timing, and I hate to be so
incredibly rude, but I have to leave. Is there any chance you
could put the photos we're talking about on a jump drive for
me?"

"If you need to leave now, no. That will take too long—
they're all high resolution." He studied her thoughtfully, his
arms crossed on his chest. "Dr. Owens, please be honest with
me. Do you think Dr. Ledbetter was killed? That she wasn't
just a victim of the attacks yesterday, but maybe a target? And
Marc Conlon might have been, too?"

She had nothing to lose by telling him the truth. He was a
sharp young man, one that Sam liked already.

"I'm starting to suspect that, George, yes."

He nodded, then turned to the side table and grabbed a
Post-it note. He wrote a few things on it, then handed it to her.

"This is the password to her account on Fotki, that's where
she uploads all of her private photos. Everything—every excursion, every excavation, every event she does is in there,
dated and explained. It's better than a diary." He thought for
another moment, then his face brightened. "Oh, hold on."

He rushed from the room and she heard him next door,
rummaging.

He came back with two books. "Here. These are the texts

she uses for SOC 102. One is pretty standard for that type of class. The other one she wrote herself."

"Wow. She's an author, too?"

"Absolutely. This book in particular is a bit of a memoir. She uses her experiences to explain how to do ethnographic research. It might give you a place to start looking for suspects."

She must have looked confused, because George tapped the cover of the book.

"That class, SOC 102, deals with her time off the grid, living for a year with a group of homegrown survivalists out in the woods. Doomsday preppers. The end of the world guys."

Sam felt all the blood rush to her head. *Conlon's status update.*

Operation TEOTWAWKI is under way.

It's the end of the world as we know it.

"George, if you ever decide you want to move on, please call me. I'll hire you in a second."

He smiled. "Thank you, Dr. Owens. That is quite a compliment."

Traffic to the airport was terrible, and Sam ended up having to run from security to the gate in the hopes of catching the flight. She barely made it; they were getting ready to shut the door to the gate when she rolled up, panting. She handed them the boarding pass, and the gate agent glanced at it.

"We're oversold. All of the coach seats are full. There's one seat left, and it's in first class. Will that work for you?"

"My lucky day."

"Here you go, then. Have a nice trip."

Sam thanked the attendant and glanced at the new boarding pass he'd generated.

1A.

Nice. A first-class window? She could handle that.

She scurried down the Jetway and into the 747, took her seat and tucked her bag under the chair for takeoff. The flight attendant was a handsome twentysomething man who gave her a bright smile.

"Want a drink?"

She nodded. "Orange juice is fine, thank you."

"Why don't I put a tiny bit of champagne in that for you? You look like you need to unwind a bit, and it is after five."

No kidding.

She nodded, and he disappeared to help the other attendants shut the doors, and grab her drink, and she finally breathed a sigh of relief. It really was her lucky day.

She wanted to call Xander and tell him what she was up to, but she was afraid that the feds might be tracking his phone, or even hers by now. Just in case, she turned it off and took the battery out, left it tucked into its pocket in her bag. She'd just have to cross her fingers that he had gone home, and she'd be able to find him before he set off back to D.C., or worse, off into the woods to search for his website friends. She had no idea how any of this worked, what a "prepper" was, or how they lived, so as soon as the flight attendant handed her the mimosa, she took a deep sip, opened Ledbetter's memoir and started to read.

CHAPTER TWENTY-SIX

Washington, D.C.
Detective Darren Fletcher

Inez was beginning to look suspiciously like Fletcher's ex-wife, Felicia, when he'd done something that met with her disapproval, which was more often than not. Her face was scrunched in anger, her toe tapping impatiently, her arms crossed. She was sending off prickly vibes, and he wanted nothing to do with it.

"What?" he asked finally, sick of pretending to ignore her.

"Where is she?"

"Where's who?"

"Dr. Owens. The agents just reported back—she's not at her house. Not at the morgue. She's in the wind, and I think you know exactly where she's gone. And Bianco is on the warpath, so if I were you, I'd start talking while we can still repair the situation."

"Stow it, Inez. Last time I looked, you worked for me here, not the other way around. I don't know where Owens is, and I'd appreciate you getting off my back and starting to help, instead of playing the Grey Spy for Madame Bianco."

"The grey spy? What?"

Fletcher just shook his head. "Before your time."

"Seriously, Fletcher. Where did she go?"

He stood and started to walk away. She tried to block his path, and he just smiled and sidestepped her. "Excuse me, Inez."

"Where are you going, Fletcher?"

"I need to take a leak. You want to help me with that, too?" He ignored her cry of protest, marched straight to the men's room and pointedly shut and locked the door behind him.

He sagged back against the door and shut his eyes. Good God above, what had he gotten himself into?

He wasn't in the habit of getting his ass handed to him on a platter. As a matter of fact, he'd had just about enough of Bianco and the JTTF. First they brought him in like it was a huge honor, then they saddled him with a bombshell case, and now they were taking him to task for letting a suspect, which they were officially labeling Sam, get away.

He wasn't sure exactly who had requested that he be put on the JTTF in the first place, so until he knew that, he wasn't going to walk out. Either someone was gunning for him and wanted him to be the scapegoat, or he'd been put on the JTTF to keep an eye on things. Until he knew for sure either way, he wasn't willing to piss Bianco off too much.

But damn, having two alpha women pushing him around all day—he'd have stayed married if he wanted to be nagged to death.

He took advantage of the lull to call his boss at Metro, Captain Armstrong. He answered immediately.

"Boy Wonder. How's things on the inside? What's all this mess happening? Aren't they treating you like a god over there at JTTF?"

"I wouldn't go that far. I'll explain in a minute. Just a quick question. Who put me up for this position?"

"I did. I thought you deserved a shot at the big time. And you'd already taken things into your own hands when you invited that M.E. into the Metro case. Why? What's wrong?"

He should have known he wouldn't be able to put anything by Armstrong. The man was smart and too good at his job. Fletcher didn't sense any strangeness or animosity, either, couldn't imagine that Armstrong himself was a part of this.

"Nothing's wrong. I was just wondering. So you came up with this all on your own? Guess I should be thanking you."

"Well, not all on my own. Chief of Police came to me and asked for a few names. Yours was the one he picked."

Ah. So it was too much to hope that this shit would have happened to anyone they sent over, not just Fletcher. The chief *had* picked him.

"What's up, Fletch? You sound like there's something seriously amiss. I can't make heads or tails of this text you sent me, either."

Fletcher took a deep breath and told Armstrong what was going down, starting with the DNA and ending with the plane ticket he'd just purchased. When he was done, Armstrong let out a long, low whistle.

"Good grief, Fletch. I can't let you out of my sight for five minutes, can I?"

"Apparently not."

"What do you want me to do?"

"Honestly? I'm out of ideas. I've stalled as much as I could, but shortly I'm going to have to come clean. I just need the DNA back first, before I go wrecking a man's life. I may not agree with him on things, but nothing about this case feels right. I'm not ready to tie the knot in the noose just yet."

"Have you stopped to consider the fact that the JTTF is right, and he is responsible for the three murders?"

"Sure I have. And they might be right. I think they believe they're going to use the evidence in the file to prove their point, and it's just not enough. But I can't get at anything outside of the congressman, nothing about the attack, nothing about the other victims, who's still sick, anything. I'm cut off, and I can't work like that. I need as much information as possible if I'm going to do this job right. I have to talk to his family, talk to his staff again. And without knowing for sure if he's responsible, or even capable of murder, I don't want to tip my hand."

"You want me to get you out entirely? I can do that. I can call the chief and ask him to pick someone else."

"So they can get another stool pigeon in to do the dirty work for them? No, I'm better off staying in and trying to control the fallout. Sam gathered some incredible information for us today. If she can stay under the radar she can be my eyes and ears. You know how people love to talk, but the minute they see a badge they hush up."

"I'm not sure why they would be undermining the investigation, Fletcher. We're all on the same team here."

A knocking began on the bathroom door, low and insistent.

"I know that. I've got to go. I'll let you know what's happening when I can. Just…keep an eye out for me, would you?"

"Will do. Watch yourself, Fletch."

He hung up, and Fletcher unlocked the door to find Inez standing there, looking slightly abashed, as if she, too, was embarrassed by their spat.

"Bianco wants you."

"Tell her I'll be there in five. I need to arrange for a couple of interviews, first."

"Fletcher, I'm sorry. I should have known you wouldn't risk

everyone's job by letting Owens go. The cameras show that she snuck out when you weren't looking. I'll deal with setting up the interviews for you. Just go talk to Bianco, okay? Who do you need to meet with?"

The cameras. They monitored their own people. He didn't know why that surprised him. Then again, nothing should surprise him about this place. It had been rubbing him the wrong way since he walked in the door, and Bianco set his teeth on edge. He didn't know why, and that was driving him crazy.

"The wife and the chief of staff. Separately. And I need to talk to the Indianapolis police who worked the original cases, before the IBI got involved. I want to start at the beginning."

"You got it. I'll get everything taken care of. The lead detective on the case is dead, but he had a junior partner, I'm sure he can help. Sorry, again, Fletch."

She walked away and he set his jaw and started toward Bianco's office.

Her door was open, and she was sitting behind the desk, glasses on her nose, looking hard at a computer screen. He knocked on the door frame to announce himself. She looked up, smiled and gestured for him to come in.

"Shut the door, okay?"

He did, then stood in front of her desk with his hands loose at his side.

"Sit," she said.

"I'd rather stand."

"Really, Darren, have a seat. We need to talk, and I hate you looming over me. Makes my neck hurt looking up."

He acquiesced, and she shut the laptop. She smiled at him, and it was different than her earlier smiles, this one looked downright genuine.

"Congratulations."

Oh boy. Here we go.

"Congratulations on what?"

"Let's see. In the past twenty-four hours you've subverted nearly all my orders, managed to gather and release a key witness, did the opposite of nearly everything I requested of you, and turned Inez into a sulking mess. So congratulations. You passed."

"Come again?"

She laughed, a low, soft sound that he found rather pleasant, all things considered.

"I need people with imagination, Darren. Talented investigators are a dime a dozen. Talented investigators who can look past the rule books and still get results, on the other hand, aren't quite as easy to find. You know what our job is here, right?"

He shrugged. "To save lives."

"Not quite. To save lives *no matter what the cost*. I need men and women who are willing to do whatever it takes to thwart attacks on our country. Men and women who won't break the law to get results, but who understand how some rules are meant to be bent, and some even disregarded in the name of the greater good. Take the congressman's less-than-savory past, for example. Just any old investigator would have taken that file at face value and gone after the man, hard. You saw it and immediately began thinking around the edges of the case. That's the kind of men and women I want on my team, ones who aren't going to make snap judgments, but will take the time to reflect, to look beyond the obvious and find the truth."

Fletcher raised an eyebrow. "I appreciate the sentiment, but couldn't you have just told me that from the beginning?"

She laughed again. "I needed to know that you'd do the right thing regardless of orders. Now, are you cool with staying? Because from what I can tell, you and your friend Dr.

Owens have made more headway into this investigation so far than my entire team."

Fletcher hated games with a passion. He was tempted to just walk out on principle. But he was too intrigued at this point, too invested in the case, to just walk away.

"Was it your folks who rolled my house yesterday?"

"What?"

"Someone did a thorough job on my house. Nothing out of place, but a light was left off that I always leave on. I figured it was you."

She actually looked surprised, and intrigued. "It wasn't on my orders. I would never invade my team's privacy like that. We should put someone on your house in case they come back for more."

He watched her for a moment, trying to decide if she was telling the truth. She seemed genuinely disturbed by the news. Which worried him even more—if it wasn't JTTF looking in the corners, then who was? No, she was lying. He could see a little muscle in her cheek twitching. A tell. Good to know.

First things first. "We can talk about that later. I'm in. But you pull another number like this and I'm gone faster than you can say bye."

Bianco smiled. "Fair enough. Now I'm going to tell you what I know, and you need to tell me what you know, and what you've done, so we can all go forward together and shut this killer down."

CHAPTER TWENTY-SEVEN

Red to red. Black to black. Yellow to yellow. White to white. Green to green.

Blue to…*careful now, this is the most important one, hold your breath, hold it*…there. Blue to blue.

He took a deep gulp of air and blew it out, careful not to jiggle anything loose. Perfection. Everything was wired up now.

He sat back on his stool, away from the workbench, and allowed himself a moment to close his eyes and breathe regularly, in and out, measured, careful. The worst was behind him. All he had left was the trigger, but that was already soldered to the back of the cell phone.

He opened his eyes and without hesitating laid the last piece in place, biting his lip, watching the metal edges as they lined up perfectly. Of course they were perfect. He was careful that way. Precision was an art, one he happily engaged in with regular practice. One must hone one's craft if one expects to be the best.

He screwed the last corner down, inserted it into the tube, carefully unscrewed the mount, then laid the finished masterpiece on his workbench.

Four identical tubes lay to the left of the current one, bringing the total to five. Five perfectly constructed bombs, any one of which could take down a large house if placed in the proper spot. All five blown together would take down a building.

By the time he hit Send on the cell phone, the world would be at a standstill, and he'd be miles away.

The perfect crime. Even better than D.C.

The idiots there still didn't have a clue what they were looking for. All the right people were dead, all the right people were sick, languishing in hospitals, giving blood samples that told contradictory stories. Chasing their tails, while the main event was yet to come.

They thought they were in the clear. They thought someone from one of those fucking medieval countries was responsible. An enemy of the state.

The enemy of my enemy is my friend.

Let them think it. He didn't care who got the blame, or the credit, so long as he had time to fulfill the last part of his agenda.

He left his workshop and went to the kitchen. He'd earned a beer. He grabbed an ice-cold Budweiser from the rack and went out onto the porch to enjoy the afternoon sun beating down from on high. Like a blessing. Like God wanted him to succeed.

He laid waste to the beer, watched the sun wither the weeds under the scrub oak. It shouldn't take him long to drive the bombs to their final resting place, only three hours at most. He'd have to use some of the gas he kept stored, but that was no small sacrifice when he weighed its use against the greater good. A tank of gas would be well used. He could be in and out of the building in less than thirty minutes if all went well. Forty-five if it didn't.

But it would. He didn't do things halfway, he'd been plotting this out for weeks. And he wasn't dumb enough to tell anyone about this part, either. That's how you got caught. That's how you ended up behind bars for life, or ended up lying on a cold steel table while grave men stood over you and poison dripped into your veins.

Not that he hadn't done a bit of misdirection, just in case.

He shifted on his bench, finished the beer. He had so much more to do before tomorrow, and the day wasn't getting any younger. He went to the kitchen and tossed the bottle in the trash, marveling again that there were people who thought they could save the world by putting glass and plastic and paper into their proper receptacles. Poor things. The world was fucked. They were all fucked. He was just going to help hasten them along the path.

"Daddy?"

The little voice startled him. He turned and saw his daughter standing in the door to the kitchen, trailing her bear with one arm, her blond hair haloed by the afternoon sun, wiping her eyes.

"What's the matter with you? You're supposed to be asleep."

"I was, but I had a bad dream."

"In the daylight? Don't you know there are no bad dreams when the sun shines, little girl?"

"I know." Her lower lip quivered. She didn't like to show weakness, he'd taught her that there was no room for weakness in their world. But she was scared, and he remembered what it was like to be a little kid who didn't understand why bad things had to happen.

"Why don't we read for a little bit. Would that help?"

"Yes, Daddy. It would."

"All right. You get the book, I'll meet you in a minute." He didn't need the book, they'd read it so many times he knew the words by heart, and so did she, but it completed the illusion to grasp the well-worn Laura Ingalls Wilder in their hands as he recited the words of another pioneer, who shared her story of life in the woods of Wisconsin, and was well loved for her stories of truth and suffering and sacrifice and love.

She disappeared from the doorway, and he washed his hands and rinsed his mouth.

He whispered the other words he'd memorized, from another book full of love and sacrifice, as he went to read his small daughter a naptime story.

"And I will execute great vengeance upon them with furious rebukes; and they shall know that I am the Lord, when I shall lay my vengeance upon them."

CHAPTER TWENTY-EIGHT

Denver, Colorado
Dr. Samantha Owens

It was dark when Sam landed at Denver International. She was tired, and overwhelmed by the information she'd gathered on the three-hour flight. She knew Xander was most likely at his parents' place, and she knew that address, so she figured she'd just get a car with GPS and drive west until she found him.

It was as sound a plan as any she'd had today.

She had an account with Hertz, so she decided to take the bus to their counter in the hopes that they could hook her up with a vehicle that wouldn't cost an arm and a leg. She was walking out to the buses past the baggage claim when she heard a voice call her name.

Xander was standing by the doors, a huge smile on his face.

She went to him immediately, didn't say a word, just let him fold her in his arms and buried her face in his shoulder.

God, that felt good.

After a few moments, she pulled back and looked up at him.

"How did you know I was coming?"

"I was trying to call you forever, and I got worried when

you didn't answer, so I called Fletcher. He told me what was up."

"And Fletcher didn't insist that you turn yourself in immediately?"

"No, strangely enough." He gave her a grin. "I'll tell you everything in the car. We've got a couple of hours on the road. There's just one little hitch. Are you ready to meet my parents?"

There was an intriguing note in Xander's voice, like he was half worried she'd say no, and half worried she'd say yes. She had to admit, the idea of the Whitfields intrigued her tremendously. She wanted to see the couple who'd created this amazing man. And she'd never been on a commune before. She had no idea what to expect.

"I'd love to meet them. You know that. I've talked to your mom before, she seems very sweet."

"They're going to go bonkers for you, that's for sure. Come on. Let me take you home."

She accepted his hand, and took a deep breath. Having him by her side would make everything so much easier. Everything.

Sam hadn't been to Colorado in years, not since a ski trip in college, and was disappointed she couldn't see the mountains as anything more than hulking shadows as they drove west into the darkness. Instead, she stargazed a bit, surprised at how close the night sky became when you were a mile up in the air. It was a moonless night, and clear as a bell, so she could easily see the stars as they wound their way into the foothills. "It is beautiful here."

"It is. Different than Tennessee. This land gets in your conscience, in your being, and you can't escape it. That's why I need to live in the mountains. The air is clearer, the whole world feels different. I wouldn't mind moving back here one day."

She let that go. Only a few months before she hadn't been able to see a life for herself outside of Nashville, where she'd relive the horror of losing her family over and over daily, her penance for surviving. Xander had already forced her from her comfort zone once. Of course, he might not want her with him when he moved. They hadn't done a lot of talking about where their relationship was headed. Which suited Sam just fine. She didn't like the idea of having to define herself right now. She was in transition, she knew that, and everything in her sphere was, as well. Maybe she and Xander would talk about it, but one day. Not now. Not with everything going on.

"You'll have to show me all your favorite places," she replied, and he shot her a smile. Enough said.

"We have a ways, right?"

"About two hours. You need a nap?"

"No. I'm going to check in with Fletcher, let him know what I found out on the plane. I'll keep it on speaker so you can hear everything. And you can share what you know, too. Save us time so we don't have to repeat it."

"Go for it. I already gave Fletcher some info to work with, I'll be interested to hear if he's made any headway."

She dialed Fletcher's number, and he answered on the first ring.

"Did Xander find you?"

"He did. Thanks for telling him, Fletch. Made my life easier."

"Well, that's my goal. Do you have anything for me?"

"I do. Loa Ledbetter lived a fascinating life. The book talks about some of the places she's gone native to research, but her particular focus was on spending a year with a pseudomilitia group in Montana who were convinced the world was about to experience an economic collapse and were preparing for that inevitability. The book is rather dry reading, there's a lot of information about food storage and preparation, weapons, setting guard duty and activity rosters. How to grow food, preserve it, find water, shelter, the works. If there is a socio-economic collapse, these are the people to be with. But what was interesting was a big run-in she had with a family who joined the group toward the end of her stay. They found out what she was up to, that she was taking extensive notes on the group, and went to the *elders* to complain about her. They raised enough of a stink that she had to come clean about her motives. Suffice it to say the group kicked her out, rather un-cordially, and there's been some bad blood ever since."

"Okay. Where's the group?"

"In the book, they're in the mountains outside of Billings, Montana. But that's not necessarily the right name, or place. After they kicked her out she assumes they changed loca-tions—having someone from the outside aware of their en-tire world is exactly what they were trying to avoid. When she wrote the book they sued, and the publisher dropped her. She went ahead and self-pubbed it, just for her own personal use, but to be safe she changed several details to protect their identities. They must have made some pretty serious threats to divert her from her course. She doesn't strike me as the type of woman who's easily dissuaded."

Xander had gone stiff in the seat beside her.

"They aren't in Montana," he said.

"What? How do you know?" Fletcher asked.

"Because I know exactly what group she wrote about. My God, I can't believe I didn't put it together sooner. They're here in Colorado. Up near Grand Junction. I knew one of the members."

"Who is he?"

"Knew. Past tense. He's dead. Taken out by a roadside bomb in Kirkuk. I haven't kept tabs on the group since, but he was an acquaintance, of sorts. Hung out with some people I hung out with, in the past, of course. Wow. It is a small world, isn't it?"

Fletcher's voice had an edge of excitement to it. "These people possibly pissed off enough about the book to stage an attack on the Metro, and take out Dr. Ledbetter in the process?"

"I don't know, Fletcher. The FBI will probably have them on their radar—they call themselves the Mountain Blue and Gray. They don't have an agenda, so to speak, and they've never been violent, are very self-contained, but I wouldn't want to roll up on them unannounced."

Sam could hear Fletcher scribbling notes.

"Mountain Blue and Gray. Got it. What else?"

Sam shifted the phone back toward her. "I started to go through her photographs, but there are thousands of them. It's going to take some time to sort through them all. I was trying to focus on the events that she had public photos of, but there's just too many. I'll keep looking, but if you have help, that would be great."

"Sure. I'll get Inez on it. But what are we looking for?"

"I don't know. Maybe nothing. But a woman so committed to detailing every bit of her life must have secrets. You're starting to think the three dead were targeted, right?"

"Right. I'm about to go talk to Marc Conlon's mother and get into his computer. Just waiting for the warrant. I need to go ahead with a warrant for Ledbetter's work as well, even though we have pretty open access already, just to make sure we don't run into an issue down the road. Should have all my ducks in a row in an hour or so."

"What about the congressman and his...other issue?" She didn't know how much they should discuss on an open cell line until Fletcher was certain about the case.

"Waiting on the DNA. Even with a rush it's going to be a day or two. In the meantime, I'm trying to talk to the cop who handled it so he can fill me in. I have an appointment with the wife...oh, crap. I gotta leave right now to go meet her. Thanks for all of this. If you get more, let me know right away."

"Will do, Fletch. Be safe."

They hung up and Sam rested her head back against the seat, suddenly exhausted.

"You okay?" Xander asked.

"Yeah. It's just been a really long couple of days."

"Why don't you shut your eyes for a little bit? I'll wake you when we're close."

She didn't need asking twice. She twisted in her seat so her seat belt was still on but not cutting into her shoulder, and lay down with her head in Xander's lap. He ran his hand along the back of her neck, kneading the knots out, playing with her hair as he drove, and the lulling rhythm of the car's tires on the highway and Xander's ministrations did the trick. She was out before she knew it.

CHAPTER TWENTY-NINE

Dillon, Colorado
Alexander Whitfield

Xander watched for deer as he guided the truck higher and higher into the mountains, thinking simultaneously about how lovely Sam looked when she slept and about the Mountain Blue and Gray.

His "friend" was named Stephen Upland. In the unit, they called him 7UP for his upbeat personality. Xander hadn't known him well—he was attached to Bravo Company and 7UP was in Charlie Company—but they crossed paths occasionally, and since they came from the same part of the world in their civilian lives, they occasionally hung out and talked about what they missed from back home. He had lived in the Mountain Blue and Gray community since he was a little kid, and had volunteered to go into the military to gain the training necessary to be the head of their defensive system should the economic collapse they feared occur.

He remembered the flack from Ledbetter's book now. She'd posited that the Mountain Blue and Gray, and groups like them, were cults. That hadn't gone over well at all. If he remembered correctly, there were some group members from other survivalist camps who'd been quite keen in showing Dr. Ledbetter what a cult was really all about.

But that had all gone down seven years or more ago. The groups weren't necessarily fluid, but seven years is a long time for a group of survivalists not to have some changes in dynamics. People come and go.

He started racking his brain to think about where those threats had come from. Not from people he knew; Xander wasn't a prepper, or even a survivalist. He didn't think the world was going to go down in a blaze of glory in the next few years. He recognized the resiliency of the American people, the ease with which governments shifted from party to party, without protests in the streets and journalists being kidnapped and beheaded and bright fires burning down the cities. In another country, the situation could easily grow dire—my God, the things he'd seen in Afghanistan and Iraq would turn any logical person into a survivalist—but in the United States, he firmly believed that even if the absolute worst were to happen, it wouldn't be as difficult to put the pieces back together as it would elsewhere. Some of the preppers were downright insane, truth be told. His friends were more a group of like-minded men and women who didn't make preparing for an unknown event the main focus of their world, just shared some handy information in case the shit hit the fan.

Which brought him full circle back to Will Crawford.

Will wasn't a survivalist, though if pressed, he could easily live off the land for days or weeks. Like Xander, his father had brought him up out of doors, with the forest to guide him. No, while Will could manage quite nicely in an emergency, that's not where his interests lay. He was, and there just wasn't a nice word for it, a hacker. An extremely talented hacker who worked with a team of very talented hackers who spent their time using their computer skills to break into government systems. Nameless, utterly incognito and rarely off taking public responsibility for their hacks, they were incredibly dangerous, and incredibly secretive. Unlike Anonymous, the group of hackers who were doing their best to destabilize the world in retaliation for the capitalist spirit that guided most modern countries by publicly claiming responsibility for their hacks and openly recruiting additional talent.

Will's group was much more subtle. They stole the information and put it to use for themselves. They were information gatherers, and for the right price, you could quietly purchase whatever you wanted to know. They didn't discriminate—so long as you could pay, you could have the info. Which meant some seriously nefarious people could wreak havoc should they choose.

The site Will ran that Xander had been on the night before the attacks was just one of thousands he had under his purview.

So who had been mouthing off about the attacks, and why had Will panicked and shut down the site? It wasn't like him to react to external stimuli—the sites he ran were so deeply off the beaten path that without strict instructions no one could even hope to find them, much less get in once they did. Which meant Will and his cohorts knew the guy who'd been talking. He must have been one of their own.

Well, of course he was. It wasn't some random guy's chatter, it was one of Will's men.

And it took him six hours to come to that conclusion. He was slipping.

The exit for Dillon was about three miles ahead. He woke Sam, who sat up rubbing her eyes like a little girl.

"I just had the most delicious dream."

"Was I in it?"

"You were, yes." She smiled at him and his stomach flipped. "Where are we?"

"About five miles from my folks' place. You ready for this?"

"Of course." She flipped the visor down and started attending to her hair, running her fingers through it lightly, then swiped on some lipstick. She didn't need much in the way of maintenance, Sam was a beautiful woman naturally who took advantage of that fact to enhance herself, rather than overload her face and hair with makeup and products. Just a touch here and there and she was incredible.

"Good. I hope they're still up. They're going to love you. I know this is an awkward way to do this. I appreciate you being so kind about it."

"Xander, meeting parents, family, friends, it's always awkward. There's no good time. So we'll just go with it. How much have you told them about what's going on?"

"About you? Or about the case?"

"Both?"

He laughed. "About you, they've heard quite a bit. About the case, though, not a lot. My dad knows more, he went to the Crawfords' with me today. Just FYI, I think I have a lead on the situation with the website. We'll go talk to my friend again tomorrow, and I'll see if he won't give us the rest of the information we need. He's not one for the greater good, but we can try."

"Sounds like a plan."

"So for the time being, I figure we can say our hellos, if they're up. My mom will want to ply you with some dandelion wine, plus a whole new wardrobe, since you didn't have time to pack a bag, then we can go to bed and start fresh tomorrow. Between the two of us we might have had three hours of sleep in the past two days, and we both need to recharge."

"I couldn't agree more. I'm beat."

She was quiet for a moment. "Dandelion wine, huh. Is it good?"

"Actually, it's not that bad." He turned off the highway, narrating about his little town, then they were up the side of the mountain and in the driveway. The lights were on in the house, inviting them in, and he heard Sam take a deep breath. It made him feel good, knowing that she cared about what his parents thought of her. He liked that feeling a lot.

CHAPTER THIRTY

Washington, D.C.
Detective Darren Fletcher

Fletcher was received—which was the only term for it, a butler was escorting him to a drawing room, for heaven's sake—in the Leighton home with a minimum of fuss, considering. The butler's name was Davis, and he offered Fletcher a cup of coffee, which Fletcher accepted with alacrity, just so he could see the china service. He was perverse that way. Money didn't bother him: some people had it, some didn't, and he knew quite well that just because you had a fat bank account, it didn't mean things were going to be easier, or better, or happier, or nicer. Quite the contrary, actually.

The Leightons' D.C. home was on Capitol Hill, tucked in behind Union Station, two townhouses side by side that had the walls between the two kicked down to eliminate the shotgun architectural style and allow for some wider, larger rooms. It had four stories and was tastefully decorated in neutral colors and dark walnut floors. Fresh flowers provided splashes of color, plus several paintings in modern, abstract style. Fletcher parked himself in front of one of these, a monstrosity that covered nearly a full wall of the room, and started taking apart the brushstrokes while he waited.

Gretchen Leighton arrived in the room before the coffee.

She was a beautiful Nordic blonde, cool, composed, athletic. She wore black pants and a sheer black blouse with a Chanel jacket over top, and jet-black pearls around her neck. She was wearing glasses, chunky tortoise frames that Fletcher didn't recall ever seeing her in before. She was often photographed with her husband, and Fletcher had gone through two pages of photos on Google to familiarize himself with their relationship. By all visual accounts, they were close, happy and, on the surface, stable in their marriage.

She approached with a hand out. "Detective Fletcher? I'm Gretchen Leighton."

She shook his hand briefly. Hers was smooth and soft and manicured. Exactly what you'd expect from the moneyed wife of a congressman.

"I'm so sorry for your loss, Mrs. Leighton."

"Call me Gretchen, and thank you. It's been a terrible couple of days. Shall we?"

She pointed toward the grouping of chairs, two soft leather Ekornes chairs and a tan suede sofa. He took one of the chairs, she chose the sofa. Davis arrived with the coffee, and they busied themselves with the service. The cups were Limoges— Fletcher knew more about china than he'd ever wanted to because of his ex-wife's obsessions with the stuff. When they were first married, she would take him on all-day outings to flea markets and antique stores looking for pieces to fill out her grandmother's four sets that had been broken up and sold off during the Second World War. He could tell the manufacturer of most any bone china, thanks to Felicia. It was a skill he rarely got to use, unless he was running a homicide investigation with the affluent set.

Bizarre, the things you pick up in life.

Once their coffees were doctored to their satisfaction, Gretchen sat back on the sofa, her cup expertly balanced on her knee, and said, "So, Detective. Have you determined who murdered my husband?"

"You think he was murdered?"

"You don't?"

"The medical examiner felt he had a massive asthma attack."

"Brought about by his exposure to some sort of neurotoxin in the Metro station. It makes sense that he'd have a problem, his lungs were so ravaged by the disease. I understand it takes several hours for the symptoms to manifest, so it fits. Whomever released the toxin into the air is responsible for my husband's death."

"On the surface, absolutely. And if more people were dead, I wouldn't be here in this capacity. But only three passed away, and that's a cause for concern. We won't know for sure if they died from the abrin until the toxicology reports are back, and that could take a while."

Gretchen looked stricken. "You need more to make it work for you? My God, what kind of man are you?"

"A careful one, Mrs. Leighton." Fletcher set his cup on the side table. "Of the three people who died yesterday, two have already been tied together. I need to ask, did your husband know a woman named Loa Ledbetter?"

The merest flicker of an eyelid.

"I'm not familiar with that name outside of the reports on the news about her death. It's tragic, just like Peter, and that poor boy."

"And Marc Conlon, as well? You've never heard of him?"

"Of course not. Why would I?"

"This is a company town, Mrs. Leighton. A lot of the kids

intern on the Hill. I didn't know if perhaps he'd been one of your husband's staffers."

"Not that I'm aware of. You'll have to talk to Glenn Temple, he'll know for sure. But surely he would have said something yesterday when you interviewed him."

"He didn't, but I'm going to speak with him again, so I can double-check. May I ask you a personal question?"

"Aren't you already?"

Fletcher inclined his head briefly. Best not roil the beast until he had to.

"More personal than we've been discussing, ma'am. Your husband shaved his body. That's not something a wife can easily miss. Can you tell me why?"

The laugh was genuine, sudden, and surprised both of them.

"Oh, I imagine that must have caused a great deal of astonishment, didn't it? Peter is a swimmer. He got in the habit in college, when he was competitive. He felt it made him faster in the water, all the boys did it. A fraction of a second could actually make a difference in those races."

"A swimmer? Does he still compete?"

"No, no. But he swims every day. He got into it as a child to help his asthma. The doctors thought it would increase his lung capacity and allow him to control his breathing better. And it worked, the more he swam the less medication he needed. His asthma had all but cleared up by the time he was an adult. Of course, the war exacerbated the condition and he was stricken again. The shaving, he's done that as long as I've known him. A bit strange, but you get used to it."

He sat back in his seat and watched her for a moment. She met his gaze frankly. She certainly believed that was the truth. Might as well see if he could push her buttons. Just in case. Something was off here, and he didn't know what it was.

Answers for everything, easy plausible answers, always made him nervous.

"You're awfully put together for a woman whose very public husband might have been murdered."

Her voice hardened. "Was he?"

Fletcher watched her for a moment before he answered. "Very possibly. That's what I'm trying to find out. So anything you can tell me will help."

Her hand went to her throat, and she sighed. The facade dropped and she finally looked like a grieving widow.

"Detective, I suppose you're right to say that, because you can't know what it's like to be married to someone like my husband. Someone who served in the military, on the front lines. Someone who has a disease that can take him at a moment's notice, who marched through deserts dodging bullets, who works in a building that has some of the highest level security in the country. Death is on our minds all the time. Life is not something that I take for granted. I've always known I wouldn't grow old with Peter. He was on borrowed time. He knew it, I knew it. The asthma had ruined his lungs, he got sick at the drop of a hat, and his illnesses were getting antibiotic resistant. He'd been battling pneumonia this winter and spring, and it was barely cleared up. He was destined to die young. We've both been prepared for this inevitability. It sucks, and I'm devastated, but I've been waiting for the other shoe to drop for years. I'm just sorry I wasn't here in D.C. yesterday. I didn't get to kiss my husband goodbye on his final day. That will haunt me forever."

"So you had a good marriage?"

"Yes, we did," she whispered, and he felt the full brunt of her grief.

"Your son died in Iraq, isn't that right?"

She stilled. "Yes."

"That changed the congressman."

Shadows passed across her face. "Many things about our son's death changed us, Detective, the least of which was losing him to a brutal, pointless war. Peter was never the same."

"And you?"

"I was his mother. Part of me died with him."

Of course it did. The answer was exactly what he'd expect.

They sipped their coffee. Fletcher needed something to take back, and he wasn't getting anything.

"Do you have any idea where the congressman's briefcase might be?"

She looked confused. "I assume it's at his office."

"No one can seem to find it. Do you mind checking if he could have left it at home?"

She stood, setting her delicate coffee cup on the glass side table. "That would be very out of character for him, but yes, we can look. I haven't been in his office since I arrived home. Please, follow me."

The congressman's office was on the other side of the house, opposite the living room they'd been sitting in. Fletcher got a much better sense of the man from his private space than he had from his congressional office. Floor-to-ceiling bookshelves lined the walls, jam-packed with titles—everything from 1970s green-and-white encyclopedias to ancient texts to modern espionage thrillers. A small Zen garden with a tinkling waterfall stood sedately in a corner, and the large dark wood desk was relatively straight, topped with just a few loose odds and ends, paper, pens, glasses, like he'd been forced to rush out and leave them behind.

She hesitated in the doorway, but just for a moment. He heard her sigh deeply, then she entered the room, went straight to the desk.

"Goodness, here it is." Gretchen reached under the desk and

pulled out a leather attaché case. She immediately opened it. She pulled out an EpiPen case, and an inhaler. Without looking at Fletcher, she asked, "If he had these with him, would it have worked? Would it have arrested the attack?"

"I don't know. He had an inhaler with him, though. Glenn Temple told me he helped him with it."

"Well, that's odd."

"What?"

"This is his primary inhaler. He does have a spare, but his security detail carries it with them, along with another EpiPen. I can't believe he left home without it. Where were his detail when he had the attack?"

"Temple said they were probably in the dining room getting coffee."

"But Glenn had the spare inhaler? Detective Fletcher, I'm sorry, but none of this makes sense. Even if my husband did leave his briefcase at home, the minute he realized it, a staffer would be sent to gather it and bring it to him. It shouldn't be here at all, and Glenn shouldn't have had the spare inhaler."

Her puzzlement was turning to alarm. Fletcher knew there could be a number of innocent explanations, but the man was dead, and coincidence was a homicide detective's best friend.

"Let me ask, does he have a day runner in there, or did he do everything electronically?"

"Electronically, but he did keep a journal. Nothing really personal, just day-to-day stuff. For when he ran for President. He liked the idea of having his letters published, after..."

She trailed off and Fletcher knew exactly what she'd been about to say. If he'd run and been elected, after he finished his presidency, he would have a presidential library, and his letters would be kept there. Even his most trivial days would be revered and dissected.

"I'd like to see that journal, if I could. And is there anything else missing from his briefcase, or the room?"

She pawed through the case. "Not that I can tell."

He had to do it. He had no choice. But he hated it like hell. He liked Gretchen Leighton. She was smart and sharp-edged and obviously respected her husband as well as loved him.

"Are you aware of the rumors surrounding your husband?"

Her eyes grew wary.

"What rumors?"

Tread careful, Fletch. You don't want to exacerbate this situation past what it's already turning into.

"Sexual rumors."

"About *my* husband?"

"Yes, ma'am."

She colored, flushing the bright pink of the peony in the vase on the shelf by her head, until face and flower were nearly indistinguishable. She set the briefcase down in the chair and squared herself.

"Detective, I'm going to ask for your discretion here. You're just going to have to trust me when I say any rumors about my husband are fabrications."

"You sound so certain."

"I am. He's been impotent for years."

Fletcher stood, as well. "Impotent?"

"Yes."

"Is that why you requested his semen from the medical examiner?"

She stilled, then straightened her spine and crossed her arms. "I think we're finished for today. Please get in touch if you have any new information to share."

She handed him her husband's journal and left him standing in the drawing room, wondering anew just what the whole story behind Congressman Leighton's life truly was.

CHAPTER THIRTY-ONE

Fletcher called Bianco from the car. When she answered, he gave her the good word.

"Wife claims he's impotent."

"Impotent?" Bianco repeated.

"Yep. She didn't go into much detail, but I got the sense that it's been going on for a while."

"They had a son, though, the one who was killed in Iraq."

"That they did. So he wasn't always having trouble. But if our recent reports are to be believed, it would be kind of hard for him to participate in a bunch of sex games with hookers. No pun intended."

Bianco actually giggled, a sound so incongruous with her station that it made Fletcher laugh, too. He just didn't know what to make of her. Sweet as pie, shrewd as hell, and cool as damn it. Not to mention one hell of a looker.

Watch it, Fletch. Don't go mixing business with pleasure.

"So where are the videotapes of him screwing boys? Where are the hookers who've serviced him? Do you have somebody in Vice you trust? Maybe the rumors are just that, unsubstantiated and worthless."

"Maybe. More importantly, what about the murders in his

home state? The DNA match was bothering me, so I went ahead and got a second sample just to be sure. The odds of them messing up are slim, but it does happen. The murders are violent, done by someone who probably didn't just quit for his health. Impotence could explain a cessation in the deaths. Any chance you took a look through ViCAP to see if anything popped from the D.C. area? If there's a murder that matches the M.O. while he's in D.C., and the DNA matches, we know for sure if Mrs. Congressman is a liar."

"There is a ViCAP search parameter that was inputted, but we haven't gotten the results yet. If you'd like to follow up on that, I'd be most grateful. Inez said she's trying to track down the detective who worked the Indiana cases, but he's over-seas somewhere and she's having trouble reaching him. His background on this would be helpful. On paper, it certainly seems our congressman is leading some sort of double life. But that's just not the easiest thing to do in this town. People are watching your every move, just waiting for you to screw up so they can swing in, humiliate you and take you down."

Fletcher got the sense that Bianco wasn't talking about just the congressman anymore.

Sleep was becoming highly overrated.

Fletcher worked all night. He took apart the file on the congressman. Looked at every single detail the Indianapolis police had pulled together from the three murders. Some-thing just wasn't adding up, and he didn't know what it was.

On the surface, the congressman looked good for the mur-ders. DNA was hard to argue with. But something was off. Something big. And Fletcher was getting a bit frustrated. He double-checked to see if the ViCAP report was back yet—nothing. He amended the file to include cold cases from Vir-ginia, D.C., and Maryland since 2000. The second round of

DNA wasn't back, either. He wished he was a detective on TV, the evidence run and returned in two hours, the trial the next day. Wouldn't that be nice?

At midnight, after reading Leighton's journal for two hours and gleaning nothing of help outside of his seemingly genuine desire to give back to the people of the great state of Indiana, not murder their co-eds, Fletcher was starting to feel he was at yet another dead end. He decided to follow Bianco's suggestion and made a phone call to a friend of his.

"Vice."

"It's Fletcher. Is Thompsen in?"

"Morgan? Nah. She's out on the streets tonight. Some hotel sting down on 14th Street. Wanna leave a message?"

"That was a joke, right?"

The guy cackled and hung up. There was little to no chance that a message left at a precinct would make it to Morgan Thompsen, much less in a timely manner. He might as well head down to 14th Street and see what was shaking. He knew the setup, they'd have Morgan, who used the undercover name London when she was out on stakeouts, walking the streets, hanging out in the high-end hotel bars, wherever the need was greatest, looking for dates. These stings usually netted a solid ten to fifteen johns in a single night, oftentimes men whose names were recognizable. And everyone enjoyed watching "London" on the prowl—Thompsen was a very pretty girl with very long legs and variable hair depending on her mood. Most johns thought they'd hit the jackpot when they rolled up and saw the "looker hooker," as she was sometimes referred to in-house, waiting for them: her hip jutted out, her hair in pigtails, or a pageboy, or teased up in a beehive, and a furtive grin on her face. Or when they found her alone on a corner bar stool, in a sleek little black dress and sky-high Louboutins, all dressed up with nowhere to go in the fanciest bars in town.

The street was hopping tonight, the shine of the streetlamps on the asphalt making little rings of safety like stage spotlights. The girls stayed in the rings as much as possible; it not only showed them off to their potential customers, but to the pimps as well, who kept careful watch over their flock at night.

Crazies liked to drive these streets just as much as the local gym rats looking to bust a nut.

Fletcher was lucky in his timing, found London getting into a black Mercedes SUV. He followed the car to an alley three blocks over, and the moment the money was produced, London flicked handcuffs on the john and stepped from the vehicle, pulling her practically nonexistent skirt down over her ass.

The rest of her team closed in, and the arrest was made. A solid bust.

Thompsen walked back a block, nonchalant, as if she were unaware of the tussle taking place in the alley, and leaned against the brick wall and lit a smoke. Fletcher rolled his car up to the curb and put down his window.

She recognized him, but stayed in character. It was safer, just in case. And he was in an unmarked, so to the naked eye, they were just a john and jill, negotiating. She let an arm trail the top of the car and leaned into the window.

"I will be poked sideways. Darren Fletcher. What the hell are you doing out here? You want a date?"

He smiled. God, that felt good. First real smile in days. "With you? London? Hell, yeah. Get in and let me take you for a ride, mama."

She flicked the cigarette onto the sidewalk and hopped in the car. Her blue eyes flashed, and she leaned back in the seat, relaxing.

"Ah, that feels good. Man, I hate the street. Give me the hotels any day. My feet are killing me. How do they wear these heels?"

"Necessity is the mother of all invention, right?"

"Yeah, but the only reason you need these suckers is to make your legs look longer and your ass stick out. For the working girls, it's kind of a moot point, they're going to get picked up regardless of their ass hanging out an extra couple of inches. This ain't the 9:30 Club."

She took off one of the stilettos and massaged the ball of her foot. He saw her wave off the team who was looking out for her tonight, a couple of sex crimes detectives he should remember the names of but didn't.

"Where should I go?" Fletcher asked.

"Head back toward the strip. You can drop me off like I got a second score on the way back. What's up with you out prowling? Just stop to say hi?"

"Nah, I got a question. Congressman Leighton. You know him?"

"You mean have I ever run across him out here? No. But word is he's into some pretty kinky shit."

"Exactly. Word is. I need to nail it down. You know anyone who's serviced him? Maybe someone who you owe a favor? Or a decent CI? I don't want someone too motivated, if you catch my drift."

Overly motivated people lied. She understood.

"You just need the real scoop, huh? He died Tuesday. Why bring this up now?"

"Because there's a bigger issue going on."

"Ah." Thompsen was a cop, she knew the drill. Cross the i's and dot the t's. "Let me think." She tapped her finger to her forehead, disturbing the bangs of her platinum pageboy-cut wig. "We had that bust back in April, they were running dope and girls through the back of that Chinese place on U Street. I hauled in a couple of cookies that are old-school, been around the block a hundred times, and then some. They're specialists, too. I know word is he likes multiples, boys and girls. Right?"

"That's what I've heard."

"The kinky ones aren't on the street as much, though. They run things off craigslist now. Everyone who's anyone just does it online. Supposed to be safer, but I don't know. I tell the girls, you don't date men whose eyes you can't look into. You can tell a lot about a john just by looking at him. But they don't all listen to me."

"Wise advice."

"What exactly do you want to know?"

"I want one of them to sit down with a sketch artist."

Thompsen leaned back against the door. "You think someone's using his name?"

"You are quick, London."

"Hey, that's why they have me out here, running the streets. It's a good ploy, it's not like the working girls and boys spend a lot of time reading *Congressional Quarterly*. If they don't know who he is, what he looks like, then it would be easy to impersonate him. So sure, I can wrestle you up a couple of cookies for that. Need them downtown?"

"JTTF."

"Ooh. Aren't you the bee's knee?"

"Hardly. I'm just trying to be sure I'm not a horse's ass. Tomorrow doable?"

"Sure. I'll bring them in once I finish this shift and grab two winks. Say, ten, eleven?"

"That sounds good. Thanks, Morgan. I owe you one."

He pulled to the curb. He was a block away from where he first sighted her.

She put her hand on the door handle. "Thanks for the interlude. We should get together, Fletch. Hang out. You can buy me a beer."

"Let's do that."

In the blink of an eye, she became London, rolling around in the front seat, a wide smile on her face. She opened the car door, hooting, "Whew, honey. I don't know who gave who the ride there."

Then she leaned in the window and adjusted her bra. She had a rather amazing rack, and he chided himself. They were colleagues. He wasn't supposed to be admiring her tits. But she was giving him a show. Maybe there was something there after all. He tucked it away to follow up on another time.

She cupped her right breast and said in a husky, come-hither voice, "By the way. If you owe me? I intend to collect."

With a smile she flounced off, and it was all Fletcher could do not to run after her and beg her to get back in the car and take him to an alley. Five minutes with her would probably be worth throwing away his entire career.

The more he thought about someone using the congressman's name on the street, the more drawn to the idea he was. It was a good ploy, and the congressman had plenty of enemies. People hated what he stood for, sure; no matter what your views, you were guaranteed around fifty percent agreed with you and fifty didn't, and the ones who didn't could get vociferous at times. And he'd changed sides on a very important issue—the military. Doves don't become hawks, they get eaten by them. So he could easily have foes on both sides of the aisle that could benefit from some well-placed, well-timed rumors surfacing in the media.

He needed more time. More time to figure out all the angles. But he didn't have that luxury. The killer may have made his latest move, or the chess game could just be beginning. The sooner he worked out Leighton's life, the closer the rest of the JTTF would be to the killer's identity.

While he digested that, Fletcher put a call in to Inez. Though it was late, she answered on the first ring sounding chirpy and fresh.

"You're chipper."

"I've got Conlon's computer."

"Oh, good. Did you call his mother and ask her to give it to us, or did she bring it in?"

"I tried her all evening but it seems she turned off the phones. I assume she's terribly upset, not that I blame her. I finally got fed up and headed out there. She was at the funeral home arranging for her son's burial, but a friend of the family was at the house and gave me the computer. I left your card with a note that you'd call her. I'm heading back downtown now. I'll have the computer guys take a crack at it."

"Good. Then go home, and get some rest. There's a lot to be done tomorrow, and I need you at your best."

"I'm always at my best. But a couple hours of sleep wouldn't kill me. I've been up for forty-eight straight."

"Go. Sleep. See you tomorrow."

There were too many moving parts to this case. He made a mental list of things that he needed to follow up: reading the congressman's journal, finding out why Glenn Temple had the inhaler instead of the security detail, why Leighton left his briefcase at home, who sent the text to his phone, getting the secondary DNA test back and talking to the detective from the Indiana cases. Not to mention keeping in touch with Sam and Xander to see what they discovered, and treading carefully around the JTTF, because he still wasn't one-hundred percent certain they had his best interests at heart.

Even though they had a whole division of people working on the case, Fletcher felt he needed to be on top of every aspect. He supposed that's what made him happy, the juggling, the rushing around. He just wasn't used to doing this without a partner—Lonnie Hart was the best sounding board and deputy a man could have. He wasn't quite comfortable with his new team at the JTTF. He knew that was only natural, and they were all feeling the pressure.

At least there was Sam. He trusted her implicitly, even when she made him see red. Her help on the case had already been invaluable. He would have loved to have her here, by his side, to bounce things off of, but his purposes for sending her to Colorado were twofold: let her feel she was helping, and get her safe in case of another attack. Truth be told, the latter had been foremost in his mind when he'd concocted the plan to send her to Denver.

He knew he was going to have to deal with his unrequited feelings for her sooner rather than later, or he'd mess up their friendship, and he'd rather have her in his life than not, even if that meant letting her belong to another man. He'd find a way to move on after this case was wrapped up.

His cell rang, and for a moment his heart sped up, thinking it might be her, that she'd been feeling him thinking of her and reached out, but he quickly saw it was Bianco.

He hit the speaker.

"You're up late."

"No rest for the wicked."

"Inez has Marc Conlon's computer."

"Excellent. Listen, I've got good news. We've caught a break. Our attacker miscalculated. He dropped a backpack and clothes in an out-of-the-way subway Dumpster that is normally emptied at eight every morning. But because of the panic, no one went in to empty it until this evening, and they were under instructions to look for anything out of place when they did. There was an address recovered, there's a team headed there now."

Finally. A break.

"Give it to me, I'll meet them there."

"You stay on our victims. We need all the information we can get on them."

"Come on, Andi. That's not fair. I want to be in on the bust. If this is our guy, I want to be the one talking to him."

He heard her talking in the background, then she came back.

"You will be. But you can't go in without the proper gear. So get your fanny back here on the double, then you can head to the scene." She hung up, and Fletcher barely refrained from screaming at her. He wasn't the only person on this team, knew everyone had their roles. But damn it, he wanted to be there when they snatched this guy up.

He gunned it. He was only ten minutes away; if he hurried he'd be able to grab his gear and make the bust.

Fletcher arrived at the scene just as the team made entry on their new suspect's apartment. They were in the Adams Morgan neighborhood, up the street from an Ethiopian restaurant Fletcher had eaten at once, at three in the morning, after a night out on the town. Run by natives, it served the traditional bread of their land, and that had been Fletcher's undoing—the thin loaf reminded him of dead skin pulled off a sunburned arm and he'd been forced to the gutter to lose the night's excess. Just knowing it was nearby made him queasy in remembrance.

There was nothing like a good SWAT entry to make your blood rise. It was especially exciting at night, when anything could come out of the darkness. Monsters and weapons and shrieking women—one never knew what would be behind that door.

He stepped from the car and watched as men bristling with weapons rushed up three flights of stairs, took the door and disappeared inside. After a few moments, he heard the shouts of the team: "Clear." "Clear."

Which meant no suspect.

He jogged up the stairs to the apartment, a tiny studio on the third floor of the building. Even without a suspect, it didn't take much to see that they'd hit pay dirt. He was careful not to touch anything—the apartment was lacking in most normal amenities, instead had a long, low desk along the wall, and a hard wooden chair, that was all. A dark-haired man was gingerly pushing a few things around on the desk with a pencil. Fletcher assumed it must be bomb-building equipment. It certainly wasn't the leftovers of someone's dinner.

"Jesus. What is all that?"

One of the SWAT men looked at Fletcher. "Sir? Do you have clearance?"

"Darren Fletcher, Metro Homicide, attached to the JTTF. Yes, I do. What do we have here?"

"Ah, Fletcher. Heard of you. I'm Brandt, lead explosives technician. Looks like someone was cooking acetone peroxide. If you look around you'll see some nails, tacks, steel ball bearings and a few leftover canisters. I'd say we have someone carrying a bunch of explosives out there. He built his bombs here and God knows where he is now."

THURSDAY

CHAPTER THIRTY-TWO

Dillon, Colorado
Dr. Samantha Owens

Sunlight streamed in the windows, making the room glow with early-morning luster.

Sam smelled bleach and felt the unfamiliar bedclothes as she rolled over, and panicked for a moment, then remembered where she was. At Xander's house.

The bed was empty, devoid of her reason for being here, but she smelled the delicious scent of bacon wafting up from the lower level, and hurried from the bed. The wood floor was warm under her bare feet. Clothes were stacked in a roughly hewn armoire. Sam looked at it in appreciation. Xander had told her his parents made everything they used, and had built everything in the house themselves, from floor studs to furniture. Sam had seen similar armoires in magazines, rustic old things that people were desperate to buy that reminded them of simpler times. She'd bet if they wanted to sell the piece it would fetch upward of $5,000.

She jumped in the shower, then investigated the clothes, which were surprisingly cute: a sundress made of soft nubbly hemp in burgundy, a lightweight tan wool cardigan, and underwear that she was convinced must have been made of freshly spun wool, as soft and fine as cashmere. Obviously Xander's mom or his sister was about her size, because everything fit perfectly. These were a bit louder than her normal earthy hues, but beggars can't be choosers. She slipped her feet into her loafers, happy to see that the neutral tan leather matched the sweater, so she looked quite put together, even if she wore another's clothes.

It had been past midnight when they arrived at the farm in Dillon. The lights were burning but there was a note on the kitchen table— "You must be exhausted. Help yourself to the plates in the fridge. See you in the morning."

Sam had been momentarily stung that they hadn't waited up, then reminded herself how tired she was, and realized it was probably a good thing she didn't have to put on a show because she was not at her best. The upset bled away and she recognized what a kind gesture Xander's parents had made in letting them arrive without a fuss.

There had been cold meats and fruit on the plates, some homemade goat cheese, flaxseed wheat bread, and of course, a small pottery flagon of the promised dandelion wine. Sam skipped it. They wolfed down the meal and headed to bed and Sam was asleep before her head hit the pillow.

Now rested and steeled for the event ahead, she was going to be fed again, which was good, because she was starving. She glanced in the mirror, gave her hair one last fluff. She was too old to be intimidated by meeting her boyfriend's parents, but she was just the tiniest bit nervous. She wanted them to like her, for Xander's sake as much as her own. The last time she'd met someone's parents she'd been twenty-four and in medical school at Georgetown. A lifetime ago.

With a final smoothing of her skirt and twist of her hands,

she headed down the stairs toward the delicious scents of her breakfast, recognizing she was walking into her future for the first time in years.

The three Whitfields had their backs to her as she descended the stairs, giving Sam a moment to appreciate the beauty of the house and the setting. The A-frame was in the alpine style; she descended into an open great room with a massive peaked two-story bank of windows overlooking the mountains and the pasture below. She was assailed by colors, a hundred shades of greens complemented by the pinks, purples, blues and yellows of the wildflowers, set off by the blatant cobalt sky dotted with cottony clouds and the browns of the woods. The windows were so clear it seemed there was nothing holding her back from reaching out into the open air. No one could have painted a prettier picture.

Then Xander turned, sensing her nearby, and his smile made it all disappear.

"Good morning. I hope you're hungry, we've got enough to feed a battalion."

His parents turned then and she saw where Xander got his dark good looks—he was the spitting image of his father, but with a more sensual mouth and slightly lighter hair, sable instead of jet, compliments of his blond mother.

Sunshine couldn't have been more aptly named; she radiated a warm happy glow. She rushed over and enveloped Sam in a hug.

"Welcome, welcome! We are so glad to have you here. I'm so sorry we couldn't wait up last night—I'm afraid once ten o'clock rolls around we are both out cold. Farmer's hours. We tried to stay awake but we both nodded off. You found the clothes, good. Yellow thought the burgundy would look nice on you, and she was right."

"This is one of Yellow's dresses? I love it. Very comfortable."

"It's yours now, and there's plenty more where that came from. If you're not wearing sustainable yet, we'll get you fixed right up. We have everything, clothes to toiletries. Once you try Yellow's soaps you will never go back to that nasty manufactured stuff. No wonder the world is—"

"Sunshine," Xander cautioned. "Hold the politics for five, would you? Let the girl eat in peace."

His mother laughed, a musical tinkle that made all four of them smile. "Oh, Moonbeam, she already knows what we believe in. I'm sure you've told her all the horror stories." She turned to Sam and whispered, "Don't believe a thing. He's such a *man*."

Roth shook Sam's hand and politely gestured for her to have a seat. He was stiffer than his wife, a little more formal, not quite the free spirit. "It's good to meet you, Samantha. Moon has spoken of you often. You've made quite the impression on our boy."

Xander blushed and rolled his eyes, which made Sam smile more.

The three bustled around for a moment then joined her at the table with a mountain of food.

"I hope you don't mind eating clean, Sam," Sunshine said. "We grow everything here, so there's none of the pollution most folks eat. It's all fresh, no preservatives, so no inflammation for your skin and bowels, and after a few meals with us, your system should regulate itself and start healing from the inside. You're going to feel better, sleep better, everything."

How could she say no to that?

"It all looks delightful, Sunshine. Thank you."

And it did. Buckwheat pancakes, sunny yellow eggs with fresh butter and herbs, lean bacon, and more of the thick dense wheat bread from the night before.

"I will admit, I expected you to be vegans," Sam said.

Roth fielded her statement. "A fair assumption, considering. But we can eat meat with no guilt, since we shoot it and skin it and cure it ourselves. We know the animals are treated humanely. Our bodies are meant to eat rich proteins, that's one of the places we get the balance of nutrients. People who don't eat meat need supplements, and that's a much less natural state of being. We understand you're a widow."

"And your poor babies," Sunshine added, reaching over and settling her hand over Sam's own. "We were just devastated when Moonbeam told us. You are quite an admirable woman, Samantha. A lesser one would have given up. I lost a child between Moonbeam and Yellow, I have had a glimpse at that abyss. You have our deepest respect."

"Sunshine, Roth! Please." Xander looked about ready to explode. He nudged Sam's leg with his in apology, and she squeezed his knee to say it was fine. She'd rather someone be honest and forthright with their questions than dance around her issues forever. This way, the sting was briefer, like a wasp that bumbled into your forearm and had no choice but to react on instinct. At least they hadn't said something stupid and hurtful, like *you can always try again,* or *what about adopting?* As if children were cereal boxes on a store shelf, just waiting to be plucked and scanned and taken home.

"It's fine. Thank you," she said, and that was all that was needed. There was a moment while everyone took a few bites, recovering, then Sunshine began again, on seemingly safer ground.

"So Moon tells us you were the one who identified the toxin in the D.C. Metro attack. Have the authorities gotten a sense of who committed the crime yet?"

"I honestly don't know. I need to call my friend and see if

they've made any progress. Was there anything new on the news this morning?"

Xander smiled through his pancakes. "No television, hon. Or internet, or wireless signal, or 3G. There's a radio but it broke years ago, and *someone* doesn't want a new one."

Roth smiled indulgently. "Too much noise, son. The local NPR stopped playing classical and went to talk format during the day anyway, so what's the point?"

She'd forgotten. "Oh, that's right. If you don't mind, we'll just have to go to the closest technology-friendly area and find out, won't we?"

"That would be pretty much anywhere that isn't the top of this mountain. We'll head down after breakfast."

"Good. I definitely want to get up to speed. What are your plans for our next steps out here? Did you find the website owners?"

"In a manner of speaking." He didn't continue, and Sam waited him out. He was just framing his argument because he knew she wouldn't like what he had to say. He finished his bacon and then cleared his throat, his course chosen.

"A guy I grew up with runs the site. His father lives on a ranch about twenty minutes from here. Roth and I went to visit yesterday, and my friend was there. He shared some disturbing information with me. He thinks the man who is responsible for the chatter on his site is the Farmer."

"That's the anarchist who claims to be friends with the Unabomber, right? If that's the case, why wasn't the JTTF all over him?"

"Well, A, no one knows where he is. And B, this is my friend's assumption. I don't know if they've drawn the same conclusion yet."

"But isn't a Metro attack a little outside his normal activities? I mean, he's known for ecoterrorism, green anarchy, that kind of stuff."

"Ah, but what bigger use of energy and consumptive materials than a subway system?" Roth put in. "They're just as bad as cars, and planes, and trains."

Xander smiled at his father. "None of us has wings, Roth. We still need transportation."

They all laughed, then grew serious again.

"Be that as it may, the Farmer is an arsonist. And he's never hurt anyone, only taken down empty buildings and that shipyard in Tacoma. This feels like a big change in M.O."

"I'm just telling you what my friend said," Xander replied.

She played with her water for a moment. "Suppose it is the Farmer. Why would he be on a survivalist website talking about his crimes? I thought those kinds of people didn't really mesh with the ecoterror set."

"They don't. Completely divergent political views. The anarchists are addicted to creating chaos, the survivalists are doing all they can to prepare to survive the eventuality of that chaos."

"So again, why would he be on that site?"

"Laying a false trail?" Sunshine chimed in.

Sam considered that. "Perhaps. Or maybe trying to make sure the blame is on the wrong people. But the Farmer has always taken responsibility for his events, hasn't he? I don't remember any media outlets, or even the cops, mentioning him yesterday. And where would he get the abrin?"

"Where did anyone get the abrin?" Xander asked.

"Excellent point. It's not something you can buy in the store. It had to be harvested and made. Ricin is a by-product of castor oil manufacture, that's why it's always been a much bigger threat—it's much easier to access, much easier to generate large quantities. Abrin is different. It comes from the rosary pea, and because there isn't a lot that the rosary pea does other than produce pretty red and black seeds, it's never been widely grown, and as such, not weaponized. I was going through the acute exposure guidelines, and everything that was listed was 'not determined.' But three are dead and hundreds sick and more may die, because there isn't a known antidote. A mass delivery system hurdle has been jumped. Whoever did this has made a technological breakthrough that no one has seen before. Does that sound like the Farmer?"

Xander shook his head. "You make a good point. No, it doesn't. And it doesn't sound like anyone else who's been making headlines in the past decade."

"Exactly. And looking at Ledbetter's memoir, and knowing there may be a link to the survivalists who make up the Mountain Blue and Gray...what's bothering me is not that he figured out a way to make it, but that he must have tested it somewhere. To know the dosages, the ratios. To make sure he had enough to really harm some people. It was airborne, so it was in some sort of propellant, which means not only did he manufacture enough to be deadly, he created a suspension that allowed the abrin to flourish. Someone somewhere has been exposed and gotten sick before this and the doctors simply didn't know what they were dealing with. It can mask itself easily as another lung ailment."

Roth had been following their conversation with interest. "What other kinds of lung ailment can it look like?"

"Ricin, anthrax, anything that would cause sudden pneumonia. Blood in the lungs, frothing, that sort of thing. We should be checking with that group to see if any of their people got sick."

"Can someone survive exposure?" Roth asked.

"Depends on the type of exposure and dosage, but yes, I'm sure they could. If the doctors found out about it early enough, they could treat the appropriate symptoms and do preventative medicine and stop it. If it's ingested, you treat like any other poison, with a charcoal lavage. Inhalation, it's primarily supportive measures. Similar to the steps taken for ricin poisoning. There's just not a lot of documentation on abrin poisonings, so it's not going to be first and foremost in the responders' minds, you know? Usually people and animals who die from it are exposed by accident—the rosary pea is often used in jewelry in the tropics and Africa. Cracked seed, open wound, ground dust, it gets in there and it can definitely kill."

Roth continued to tap his chin thoughtfully.

"What is it?" Xander asked.

"Oh. You're thinking about old man Gerhardt," Sunshine said.

Roth nodded. "About a year ago Crawford's buddy Sal Gerhardt got real sick, all of a sudden, and no one could pinpoint what was wrong with him. They thought it was lung cancer, but then it cleared up. A couple of months ago, he got sick again, but this time he died, and so did some of his animals."

"What kind of animals?"

"Cattle. Some calves and cows. The bulls were fine. They felt it was grass tetany. Low magnesium levels. Common in the spring. Everyone around took measures to make sure the stock was fed the proper balance of food, and it ended."

"Did they necropsy the cows?"

"I believe they did. They had to—they found them dead in the fields, if I recall correctly. Back in April. It was a warm spring, they put the cattle out in the high pastures early. Tetany sometimes happens with the new grass."

"If the cows died from…what was it again?"

"Grass tetany."

"Okay. I need to look that up. I'm assuming Mr. Gerhardt didn't eat grass. What was his cause of death?"

"Don't know."

Xander pushed back from the table. "I know how we can find out. Sam, are you about finished?"

She took a last bite of bacon. "I am now."

"Good. We have a lot to go do." He looked to his parents. "If you will excuse us, we should get into Dillon. Will the Chief have the information on Gerhardt, you think?"

Roth nodded. "I would assume. Will you be back for lunch? Sun is making her special stew in your honor, Sam."

Sunshine lit up again. Sam couldn't help but feel happy around her—the woman was better than a bottle of antidepressants.

"You will love it, Sam. Every root vegetable we grow goes in it, plus a number of spices I can't reveal, and we have that fresh venison for extra flavor, and a few extras."

"It sounds delicious, thank you."

Xander gave his parents an affectionate glance. Sam was glad to see that they got on so well. It was nice being with a family again. She'd lost her own parents a few years back, and she missed the normalcy of meals, or just having someone to talk to when you needed to hear a friendly voice. She'd adored her parents, and they her, and she felt their loss daily.

Xander hugged his mom, then his dad. "We'll do our best. Maybe one or so, okay?"

"Sounds good, son. Do you want me to come along?"

"I think we'll handle this morning, Roth. But we may need to go see the Crawfords again, and if that's the case, I definitely would like you there."

"Of course. Anything you need." He patted Xander on the back and took his plate into the kitchen. Sam followed suit, but Sunshine scooted her away. "No, no, that's my job. You go on with Moon. I'll take care of this. It is lovely to finally meet you, Samantha. You are a very special girl. You're going to fit in with the family perfectly."

"Good grief, Sunshine, we aren't married yet."

Xander realized his slip just as Sam whipped her head toward him. Marriage? Did he just mention marriage? She felt a little faint. My God.

Sunshine waved a hand at them. "Like that was ever a question. You can see it written across both your faces. Love is a beautiful emotion, and it makes me happy to see you both basking in it. Now go find out about Gerhardt, and be back by one."

CHAPTER THIRTY-THREE

Xander was quiet on the drive down the mountain, simmering in what Sam took to be embarrassment. She understood completely. She'd been overwhelmed by the breakfast conversation and energy, for sure. His family was amazing, warm and open and too frank for their own good. Sam was more used to the way people treated her after the flood, how they were so reticent to meddle in her affairs, how they didn't ever suggest she do something so crass as moving on, or even ask how she was feeling about the situation. That was just the Southern way; while she knew everyone was discussing her situation, they'd never be so uppity as to do it to her face.

Sunshine's and Roth's personalities precluded them from that kind of approach. They were open people who didn't have much to hide and felt others shouldn't, as well. It was refreshing, in its own way.

She'd lost a part of her in the floods, more than just a husband and children, but the dream of her life, her future, her place in the world. She'd spent years planning out her life, knowing where each step would be placed, like ancient stones across a river. And then that river had risen up and swept the stones away, leaving her alone on the bank, watching for the stones to reappear, not knowing how to reach the other side without them, or even whether she wanted to try.

Fate had different ideas for her. It had steered her away from the prophetic river, brought her to D.C., to the home of another she'd loved and lost, and then to his friend and fellow soldier Xander. She didn't know why they'd been brought together, and it was still so early in their relationship that she rarely questioned it, was just enjoying not being sad all the time. But the word *marriage* held some significant connotations for her.

He was getting serious about her.

She loved Xander, of that she was sure. He was a good man, a decent man, even with his demons. She had demons, too, she could hardly begrudge him his. But marriage...she didn't know if she could ever commit like that again.

But there were more important things going on right now, lives to be saved.

The rest would just have to wait.

He finally broke the awkward silence.

"You have to forgive my mother. She thinks she knows me better than I do sometimes."

Safe territory was needed. Neutral ground. "That's what parents are for. Why don't you call them Mom and Dad?"

"Oh, that. I know it must seem strange. Part of our childhood equality lessons. If we called them Mom and Dad, that gave them power over our actions and emotions. An open command structure that flowed from adult to child. Instead, we all used our first names and we all worked together to get things done instead of them relaying orders, as they saw it, for us to do chores, our homework, to be pushed to read, to play the piano, or violin. Everyone had—has—equal footing in the family. It was designed to help us self-motivate, and it worked. Both Yellow and I excelled at most anything we tried, and there were no limits set that said we couldn't try something because we weren't old enough, or mature enough, or it wasn't time to get out the finger paints, or we might spoil our supper.

"It seemed totally normal to me until I got out of the house and saw how other kids lived, with all these rules and regulations. I remember when Will Crawford got grounded for not cleaning his room. He had to explain what grounding was to me. It all seemed very unfair."

"And yet you end up in the military, with possibly the most stringent command structure in the world. Why?"

"It wasn't because I wanted more structure, that's for sure. What was it Fletcher said to you that time? Don't let the *romantic warrior full of valor* get in the way of your emotions?"

"My common sense, I think he was intimating. But yes, that was the quote."

"Well, when I was a kid I read *The Red Badge of Courage,* and everything Hemingway wrote. There *was* something romantic about the idea of courage, of standing shoulder to shoulder with your brothers in arms, of being willing to lay down your life for that which you believed in, and procuring freedom for the masses. My parents swung between anarchy and apathy depending on their moods, and of course encouraged us to make our own decisions, never imagining that either Yellow or I would ever arrive at a different conclusion. It about killed Roth when I said I wanted to enlist. That was not the life he imagined for me."

"Yet you've put your differences aside. You seem to have a solid relationship now."

"Part of encouraging autonomy means accepting the choices your offspring make. He didn't do what his father wanted either, so he couldn't get too fired up at me for choosing my own path."

"What about your grandfather? Do you know him?"

"Only through news reports. He cut Roth off the minute he and Sunshine said 'I do' under the willow tree in their backyard."

"Have you ever been tempted to look him up?"

"No. Here we are." He had pulled up on the main street in downtown Dillon in front of the Arapahoe Cafe, stunningly backed by the shimmering blue lake. The scent of pine smoke permeated the truck, and despite her recent breakfast, her stomach growled in response.

"That smells amazing."

Xander smiled. "Don't you dare tell my parents, but this place has the best cheeseburgers I've ever eaten."

"Naughty boy. Your secret is safe with me."

"Good. Sunshine would never forgive me. Do you want the internet first, or the Chief?"

As if it knew she'd arrived back in civilization, her phone chirped to tell her she had missed messages.

"Guess I better hear what Fletcher has to say before we tackle either."

She hit 1 for her voice mail and listened.

There were actually two messages, one from her best friend back in Nashville, Taylor Jackson, who was checking to make sure Sam was okay. She'd call her back later, they had things to talk about, to catch up on. The second was Fletcher, with an ominous, "Call me the minute you get this message."

"Uh-oh. That doesn't sound good."

"What's the matter?" Xander asked.

Sam was busy dialing Fletcher back. She held up a finger. Fletcher answered right away, his voice jubilant.

"We think we got him."

"The Metro killer? Wait a minute, let me put this on

speaker so Xander can hear." She pressed the button then asked, "Who is he?"

"Moroccan national. FBI's been tracking him, working on a deal with him for months. He dropped off their radar last week, they figured they lost him. D.C.'s been locked down tighter than a drum, no one was getting another attack through. They mobilized everything when they figured out who it was. He was online overnight saying his goodbyes, they picked up the chatter, and they popped him this morning heading to the Capitol with a vest on full of explosives. We found a backpack in a Metro Dumpster that had an address, and found his apartment. It was full of bomb-making materials, and other stuff that's being tested right now. The bombs he was making weren't real, of course, he'd been duped. The FBI's been posing as al Qaeda agents and recruited him to do a bombing. Looks like he might have branched off into the abrin without them knowing. It will be on the news any minute now."

"That makes no sense, Fletch. That he'd been able to manufacture the abrin, slip their grasp and plant it in the Metro?"

"That's how it all looks, though. We found a canister at his place that could have been used to fill an aerosol can—they're testing it right now—plus workman's clothes from the subcontractor who's laying the Silver Line. The Metro cameras have spotted the suspect leaving the Rosslyn station, he matches the build of the Moroccan. They're looking through the Dumpsters for more. It's starting to look like an open-and-shut case."

"So he was working with more than just the feds on his plans?"

"We're looking into that."

"A self-actualized radical? Or part of a group?" Xander asked.

"Loner, it seems. You know how they crawl up out of the

gutters. He's been in the country for over five years, came over on a student visa and dropped off the face of the earth. According to Bianco, he got on their radar a couple of months ago wanting to execute a major attack, and their agents strung him along. They figured he'd been tipped, that's why he went to ground, but he was just getting his rubber ducks in a row."

"And the ties between Ledbetter and Conlon? And the congressman's background issues? Just happenstance?"

"It's a small town, Sam. The good news is, you're off the hook. You and Xander can come home without any worries. Bianco won't make any trouble for you. Listen, I've got to go, wrap up a few things. But call me later."

He hung up, and Sam looked at Xander. He had his hands on the steering wheel and was contemplating them, squeezing first one, then the other. Sam had seen him do that before. It signaled he was lost in thought.

"Well, that's good news, don't you think?"

He looked over at her. "Absolutely. If they're right."

"Meaning?"

He shook his head. "FBI and Homeland need to save face. An attack happened on American soil on their watch. It's not fair, because they prevent a ridiculous number of attacks, but the only time they make the news is when one slips through their net and something bad happens. You notice they're releasing more and more information about events they've thwarted? PR, pure and simple. They have a thankless job, and the people of our country haven't the first clue just what happens behind the scenes to keep them safe so they can drive their minivans and go to the movies and complain about their injustices on the internet."

"I follow. What are you saying?"

"If a Moroccan national committed this crime, I'll eat my hat."

"You're not wearing a hat."

"Euphemism. I have plenty back home. Seriously, Sam. No way. *No way.*"

"Xander, I hardly think the entire jurisdictional force of the JTTF and the FBI and Homeland are going to make a mistake. Why do you think they're wrong?"

"You don't?"

"I asked you first."

He wrapped his hands around the steering wheel again, sat in silence.

"Xander, I think you're keeping something from me. What's going on in that gorgeous head of yours?"

That got a smile out of him. "Why don't we grab some coffee and go talk to the police first. It just feels too neat, too easy. Someone already on their radar manages to slip the net and commit an attack? It doesn't feel right."

"You're borrowing trouble, my friend."

"Maybe. Maybe I'm just paranoid. But I can't wrap my head around why Will Crawford would shut down his site if there wasn't a tie directly to him."

"Maybe he was doing something else wrong."

"Maybe. Come on. Coffee. Police. Then we can tackle Will."

"Police first, Xander. The coffee will wait."

He groaned but walked past the entrance to stairs that led to the cafe. She saw him cast a wistful glance back toward the restaurant's door.

"We'll make it fast. I promise."

CHAPTER THIRTY-FOUR

The police chief, Reed McReynolds, had sun-bleached blond hair and a round face decorated with a darker goatee, broad shoulders and long, rangy legs. A surfer cowboy, plain and simple. He sprang out of his chair when they walked in, a smile a mile wide across his sunburned face. She liked him immediately, his open laugh and surprised eyes made him look even younger than he was, which Sam assumed must have been around thirty.

"Well, I'll be damned, if it isn't Xander Moon. How the hell are you? Your parents know you're back in town? And who's this stunning creature?"

"I'm good. Yes, they do. This is Dr. Samantha Owens."

McReynolds shook her hand. "You can do better than this piece of chum. You know he can't even keep himself upright on a board? Falls over on his ass every time."

Xander was grinning, easy, comfortable. She hadn't seen this side of him before—he was always so serious and buttoned up. He was home. Home among his people, his family, his friends. She liked it. Liked him loose and happy.

"Don't you start, you know that's not true. It was only that one day, and I had an ear infection. Couldn't keep my balance on flat ground much less a piece of fiberglass hurtling through the pipe."

Snowboarding, Sam came to find out, was McReynolds's passion, existence and reason for living. The law enforcement gig was secondary, just a little something so he didn't get bored.

"You ever been snowboarding, Dr. Owens?"

"It's Sam, and no, I haven't. Skiing, yes, but I'm no daredevil. Give me a nice blue run and I'm perfectly content."

"Ah, you gotta get this cheek to teach you. He's pretty good. Or used to be, before he had his *wittle bitty ear infection.*"

"God, Reed, let it go."

"Fine. How long you here for? They've got the grass skiing open. We could take a few runs after I get off today."

"Would that I could, man. I need to chat about something else. You familiar with the Gerhardt case?"

"How'd you hear about that? Your dad?"

"Yeah. He mentioned it this morning. What do you know?"

McReynolds sat on the corner of his desk and crossed his arms on his chest. "Why do you want to know?"

"Sam here has a hunch. Any chance we can get his autopsy records?"

"What kind of doctor are you anyway, Sam?"

She smiled. "A forensic pathologist. I've been working on the abrin attack in D.C. I think it's reasonable to assume the killer tested the abrin before he set it off in the Metro, because he'd need to have an idea of just how much could kill a human. It seemed odd that Mr. Gerhardt and his cattle would die at the same time."

"It was damn odd, but the coroner felt the cancer had returned, and progressed incredibly fast. They sent him up to Golden for an autopsy. And the cows, well, the vet thought that was tetany. Rare in these parts, but it happens. You think it was a test run for the attack?"

"I don't know. But if I could get my hands on the files, it would certainly help. I'll know rather quickly if Mr. Gerhardt was exposed. And if the vet who did the necropsy is still around, I'd love to talk to him, too."

"Her. Name's Carly Skinner."

"No kidding?" Xander asked. "Carly's the large animal vet around here now? I figured she was gone for good when she went to L.A." He gave his friend a sly smile.

"She was. But remember when she came back a few Decembers ago? She decided to set up shop instead of acting. More important things here."

"Yeah, I get it. It's nice to come home again."

"It wasn't home she came back for. It was me."

"You? She threw over her acting career for *you?*"

Reed punched Xander's shoulder, hard enough to make him suck in his breath. "Yes, you asshole. And I married her. See what you miss living up in the rocks alone? Carly Skinner McReynolds was too much of a mouthful for her so she stuck with the maiden name."

Xander grinned at him. "About damn time that girl found some sense. That's great, Reed. Congratulations. You guys were meant for each other, we all knew it."

McReynolds smiled, shyly this time, pleased with Xander's obvious happiness for him. "Ah, go on. You know how much she loves to ski. There was no keeping her away for long. I'll go call her, you all wait here for a minute. I'm sure she'll be happy to go over the stuff on Gerhardt's stock. And I'll get the records pulled from Gerhardt himself. Might take a little bit though. Where will you be?"

"Back at Arapahoe Cafe. We need the wireless to look at some other stuff."

"They caught the guy who did it, you know."

"That's what we hear."

McReynolds pushed himself off the desk. "All right. Let me go get your info. Meet you back here in an hour, say?"

"That's perfect. Thanks, Reed."

"Oh, you owe me. I've got a list the length of my...arm of things you're gonna do to repay me."

"Yeah, yeah. Whatever." They jostled each other shoulder to shoulder, the grown man's version of a hug, then Xander took Sam's hand and they walked back out onto the street.

"What's next, madam?"

"Well, you need coffee before you faint. And I'd like to go through Loa Ledbetter's photos more thoroughly. I can do it on my iPad. So let's settle in at this cafe for a bit, see what we can't uncover."

CHAPTER THIRTY-FIVE

Washington, D.C.
Detective Darren Fletcher

Fletcher hung up the phone and stowed it in his pocket, then turned the sound up on the television in Bianco's office. The announcer was holding back a smile, trying to look serious while also relieved.

"We are here with breaking news right now, good news, as we've learned that the Metro attacker may have been caught. A suspect was arrested by police on his way to stage another attack, this one on the Capitol building. This news is just coming in to us over the wires. Again, it seems the Metro attacker suspect has been identified and detained by police. Stay with us, we'll be right back."

Fletcher watched as the station went to commercial, in awe of their audacity. If this backfired, they were all fucked.

Bianco stood to his right, a grim smile on her face.

"I hope you know what you're doing," Fletcher said.

"It's better this way. He won't know that we know. He'll think we've backed off, and he will relax, and then he'll slip up and we'll catch him."

"Disinformation is a tricky thing, Andi. You're going to have to admit you were wrong about the Moroccan."

"I'm not wrong about the Moroccan. The FBI *has* been working him for several months. He *was* on his way to the Capitol with a backpack full of what he thought were explosives loaded with shrapnel and ball bearings, all puffed up on the idea of a second attack in as many days destabilizing us. The material found at his apartment makes him a strong suspect in the Metro attack."

"But it's not him."

"We don't know that. We still need to run the prints we found. There is a mountain of evidence that puts him together with the attack. The problem is, even with him off the street, there's going to be yet another wacko waiting in the wings. Our people are working day and night to mislead these lone wolves. We're watching three others right now, just to make sure they aren't making friends with the wrong people. It takes months, years, to set this up. And yet somehow, someone has slipped in under the radar and manufactured enough abrin to make a weapon. God knows what else he has planned. We have to catch up to him before he does something else, and this was our best shot. Even if the Moroccan wasn't responsible but knows who is, we're golden. And if there *is* a third party and he thinks the pressure is off, he might make his move. We've got eyes everywhere, just waiting for it. And when we catch the bastard who did this, no one will be the wiser until all the details emerge. We control the game now, and we will explain our reasoning once the shit is in custody. Okay?"

"Big gamble. Your ass, not mine."

She smiled. "Exactly. So we have work to do. Where are we on Conlon's computer?"

"Inez and the boys are going at it. They were like a bunch

of locusts. Do you ever get the sense that we're becoming obsolete?"

"No. They may have the technological advantage, but we're the adults. We know that you don't get a blue ribbon for trying. They may not have that figured out just yet."

Fletcher laughed. No kidding.

"What's the next target?"

"No earthly idea."

"And yet you're calm as a deep blue sea."

"You know that all the motion in the ocean goes on underneath the surface, right?"

"Meaning?"

She sat back in her chair and sighed. "I'm sick inside, Darren. It eats at me. I don't sleep, I subsist on coffee and carbs. The fact that we lost three people is killing me. But I have to keep treading water, conserving energy, knowing that in a few hours, or a few days, or a few weeks, I'll have to strike off and swim my way to the shore, dragging their bodies with me, hoping we don't all drown."

Fletcher looked at her, really looked. Past the artfully applied makeup and the styled hair to the dark circles under her eyes, the small worry wrinkle between her eyebrows. He suddenly found himself wanting to smooth the troubled look away with a few gentle strokes of a finger, and turned away to gaze out the window. They had no view up here, but the city still shimmered beneath him, the warm haze of summer descending. There would be rain tonight, washing clean the sins of the great city.

Bianco got up and came around the desk, set a hand on his arm.

"Darren, this is going to work. I can feel it. We just need to keep treading water a little longer, and we'll catch a great wave."

Inez knocked on her boss's door. Fletcher could see the excitement bubbling off her.

"Ma'am? I'm sorry to bother you, but we have something you need to look at."

Fletcher drove back to Falls Church with some interesting information under his belt.

The skies were gray and low, threatening. Fletcher didn't care. It was good to get out of the confines of the JTTF, out from under Bianco's eye. He still thought they were playing with fire, announcing the culprit had been caught when they weren't one-hundred percent that he was solely responsible, but it wouldn't be his ass in a sling should the story blow up in their faces.

Instead, he needed to find out more about Marc Conlon, in light of the fact that his computer files showed the mind of a very disturbed young man.

Very disturbed.

The kind of disturbed the JTTF could hang their hat on. The Moroccan may have been publicly trying to blow up the Capitol, but it seemed Marc Conlon could very easily be the accomplice they were looking for instead of an innocent victim.

The Conlons' house had double doors on the front, a regular wood door behind a glass storm door. The wooden door stood open, allowing easy access for multitudes of people who were coming to pay their respects to Mrs. Conlon and her son.

Fletcher knocked on the glass, then pulled the door open. There were noises coming from the back of the house, a television, most likely. He called out, but no one answered. He tried again, and this time, there was a thin, reedy voice that answered, "In the back."

Lucy Conlon was a mouse of a woman, small eyes and

twitching nose and graying hair cut in an unflattering bob. There was none of her in her son outside of the small stature—he was dark where she was light, gregarious where she was shy, outspoken where she was strangled. She was curled on the sofa facing the television, which was running some sort of infomercial. Maddening if you were in a normal frame of mind, blank distraction if you weren't.

She turned her head back to the screen when she saw him. "You must be the detective who called. Sit down if you like. What's wrong with Marc's computer?"

Fletcher had called before he drove out, just as a courtesy, so she wouldn't be too blindsided. He may have understated his reason for calling.

He sat in the chair across from her, set the laptop on the table between them.

"Mrs. Conlon, I'm afraid I have some more bad news."

CHAPTER THIRTY-SIX

Falls Church, Virginia
Detective Darren Fletcher

Fletcher was astonished. Lucy Conlon may have been a mouse, but she was finding her inner reserves right now. She leaned forward with her finger in his face, every inch of her body shaking in anger.

"I will not repeat myself again. My son was not a terrorist. If you say that he was, I will sue you and everyone you're associated with. He's never had any contact with that man who was arrested."

Fletcher ran his palm across his forehead. They'd been at it hammer and tongs for nearly twenty minutes now, and he was getting tired of the battle.

"Ma'am, no one is saying he was a terrorist. But your son's computer contains some rather disturbing information. You can't deny he was working on some sort of manifesto. It's all right here." Fletcher tapped the lid of the laptop.

"I told you. It's not a manifesto, it's a research paper. He was studying their lifestyle. He wanted to be an anthropologist. That Ledbetter woman got him all turned-on with her book, and he struck out to repeat her findings. He was starting his master's degree work early. They let them do that now, work on credit toward a master's while they are doing undergrad. That's all this is."

Her voice finally wavered a bit. No mother wants to find out that her son could be involved in a crime, especially one so heinous as an attack on a mass transit system.

"Mrs. Conlon. Please understand. Right now, no one is accusing Marc of planning the Metro attack. But the material we found in his computer makes it quite clear that he was on a bad path. He had contact with several less than savory people. He was exploring converting to Islam. He was talking to white supremacy groups. This is not the computer of some innocent who played Dungeons and Dragons in his spare time. This is the computer of a quiet revolutionary, gearing up for a serious change of routine."

She shook her little mousy head and her wispy hair barely moved. "I'm telling you, he is innocent in all of this. He was a curious boy. He liked to see what made people tick. He wanted to live a hundred lives. Church, for example. He's been to services at just about every single church in the metro area. It didn't matter what the religion was, he was interested in how the people who attended responded to their environments. He wasn't planning anything. He was just studying them. Studying the people and their actions. I know it in my heart."

This was getting him nowhere fast. She would never admit her son could be involved in the attacks. He decided to try a different tack.

"Okay. Say I believe you, and Marc was doing research because he wanted to do a master's thesis."

She crossed her arms and gritted her teeth. "You'll have to believe me, because that's what he was doing. He had plans to finish college early and get his Ph.D. before he was twenty-five. He was a really smart kid."

"Mrs. Conlon, please. In the course of his research, Marc came across some very nasty people. Did he ever mention being afraid of anyone in particular? Did he get calls late at night? Was he upset about anything?"

"My God, the boy was nineteen. He got calls at all hours, and was always upset. His hormones hadn't settled yet."

"Where is Marc's father?"

She glanced at the floor. "Dead. When Marc was just a boy. I raised him myself. And that's why I can assure you that he was not a bad kid. And he's gone now. My baby is gone."

She started to cry, and Fletcher stood. Nothing like brow-beating a grieving mother to tears. There was nothing more to be learned here. He handed her his card.

"Mrs. Conlon, I may call on you again. I truly am sorry for your loss. I'll show myself out."

Driving back downtown, Fletcher couldn't help but wonder if Marc Conlon had duped everyone in his life, or if his mother was telling the truth. If that was the case, it was entirely possible that his research had gotten him killed. Which meant Fletcher was back at square one. Again.

CHAPTER THIRTY-SEVEN

Dillon, Colorado
Dr. Samantha Owens

Sam found Xander's world more and more charming the longer she spent in it. And for someone who liked to keep to himself, he was practically a rock star around Dillon. Everyone knew him. Everyone welcomed him back with open arms. It was a good thing they weren't trying to be subtle, because that would have been near on impossible. Sam understood why he'd chosen to hide out in the Maryland mountains instead of coming home. There, he could be alone. Here, that would never happen.

She got that. Entirely. It was one of the big reasons she'd chosen to move to D.C., just to get away from the constant noise of people caring.

After running into three more people who were happy to see him, they finally got settled at the restaurant with thick dark roast coffees, mouths watering at the smells emanating from the grill. Sam hooked into the free wireless and opened the website George had sent her to, Fotki. She pulled the Post-it note with the username and password from her wallet and logged into Loa Ledbetter's account.

There were more than ten thousand pictures to sort through. Sam stifled an inward groan and remembered her plan—look to the events Ledbetter had immortalized on her walls first. Xander watched over her shoulder as she started sorting through the photos.

If the pictures were any indication, Ledbetter lived an amazing life. There were folders from every continent, every major city across the world. She did a search for Hawaii, and four separate folders popped up. She searched through them until she found the shot of Ledbetter on the plain below the volcano, the rosary pea plants next to her.

"I find it highly ironic that she's the key to realizing the poison was abrin," Xander said.

"No kidding. The simple fact that she's been in contact with the plants makes me wonder what she might have had to do with this. And why a killer would go so far off the beaten path to discover how to weaponize the abrin, and use it to murder three people."

"It's looking more and more like a targeted assassination."

Sam took a sip of her coffee. "I agree. There are just too many coincidences. And if we look at Ledbetter as the primary target, not Peter Leighton, the whole story shifts. I think Fletcher is off on the wrong trail, and we're on the right one. But one thing doesn't work for me."

"What's that?"

"The three must have been exposed to more abrin than the remainder of the people who were sickened. Leighton had asthma, so it's conceivable that he would react more intensely than the others to the effects of the poison in the Metro, but he was all the way on the other side of town, and there are plenty of immunosuppressed people with lung ailments who

take the Metro. The odds of it only affecting him and Conlon and Ledbetter are astronomical."

"So what are you thinking?"

"That we're missing something major. A delivery method.
This killer disguised the murders in an attack on the masses, so
he was desperate to cover his tracks. He doesn't want recogni-
tion for himself, he just wanted three people dead and didn't
want to be caught. This took so much planning, he couldn't
leave anything to chance. I think there must be another delivery method for the three dead. I'll bet that the abrin levels
are much higher in their blood work than any of the people
who got sick from the Metro attack."

"Can you test for that?"

"The concentration levels will show clearly on the tox
screens. Let me call Amado. He might be able to shed some
light on this."

She dialed Nocek's number, and he answered right away.

"Samantha. It is good to hear from you. I understand you
have been traveling."

"Hello, Amado," she said warmly. "Yes, I have. May I ask
a question?"

"Of course."

"Has the lab returned the blood work on the victims yet?"

"It has. Are you interested in something specific?"

"Yes. What were the concentration levels of abrin in the
three dead?"

She heard him flipping pages. How convenient, he had the
records there on his desk, almost as if he'd known she might
be calling. Then again, Nocek had always been able to inter-
pret Sam's next move. He was special like that. Highly focused.

"The estimated human fatal dose is 0.1–1 microgram per
kilogram. The three dead had concentration levels over one
microgram. Ten times the amount necessary to kill them."

"Goodness. Were there any findings from the people sick at GW?"

"The CDC has been running tests on them. From what I've heard, the levels were under 0.001–0.003 micrograms."

"Enough to sicken, but not enough to kill. Excellent."

"Excellent?"

She heard the questioning tone in his voice. She must have sounded rather heartless.

"I don't mean it like that. You've just proved my theory. I believe Leighton, Ledbetter and Conlon were all dosed separately to make sure they got enough abrin in their systems to kill them, and the Metro attack was simply to cover the killer or killers' tracks. The question is, how were they dosed?"

"You have a keen mind, Doctor. When I saw the concentration levels today, I was wondering the same thing."

"Ledbetter smoked. Did Conlon?"

More papers rustling. "The list of personal effects includes a pack of Camel Lights. So yes. Dr. Ledbetter does not have cigarettes within her personal items, but she was at work, so it is entirely possible the cigarettes were already in her office."

"She was supposed to have quit, but you know how easy it is to slip up. And what's the first thing you do after a long trip, or before you go to work, or into class?"

"As a former smoker myself, I would have to say smoke a cigarette."

"I would suggest you get those tested, Amado. It's entirely possible that's the delivery method."

"But what about the congressman? He was not a smoker— on the contrary, he would be doing all he could to make sure his lungs were not compromised."

They said it at the same time.

"The inhaler."

"Samantha, I will endeavor to retrieve the inhalers from the

Leightons as well as the cigarettes from Conlon and Ledbetter and have them tested immediately. Thank you for this information. Would you like to share it with Detective Fletcher, or should I?"

"You feel free. I have a few more things to work on before I check in with him."

"I will take care of this. Be safe, Samantha."

"Thanks, Amado. You, too."

Sam was enjoying the adrenaline rush she was feeling. Mildly euphoric, she soldiered on.

"Okay. The pieces are starting to come together and make more sense. Back to the photos."

"Does she have any pictures of her time with the Mountain Blue and Gray?"

Sam clicked out of the Hawaii folder and did a search for Colorado. Forty folders showed up. "Wow. Let's see here..."

She looked at the dates, opened the folder dated 2006.

The pictures were of what seemed to be beautiful but inconsequential things—gardens, trees, flowers. Spring in the mountains.

"She set up shop with them in the winter. This could be after the first big thaw."

"Makes sense."

"Interesting that she got into it with them, that she was trying to stay below the radar and fit into their world."

"They wouldn't be likely to accept just any stranger off the street. She must have been working an angle for a while to get invited in. Usually they have specific people with specific skills, and some redundancy. Like a SEAL team. Twelve men with expertise redundancies so the group can be broken into two teams of six if necessary, or further split into four teams of three. Electronics, communications, weapons. The survivalists are similar in makeup, only twice the size. So she must have brought something to the table."

Sam thought back to the memoir. "She was a gardener. She apparently could grow most anything."

"That's a useful skill, for sure. Sustainability is vital. It would be interesting to see how she made contact, though."

"Here, read it." Sam pulled the memoir from her bag and handed it to Xander. "I was skimming for information, I didn't really know what to look for."

There was nothing good in the first folder, nor the second. But the third held a treasure trove—close-ups of weapons, cabins equipped with root cellars, walls lined with lockers and shelves full of dried foods, and a group photograph.

"Ah, here we go." Sam blew the picture up. There were about twenty-five people in the photo, and each person held either a gun or a tool of some sort, except for a young teenager front and center who held a flag. It was blue and white with an embroidered columbine framed by snowcapped mountains.

Ledbetter, one of the taller people in the camp, was in the back row. Sam was surprised by how many children there were—at least six, by her count.

Xander was staring at the photo.

"Do you see your friend?"

"No, he's not in this. Must have been taken while he was overseas. Go close up on the girl in the front. She looks familiar."

Sam dragged her fingers across the photo again, making the girl bigger.

"Who do you think she is?"

"Look at her eyes, the shape of her face. Then look at Ledbetter."

Sam compared the two, swiping back and forth on the picture. There was a distinct resemblance between the two. The girl was wearing a baseball cap, so it was impossible to see the color of her hair, but her mother's fiery red tresses stood out. If you imagined them haloing the girl's face, the likeness was clear. Sam thought back to the photo she'd seen on Facebook but couldn't make a visual connection.

"Ledbetter has a daughter," she said. "But she wasn't mentioned in the book as a member of the group. George told me they were estranged and she inherits everything."

"Could have been trying to keep her family life private."

"That's true." Sam stared at the photo a few moments longer, then backed out to the main screen and did a search for "Loa." Multiple folders popped up, and Sam went through several of them. They left no doubt. The girl in the photo was definitely Ledbetter's daughter.

"Answers that," Xander said.

"Yeah." Sam went back to the main screen and another folder caught her eye. Africa. 1990. Ah, that must be where the photo Ledbetter used most prominently, her winning smile as she was surrounded by Maasi tribesmen, resided.

Sam clicked open the folder and started scrolling through the pictures. She was near the bottom when she recognized another face. Her excitement began to build.

"Xander, look at this."

He set down his coffee and leaned in close. She could smell him, the indefinable scent of man coupled with the lemon soap his mother left in the shower for them and the barely perceptible tang of his sweat. She took a deeper breath, just for the pleasure of it. He smelled good, and she had to check herself from snuggling up against him. Pheromones were a fascinating thing.

As if he sensed her sudden lust, he set his hand on her forearm, making a connection between them. A promise for later.

"What am I looking at?"

"Third man from the right. Sort of angled away from the camera. Is that who I think it is?"

He stared at the photo for a minute. "I think it is. How about that."

"How about that indeed. Ledbetter and Leighton were in Africa together in 1990."

Sam scrolled through some more pictures, hoping to find a smoking gun, but the one with Leighton in the background was the only photo she could find that proved they were in the same place at the same time. It was a tenuous thread at best, but a thread nonetheless.

She dialed the number of Ledbetter's office, hoping to catch George. She was in luck, and he came to the phone after just a few moments.

"Dr. Owens. It's lovely to hear from you. What can I help you with?"

"Hello, George. Do you mind if I put you on speaker? I have someone here who needs to hear our conversation. His name is Xander Whitfield, he's a former Army sergeant who is familiar with the Blue and Gray."

"That's convenient. You've been busy."

"We're tracking down a few leads. And as it happens, he's my significant other."

"By all means, then. If you trust him, I do, as well."

"Thank you." She hit the speaker. The cafe was crowded enough that the background noise would cover their conversation, but they were off in a quiet corner, so they were still able to hear.

"I've been going through the photographs, and I have a couple of questions. I found a group photo of Dr. Ledbetter's time with the Mountain Blue and Gray. I wasn't aware that her daughter had been on the excursion with her."

"Ah. Yes, she decided to keep that part of the story out of the book. It's the reason they're estranged, actually."

"Really? Can you tell me more?"

She heard him closing a door. Discretion. George was a commendable employee. Sam really needed to find a way to steal him for herself.

"This was before my time, so I've only got pieces of the story. You read the memoir?"

"Yes. I know she was forced to leave and they sued to have some of the details changed to protect their identities."

"That's close enough to the truth. But of course, there's always more. The gist of it is, once she'd been found out and was asked to leave, her daughter refused to return to civilization with her. She'd made a connection with one of the men, and wanted to stay with him."

"One of the men or one of the boys?"

"From what I know, he was older than her by a good ten years."

"She looks very young in this photo."

"Thirteen at the time, yes. Dr. Ledbetter was adamantly against it, both the relationship and her staying behind. They had several terrible arguments. Dr. Ledbetter wasn't about to leave her young daughter out in the woods with a bunch of strangers and at the mercy of a man nearly twice her age. But Loa had other plans. She and the man left in the night, ran away, and though they did an extensive search, Dr. Ledbetter was forced to come home without her. The group leader assured her he would find them and be in touch the moment he knew anything."

"I can't imagine leaving my child behind." There was ice in her voice.

"Neither could she, believe me. She canceled several months of work to stay and try to find Loa. She was holed up in a hotel with basically no help, though. It was terrible for her. In the end, they simply didn't want to be found, and she had no choice but to return to her life."

"But Loa came back."

"That she did. When I saw her, probably six months after she returned, she was thin and tired and silent as the grave as to what had happened. She was fifteen when she came back. She'd been gone for two years."

"No chance you know the name of the man she'd been with, is there?"

"Not off the top of my head. I can go through some of Dr. Ledbetter's things and see. Or you could just contact Loa yourself. Maybe she'd be willing to talk now, especially since her mother is gone."

"I left her a note on Facebook asking her to get in touch, but she never returned the message. But it's only been a day."

"Here's her direct number. You can try that instead of waiting." He rattled off ten digits, and Sam scribbled them down on a napkin.

"Thank you. There's one more thing. Remember I asked if Dr. Ledbetter knew Congressman Leighton?"

"Yes. As far as I know, she didn't."

"What was she doing in Africa in 1990?"

"Peace Corps. She dropped out, though. It wasn't for her. She wanted to scale all the mountains, not be stuck in one place. That's what she said about it."

"Are you near her computer?"

"Yes, I am."

"If you look in the Africa folder from 1990, at photo number 7679, you'll see a group of people. Do you have it?"

She heard him clicking away, then he said, "Yes. That was taken about a month before she left Kenya. She'd only been there for about three weeks at the time."

"The man facing away from the camera. We believe that's Peter Leighton."

George was silent.

"Are you still there?"

"Yes, sorry. I was just looking. It does seem to be him. That's weird, though. She never said anything about knowing him to me."

"Well, maybe it didn't come up."

"Actually, it did. She was invited to a fundraiser last month that he was speaking at. Normally she accepts all those invitations—they're good for drumming up new business. But when she saw it on her calendar, she flipped out. Told me to cancel, which I did. I asked her why and she said she thought Leighton was a pompous ass and didn't want to be associated with him or his policies. That was enough for me. I canceled it, and we never spoke of him again."

"That's interesting. Just one last question. Who was Dr. Ledbetter married to?"

"She's never been married. She didn't want a man tying her down, but she always wanted children. For lack of a better term, she used a turkey baster to get pregnant with Loa. The father was a friend of hers from college."

"Do you know his name?"

"No. He wasn't part of her life. He just did her a favor once, as she put it."

"All right, George. Thank you so much. You've been a huge help, as always."

"You're welcome, Dr. Owens. Call me again if you need anything more."

She ended the call, raised an eyebrow toward Xander.

"Well?"

"Very interesting."

"I'll say. I think it's probably time to call Fletch, give him some information."

"Probably. Hopefully Reed will be back with the details on Gerhardt soon, too. More coffee?"

"I don't know how you can handle all that caffeine."

"That's a yes?"

She smiled. "Yes."

He bussed her on the forehead and went in search of refills. Sam watched him go, just happy to be near him. Then she dialed Fletcher's number, and gave him all the news.

CHAPTER THIRTY-EIGHT

Washington, D.C.
Detective Darren Fletcher

Fletcher was back at the JTTF when his cell phone rang. He was surprised to find Mrs. Conlon on the other end of the line.

"Detective, I apologize for my tone this morning. I am not mentally prepared to think about anything other than the fact that my Marc is gone, and I'll never see him again."

"I understand, Mrs. Conlon. There's no need to apologize."

"Thank you. I thought about what you said, about Marc's research, and people he might have come in contact with who upset him. There was a boy who Marc talked to a few times on his computer. I don't remember what they call it."

"Skype?"

"That's it. Yes. He was on the computer with this young man and I was bringing some laundry up. They were having an argument."

"Do you remember what it was about?"

"No, sir. The minute Marc realized I was in the room he shut the computer. I asked if everything was okay and he said it was, that he was just talking to a fellow student who needed some help with his thesis."

"Why did this moment in particular stand out to you, Mrs. Conlon?"

"Because he was lying to me. He didn't lie much, we had an understanding. You don't need to lie, you can just say it's none of my business and so long as it's clear no one is getting hurt, I'll leave it alone. But he was upset, angry, and when I left the room I heard him slamming around upstairs."

"When was this, ma'am?"

"Oh, a couple of months ago. The thing is, looking back, I think I recognized the boy. He was hanging around our neighborhood a few days ago. I didn't know who he belonged to, he was like a stray dog just hoping someone might take him in. He was sitting in his car like he was waiting for something. That's all I have, Detective."

"Mrs. Conlon, would you mind sitting down with an artist and letting us get a composite of this boy?"

"I don't know what good that will do. I can barely remember what he looks like, I just recognize that he was the same person Marc fought with."

"Anything might help us, ma'am. You'd be amazed at what you do remember, even though you don't think you do. I can arrange for an artist to come to your house right now if it would be convenient."

She sighed. "I guess that would be fine. Better than sitting here grieving. At least it will give me something to do."

Fletcher told Inez to get an artist with an Identi-Kit to head over to the Conlon house, then sat back in his chair and tried to piece things together. Just as he decided he'd be better off chucking it all and starting from scratch, and maybe grabbing a sandwich and some coffee to go along with that, his cell trilled.

It was Sam.

"Hey there. How're the mountains treating you?"

"Very well, thank you. Have you talked to Amado?"

"About the delivery methods of the abrin? Yes. Great catch. It's all being tested now."

"Good. Listen, I have something else that you're going to need to check out. Something that now ties everyone together."

"Hit me."

"The congressman was with Loa Ledbetter in Africa in 1990. She was in the Peace Corps briefly, and apparently so was he."

"That's it?"

"Yes."

"That's interesting. But I'm not sure how to use it. That was a long time ago. He wasn't on the public radar then. He was just a kid, really."

"He'd be, what, twenty-two or twenty-three. About her same age, actually. I'm just here looking through Ledbetter's photos, and up pops the congressman. They were definitely in the same place at the same time. They knew each other."

"That helps, but, Sam, you're giving me precious little to go on."

"Precious little is an understatement. But there's something here, I can feel it. Ledbetter uses the photos from her trip to Africa, specifically the day she was with the Maasi, on a lot of her stuff—it's the focal point at her office, it's her Facebook photo."

"Maybe she just liked it of herself."

"And maybe that photo held special meaning for her. Come on, Fletch. Think about it. Twenty-three years later, Ledbetter and Leighton are both murdered on the same day? There's a connection here."

Fletcher thought about his meeting with Gretchen Leighton, and her infinitesimal reaction when he asked if she was familiar with Loa Ledbetter or if her husband knew her. The tiny eyelid flutter. He'd wondered at the time whether she was hiding something. But if your husband is a congressman, he's going to know a lot of people.

"There's one more interesting thing. Ledbetter's daughter, also named Loa, was with her during her year she was sequestered with the Mountain Blue and Gray, but she never mentions her daughter in her memoir of that time. This is the daughter she's estranged from and who inherits everything."

"Where's the daughter?"

"In D.C., I think, or thereabouts. From what I've ascertained, Ledbetter had to leave the girl behind because she fell in love with one of the men in the camp, and ran away with him. She showed up back in D.C. two years later. I've got her phone number if you want to talk to her. She might be able to shed some light on things."

"Where did you get this information?"

"Ledbetter's assistant, George. He's a treasure trove of information."

"All right. Thanks for this. When are you coming back?"

"Soon. But we have a date with a large animal vet and some autopsy reports first. A man out here, name's Sal Gerhardt, died a few months ago, along with several of his cattle. A lung ailment. I just want to check and see if there's a chance our killer tested his abrin out before the attack. Has the Moroccan dude talked?"

Fletcher double-checked that he was out of earshot from anyone else at the JTTF before he spoke again. He kept his voice low.

"This is for your ears only. I'm pretty sure it's not him. It's a diversion. They're trying to lure the real killer out. So you keep on your trail, and on your toes, and tell me everything you find out."

"I figured as much. Will do, Fletch. Talk to you soon."

She hung up, and Fletcher put his phone back in his pocket.

He felt better now that he'd told Sam the truth. He didn't agree with the tactic of allowing the media to think they'd caught the man who did this. He thought it was a dangerous ploy, one that could easily backfire on them.

But that wasn't his problem, that was Bianco's. He had another focus.

Who the hell was behind the murders of the three Indiana girls? And how was that connected to Tuesday's Metro attack?

CHAPTER THIRTY-NINE

Loa Ledbetter the younger lived on Connecticut Avenue, near the Washington Zoo. Inez tracked her down, asked her to make herself available for an interview. She was actually coming downtown to meet a friend for lunch at Old Ebbitt, and said she would be happy to stop by the JTTF for a chat.

Fletcher realized he needed to start thinking about this case differently. Sam emailed him the photographs she had found, and he had Inez start going through them. Finding a connection between the congressman and Ledbetter was a good step. It at least proved they knew each other. He wished there was a direct and contemporary correlation between Leighton and Conlon, then they'd really be cooking with fire.

But he still couldn't figure out why and how the subway attack figured in. If you want to murder three people, why run the risk of killing hundreds?

Sam's theory was as good as any he'd come up with. The point was to attack hundreds and mask the true targets.

If he was a profiler, he'd start looking at this killer more like a workplace shooter, someone with an ax to grind, who felt he was being disenfranchised. Someone whose world was falling apart, and blamed the people around him for that downfall.

Congressman Leighton, Dr. Loa Ledbetter and Marc Conlon.

Each knew the other in some capacity. But where was their overlap? Who had come across all three of them in such a way that he, or she, was infuriated enough to kill them all?

"Inez, where's that list of staffers from Leighton's office? And I want to start talking to the people who were with him the morning of the attack. I don't care what Temple said, one of them could have had some sort of access to him."

"Right here."

She handed him a file folder.

"What about the damn detective from Indianapolis? Has he ever surfaced?"

She glanced at her watch. "Yes, he did. He's supposed to call at three. He's at a conference in Berlin, and won't be free until this evening." She perched on the edge of his desk. "You look like a man with something on his mind."

"You can say that again. Too much information coming at me from too many quarters. But that's good. The artist off to Mrs. Conlon?"

"Yes. You probably have an hour before Ms. Ledbetter joins us. Can I get you anything?"

Answers.

"I need something else from you. You've been looking at those photos Sam got you access to, right?"

"Yes. Dr. Ledbetter was a wonderful photographer."

"If nothing else is leaping out at you, set them aside for now. I want you to find everything you can on the congressman's past, especially around 1990. I want to know what he ate for dinner, where he shopped, the works. And not just details, I want assumptions, too. Go through his life with a fine-tooth comb. Everything that you think could be relevant to his murder. I need a second set of eyes and hands on this, so consider yourself promoted. No more fetching me coffee. Unless you're absolutely itching to continue being secretary of the year instead of doing the heavy lifting."

Inez smiled. "Seriously?"

"Seriously."

She brightened, and pushed her glasses back up her nose in excitement. "I was hoping you'd ask. I've actually already started looking into him."

He smiled at her. "I figured. What do you have?"

"Well, Africa, for one. His military record is pretty straight-forward. He was in Liberia in 1990, supposedly part of the reinforced rifle company that went in to protect the embassy in Monrovia. Now that's on the other side of the continent from Kenya, where Ledbetter's photo was supposedly taken, but I think Dr. Ledbetter was actually in Liberia when that picture was taken, not Kenya. The Maasi travel, of course. Plus they're trotted out for national visits and things, they're one of the most recognizable tribes in Africa. It's plausible that the whole Peace Corps thing could be a front for her. It would help her life take on some perspective."

"What are you saying? Ledbetter was a spy?"

"I think she might have been, yes. She was a world trav-eler, never stayed in one place more than two or three years. State Department doesn't have a record of her working for them, but that means nothing. But they do have a record for Leighton. And it's redacted. That's why he would have been in plain clothes in Liberia instead of military—he was attached to the embassy, and so was she. The Maasi shot could even be cover for where she really was in Africa. And it would be very hush-hush, of course. Not something you talk to your friends about. But lots of people get recruited out of the Peace Corps. Or are placed there to start their careers."

Fletcher had to give it to Inez, she was showing what Bianco liked to refer to as "real imagination."

"So if Leighton's job in the Army was to run interference for CIA operatives, wouldn't that kind of information get out during a congressional run?"

"Not if they covered their tracks pretty well. He was a popular candidate, didn't have a lot of opposition that stood a chance. His first election was relatively painless, and in his subsequent elections he ran unchallenged. So it's very possible that no one dug deep enough to find this. It's not the kind of thing your run-of-the mill journalist can get his hands on—I'm lucky State was willing to play ball. I think the only reason they were was because he was dead. And I agreed to have dinner with the watch officer who pulled the file for me."

"He cute?"

"Very." She shared a wicked grin with him.

"That is all very compelling. What else do you have?"

"A lot that doesn't make sense. The murders, for example. He couldn't have done them."

"Yeah, I already suspected that."

"You did?"

"Just a hunch. As soon as that DNA comes back, we'll know for sure, but it just felt too convenient."

"Convenient, for sure. His schedule matches up perfectly to the estimated dates of the crimes. But the last two girls went missing for a day or two before they turned up dead, so there's some leeway on exactly when the crimes occurred. Twelve hours in either direction casts some pretty big doubt on his whereabouts. He leaves town before they're found, but they're all dead for almost one day *before* he comes to town. Now remember time of death is somewhat unreliable when you're talking days, rather than hours. All they can really tell is what day they were killed based on insect activity on the bodies, not what time exactly. So it's feasible that he was there and the first thing he does when he lands is go out and find a girl to kill."

"Tell me more about him."

"I started in 1994. He'd just left the military, and wed Gretchen Dasnai. She was his hometown honey from high school. They'd known each other for years, had been dating since they were in their late teens. They got busy having a baby—that's Peter Junior, the one who died—and got Peter Senior settled in her father's law practice. He went to night school while he paralegaled for the firm. When he graduated and passed the bar, they brought him on as an associate. By 2000 he was a partner, and he made his first Congressional run in 2002. The rest I think you know."

"So he's been time-sharing his life with Indiana and D.C. ever since. Thirteen years. Unlucky thirteen."

"His son died in 2011, and that's when he did the big turn-around on his stance toward military funding."

"Did they have the vote today on the appropriations bill?"

"They did. It didn't pass."

"Just like Glenn Temple expected. Who is he in all of this? He was a bit autocratic when I met him, and crass to boot. Seemed more upset about the fact they'd lose the votes on the bill than his boss's death."

"Ah, see, now that's where things get interesting. Temple is a hometown boy, as well. He's known the congressman as long as his wife, maybe more. They went to elementary school together."

Fletcher whistled. "There could be some animosity there. Always playing second fiddle, that kind of thing. And Mrs. Leighton mentioned that it was odd that Temple had helped the congressman with his inhaler. That was supposed to be the security detail's job."

Inez shrugged. "Who knows? That's all I have right now."

"That's one hell of a good start, kiddo. Now go get me some more. Don't forget the finances."

She glowed with the praise, and said, "Yes, sir. I'll be back to you with anything else I can dig up. The boys have been working the financials, I'll get their report to you as soon as it's finalized."

She practically skipped off to her desk and settled behind her computer, her fingers a blur as she continued her research.

Okay. One step taken.

Morgan Thompsen waltzed into the JTTF at half-past ten with two seriously bleary-eyed women in tow. Thompsen looked great, like she'd been sleeping in cotton wool for the past ten hours, not up all night roaming the streets. Age, Fletcher decided. That, and good genes. It certainly wasn't clean living.

Inez got them situated in the conference room and passed around steaming mugs of coffee. The working girls, introduced as Alexis and Rosie, slumped in their seats, not happy to be there.

Tough. This was more important than their comfort.

Thompsen set her mug on the table. "Okay, ladies. Tell us what you know about Congressman Leighton."

Alexis glanced at Rosie. "You mean Peter Peter Pumpkin Eater, right?"

"Seriously?" Fletcher asked. "That's what you call him?"

"That's what he calls himself. He's a nutter, but normally harmless. Likes shows, doubles, triples, club sandwich, but sometimes all-nut threesies, too. He's generally up for anything, if you catch my drift."

"Does he prefer men or women?"

Rosie shrugged. "Always thought he was caught between the pointers and the setters, if you catch my drift."

"Oh, my God, he liked doing it with dogs?" Inez was almost apoplectic, and Thompsen leaned over to her and explained.

"He was bisexual, but didn't seem to know which he preferred, men or women. And he liked multiple partners at once."

"Oh. Okay. Well, that sounds…adventurous." Inez was embarrassed by her outburst, but gamely trying to recover. Fletcher bit his lip to stop himself laughing; despite her nonchalant tone, the poor girl's eyes were wide as saucers. She was trying to act blasé, but the more the hookers explained "Peter Peter's" proclivities, the pinker her face became. Oh, to be young and innocent again.

And when the hookers realized they had a captive audience, they went all out, even offering to act out a few of the concepts for their inexperienced companion.

Thompsen was openly laughing now, and Fletcher cut them off with a smile. Inez hastily closed her mouth and composed herself, still bright pink.

"Okay, okay. No more playing," Fletcher said. "I'm going to show you some photographs, and I want you to tell me which one is Peter Peter."

He'd made up a six-pack of pictures, a small card with photos of six men on it. The congressman's face was third from the left. He slid the composite to Alexis, and she stared at it a minute and shook her head. "Rose, you see him?"

Rosie looked and shook her head, as well. "No. He's not any of them. But remember that one, on the bottom right, Lexie? He wanted us to rob the liquor store for him."

Normally, that would be of interest to all involved, but Fletcher needed to stay focused.

"You're sure you don't recognize him."

"No, sir," the girls said in tandem.

Fletcher glanced at Thompsen, who was nodding. Fletch's hunch was right on: someone was claiming to be the congressman, but it wasn't him.

"Tell me what he looks like."

Alexis scratched her left ear. "He's slim build. Short hair, parted on the side. Puts that smelly cream in it so it will lay down. Handsome, but seems like he could pop his top anytime. He really seems like a congressman, you know? His attitude. Like he's really important."

"Important. That's it, Lexie," Rosie chimed in.

Something in Fletcher ticked. He'd met a man very much like that just the day before. A man who would know enough about the congressman and his day-to-day life to impersonate him with ease.

But if that were the case...

"Hold on, ladies. I'll be right back."

Fletcher left the conference room and quickly traversed the floor to his desk, toggled his mouse and typed in the website for the congressman. He clicked on the Staff button, and up popped a bevy of people. The man at the top was the one he wanted. He captured the image and sent it to print, anxiously tapping his forefinger on the mouse, making the pointer jump herky-jerky all over the screen.

Once the printer spit out the paper, he took it and went back to the conference room.

He had no idea what he'd interrupted, Inez was pink again and Thompsen was nearly doubled over laughing, but he ignored them and shoved the paper toward Alexis.

"Do you recognize this man?"

Alexis nodded right away, handed the paper to Rosie, who said, "Yeah, that's him. That's Peter."

Thompsen took the paper from Rosie and glanced at it. "Who is he?"

"Glenn Temple. The congressman's chief of staff."

CHAPTER FORTY

Dillon, Colorado
Xander Whitfield

Sam was bent over the files Reed McReynolds had brought them, lost in a world Xander barely understood. He watched her read, her eyes flitting across the pages as she absorbed the autopsy report on Sal Gerhardt. She made little noises every once in a while, *hmm*s and *oh*s which could only lead him to believe she was finding the information of some worth.

He tried to ignore her and read through the memoir Loa Ledbetter had written. As far as he could tell, she'd come across the Mountain Blue and Gray through a private message board and reached out. She knew all the right lingo, used the acronyms that he was familiar with liberally throughout the text. TEOTWAWKI came up often, but she got into other details—bugout bags and humanitarian daily rations and INCH communications. Xander, too, had these items in his arsenal— in addition to the guns and rations and stored water and iodine pills and batteries, he had a solid escape plan should he ever have to bug out of the cabin in the Savage River mountains, and a way to send an INCH letter that told people "I'm never coming home." He'd never really talked to Sam about his preparations, knowing they were paranoid at best, but better safe than sorry. He could safely get them to his parents' farm within three days in a car and two weeks on foot. He figured Dillon was as safe as anywhere, and at least he knew the land like the back of his hand. His parents already had everything they'd need to live, and they'd all be happy and safe.

Honestly, one of the reasons he'd headed willy-nilly down to D.C. Tuesday in the first place was to evacuate Sam back to the cabin and assess the situation from there. At least he had a bolt-hole high up in the mountains that could keep them safe temporarily, if not permanently.

But nothing like that was going to be necessary, unless a giant asteroid came out of nowhere and hit the earth, and the odds of that were astronomically high, which made him feel pretty comfortable with his plan should it be needed for any other sort of man-made or natural event. His prep was as useful in the event of a tornado slashing through the woods as it was for the end of the world.

He hadn't told her because she would look at him with that grin in her eyes that she got when she wasn't taking him seriously, the one that made him want to chase her all over the house then throw her down on his bed. And he wouldn't blame her one bit.

But he was a good Boy Scout. And there was no reason in the world not to be prepared in case of a "what if" scenario.

Sam closed the file folder and stretched her back, the light from the windows catching the ends of her hair, making them reddish in the morning sun. She was a truly beautiful woman, even if she didn't see it in herself.

She caught him watching her and smiled.

"Hi."

"Hi yourself."

"Anything good in that book?"

"Anything good in that autopsy file? You sounded like a French chef going over the last-minute details for an enormous meal."

That surprised a laugh out of her.

"I can get lost in my work sometimes. The pathologist in Golden did a good job. He was thorough and methodical, especially since he wasn't sure what he was dealing with. Took tons of samples, which we'll have to unearth to have run, but with the visual findings—the frothy blood in the lungs, the edema, the organ engorgement—I'm willing to bet good money that Gerhardt was exposed to abrin, and that's what killed him. We have to buy your dad a nice bottle of wine or something for pulling the pieces together. If the cattle had some of the same findings, we may have found our staging ground."

Xander nodded. "It was a smart catch. But then again, he is a smart man. We need to go talk to Will Crawford sooner rather than later."

"What do you think he knows, Xander? What is he holding back?"

If I only knew.

"I think he might have an idea who is behind this. And might know what he plans to do next. The more I think about our conversation yesterday, the stranger it all seems. It's one thing to shut the site down and go dark for a while to protect yourself—that I understand. But to come back here, to be close to home…and with the connections to the Mountain Blue and Gray, who he has friends in, that tells me he's worried. Worried about his own family."

Saying it out loud felt good. That's exactly what had been bothering him, that Crawford ran back home to Daddy when things started coming off the rails. Either he knew something and was trying to protect his own, or he was afraid of an attack, and was hiding out.

Whichever the case, he was acting pretty damn strange, and Xander felt he might be the key to all of this.

"Why don't we go there now, then? See what we can find out. Maybe the vet could meet us back at your folks' house?"

"That sounds like a great idea." Xander stood, began to gather their things, then saw a flash out the window. He couldn't help the wide smile splitting his face. Damn, the girl hadn't changed a lick.

"Sam, hold up. Here's Carly now."

He watched her run lightly up the stairs and enter the restaurant, blue eyes searching for him. She was still cute, still lithe and trim and bursting with energy. When she found him, she ran across the room and launched herself at him. He had to drop his bag to catch her. Good grief. Ever the cheerleader.

She laid a big fat kiss on him, then, still clinging, looked up at him and said, "Xander Moon, you get handsomer every time I see you."

"And you get prettier." He disengaged himself and set her gently on the floor. "Dr. Carly Skinner, meet Dr. Samantha Owens. Sam's one of the best forensic pathologists in the country."

Xander was surprised when Sam simply nodded her head and said, "Hello."

The reticence Sam was showing was unusual. He'd never seen her be anything less than cordial to anyone before. Carly didn't seem to notice, she just started prattling on about coming back to Dillon and marrying Reed and "Don't you remember that time, Xander, when we all went skinny-dipping…" and Sam pulled into herself more and more.

Xander didn't quite know what to make of it, so he just nodded and smiled and tried to catch Sam's eye, but she was assiduously avoiding his. He listened to Carly reminisce for a bit, reminded himself again that she was a total jaybird, then pulled her back to the matter at hand.

"Sam wanted to talk to you about the cattle lost over at Gerhardt's place. Were you able to get the records?"

"Sure, I've got them, right here." She patted her backpack. "That was a big ol' mess, I'm telling you."

She turned to Sam. "I'm sorry to fawn all over him. I just haven't seen Xander Moon in forever. We haven't had a catch up in ages—what, was it when you got out of the Army? What's that been, three years? You came home and we had dinner that night and you were gone again, lickety-split. Didn't even give me a chance to sink in my claws. And I pined away so much Reed took pity on me and asked me to dinner, and I married him just because I couldn't have you."

Xander was finally catching an inkling of what the problem was. Sam wasn't enjoying hearing about this aspect of his past. It hit him like a ton of bricks. Oh. *Oh!*

He stepped closer to Sam and put an arm around her, but the damage was done, she just stood there.

"You are so full of it, Carly. You never had eyes for anyone but Reed."

"Yeah, yeah. You could have given him a run, Xander, if you hadn't run off."

"Let's talk about the cattle, shall we?"

Carly nodded enthusiastically. "Sure thing. But I think we need to go somewhere a little more private for this. Don't want to freak out half the town with the photos. It ain't pretty."

"Let's just head over to Reed's office, then."

"Sounds good." She punched him in the shoulder. "Tag. You're it."

She took off at a jog and he damn near followed, reinstituting the game they'd played as children on the mountain.

Sam's gaze was mutinous though, so he offered her his hand in a peace gesture. She ignored it, watching the door where Carly had disappeared with a combination of anger and longing etched on her face.

He realized he was in serious trouble. She was righteously pissed off.

"Uh, sorry about that. Carly's always been a little enthusiastic."

"No worries. Let's just go ahead and get this over with." She wouldn't meet his eye, and all he could think was uh-oh.

Uh-oh, and by God, she loves me.

CHAPTER FORTY-ONE

Washington, D.C.
Detective Darren Fletcher

With Glenn Temple identified as the man who was passing himself off as his boss in the D.C. underground sex scene, Fletcher felt the edges of the case start to come together. He sent Inez off to do a complete and thorough background on Temple, but she was back a few minutes later with a printout.

"ViCAP results. Thought you'd want to see them."

"Let me guess. We have matches."

"Six of them. All from the tri-state area. It looks like whoever killed the girls in Indiana is killing here, too."

Fletcher whistled.

"Still a very good setup to hang on the congressman. I'll bet you dollars to doughnuts the murders all coincide with times he's in the city for session. Okay, Inez. Work quickly. We are going to have to find everything and anything on Glenn Temple. We'll need DNA from him as well, so get creative. We don't want to screw up, here. I need to brief Bianco, too, so I need details."

"Do you really think that he would set up his oldest friend to take the fall for his crimes?"

Fletcher nodded. "Wait till you meet him. The man is cold as ice. Yes, I can totally see it. And what better way to clear yourself than hang the stink of suspicion on a public figure? Who has more to lose? If it is him, he probably planted the DNA—they got the sequence off a straw from a fast-food drink. That's easily manipulated. Temple hasn't returned my calls, so when you have everything, we'll go at this from the other side. You can call the office and say it's Gretchen Leighton for Mr. Temple. They had an intern on the phone last time I was there. They won't know the difference."

"And then?"

"We're going to make every detail from our end seamless and airtight. Once we're all set, I just want to establish his whereabouts, then we go in and grab him up. But we have to move quickly. The hookers aren't exactly known for their discretion. Word will go around fast. So get going."

Inez scooted away.

Fletcher chewed on a pencil, thinking. Could Temple be behind the Metro attack?

The answer came to him disturbingly quickly. Yes, of course he could.

The phone on his desk rang. He jumped; he'd never heard it before, and the ringer was set on ten. People half a world away had probably heard it. He hit the speaker.

"Yes?"

"Detective, a woman is here to see you. Her name is Loa Ledbetter."

"I'll be right there." He hung up and looked over at Inez. "Conference room still free?"

"Should be. Bianco is caught at a meeting over at the FBI about the Moroccan. I hope she's not in trouble."

I hope she is.

"All right. I'm going to be in there. If the artist shows up with the Identi-Kit, let me know."

"Yes, sir."

He left her happily tapping away and went to meet Ledbetter's daughter.

Time to get some damn answers.

"I just can't believe she's gone. When I found out, I thought it was some sort of bad joke."

Loa Ledbetter was the spitting image of her mother in her photos from twenty years earlier. Fiery red hair barely tamed, milky skin, hazel eyes. She had an unaffected speech pattern, soft and sweet, with a touch of Southern, probably from the girls' school she'd attended in rural Virginia, and hardly fit the bill as a scheming heir. She seemed rather calm, all things considered, but was certainly grieving—beneath her elegant makeup, Fletcher could see dark circles and puffy eyelids, a sure sign of extended crying.

Losing a parent is always hard. To have one murdered was worse, and to be estranged from them? Either you were a heartless wretch and couldn't care less, or there was remorse, or regret, and maybe even some self-loathing driving your every waking moment. Ledbetter seemed to be suffering from all three.

Fletcher sat across from the girl and watched her carefully. Even the best investigator could be taken by a pretty face, but Ledbetter didn't seem out to con him. She seemed genuinely upset, and willing to help. Well, he thought, let's see just how willing she was.

"Ms. Ledbetter—"

"Loa, please."

"Loa. What can you tell me about your mother's life? She was a big traveler, wasn't she?"

"She was. A different city every summer, and we'd park it in some weird hotel or silk-covered casbah or tent in the middle of the desert, and she'd spend all her time digging in the sand while I entertained myself. It was a hard way to grow up, but not too unpleasant. I saw a great many things, and experienced a great many cultures. But I'm a bit of a homebody. I avoid travel if I can. Anything more than a three-hour drive away gives me hives."

"Was there ever anything strange about her trips?"

Loa laughed. "There was never anything normal. We dined with heads of state and footmen alike. My mother was fascinated by people—everything about them turned her crank, from the littlest bit of perfume to their shoes and cars and horses and goats. She wanted to know everything. She was damn good at her job, which was basically to ask a few well-placed questions and let people spill their guts. Then she'd hurry us home so she could write everything up while it was still fresh in her head. I'm sure you already know she was the preeminent ethnographic researcher in the field. There wasn't a soul who wouldn't open up to her. Five minutes with someone and she'd know their lineage, their wives' names, how many children they had, what sort of donkey they owned, whether they liked sweets, what their favorite dish was, whether they'd had an affair, or a miscarriage. She was astounding."

"And yet you two were on the outs. Why?"

Her mouth formed a thin line. "I'd rather not get into that."

Fletcher leaned back in his chair and crossed his hands on his belly. Unassuming. Friendly.

"Loa, please understand. All I'm trying to do here is find out who killed your mother."

Her eyes flashed. "She was on the Metro. She went through

Foggy Bottom every day. Whoever set off the abrin killed her."

"We think it may be more than that. She taught one of the victims, Marc Conlon. He was a student of hers at American last semester. And we think she may have known the congressman who died, as well. Are you familiar with Peter Leighton?"

"Well, yes. Of course. He's been all over the news. It's almost as if he was the only one who died. Every once in a while they'll throw in a statistic, say three dead, but they never even mention their names."

As was often the case.

"But did you know him before the attack? Was he friends with your mother?"

"Not that I'm aware of. She was pretty apolitical. She had to be, to be able to get along with everyone."

Dead end. Either she was lying through her teeth, or there wasn't an open connection there.

"Do you know anyone that might want to hurt your mother?"

"My mother and I hadn't talked in quite some time, Detective. I am very, very sorry that she is dead, and that I will never be able to tell her how much I loved her, despite the fact that she made me crazy. But I was no longer a part of her life, so no, I really don't."

A sad speech. He thought she was being genuine, too. A shame, really. He made a mental note to call his own mother; it had been too long since he'd spent time with her.

"You inherit everything. Twenty million is a lot of money."

"Yes, it is. And I'll be setting up a charitable organization in her name with that money, and making sure her company continues to run. I won't be benefitting from it personally, if that's what you're asking."

She had all the answers. Fletcher decided to rattle her cage.

"All right. Tell me about your time in Colorado, with the Mountain Blue and Gray."

The change that came over her features was remarkable. One minute a soft, grieving child, the next a battle-scarred soldier. She stood up, looking like she was going to run from the room.

"We're finished here."

"Loa. Please. Sit down. We already know a great deal about your time there. That you had a boyfriend, and you ran away with him. That you were gone for two years. I just need to know how that pertains to your mother. I think you've already assessed that we don't think this was merely an attack on the Metro, but a targeted assassination. We are drawing parallels between the three victims, and your mother is at the core of our investigation."

She didn't sit, but she didn't bolt, either.

"Please, Loa, sit back down. I understand that it might be a difficult thing to relive. I promise that nothing you tell me will go any further than my investigative team. But if we're going to find who murdered your mother, we need to know the whole truth about her life. And you were a very important part of her life."

"So *important* that she couldn't even give me my own name. She had to give me hers."

The bitterness was finally coming out, along with a smattering of tears.

"You have her name, which is heavy enough, but forevermore you're going to be associated with her, mistaken *for* her. All because you share her name. So why don't you tell me about that. I assume your running away was an attempt at some real autonomy? What were you, thirteen?"

She sat back down at the table, but still looked like she was ready to bolt.

"Nearly fourteen. Just shy of my birthday."

"What happened?"

"It's a very silly thing to say, but I thought I was in love. And I was sadly mistaken."

CHAPTER FORTY-TWO

Dillon, Colorado
Dr. Samantha Owens

Carly Skinner barely looked strong enough to lift a piece of paper, much less handle horses and cows. But Sam knew strength was easily disguised. And she figured Skinner's small hands might come in handy when it came time for birthing. Animals, like human children, sometimes didn't want to come into the world headfirst, and needed turning in the womb. It was a delicate process, and not one for arms like tree trunks.

No, her size wasn't the problem. The problem was, Xander and Carly clearly had some history.

When they'd been reminiscing like a couple of school kids at their first reunion, Sam was annoyed to feel her blood begin to boil, because for a moment, she felt utterly invisible.

Her internal radar was singing, and she fought hard against it. She had no claim on Xander. She especially had no claim on the years before she'd met him. She was acting like a child. She knew it, and yet something in her just wouldn't quite let go.

When Carly had cried, "Tag," and taken off at a jog, Sam swore she saw Xander tense, as if he was about to sprint after her but then remembered that he had an anchor that would hold him back.

Sam began to gather her things with exaggerated slowness. He grabbed his bag and said, "All right. Let's go nail this down."

"You feel free to go on ahead. I'll catch up. I wouldn't want to hold you back or anything."

"What are you talking about?"

"Nothing."

"Nothing? You look about ready to murder someone."

Sam hastily rearranged her features. *Great, why don't you just announce it to the world? Grow up, Sam. You don't own him. You've never even officially defined your relationship.*

She was pouting. She could feel the waves of disapproval oozing off her body, and tried to pull it back in. *Stop being silly, Sam.*

Xander took a step back and watched her carefully. Then a grin split his face, and he started to laugh.

"You're jealous, Owens."

How dare he laugh, like this was all a good joke? She turned her back and picked up her bag, then started to walk past him.

"I'm not. I have no claim on you. You can talk to whomever you please."

Xander shook his head. "Oh, my dear, darling Sam." He grabbed her wrist and turned her around so swiftly she felt dizzy, then pulled her close and kissed her, hard, right in front of everyone in the restaurant. It went on and on, and she was vaguely aware of a few good-natured snickers, but she didn't care, it just felt so good to be in his arms, to have all of his considerable personal sunlight pouring down on her. She *was* jealous, damn it. The thought of him with another woman tore her into pieces.

Damn. She cared for him even more than she thought.

When he let her loose, he had a smug smile on his face. She wanted to hit him, to smack that grin right off, but part of her smiled back. He'd just laid claim to her in public, with a bunch of witnesses. Old girlfriend aside, it was clear who he wanted to be with.

He touched the back of her neck, then rubbed the pad of his thumb in circles on the delicate skin on the inside of her wrist.

"Okay?" he asked, clearly needing to be forgiven.

"Okay," she answered.

"I'm glad you care," he whispered.

"I care more than you know," she answered softly, and he kissed her again, very briefly.

"Let's go deal with the bovine attack, so we can get on the track to finding this yahoo. Because once this case is put to rest, you and I have some things to talk about."

They walked to the police station hand in hand, and Xander told her all about his relationship with the mercurial teenage Carly, who would be interested in him one day and not remember his name the next. She'd always wanted to be an actress, felt drama was her future. But she'd also been deep into science and managed to conquer acting school and a B.A. in molecular biology, then realized she missed Colorado, her life and her friends too much.

"She's a nice girl, but way too flighty for me. I like a woman with her head on her shoulders. We went on one date, when we were sixteen, and she spent the whole night talking about Reed. She's always been in love with him. And he's always had it bad for her. They are perfect together."

Sam was feeling much comforted, and they finished the quarter-mile walk from the restaurant to the station in companionable silence.

By the time they arrived Carly had already spread her

unique brand of pixie dust all over the station. Every man in the place was smiling, and Carly had her back to the door, pinning up rather grotesque pictures of cows in various stages of dissection on a wall-mounted corkboard.

Xander leaned his head in close. "See? It's not just me. She's like this with everyone."

"What's the divorce rate among your cohort?" she whispered back, and he started to laugh.

"Oh, Sam, Xander Moon, there you are. You guys took forever getting here. Stop off for a quickie on the way?"

McReynolds was lounging against the wall of the conference room, arms crossed on his chest and one cowboy-booted heel flat against the wall. He looked like a very tall, very tan crane. "Lord, Carly. They're going to think you don't know your stuff you keep after him like that. Hush and let's talk about cow innards."

She blew her husband a kiss and stood in front of the board while Sam and Xander took seats at the table.

Satisfied she had everyone's attention, she addressed Sam directly.

"Have you ever necropsied a cow?"

Sam shook her head. "I've never had the pleasure, no."

"Damn hard work. Cows have a lot inside of them. The rumen itself takes forever to get through. You have to pick them up out of the fields with a crane. I was in luck, when Gerhardt's stock went down, the NTSB had their portable crane they call Godzilla here in the mountains dealing with a plane crash. They came and helped us. We were able to use it to move the cows up the hill so we could do the necropsies behind Gerhardt's barn. Level ground there, a nice wide concrete slab."

She pointed at the first of the pictures. Sam saw the pasture running downhill, and the dead cows dotting the green grass like gigantic black-and-white spotted mushrooms. It wouldn't have been an easy feat to move them. She imagined herself, grimly prepared to necropsy the cows, marching off down the hill with purpose, and her respect for Carly upped a notch.

"How many died?" Sam asked.

"Five. Four cows with new calves and a newly weaned winter calf."

"And your findings were consistent with grass tetany?"

"Honestly, that was the only thing that made sense." She started moving down the line of photographs. Sam got up to see better. The first was of a cow on its side, then wide open, on its back, its legs splayed wide as if the cow had spun out on some ice and landed upside down.

Carly continued a painstakingly detailed recitation on the dissection, walking Sam through every step with her on the photos. She was a good teacher, though once you got past the rumen, things were pretty self-explanatory. Hearts were hearts and lungs were lungs and guts were guts on mammals.

"See this? The rules on an animal this size are easy—if it's hollow you lay it open, if it's solid you cut through it. Once I got into the rumen, I started opening things up, and found there were lesions in the abdominal track, as well as blood in the lungs and more lesions on the snout and tongue. It stood to reason it was something they ate, and their magnesium levels came back as low. We gave the herd supplements in some fresh grain and that seemed to fix the problem. We didn't lose any more."

"Are the samples you took still available?"

"I seriously doubt it. We sent it all to the lab at Colorado State, and since it wasn't a herd disease, something communicable that could spread across the stock, there was no reason to keep it on hand once we made the diagnosis. Tetany is dangerous, but only to the cows that aren't getting the right nutrients. I take it you think I'm wrong?"

"I do. But damn if I know how to prove it."

"So what do you think caused their deaths?"

"Abrin. Most likely in their grain. Cows are four to eight times the weight of an average man. The killer would want to be sure the dosage was enough to kill. If it would take down a cow, it would take down a human, without a problem. Personally, I'd have tested on pigs, they're closer to humans point for point. Cows seem overkill, honestly."

"Not a lot of pig farms up here, though."

"Maybe he had a vendetta against Gerhardt," Xander offered. "Reed, did the old man have any threats against him, or problems with people?"

"You know Gerhardt, Xander Moon. He had problems with everyone. But no one wanted him dead as far as I knew."

Carly was walking along her line of photographs, thinking aloud. "Gerhardt could have just been a wrong place, wrong time casualty. If the poison was in the grain, anyone who fed those cows could have gotten sick. The dust that comes up when you pour it out of the carrier is bad. Jeez, I fed the stock myself when he was laid up—it could have been me just as easily. Assuming the killer was testing things." Her hand went to her throat and her china-blue eyes grew wide, and Sam remembered, *drama lessons*.

"What about poachers?" Sam asked.

"You're thinking about how they could get on his land unseen?" Xander asked.

"Yeah."

Reed shrugged. "They're out there, but we don't have too many problems in this area. We mostly have fools who are fishing without licenses and taking a buck out of season rather than people trying to get at the mountain lions and brown bears without a care. It's been known to happen, but it's rare."

Carly was watching her husband. "What about the bandit, Reed?"

"What bandit?" Xander asked.

Reed stepped himself off the wall. "You haven't heard about this? Been going on for a couple of years now. Summit, Jefferson counties, pretty widespread. Someone's been breaking into the cabins and barns and helping themselves to some very nice stuff. Everything from weapons to axes to food. Even a cell phone here and there. We thought it was kids for the longest time, but last month, one of the camp owners got smart and rigged an outdoor camera. We caught the bastard on tape, dressed head to toe in BDUs, sporting a rifle on one shoulder, a coonskin cap and snowshoes. Got him dead to rights coming into the camp, breaking into the cabin and walking out with groceries. Owners were at some kind of party, came home to find they'd been burgled. They called me and since the trail was so fresh, we tried to go after him, but we got nowhere fast. Trail ended at Ridge Road. He must have taken off the snowshoes and hiked along the asphalt for a good ways, because we went up and down the ridge and never got another whiff of him. He hasn't been spotted since, and we've had no new reports."

"What exactly was he stealing?"

"Tools, supplies, food, you name it."

"Did he ever hit Gerhardt's place?"

"You know, come to think of it, he did. Last year. Around the time Gerhardt got sick the first time."

Sam chewed on her lip. She didn't believe in coincidences.

"You still have the video, right?"

"Sure. It's an open case."

"What are you thinking?" Xander asked.

Sam smiled. "Depends on what he stole. Are we talking tuna fish, or are we talking real supplies?"

Reed went to his desk and pulled out a wide file from the cabinet.

"Let's see here—it's mostly food, but when he does take things, it's always really odd stuff, things that don't match. The first one was fertilizer, potting soil, metal pipes, gardening supplies. The second was all kinds of food and vitamins. Kids' vitamins. The third was weapons, the fourth he took the mufflers from the cars, and a whole wad of stuff from the garage—nails and tacks and PVC. The list goes on and on and on. He's like our very own barefoot bandit. We haven't decided if he's harmless or not."

Sam raised an eyebrow at Xander. "I'm going to vote for not. None of those things sound random to me. That's all the makings to cultivate a crop of rosary peas, and build some delivery vehicles."

Xander nodded. "Among other things."

Reed's phone began to squawk. He apologized and went to answer it. Carly followed him.

Sam and Xander sat down together at the table.

"I can just see Carly, marching off down that hill to necropsy the cow."

"She's very determined," Xander said carefully, unsure of whether Sam was being serious or flip.

"Takes a special woman to treat animals," she offered. Olive branch. Carly may have looked like a piece of fluff, but she was obviously smart, and obviously in love with her husband. Sam stowed her animosity and thought aloud about the bandit.

"I bet he has a greenhouse. That's how he's been growing the rosary peas. They need warmth. A hothouse would work just fine for that, especially up here with all the sun. Could be solar, or on a geothermal area—you've got lots of those pockets this high in the mountains."

"How do you know that?"

She smiled at him. "Ledbetter's book. It was one of the tricks they used for keeping themselves warm without having to use fire, since the smoke is a dead giveaway if you're trying to stay invisible. They build their camps near a natural geothermal and pipe the hot water in."

"Whoever is doing this was in the Mountain Blue and Gray when she was."

"I agree. And growing rosary peas is hardly illegal, so anyone who happened upon it thinking it might be a marijuana operation would be sadly surprised. If he's stealing the materials, he's trying to stay off the radar. So there will be no records of him buying the makings."

"You're right. He's totally off grid."

"So it's time to visit your friend and see if he can identify the people in the picture."

Xander nodded. "Let's go then."

Reed and Carly came out of his office. "Man, I'm sorry, I gotta run. Accident up in Breckenridge, I'm gonna take Carly up there. They want someone from ski patrol. You have what you need?"

"We do. We're heading up to Crawfords' Ranch. Will is in town. When we push him with this new information, he might share more about what's going down. He didn't give me the whole story last time we talked."

Xander and Reed shared a look that Sam couldn't decipher.

"Careful up there," Reed finally said. "Crawford's all kinds of crazy. Dementia."

"I know."

Sam turned to Carly. "Thank you for the necropsy primer. I appreciate it."

"No problem. I'll check and see if those samples are still around the labs up there in Fort Collins."

"Thanks."

They all walked out together. The sun beat down, the blue sky close and watchful, and Sam couldn't help but feel like they were one step closer.

Closer, and even farther away.

CHAPTER FORTY-THREE

It amazed him that an office building in Boulder could have better security than the Metro in D.C., but there you have it. It didn't matter, really, he had the appropriate ID and equipment and uniform. No one would give him a second glance. But it was ironic.

He showed the badge at the front desk, grunted noncommittally when the guard asked him to sign in, scribbling something with the pen, careful to wipe it on his sleeve before he set it down, to smudge any possible prints. Going about in gloves at this point was too suspicious, but the minute he was in the elevator he slipped them on.

The higher the elevator rose, the more the bombs seemed to come alive in his bag, chittering to him, though he knew that was impossible. They were each swathed in the devil's own Bubble Wrap, tucked tightly together without a chance for connection until he was ready to make them sing. They couldn't clank or whisper, he'd made sure of that.

At the top floor, he got out and made his way to the end of the stairwell. He had a large fluorescent light in one hand, his bag in the other. He looked every bit the part of an electrician, replacing a specialized bulb.

He started at the top. He had five to place. Five tubes of life-ending hell, all ready to unleash their fury upon the heathens who created their horrors within these walls.

He worked his way down the stairs, tucking a bomb into the ventilation shafts every third floor. No cameras in the stairwells, the dummies. Though he assumed they made their devil deals out here, which was why it was the perfect spot, private, load bearing and the main escape route from the building in case of emergency. He'd be sure to capture everyone. When he was finished, all he had to do was pull the fire alarm and hightail it out of there. Count thirty to allow for maximum confusion, then hit Send on his cell. He'd already be a block away before anyone knew what hit them, and on his way back to the camp before the first responders arrived.

It was a shame he couldn't stay to watch, but Ruth was waiting in the truck. She was a good girl, she was on the floor with her book and the windows were tinted so there was no way she could be seen from the outside. She'd happily play there for a good hour or so, more than enough time for him to set his trap.

He liked this "making a statement" work. Truth be told, in the beginning, he had been planning to stop after D.C., where things had gone so well, but he had the leftover abrin, and the material to make some serious boom-booms, so why not? He could get used to this—eliminating those who pissed him off. Obviously no one in D.C. had any idea of what was going on. They'd arrested some raghead, and he was happy to let them. It gave him more freedom, and that's all he was trying to do, anyway, was fight for freedom. Damn government tried to interfere in everything now, and he was sick and tired of it.

They made laws that allowed the most terrible things to happen, from allowing children to die in their mothers' wombs to the rape of the land to the secret stores of stem cells they were using behind the doors, twenty feet away, to build a genetically perfect army, clones who were unstoppable, things that would heal within minutes and rise to fight again. Like zombies. Once they'd figured out how to re-create a woman's eggs from stem cells, it was all over. There was no more slippery slope: they'd all arrived at the bottom, and the only way to recover was to scrabble around in the mud and build their wall again, sailing to the top on the backs of the unborn, carefully crafted and modified children.

They would interfere with the people next. The evil-loving societies, and their desire to be sheep, led to the slaughter. They didn't care. They wanted to be fattened and allowed to live their useless little lives, with their cars and electric toys and drugs and sex. They were an abomination. They epitomized sin. They reveled in their greed and sloth and envy. He'd fallen prey to one of the seven deadlies himself, been captured by the bonds of lust, and knew just how powerful that pull could be. And look where that got him.

Things went black, a rage he couldn't control panting through him, taking him away. He had to fight for control. Tears pricked the corners of his eyes. The injustice of it all overwhelmed him.

Not now. Not now.

His breathing slowed infinitesimally, enough for him to catch some air.

He wouldn't allow the sins of the father to be visited on his child, no matter that she was the direct result of those sins.

No one would ever hurt his Ruth.

And so he became wrath.

Because it is not a sin to be living proof of God's will.

He realized he was standing stock-still in the hallway, and people were filing past, some in scrubs, all looking at him queerly. He carefully tucked his hands in his pockets and went to the elevator, the now empty backpack on his shoulder.

It was done. In fifteen minutes, they'd all be dead, and the ones who didn't succumb in the blast would get a nice whiff of abrin and die later.

Die, mother...*fuckers.*

He stopped himself from giggling. He didn't use bad words often. Just thinking one was tantamount to shouting it at the top of his lungs, but that thought felt very, very good.

The elevator dinged and the doors slipped open. He kept his gaze averted and entered, ignoring the two nurses inside. He counted it down.

Thirty.

Twenty.

Ten.

Ding.

He walked straight out and made a beeline for the doors.

"Hey! Hey! Electrician dude."

Stop walking. Turn around slowly. Don't look anxious.

He followed his own advice. The security guard was on his feet, pointing his long finger right at his...oh, the badge. They wanted their badge back.

He allowed himself half a breath, and detached it from his pocket, walked it back to the security guard, who grunted thanks and took it.

He turned and hightailed it out of there. At the door he hesitated for a second, looking over his shoulder. The fire alarm was on the wall to the right of the glass door. No one was looking.

He pulled the white bar, and the sirens sang out. Quicker than a breeze, he stepped out the doors and began a quick march away from the building.

The previous glee returned. He was golden.

The truck was parked five hundred yards away, and he glanced at the gorgeous, sunny summer sky, wondering what the people inside the four walls of perdition were thinking.

Panic.

Fire.

Apocalypse.

He bet they'd been looking outside their windows, gloating about their advances, cheering each other with their test tubes full of the abominations they created, reveling in the sun, thinking it signified God's pleasure at their interference with his plan, and yet they had no idea that they were staring into the brimstone sky of their real creator. And then the warning system kicked in, and they'd have to abandon their work, scramble into the stairwells, where his vengeance lay in wait.

He would show them. *Breathe your last, hellspawn.*

He counted the steps to the truck. Reached the door. Opened it, and swung his big body into the cab.

"Ruthie, my darling…"

The truck was empty.

"Ruth? Where are you? Ruth?"

No answer.

And the cell phone, stashed so carefully behind the gearshift, was gone, too.

Terror filled him, bleeding into his blood, and he went ice-cold before breaking out into a flop sweat. His breath came fast, and he couldn't see. The blackness was coming, it was going to take him.

Breathe, man. She can't be far.

Ruth was going to be in some serious trouble. She had strict instructions not to move. She had defied him, and stolen the phone from him, as well. He would tan her hide the minute he found her.

Think. *Think!*

He got out of the cab of the truck and scanned the street, up and down. The office building was the only one on the street, and people were actually starting to stream out of the doors, white lab coats flapping in their hurry to escape.

Oh, God, where was she?

He searched up the west side of the street, saw nothing, then turned and scoured the east side. Half a block away on either side were some of the college's classrooms. The University of Colorado campus was extensive, stretching all over Boulder, their octopus-like tentacles spreading through the streets and into the businesses. She could be anywhere, in any direction.

And she had the detonator.

CHAPTER FORTY-FOUR

Washington, D.C.
Detective Darren Fletcher

Fletcher had to coax the story out of Loa, a little bit at a time. It wasn't terrible, by any means, but he could see how much it hurt her to relive.

"You can't know what love is when you're thirteen. My mother kept trying to tell me that, and I kept trying to make her see that of course you can. But she was right. She was almost always right."

Loa was calm again, settled in. She had leaned her head on her right hand, was idly playing with the ends of her hair. She seemed strangely disconnected from the story as she told it, clearly a self-protecting device. Either she'd told this story a hundred times, or she'd rehearsed how she would relay the details.

Fletcher wasn't so bad as an ethnographic researcher himself. He pulled the pieces from her, slowly at first, as if he'd been digging for days in the desert, and the shovelfuls of information hit the screens, and the sand sifted out, leaving the remnants to expose themselves.

He let her talk, gave her a push here and there, and the rest of the story flowed from her mouth. She seemed almost relieved in the telling, unburdening herself. She had nothing to lose anymore.

"You know they found out she wasn't really a survivalist, but a researcher, right? They actually shut her up in the cabin for a few hours to discuss things. When they let her out, she raised all kinds of holy hell, trying to explain herself, but it wasn't working. They were pissed. They told her to get out, and stay out.

"When she told me it was time to move on, I balked. I wanted to stay. I liked the group, they liked me. They treated me as an equal, not as a child. Mother never understood that— she thought that just because she let me stay up late and try champagne and travel the world that she was giving me equal status, but she would flip between friend and mother in a flash. If I didn't do as she asked immediately, she treated me like a petulant child. Do you know how embarrassing it is to be grounded in front of a crown prince?"

Fletcher just shook his head.

"That was my mother. Hot and cold. I don't think she ever really wanted to have children, I was most definitely an accident. One she gamely tried to stuff into a backpack and take along just like she did her camera and fresh underwear and toothbrush. And when I was little, that worked. But as I got older, started having my own opinions, wanted to play with my friends, go to school…well, we were destined to clash. She was used to getting her way. I was used to having a lot of freedom. When she laid down the law on me, for the longest time I would acquiesce. But in Colorado, that all changed. I didn't want to let her bully me anymore. And I had my special friend, and when she tried to force me into something I didn't want, he would take me aside and explain why I didn't have to listen. That I was an adult in the eyes of the group, and should anything ever happen, I'd be expected to pull my weight accordingly, so she needed to start treating me as a real equal, like the rest of them did."

"And that 'special friend' was the one you ran away with?"

"Yes."

"Why didn't the group kick you out along with your mother?"

"Because I was thirteen, and they knew I was just along for the ride, not playing a part in the charade. They left the choice to stay up to me. And I wanted to stay. For the first time in my life, I felt like I belonged. Remember, this sort of continual assimilation was par for the course for me. I normally just melded into whatever situation we found ourselves in. But the group was different. They wanted me for me, and I had found a place where I could be comfortable, be myself."

"Who was your friend?"

"I'd rather not say."

He let that ride for now. He would come back to it in a bit.

"Your mother posited that the survivalists are all cults."

"And in many cases, she'd be right. Especially when you look at the groups that are promoting violence, or hate wars, or finding some way to exclude people should the end of days come. But the Blue and Gray were just a bunch of normal people who decided to live life their way. They had no charismatic leader, didn't have church services and stuff like that. They were totally normal."

"I'll take your word for it. So you ran away, they threw your mother out, and then what happened?"

She was growing visibly uncomfortable.

"Let's just say things didn't work out according to plan." She looked at her watch. "Oh, my goodness. I am so late. I really must be going, Detective." She stood again, this time determined. She was finished talking. He couldn't make her stay, really; it wasn't like she was a suspect.

Then again, twenty million was enough to lay the suspect carpet in front of anyone's door.

He shrugged and rose himself.

"If you think of anything more, I would really appreciate it if you could call."

There was a knock on the conference room door. Fletcher looked over Loa's shoulder to see Inez. She had thick white art pages with her. He assumed it was the Identi-Kit.

"I'm sorry to interrupt, Detective. The artist rendering you asked for has come in."

"That's fine, Inez. Ms. Ledbetter was just leaving. Would you mind showing her out? Thank you."

"Of course. Ma'am, if you'll just follow me." Inez handed the drawing over, and he glanced down at it. It was a man. Just a man. He didn't know if he was expecting horns and a forked tail, or a sign that blinked neon and screamed: *I did it*. This was just another run-of-the-mill schmo with a square jaw, short hair and shaded cheekbones. Caucasian features. It could be anyone.

Then he had a thought.

"Wait a minute. Loa, will you give this a quick once-over, see if it's anyone you might recognize?"

She squared her shoulders. "Is it a picture of the man who killed my mother?"

"Possibly. We're looking at every angle, and this man had contact with Marc Conlon recently. It's worth a shot, just in case."

He handed the paper to Ledbetter and watched her eyes grow wide, and her face drain of color like someone dropped a black-and-white screen over her. Two seconds later her eyes rolled back in her head and she started to fall.

"Whoa, whoa, whoa!" Fletcher tried to catch her and missed, and she hit the floor, surprisingly hard for such a small woman. Inez hurried back to them.

"Wow. That gives a whole new meaning to fainting dead away. I have never seen anyone go down like that before. What did you do?"

"What did *I* do? Thanks for the vote of confidence, Inez."

Fletcher knelt down next to her, felt for a pulse. It was just a faint, she was already starting to come to. Inez got on her knees and pulled Ledbetter's head into her lap.

"Little help here," Fletcher called out. One of the young guns appeared in the door.

"Holy crap, is she okay?"

"Just fainted. Get her some water, will you?"

He looked at Inez, who was smoothing Loa's hair back from her forehead with one hand and fanning her with the other, all while shushing her like she was a scared puppy.

"I think it's safe to say she knows him," Fletcher said drily.

Ledbetter was back among the living in a few minutes. They got her seated at the conference table, and she clutched the bottle of water, pale as a ghost, a look of sheer, unadulterated fright on her face.

Fletcher sat down next to her.

"Loa, who is he?"

She shook her head like a child who doesn't want to rat on her friend, quick and with her eyes closed.

"Loa. You obviously know this man. That in and of itself makes him more than just another pretty face. Come on. Who is he?"

She kept her eyes closed and whispered, "He told me his name was Ryan. Ryan Carter."

"How do you know him?"

She took a big, deep breath before she spoke again, then finally opened her eyes.

"He was my husband."

CHAPTER FORTY-FIVE

Dillon, Colorado
Dr. Samantha Owens

Sam was quiet as Xander drove them back up the mountain. She felt like they were going in circles, and had no idea if they were on the right path. If they were, why weren't Fletcher and the rest of the JTTF here, combing these mountains? Unless they really did feel the man they'd arrested was responsible for the attack. She was getting really frustrated and didn't know what to do next. She didn't want to call him again and get another *well done you,* not until she was sure they were totally on to something. But she needed him to call out the troops, to get the CDC to Sal Gerhardt's farm, and the FBI and Homeland here to deal with this. She was only one person, and there was no way she could handle all of this.

But she knew they *were* on to something. Something bigger than what they originally thought they were dealing with.

Clouds were gathering, blotting out the sun with unholy speed. Summer in the mountains: one second sunny, the next a torrential downpour. It fit her mood. She'd been all over the place today, exaltation and sorrow, jealousy and possessiveness.

She guessed that's what love was supposed to be about, but wow, she wasn't sure if she was ready for this again.

It scared her. She didn't want to belong to someone again, to have him belong to her. Belonging meant there was a chance of loss, and she didn't think she had the strength to go through it once more.

But she couldn't deny that her feelings for Xander had gotten completely out of her control. They were wild and untamed and so strong it took her breath away.

And she knew he felt the same way. It was becoming unavoidable. They were rushing toward a huge brick wall, and it was going to be up to her to either slam on the brakes before they hit the barrier, or make herself malleable and willing, and let a door open that would allow them to pass through safely to the other side.

She wondered what had driven Loa Ledbetter. Was it love, or heartbreak? Was she running away from something, or toward it? The constant travel, the desire to live off the land, to disappear into other cultures, other lives. What was she looking for? Why would she take her only child into that world with her?

"Penny for your thoughts."

She wrapped her hand around Xander's. "I was just wondering why Loa Ledbetter felt so compelled to be on the move, to expose herself to so many different worlds. It seems exhausting."

"I was thinking about that, too. She may have been on orders."

"What do you mean?"

"I ran into people like her from time to time while I was in the Army. They were the ones with actionable information that we used to topple governments, or steal weapons caches."

"A spy?"

"Of sorts. Versatile. More an information broker. She had the perfect cover if she was, her 'research' allowed her to travel the world, to go anywhere, with impunity. Some of the terms she uses in her book are ones I'd attribute to a broker. Or a spy."

"So what did she want with the Mountain Blue and Gray?"

"I think she wanted Will Crawford."

"Your friend? Wait, the one we're heading to see right now?"

"Friend is a loose term. But yes. This is between us, okay? I don't want you sharing it with Fletcher."

"I can't promise that. If it's vital to the investigation, Xander, you know you can't ask me to withhold information."

"I'd never ask that of you, Sam. Not if it mattered."

"Okay, then. I promise not to breathe a word."

He smiled at her. "Thank you. I think Ledbetter was trying to find Crawford. She wouldn't know his name—no one does. But Will…how to best put this? You've heard of Anonymous, right? The group of hackers trying to bring down big government across the world by creating as much chaos as possible?"

"The ones who use the mask from that movie, *V,* as their symbol."

"Right. They are practically an open group, anyone who's into hacktivism can join. But Will is also an anarchist. He is antigovernment, antijudiciary, anti–just about everything. He unconditionally rejects the concept of centralized political authority, and authority in general. His groups work behind the scenes to hack into the computer systems of the major corporations and governments who support democracy. It's a war to him, just as sure as boots on the ground in Iraq was to America."

"He's the head of Anonymous?"

"No. They're the kiddie pool. Will's actions are much bigger, and much stealthier. His hackers wouldn't dare draw attention to themselves. They get in, get the information they need, and get out with no one the wiser. They aren't merry pranksters, or looking for any sort of vindication. Their reward is destroying the concept of a government by the people and for the people from the inside."

"Good God. He's not an anarchist, Xander, he's a terrorist."

"That may be," he said. "But he wasn't always like this. He used to do work for the alphabet suits. CIA, FBI, NSA. Something tripped his switch and he went out on his own, working against them instead of for them, stealing the information they'd need right out from under them."

"So he's a wanted man."

"Yes. But he'll make a mistake, and the feds will bring him down. That isn't our problem."

Sam disagreed wholeheartedly with that sentiment but kept her tongue. Xander continued.

"No, our problem is Will knows the attacker. Knows where he is, too. I'm sure of it. He lied to me before, sent me off thinking it was the work of the Farmer, but he's covering for someone. I'm not sure why, though. I've never known Will to have any allegiance to anyone but himself."

"Maybe he *is* the Metro killer, and he's just trying to send you off his trail."

"I thought of that. And I haven't ruled it out completely. He wasn't a part of the Blue and Gray, but it's possible he has something to do with them that Ledbetter was after. The key lies there. If she is a broker, he would have been a massive coup."

"What are you going to say to make him talk?"

"I have no idea."

"Xander, think about it. He could easily have ties to all the victims. Marc Conlon was talking to someone who he thought he could research and write a thesis about. Loa Ledbetter was trying to broker the information to take him down. And Congressman Leighton's appropriations bill has funding for massive increases in military spending. I'd say the three would be an anarchist's field day, especially if one of them identified who he really was. Conlon might have picked up the banner where Ledbetter left off. If she lost her daughter in the process, maybe she threw up her hands and quit, went back to her research and stopped her spying because the cost was too great. And Conlon, having studied at her feet, was in the perfect position to follow in her footsteps and keep searching for answers. And he found them, so he had to be killed."

"That's a solid theory, Sam. I won't discount it."

"But?"

"Will isn't a murderer."

"You don't know that. You of all people understand how hate changes a person."

They were pulling into the Whitfields' drive now.

"We getting your dad to come along?"

"Among other things."

His tone was dark, and Sam could only imagine what he meant.

The dogs bounded up to the car, happy to see them. She assumed it was going to be the last welcoming committee they'd encounter for a while.

CHAPTER FORTY-SIX

He was running now, fighting to keep himself from screaming her name. If he could find her, there was still time. She
was small, she couldn't have gotten far. But he didn't know
that, not for sure. He had no idea when she'd gotten out of the
truck. Had someone come by and seen her? That would have
been impossible, she was on the floor. They'd have to climb
the hood of the truck and look in the windshield to see her.

No, she must have gotten out by herself.

He felt for the keys in his pocket. He had locked the door,
thinking that was enough. He should have chained her. Damn
devil's spawn. He should have chained her to the arm rail like
he'd done with her mother, though that stupid bitch had broken
her own wrist to slip out of the handcuffs and make her escape.

Stop. Regroup. Think. Look.

He scanned the sidewalks. Estimated in his head, used the
geometry that flowed through his brain like a second nature.
If she'd gone half a mile in twenty minutes, a mile in thirty...

How could a little girl walk away unnoticed on the busy
streets of Boulder? Especially one with fire-red hair?

He needed to start looking inside the businesses, then he'd be forced to ask about her. It couldn't be helped. Decision made, he opened the door of the nearest shop and stuck his head in.

Nothing. He ran to the next, and the next. A wail built behind him. The fire trucks. First responders. Coming to see why the alarms were blaring at the baby-killing business.

Oh, no. His bombs. His beautiful, precious bombs. They'd comb the building and might find the devices. Hurry, hurry, hurry.

Two more businesses empty, devoid of his daughter.

He ran back onto the street. There was a flash of red, in his peripheral vision.

There she was. One hundred yards away, talking to a grandmotherly woman. He would be able to make it, to grab her, to get her back to the truck, to hit the Send key. It would all be okay. She must have wandered off, trying to find him. Lost without him. He knew she was a good girl.

His breathing evened, and his strides grew long, eating up the distance between them.

He watched them turn. The old woman took Ruth by the hand and led her through a small blue wooden door.

He didn't want to run, didn't want to draw attention to himself.

One hundred feet.

Fifty.

As he put his hand on the door to follow after them, the ground began to shake. The roar of the explosion hit him a moment later. A million years of instinct took over and he hit the deck.

His ears were ringing. And a single sentence kept flowing through his brain, competing with the noise.

My daughter triggered the bombs.

He froze facedown on the concrete sidewalk. Wails grew, and shouting, and the alarms on the cars nearby began to sing, their very cores shaken.

My daughter triggered the bombs.

A clock started counting down in his head, and his mind began measuring wind speed and distance. He had to get out of there.

He got to his feet. Didn't look back. There would be no way to trace this back to him. Ruth was gone to him now, in the hands of the devil. She had committed the ultimate sin—was dirty with it. It was too late for her. She wouldn't have any idea how to find him; they had no address or phone number or driveway. She was lost in a world that he devised for her, an innocent. She couldn't lead them back to him.

And in ten minutes or so, none of that would matter. She was beyond his help now.

He couldn't worry about her anymore. He needed to save himself. The abrin would be floating in the air, and everyone in the vicinity would be affected. Those who hadn't made it out of the building would be pulverized, those who did were breathing deep the venom, molecules of death that coated their souls. He had to get out of there, he didn't have his mask on.

Get out, get out, get out.

How could this happen?

His daughter had triggered the bombs.

He was back at the truck now. Fumbled with the keys, realized he was only half upset. She'd become a handful anyway, always needing attention, always wanting him to read to her, tuck her in, feed her, protect her. He was better off alone. He could always snatch her again, should he want to. If she survived. But for now, he just needed to get the hell out of there, back to his camp, to the soothing trees, the warm summer sun catching the rumps of the deer and squirrels, the flowers, the field of columbines he'd planted, glowing blue and yellow.

Leave now, and live to fight another day.

The sirens were shrieking now, close and vivid, but he ignored them. Got in the truck, turned over the engine and slammed it into gear.

He was gone.

CHAPTER FORTY-SEVEN

Washington, D.C.
Detective Darren Fletcher

Once Loa had admitted the man in the drawing was her husband, the rest of her sad story came out. Fletcher listened in awe, knowing if he pushed her too hard she'd shut down. So he let her tell the story at her own pace, only interrupting when he needed to clarify a detail.

"At first it was fun. Defying my mom, being out on my own. The first thing we did was 'marry,' if you want to call it that, basically handfasting, declaring ourselves. That was legal in the camp, it was how everyone officially married. Because I'll tell you, he wasn't about to mess with God's will by taking me to his bed out of wedlock. And the moment we were official in his eyes, that's when things got really intense. He was rather single-minded about the whole thing. He discovered he liked sex. A lot. I did, too, in the beginning. But then it became his thing—finish dinner, go to bed, do it three, four times a night, whether I wanted to or not. Then as soon as we woke up, too, and after a couple of weeks he'd come home for lunch and we'd do it again. I wasn't allowed to say no. He believed in the concept of obeisance quite literally.

"After about a month, I was a mess. I said no once and he beat me to a pulp. I didn't bother again. I started realizing I'd made a mistake pretty quickly, wanted to go home, but then I got pregnant. When I told him, he was ecstatic. I've never seen anyone so happy. He treated me differently then, reverently. No more forcing me down and having his way whether I resisted or not. He'd ask nicely if I would be willing to lie with him, and if I wasn't, he'd ask nicely for me to do…other things. It was a bit more bearable, but I would be damned if I was going to have a kid all by myself out in the woods. I asked if we could get a midwife, go to the city for the birth, go to a hospital, but he was adamant that he'd handle it himself.

"I ran away once, but he caught me. I was about three months then, and he beat me black and blue, careful not to touch my stomach. So I started doing things so I would miscarry, throwing myself against trees, hitting myself in the stomach, anything that would give me freedom. He caught me at it and started handcuffing me. We went to town one day and he handcuffed me to the door handle while he was gone. He didn't trust me not to say anything to someone. As soon as he was gone, I started working on the handcuffs."

Loa wore a thin white oxford shirt over a tank top. With a sigh, she folded back the cuff to reveal an angry scar across the top of her right wrist.

"Broke my wrist, and slid right out of them. Compound fracture. Hurt like hell. But if I'd known that's all it would take, I would have done it sooner. Walked to the police station and told them I was a runaway who wanted to go home. No one asked any questions, just got me to the doctor, into surgery, and a cast, and Mom flew out that afternoon. I was back in D.C. the next day. To hot water and television and my pink comforter and dolls. It was like the two years I'd been gone was a really bad nightmare. It didn't feel real."

"And the baby?" he asked quietly.

She smiled. "I gave her up for adoption. I couldn't keep her, I mean, my God, the man raped me four or five times a day, and she was the product of that. Not only was I barely sixteen, I had some pretty complicated feelings toward her. I knew in my heart I couldn't be fair to her, give her a life that wasn't tainted by his violence. She went to a great family, they told me, and I got back to my life. Mom went on like nothing had happened, but I had myself declared an emancipated minor and got a job doing hair. Got into therapy. Tried to go to school down south, but I didn't fit in at all, so I came back and finished college at night. I'm a CPA, by the way. You never asked."

"And you've never heard from him since?"

She paled a little more, and he saw her shudder.

"He found me here in D.C. Confronted me on the sidewalk outside my apartment, pushed his way into my place. Demanded I give him the baby. I told him she was stillborn. It was all I could think to do. He was a crazy, mean asshole, and I didn't want him anywhere near her. Even if I could have told him where she was, I wouldn't. But it was a closed adoption. I don't know who she went to or where she is. I did that to protect her." She shuffled her feet like a little girl. "He didn't believe me. He made me tell him the truth. That she lived. That I gave her up. He realized pretty quickly that I honestly didn't know where she was."

She was wiping her hand slowly across her cheek, and Fletcher knew exactly how she'd been forced into giving up the information.

"Will you tell us where he is, Loa? Where Ryan Carter might be now?"

"Please, don't say his name again. Every time it's spoken aloud it's like he's being summoned. Though from what you're saying, it seems he already has been. I'm not sure I know where he is. I can try to pinpoint it on a map, though. At least give you the right area where we were. But, Detective, remember, this was six years ago. He may have a new camp now."

"That's fine, Loa. Anything you can give us, we can work with."

She shuddered a little again. "Then I need a map of Colorado."

Bianco was back at long last, and she was not in a good mood. Fletcher was watching Loa write up a statement, and Inez was fetching them a map of Colorado. Bianco stuck her head in the conference room and said, "Detective? May I speak with you? In my office, if you please."

His balls shrank at her tone. He'd heard it too many times before not to know exactly what was coming. A dressing-down. But for what? He'd done nothing but nail this case to the wall. He had an actual suspect. What did the rest of her team have?

Loa recognized the tone, too, because she flinched and looked at Fletcher with wide eyes.

"Loa, excuse me. I'll be right back."

She nodded, and he gathered his notebook and went to join Bianco in her office.

She was sitting at the desk, emanating fury. Inez was sitting in one of the chairs in front of the desk, back stiff like she knew they were in serious trouble. But for what?

Bianco glared at him and said, "Shut the door."

He did as she asked and joined Inez. If he was going to be yelled at, might as well be comfortable.

All of Bianco's earlier friendliness and congeniality and "rah-rah team" attitude was long gone.

"Am I to understand that the two of you went to the State Department and the CIA asking about files on both Congressman Leighton and Dr. Loa Ledbetter?"

"It was me, ma'am," Inez said. "I requested the files."

"Did it ever occur to you that there might be a reason for chain of command? Did that not seem like something you should let me know about before you trotted off to State?"

"I was just following a hunch, ma'am."

Fletcher wasn't about to let Inez take the fall for this. "A solid hunch that paid off. We found out Ledbetter and Leighton were in Liberia together. She was definitely working for us, and they had a—"

"Shut up, Darren. Inez, after you unearthed this information, you discussed it with whom?"

"With Detective Fletcher, ma'am."

"Then would you like to tell me why the *Washington Post* just called me looking for a quote on the story they're about to run about Dr. Ledbetter and Congressman Leighton's time in the CIA and how they both were forced out after having a child together?"

Both Fletcher and Inez said "What?" at the same time.

"Don't play coy with me. Inez, they're naming you as the source. They said you gave this to them on background, as a well-placed source in the investigation. When they asked if they could use your name you said 'certainly.'"

"That is preposterous," Fletcher said. "We never even discussed this. This is the first I've heard of Ledbetter and Leighton having a child. It wasn't from us, Andi. I can assure you of that."

As he said it, his mind went *click*. Click. Click. Click.

Loa. Loa was the child.

Fletcher hurriedly counted back. Twenty-two years ago, Ledbetter and Leighton were in Liberia. Loa didn't know who her father was. That imperceptible twitch when he asked Gretchen Leighton about it.

Son of a bitch.

"What do you have to say for yourself, Inez?"

The girl had tears in her eyes. "It's not like it sounds. It had to be the guy at State who leaked it. I requested the files. He asked me to dinner. We chatted a little. That was it. He has beyond top-secret security clearance. I never imagined he'd go to the press."

Bianco slammed her hands on the desk. "Do you realize what you've done? You've besmirched the name of a man who was a patriot, who can't fight back. You've brought into question everything he's done in his career from the time he was a soldier until now. And Dr. Ledbetter has been outed as a CIA asset. All because you wanted to play patty-cake with some night watchman from a file room."

Fletcher's back went up. That wasn't fair. "Oh, come now, Andi. You're being way too hard on the girl. And you were all-fired ready to call Leighton a serial killer twenty-four hours ago. That might have done a bit more damage to his reputation than this will."

"I'd rather him be a serial killer than people find out he was an asset. A couple of dead girls is nothing compared to the fact that everything he and Ledbetter did is now compromised. Every single mission will now be trotted out, taken apart. You have no idea what you've unleashed. I just got my head handed to me. And the fucking *Washington Post* has the story!"

Bianco wasn't being shy now, she was bellowing at the top of her lungs.

"Both of you, pack your things and get the hell out of my building."

There was a tentative knocking at Bianco's door.

"What is it?" she shouted.

A young man Fletcher didn't recognize opened the door, practically shaking in his boots.

"Ma'am? Detective Fletcher? There's been a bombing in Boulder."

CHAPTER FORTY-EIGHT

Dillon, Colorado
Dr. Samantha Owens

When they'd arrived at the house, Roth was waiting for them, looking exceptionally uncomfortable.

"What's the matter?" Xander asked, batting the dogs away.

"Glad you're back, son. Crawford was here, right after you left. Man's nutty in the head at the best of times, but he went off, yelling that we'd caused some sort of trouble yesterday when we came by. That Will got his gear together and left last night, drove off and hasn't come back. Stu wasn't entirely lucid, I tried to calm him down but he was all over the place, ranting and hollering, then he took himself back to hell where he probably came from. Sunshine is terribly upset."

Sam gave Xander a pointed look. "Are you absolutely sure Will isn't the one we're looking for?"

"No, I'm not." He explained their theory to Roth, who shook his head.

"I don't know, son. It breaks my heart to think that Will could be involved in this. Something isn't right with the Crawfords, though."

"He had all his gear?"

"That's what Stu said."

Xander rubbed his chin with his hand. "He's only got half a day's head start. We take the dogs, we can probably catch up to him."

Sam felt alarm spring up in her chest. "And why would you be the one going after him? Let's call Fletcher, let him send some JTTF people out after him. It's too dangerous for you to go hunting him, Xander. We don't know what he's capable of."

"Sam, honey, I know these woods like the back of my hand. I'm the only one that remotely makes sense to go after him. I've got the skills and the training to find him, and find him fast. Will may know how to hunt turkey and elk, but I have some more…unique qualifications."

Like how to hunt men.

"And then what, Xander? What do you plan to do? Shoot him? Sit down and make a pot of tea over the campfire? We don't even know he's involved for sure."

"He ran. That's all I need to know. If he was innocent, he wouldn't be here in the first place, much less off going to ground. He's in trouble. Either he's responsible, or he knows who is. There's a damn good chance he's going after him, and if we hurry, we might catch him. Or them."

"We'd best get a move on, then," Roth said.

"You need to stay here with Sunshine."

"You need someone to watch your back, son."

Xander hesitated, then nodded. "All right. Let's load up."

Roth smiled. "I figured you'd want to go out. I'm three steps ahead of you. Already have most of the gear pulled out. I think we should leave the dogs, they might announce our presence before we're ready to be known. Sam can stay here and keep Sunshine company."

"No."

Both men looked at her.

"I'm going with you."

Roth barked out a laugh. "Sam, you have about as much survival training as you can fit in that pretty leather bag you carry. No offense meant, of course, Samantha."

Sam glanced at her Birkin bag, and all in all, thought Roth was being rather generous in his assumptions.

Xander was a bit gentler, but firm. "Sam, Roth's right. This isn't going to be easy."

She barely kept herself from stamping her foot.

"I *am* coming, and we *are* going to tell Fletcher what we're doing. We aren't above the law, Xander. We aren't the law, either. You need to call McReynolds and tell him what you're up to, as well."

"Sam, we're losing valuable time here. I don't want to argue with you about this."

"There is no argument, Xander. This is how it's going to be. I don't care if you think we're out here in the wilderness playing with a different set of rules. No way in hell you're running off half-cocked."

Roth was watching her with half a smile quirked on his lips. She thought he was enjoying seeing his son reined in a bit. But damn it, amusement or not, this was dangerous, and she'd be damned if she was going to let them tramp off into the forest after a killer without backup.

Xander looked like he was going to argue again, but Sam help up her hand. "Non. Negotiable."

He sighed.

"Fine. Let's get you outfitted and make some calls."

Sunshine had dressed Sam in several layers of Yellow's creations, plus a pair of sturdy hiking boots. Thankfully, Sam and Yellow wore the same size shoe and the boots were already broken in, but Sunshine gave her moleskin and Band-Aids anyway.

Roth and Xander were at the kitchen table, poring over maps. They were looking for the closest geothermals that were in desolate areas, ones only accessible by foot. That's where they thought the camp would be. There were only three or four areas that fit the bill, almost all up in Eagles Nest, in the White River National Forest.

Sam thought they were crazy to try to go in without more of a plan, but as Xander always said, once a Ranger, always a Ranger. He could plan a mission through a minefield in his sleep. What looked utterly insurmountable to her was a cake-walk for him.

He'd given her permission to call Fletcher only once they were ready to rock and roll, and it looked like they were about at that point. Xander was rolling up the maps. The trailhead they'd be using was fifteen miles away, up Colorado State Road 9, so they'd have plenty of time to catch a cell signal to make their phone calls.

They spooned a bit of Sunshine's famous stew into their mouths and took the rest in thermoses and, at three in the afternoon, headed off.

Sam was incredibly uncomfortable.

She was in the backseat of the rented SUV, and felt as if there were guns and arrows and bolt-throwing crossbows pointed at her back. Which there were. Xander had loaded up the truck with gear: weapons, backpacks and tools. He wouldn't tell her what everything was for. He and Roth were in the front, organizing, planning, discussing trailheads and alpine zones and bivouacs and longitudinal areas and taluses and walking-in.

She started thinking some hot tea and a warm fire sounded

like a much, much smarter plan than the one she'd deter-
minedly forced herself into.

She was going to hold them back, no doubt about it, but
that was important, she thought. She hated that Xander was
so willing—hell, excited—to run headlong into danger. At
least his father was along—his pacifist father, who didn't blink
as his son loaded enough ammunition to take down a herd of
moose in the back.

Great.

They were climbing now, and Sam glanced at her phone.
She had bars.

"Who do you want me to call first?" she interrupted.

Xander harrumphed, but Roth said, "McReynolds."

Sam grabbed the card Reed had given her earlier and dialed
the number and, when it started to ring, handed the phone
to Xander.

"Reed. Xander. Hey listen. Crawford took off into the
woods last night, and his dad came by all sorts of agitated.
We're going up after him. We just wanted to let you know
what was going on, just in case."

Silence, then Xander laughed. "Yes, Sam made me call.
She's a stickler like that."

He listened some more, then gave Reed the coordinates
they were heading toward.

He listened for a minute, then Xander's voice changed.
"No, I hadn't heard. Thanks for telling me. Right. Right.
Good idea." He paused for a minute. "Yes, I will. On my
honor. Okay."

He handed the phone back to Sam.

"You better go ahead and call Fletcher."

"Why. What's wrong?"

He caught her eye in the rearview mirror.

"Someone just blew up a reproductive services center in
Boulder."

CHAPTER FORTY-NINE

Washington, D.C.
Detective Darren Fletcher

Bianco put her tirade on hold long enough to let the aide fill them in on the details of the bombing, but Fletcher could feel the waves of anger coming from the other side of the desk. Poor Inez was shriveled up in her chair, completely stricken. He thought Bianco had been overly hard on the girl—it wouldn't be the first time a little pillow talk had resulted in an embarrassing story gracing the pages of a newspaper.

Fletcher had a hard time believing the accounts he was hearing. A man was seen leaving just as the fire alarm went off. The building was evacuated successfully—thankfully, he'd struck in the afternoon instead of the morning, when the surgical procedures were normally done. Many more would have been hurt if the operating suites had been full.

There were no reported casualties, though several people had been taken to the hospital with respiratory issues. But the building itself was decimated. It was a combination research hospital for reproductive endocrinology and a fertility clinic, but not just for everyday women with fertility issues. They were doing cutting-edge work, stem cell transplants and clinical studies for in vitro fertilization in addition to the run-of-the-mill fertility treatments. The center was internationally recognized as a leader in reproductive technologies. Couples flew in from all over the world to have the very best possible care, and they had the highest success rate of any clinic in the country.

But the bombing wasn't the weirdness. That came in the form of reports of a small girl, around six or seven years of age, who the police were convinced had set off the bomb.

According to witnesses, she'd been lost on the street, walking up and down the sidewalks crying, looking for her father. She had a cell phone in her hand, and one woman thought she meant to call her father with it. So the business owner had taken her into her store, sat her down on a stool and told her to call her parents.

The girl had no idea how to use the phone, though, no real concept of what a phone was, either, which seemed strange. The woman looked at the phone and saw a number already programmed in. Assuming that was the parents' number, the woman told her to press the green button to send the call, and the girl, who seemed more than willing to please, did. Moments later, the building, less than half a mile away, went down in a pile of rubble at the feet of the people who'd just evacuated it.

The Boulder police had sent photographs of both the child and the cell phone detonator. The aide handed them to Bianco, who glanced at them and tossed them onto her desk. Fletcher reached over and picked them up, and felt the punch in his gut. He showed the photo of the girl to Inez.

"Oh, my God. Do you think?" she asked.

"What? What does he think?" Bianco snapped.

Fletcher pointed toward the conference room.

"I'd say the chances are pretty high that her mother is sitting in the conference room."

Bianco's tune changed a bit when she realized the link to the bomber was sitting five feet away from her office. She was still obviously pissed at Fletcher and Inez, but she put her indignation aside long enough to allow herself to be briefed on the rest of the story.

When Fletcher finished, she sat back in her chair. Anger turned to incredulity.

"So let me get this straight. While I was getting my head handed to me for letting my staff run amok with highly sensitive information that can compromise national security, you two were busy finding the wife of the bomber. Who happens to be the daughter of two of our victims."

"It looks like that's the case, yes, ma'am." Inez was paddling, anything to get back in her boss's good graces. Fletcher wasn't quite as anxious.

"Well, we don't know that she's the congressman's kid, though." Fletcher was still a little unsure of that, but the more he thought about it, the more it made sense.

Bianco gave him a look as if to say *keep up, stupid,* so he shrugged. "Okay, she's their illegitimate love child. Fine. The *Post* never got *any*thing wrong, ever."

"Don't get fresh with me, *Detective.* You are still on my shit list. But you can't leave yet. I want to meet this girl."

"Before we do, *Andi,* let me reiterate something. There is no way the paper got that story from Inez. Neither one of us had that connection until you told us just now. We were still piecing together the CIA connection, as well. I'd say an apology is in order."

Bianco's eyes were still simmering, but she raised her hand, palm first, in apology.

"Fine. Inez, I'm sorry. I ever find out you leaked something from this office, you're fired. Happy now?"

Inez nodded meekly.

"Good. But before we go singing 'Kumbaya,' where the hell did the leak come from?"

"I don't know," Fletcher answered. "But there're only a few people who could have this level of detail. While you were out, we discovered that Glenn Temple has been impersonating the congressman on the street with the working boys and girls. Hence the rumors that the congressman has a few interesting proclivities. They don't know what the real Peter Leighton looks like, Temple has been careful to pick from the low end of the spectrum, the specialists. I'd wager some of the higher-priced call girls would know who he was, primarily because they service the same level of clientele, and part of their job is to be savvy about the daily goings-on in town and on the Hill. But Temple would know that, too, so he made sure that his playmates weren't following the news closely."

The look on her face was priceless. "Glenn Temple, the congressman's chief of staff."

"Yes, ma'am. There's more. ViCAP came back with some matches to several unsolved cases here in the tri-state area. Mostly working girls, strangled, raped, left out in the open. We are thinking Temple might be responsible for these murders as well, but has been trying to lay the blame on his boss. Who happens to be one of his best friends, as well. We need DNA from him, and we were in the process of following that lead, so we need to make that happen sooner rather than later."

Bianco was totally back on board.

Yeah, you don't mess with the Fletch.

"Where is Temple now?"

"Don't know."

She gave him one of her more unfathomable looks, then hit a button on her phone. Sutton came into the room.

"Would you be so kind as to have Cusack and Halder go pick up Glenn Temple for a chat? Inez will give you the information. Thank you, Inez. You and Sutton may go."

Inez didn't waste any time. She threw Fletch a grateful glance and hightailed it out of there. He didn't blame her for a second.

"You are so damn lucky, Fletcher. If you didn't have case-breaking information right now, I would have you tossed out on your ear."

"You're welcome," he said, biting back a few choicer words. "Tell me about Ledbetter's kid."

"Shouldn't we figure out where the leak came from?"

"Surely it was Temple. Right?"

He shook his head. "Honestly, I think it's even closer than that. Think about it. Who stands to gain from this sort of information getting out?"

"Leighton's enemies."

"Leighton's dead, and his grand wide-reaching appropriations bill has been tabled indefinitely. His enemies don't have anything more to work with. But someone's going to have to fill his seat. And there is a tradition in this town. I'll bet you good money the powers that be have been knocking on Mrs. Leighton's door already, asking for her to do the right thing and step in. I don't know how Indiana works, if they can appoint her to fill out his term or if they'll call for a special election, but either way, she has a lot to gain by keeping her husband and his life in the news cycle. It's completely feasible. If it's true, it just means she was a little more ambitious than I gave her credit for. According to her, she and her husband knew he had a death knock coming, it was just a matter of when. Besides, who else would know about the kid?

It wouldn't be hard to keep a record of work with the CIA under wraps, they wouldn't be in business if they couldn't keep a decent secret. But an illegitimate kid—that's the meat and potatoes of any decent opposition researcher."

"Maybe the kid did it herself?"

"Come talk to her. I think you'll see that isn't the case."

"And we're sure that Gretchen Leighton isn't behind this whole thing?"

"Andi, I'm not *sure* of anything right now."

She started to pace. "So, why were they murdered? Why the grand cover-up of a Metro attack if the point was to knock off the three people? Why not just take them out and walk away?"

"I'll give you my best guess. This is personal. It has felt personal from the get-go. The delivery methods, the timing, everything. I think the killer was trying to win back his lady-love in there. He had something good going, out there in the woods, with just the birds and the trees and his perverted faith as their best friends. Then she got knocked up, scared and ran away. He hunted her down, found out she'd given the kid up for adoption. I have a good feeling that when we look into this kid they have in Boulder, we're going to find that it's the child they conceived, and he took her from her adoptive parents. With the kid back under his roof, mommy makes three. He probably didn't know she was estranged from her mother. He probably figured Dr. Ledbetter was influencing her to stay away from him. So he eliminates the two authority figures that are keeping her from him—mommy and daddy."

"And Conlon?"

"He thought Conlon was his friend. Everything on the boy's computer says he's been drawing information out of Carter for months. Carter felt used, and while he was eliminating the people who made him unhappy, decided he might as well take care of the friend, too."

"That's insane."

"From what Loa has been telling me, he's *not* sane. Not in the least. He's a religious zealot who takes great pains to follow the words of the Bible without understanding the actual message, just takes the lessons and makes his own kind of sense from them. I'm betting he's got a touch of schizophrenia. It fits. Brilliance and madness all bundled together. No one said it had to make sense to us, it only has to make sense to him. Murder rarely does have its roots in logic."

Bianco sighed.

"You're one hell of an investigator, Fletcher. So where is this whack job now?"

"That I can't tell you, outside of I'd lay bets he's within a four-hour radius of Boulder."

His cell rang, and he looked at it, relieved. He'd tossed a lot of that off his head, theories that came together with the details Bianco had thrown at him, and now he had to go make it all stick.

The call was from Sam.

He excused himself and answered it, shocked to hear actual fear in her voice.

"Fletch? Thank God I caught you. My cell signal sucks. Listen. We think we know where the bomber is."

And the phone went dead.

CHAPTER FIFTY

Eagles Nest
White River National Forest, Colorado
Dr. Samantha Owens

"Oh, hell. He's going to kill me." Sam shook her cell phone as if that would help her get service again. The farther into Eagles Nest they drove, the worse the mobile service. She'd finally managed to get through to Fletcher, and the minute she dropped the news, she dropped the call, too. They'd been flirting with the rain for a while now, heavy downpours interspersed with rumbles of thunder and some foggy virga hanging low over the mountains, but the storms now seemed to be passing without too much bother. They should have clear weather into the night.

They'd found Crawford's vehicle, and Sam had to admit, Xander had been right about where Crawford was headed.

"Don't worry," Xander assured her as he tied a backpack on her. "Once we get above 7500 feet, we should have a nice clear signal coming across the mountain."

"And how long's that going to take?"

"I don't know. What do you say, Roth? Day? Day and a half?"

She shot daggers at him.

Roth shook his head. "He's teasing you, Samantha. I'm sure we will find service along the trail. They have better signals out here now for hikers, have cell towers strategically placed so they don't get too lost. How's that pack feel? Too heavy?"

"I think I'll be okay."

Xander raised an eyebrow at her. "I can take out that nail file you insisted on. That might make all the difference."

Sam stuck her tongue out at Xander, who, laughing, went back to the car for another load, and put the phone in her pocket. The pack *was* a bit heavy, but she moved it around and figured it wasn't anything she couldn't handle. They had four hours of daylight left, and Xander wanted to get them as high up the trail as he could before they made camp for the night.

Sam thought about what her best friend would have said to all of this a year ago. "You, camping? Ha!" Yes, well, falling in love with an outdoorsman meant she was now more than accustomed to roughing it.

Hiking a vertical to 7500 feet on the trail of a killer? Maybe not so much.

Satisfied they had everything, Xander locked the truck, and they started off, Roth leading, Xander taking the rear. After a few choice comments about the view, and a few well-aimed kicks toward his midsection, they settled into a steady pace.

They'd been hiking for an hour before Sam got a decent enough signal to try Fletcher again. She was more than relieved to take a break. Roth and Xander fidgeted with their things, checking weapons and straps, while Sam dropped her pack, drank some water and made the call back to D.C.

Fletcher answered immediately, annoyance and relief bleeding through the phone. His voice was at a decibel she recognized as his version of DEFCON One.

"Whatever the hell you're doing, Owens, stop. Cease and desist, immediately. We have teams converging on the area to go after the killer. His name is Ryan Carter, by the way. We have his wife here at the JTTF. I'm sending you a photo. Where are you?"

"Halfway up a mountain, on our way to where we think his camp is. How did you get his wife?"

"You're doing *what?*"

"Xander knows the area, and his friend Will Crawford knows the killer. He took off after him yesterday, and we are following his trail. How'd you get the killer's wife?"

"It's Ledbetter's daughter, Loa. Not only that, Congressman Leighton is her father. Long story short, she ran off with Carter, got pregnant and changed her mind about living in the woods, ran away, gave the kid up for adoption and started her life over. There was a bombing a couple of hours ago in Boulder, a reproductive clinic. We believe we have Carter and Ledbetter's daughter in custody—he left her behind."

"We heard. Xander, how far are we from Boulder?"

"About a hundred miles, maybe one hundred and ten by road. Less than forty as the crow flies."

"It's possible he's ahead of us, and it's possible we're going to walk right in on him. Xander, here. Talk to Fletcher. Tell him where we are."

She handed the phone to Xander, who pulled a face but put the phone on speaker and said, "Hey, Fletch. Think you got him?"

"We do. Where are you?"

"Halfway up to Eagles Nest. We took a vertical trailhead off Colorado State Road 9, about fifteen miles south of Kremmling. Rumor has it there's a geothermal hot spring in this area, it triangulates to the most logical spot to have a private camp.

It's basically uninhabited, hard to find and harder to hike, so there's not going to be any foot traffic accidentally stumbling into his camp. We're following the steps of a friend of mine who I think knows where this guy is—"

"Ryan Carter's the name."

"Roger that. My friend took off after Carter, like Sam said. He's got half a day on us. We're three hours on foot from the site where we're assuming he's hunkered down."

Fletcher didn't hesitate. "You turn around and go back down that mountain. We are sending teams in. Just give us your coordinates and we will have them there shortly. Loa Ledbetter gave us a pretty detailed map of the area, we know exactly where we're headed."

"At this point, Fletch, you're going to have to fly them in to make it in time. And that's just going to spook him. Coming in on foot from below will take too long. My friend will have eliminated the problem by then. I'm assuming you want him alive?"

"We do."

"Then we're your best shot. I arranged for backup, the police chief in Dillon, Reed McReynolds, is probably already on our tail. And we're losing daylight."

Fletcher went ballistic. "Goddamn it, Xander, you are not a cop. Park your ass and wait for the cavalry. That's an order, soldier."

Sam watched Xander's face shut down. It got blank as an empty sheet of paper. Uh-oh.

"Can't hear you, Fletch. You're breaking up."

"Whitfield, so help me God, you get one hair on her head hurt—"

Fletcher's voice was drowned by static, and then there was silence.

"Whoops," Xander said, grinning. "Looks like we dropped

the call. Maybe you should switch carriers when we get home, Sam. This one really sucks."

He handed her the phone and she didn't know whether to laugh or hit him. A small ding indicated she'd received a text. It was the photo of Ryan Carter. She passed it to Xander and Roth so they could see who they were hunting.

Xander stared at the photo for a moment, then handed her the phone. "Okay. Break's over. Time to go." He and Roth shouldered their packs.

"Xander. You heard Fletch. We really should stay here, or go back down."

Xander fingered his M-4. He looked incredibly formidable, and she wouldn't want to have him tracking her up the side of a mountain. He was not fooling around.

"Darren Fletcher is not my commanding officer, Samantha. We are his best chance of capturing this Ryan Carter character alive. Crawford didn't set out to have a fireside chat. If he gets to him first, we're screwed. The fact that Carter's coming in from Boulder is probably the only reason he's still breathing, if he actually still is. So let's quit jawing about it, and let me go make sure a friend of mine doesn't go to jail for life for homicide. Okay?"

Sam took a deep breath and sat back down.

"What—"

She cut him off with a sigh. "Just give me two seconds. I'm putting a Band-Aid on my heel, just in case."

She got out the bandage and unlaced her boot. When Xander and his father bowed their heads over their map, she took their moment of distraction to send Fletcher a text.

Didn't work. We're going in. Hurry up.

Two hours later, the hike became a study in pain. It was getting dark, the moonrise only just beginning, shining flat and silver through the trees. Not only was Sam scared and tired and hungry and worried, the pack had grown much too heavy on her shoulders and the imaginary blister she'd patched up when they'd last stopped had become a reality. There was no service on the cell now, and the forest had grown dense and dark around them. Little scurries in the bushes made her jump, and the lonely howl of a coyote twenty minutes earlier had completely freaked her out.

Xander and Roth seemed completely unfazed by their surroundings. Sam was a bit embarrassed, chalked it up to the fact that they were alone in the woods with a killer.

The irony of the fact that her boyfriend could be called by the same moniker wasn't lost on her.

She glanced at him over her shoulder. He looked dark and dangerous, his beard growing in, the weapon cradled in his arms like a baby. He was carrying a modified M-4 assault rifle, and she knew he was more than accustomed to using it. It was simply an extension of his body, an extremely lethal metal hand. Part of her grieved for him in that moment, knowing what he'd been forced to do in the name of securing freedom, how he became so intimately familiar with the weapon, probably knowing it better than he knew the curves of her body.

She wouldn't want to be on the wrong side of him, that was for sure. He was so very different from her late husband, mild-mannered Simon Loughley: scientist, romantic, appeaser. They shared an incredible intellect, but that's where the similarities stopped.

Life with Xander was never going to be boring, of that she was absolutely certain.

Just when she thought she was going to have to ask them to stop for a break so she could catch her breath, Roth whistled once, freezing in his tracks, his right hand up in a fist.

She recognized that move from the movies. It meant stop.

She did, grateful for the break, but her concern rose when Roth ducked down to his knees and gestured for them to do the same.

She listened carefully, trying to ascertain what had drawn his attention. All she could hear was the low hooting of an owl. A parade of goose bumps ran up and down her arms. Death was coming. She could feel his cool embrace on the wind that started rustling through the trees. The temperature dropped, and she realized the breeze had increased.

Xander slithered away, practically on his stomach, and Roth leaned back and squeezed her shoulder, whispered so quietly she had to strain to hear him.

"I smell a fire. We thought he would be farther up the mountain, but looks like he, or someone, is here, about a quarter of a mile to the west. Xander's going to investigate."

They stood carefully, quietly, and she followed Roth off the path into the woods, where they stood against a tree. Xander was back in a few minutes, speaking low so he wouldn't be heard over the wind.

"I think this is it. There's a cabin, and a barn. The fire's down to embers, though, and I can't see anyone there. It looks deserted. Could be Crawford was waiting for him. Maybe he banked the fire and took off when he wasn't here."

"Or it's Carter, and he heard us coming and scatted."

"Would he have lit a fire to eat or something?" Sam asked.

"Possibly. Or get rid of evidence. But if you don't put a fire out properly, it can take hours to settle down and that's damn dangerous in these woods. I think we should walk past and swing back around, come down from the high ground. He may have come back and gathered things and set off again in a hurry, worried he was being followed."

"Or Will got to him," Sam said.

"Or that. Let's do some recon before we make any decisions, okay?"

They regrouped and started again, stealthier this time, off the trail, careful not to make too much noise. Sam thought they were a damn sight noisier than the rabbits or grouse or turkeys or whatever they kept passing on the trail, but for a tired, scared mad bomber, who possibly had some percussive damage to his eardrums from his latest blast, maybe they wouldn't be noticeable.

Sam could smell water. There must be a lake nearby. Sure enough, fifteen slow paces later, the edge of the forest began to slope, and below them shimmered a moonlit mountain lake. Sam had never seen anything so stunning. She couldn't help but stop and stare. Wildflowers paraded down into the valley below, marked like gray frost by the moon's path, and the water lapped gently at the edges of the soil, which looked nearly black.

They stayed still, watching. An elk, a stag by the size of him, ventured to the water's edge, drinking long and deep, secure in the knowledge that he was safe from predators for the moment. Then the wind shifted, and his head jerked up in surprise, and he crashed away into the brush, sounding like a small army moving through.

They took advantage of his thrashing to move again, traced their steps back and up the hill, and Roth found a sinuous deer path, which they started up. There was a small clearing ahead, Sam could see where the branches lessened, and knew that would be the right place for them to stop and regroup before entering the camp again.

They stepped from the trees and froze.

Ryan Carter was squatting next to a man Sam had to assume was Will Crawford, who was on his back, blood bubbling from his mouth and nose. He wasn't dead, but damn close to it.

Carter reminded Sam of a child who'd just pulled the wings off a fly and was watching, mildly curious to see what would happen next, not understanding or caring about the pain the fly was experiencing.

He didn't seem to hear them, or mind their presence if he did. Crawford, on the other hand, seemed to sense movement and tried to turn his head to see what was happening.

Xander swung his M-4 toward them and used a tone Sam had never heard before, his voice ringing with authority. She couldn't imagine anyone hesitating for a moment to obey him.

"Carter. Step away. Step away and get on your knees, facing me."

Carter didn't move. Crawford whined, a high-pitched sound laced with pain, and it was all Sam could do not to rush for him, to help.

Xander tried again, louder and more forceful, and this time, Carter turned his head, slowly, to face them. Sam was surprised by how normal, how plain he was. He didn't have the face of evil that she'd seen before. He just looked like a man, a regular guy, neither handsome nor ugly, just plain. His face didn't change, or even acknowledge that he was looking at the business end of a weapon.

Before she could blink, he took off, leaping to his feet and rushing away through the trees. With a muttered oath Xander followed, and Sam heard the shouts and shots as he tried to catch him.

Roth followed his son into the darkness, and Sam was left there, motionless, until her system finally responded to her mental commands and her legs started to work again. She ran to Crawford and fell to her knees at his side.

She ripped off his shirt and saw the entrance wounds, three

of them, a tight grouping midsternum. He was losing a lot of blood, and having trouble breathing. She used the shirt as a compress, pushed hard with her palm to stop the bleeding. But she could see the damage was done. The blood coming from his mouth and nose was the indicator; without some sort of serious intervention, he would drown in his own blood.

She ripped apart her pack until she found the first-aid kit Xander had packed. His was a bit more sophisticated than the average bear's, and was full of trauma items necessary to save a man's life. She assessed the wound in the moonlight, listening to the man's breaths shorten. She didn't have much time.

She ripped a wound-seal kit from the pack. She yanked it open, pulled out the clear thick shield and slapped it over the wounds. It molded to his skin, and the horrible sucking sound from the air moving through the holes stopped. She ripped open the brown packaging of an Olaes bandage, hurriedly wrapped his chest, effectively putting a second sealed compression dressing on the open wounds. There was also a catheter and scalpel in the kit. She threw on some gloves and doused the side of Crawford's chest in alcohol, then made a deep cut into the flesh, ignoring his high grunt of pain, and stuck her fingers in behind the scalpel to get to the right spot. Confident now, she inserted the tube into the fifth intercostal space. Blood poured from the catheter and Crawford took a huge, deep breath as his lung began to inflate.

It was a temporary fix—he needed real medical treatment, immediately, or her efforts would be in vain. She stood and looked for Xander and Roth, saw only silvery blackness. The shouts and gunshots were gone, and it was just her and Crawford—Crawford lying on the ground, going into shock, trying to stay alive.

A cloud passed across the moon and it was suddenly pitch-black. She shut her eyes for a moment then opened them, knowing they'd adjust in a few seconds.

He came out of nowhere. She didn't hear the footsteps, just a sudden weight against her, forcing her back against a tree, his forearm to her throat. She couldn't swallow, couldn't breathe, and started to kick, clawing at his arm with her hands. When that did nothing, she reached out for his eyes, his face, anything she could get a grip on. She connected with something, heard him gasp, then snarl, "Fucking bitch."

His hand replaced his forearm, choking her, pressing down hard on her windpipe. She started to see stars, the edges of her vision blackening. She could see his outline now, and smell the coppery tang of fresh blood. It was Carter. At least one of Xander's bullets had found its mark; Carter stank of blood and fear. She struggled against him but he was too strong, too big, and she was losing strength, losing her balance, her will. The bark scraped painfully against her spine, tearing the flesh, and she knew she was close to passing out.

Go limp.

It was her best friend Taylor's voice in her head.

Go limp, and the second he shifts, jam your hand into his throat, that spot I showed you, and run like hell.

Sam sagged back against the tree, let her arms drop to her sides, deadweight against him. The sudden lack of activity made him shift his hand to get a better grip, and she lashed out like a cobra, hit him square in the windpipe with her stiff fingers. He let go, stumbled backward coughing, and she took off. She could hear him behind her, running, cursing, coughing. She veered off onto the main track. Where the hell was Xander?

She was afraid to call out, she didn't want Carter to know where she was. She ducked under a fallen tree and froze there, a spiderweb brushing her face. She imagined small things climbing up her arms, and it was all she could do to stay planted, to stay hidden. She heard him coming, crashing through the brush, and prayed he couldn't see her.

He stopped, growing quiet, the noises of the forest dead, too, the silence so pervasive she thought maybe he'd succeeded; maybe she was lifeless, lying at the base of that tree, and her flight was just a dream.

Then she heard him start again, slowly, carefully. Stalking her. Hunting her.

Her heart took off. She bit her teeth together so she wouldn't cry out. She should have taken the gun Xander wanted her to carry. Stupid not to carry it on her, like he wanted. *Stupid, stupid, stupid.* She'd thought she was safe with him and Roth to guard her. She didn't think Carter would come after her.

His voice was soft, cajoling, and no more than ten feet away. "Come out, come out, wherever you are."

Something was definitely crawling on her now, along her neck. She tried not to shudder and hoped to God whatever it was wasn't poisonous.

"You're a pretty little thing. You and I could have a lot to talk about. Do you believe in God, pretty thing? Have you ever given much thought to your great Creator? He made you for me, from my rib. You are imperfect. You are sin. But you can be cleansed. I can show you the way. I know things. About how the earth moves, and the stars spin. How he made them, and how we can honor him."

Where was Xander? The panic was building in the back of her throat, and the soft, feathery touches of many-legged things quested across her cheek.

"I think we can risk it. Just a little light." She heard a small click. He'd turned on a flashlight. "The two you came with are gone. On their journey to the great beyond. It is just us now. Come out from your hiding spot. We will go back to the house, and I will feed you, and honor you in the way our God has taught me. You know how to say the words, don't you, pretty thing? Were you properly taught? Try them with me. *Our father, who art in heaven…*"

Her heart constricted. She couldn't allow herself to think that he might be telling the truth, that he'd bested Xander and Roth, or she would begin to sob and give herself away.

He was getting closer. Two more steps and he'd see her. He was still singing out The Lord's Prayer, one she was more than familiar with. She said the words with him in her head.

Thy Kingdom come, thy will be done, on earth as it is in heaven.

She made a snap decision. She didn't want to be dragged out from under the log kicking and screaming. If she was going to go, she was going to do it facing the man, looking into his eyes.

She rolled out from the log and stood, the words coming from her mouth, a terrible prayer.

"Give us this day our daily bread, and forgive us our trespasses, as we forgive those who trespass against us."

He stopped, five feet from her, a look of sheer delight on his face.

"There you are. Go on."

Her voice didn't shake, though she hardly knew how that was possible, she was shivering in fear. "And lead us not into temptation. But deliver us from evil—"

"Ah, see. Now that's where all of you pretty things seem to slip up. Temptation. A concept that you don't understand. We are bound by temptation. We are burned in hell for it. We must cleanse ourselves of our sins and be reborn in the image of our father." His voice was getting louder and louder, until he shouted, "Go on!"

"For thine is the kingdom, and the power, and the glory, for ever and ever."

"Amen," he said, then leaped at her, shooting, bullets scattering the leaves around her.

She couldn't help herself, the scream ripped from her throat, and she braced herself for the sear of the bullet, the impact of his body, but it didn't come. Instead, she heard a loud thwang, and Carter stopped moving forward, almost midair, like Wile E. Coyote over a gorge, when he realizes he is going to fall, but stays suspended in the air for a moment, just long enough to wave goodbye. He met her eyes and a smile came over his face, a secret revealed to him alone, then he dropped, all of a piece, face-first onto the forest floor. She shut her eyes and took a breath, then opened them to see the shaft of the arrow buried deep in Carter's back. He wasn't moving.

"Sam, are you all right?"

Xander.

"Xander," she cried. "I'm here. I'm okay." Her voice had a ragged edge, and she could feel the swelling beginning around her trachea. She was going to have one hell of a set of bruises in the morning.

He came from the woods, limping. She rushed to him. She ducked her shoulder under his arm and helped him sit. He was white as a ghost and she felt the wet of blood on his thigh.

"What happened? Are you okay? Where's Roth?"

"He's at the camp. We were trying to circle him, and the bastard slipped through. Are you okay?"

"I'm okay. You're not. You're hit."

"Yeah. In the thigh. It's not bad, a through and through. No bone or arteries. Hurts like shit, though."

"Let me get the kit. And your dad."

"No, honey. Let's just sit here for a minute. I want to talk to you about something."

"Xander. Now is not the time for talking. I need to patch you up."

He clung to her shoulder and buried his face in her hair. His voice was odd, lilting, gaining strength then fading. "Really. Samantha, I love you. I want to marry you. I want you to have my babies, and be my woman, and build my life with you. I can't imagine being without you. When I heard you scream I thought it was all over and I ran right into a hail of bullets so I could get to you because if you were dying I wanted to die with you. I love you, so much. I love…" His voice drifted off and he slumped against her.

"Xander?" She slapped his face a little, trying to rouse him, but he was out.

"Roth!" she shouted. "Roth, if you can hear me, I need you!"

She heard a faint answering shout, and felt a tiny bit of relief. Xander had been in shock, his wound must be more serious than he was letting on.

She eased him gently to the forest floor and started to feel around. Yes, he was hit in the thigh, but also in the stomach, and his upper right arm, as well. Holy crap. He was losing blood rather substantially through the wound in his stomach—it had probably nicked an artery. She needed to run back up the hill to the first-aid kit, but just as she stood to do so, Roth announced himself and stepped from the woods.

He saw his son and his face paled.

"Jesus, he's hurt bad."

"I need your medical kit."

He swung his pack off his shoulders and dug in for the kit. He handed it to her and she knelt beside Xander again, started to work.

"How bad is it?"

"Bad enough. He's lost a lot of blood. He passed out on me before I could get a read on things, but I daresay he's just in a faint from blood loss."

"That hurts," he groaned. "I didn't faint. I can hear you fine. Tell me you'll marry me."

Roth chuckled under his breath. "Careful there, Samantha. He gets stubborn when he's hurt."

"He's delusional and rambling incoherently."

"Samantha," Xander moaned. "Dad, tell her."

She shushed him. "Xander Moon, you quit it right now. Let me do my job."

"Your job is to cut open dead people. Ow!"

She'd pulled his jeans away from his thigh, the sucking crackling of dried blood started the wound bleeding all over again. He started to roll toward her, like he was going to embrace her, and she fought him back to the ground.

"Hold still, I said."

She tempered her tone with a gentle palm to his forehead, brushing his hair back from his face. She leaned down and kissed him. And he passed out again with a smile on his face.

She worked on his wounds, saying prayers of thanks that he was still with her. He was hurt badly, might lose his spleen, but he would live.

The *whump, whump, whump* of a helicopter's rotors became audible.

Roth touched Sam on the head.

"He must be in a bad way if he called me Dad. You take care of him. I'm going to go drop a flare so they know where we are."

She smiled at him. "He'll be fine. I promise."

"If he has you, Samantha, I have no doubt of that."

He walked ten feet away and she heard the whispering crack of the flare, then an eerie green light filled the forest.

It only took a few minutes for the helicopter to see them and start a hover, men snaking down nearly invisible lines to the ground. Roth briefed their leader and they came to Xander first.

She'd never been so happy to see a bevy of men with guns in her life.

FRIDAY

CHAPTER FIFTY-ONE

Denver, Colorado
Swedish Medical Center
Dr. Samantha Owens

Sam was reading in the soft sunlight flowing through the window of Xander's hospital room when the attendant came in with a plastic tray and cheerfully sang out, "Chow time!"

Xander gave her a hateful glance. "I don't want that. I want real food. Solid food." He turned to Sam. "Please, Sam, tell them to quit torturing me. If I see one more bowl of broth, I swear I'm going to—"

"You're going to what? Eat it? The broth is definitely in danger today, I can tell." Sam stood and went to the tray, which housed a bowl of clear broth and little else.

"You're feeling better?" the attendant asked.

"Yes," he growled. "Tell them I want actual food."

"I'll see if they'll let you have some Jell-O for dinner."

"Oh, goody."

"Xander, be nice to the girl. It isn't her fault you managed to get shot in the stomach and lost your spleen and part of your colon. These things take time to heal. At least they aren't forcing a feeding tube on you."

"But I'm starving."

"And that's an excellent sign. I've got it from here, Eunice."

The girl left with a grin, and Sam sat on the edge of Xander's bed and picked up the soup spoon. "Choo-choo or airplane today?"

His face turned puce. "Samantha Natalie Owens, if you dare, I will—"

She cut him off at the pass with a kiss, which placated him enough to take the spoon from her hand and feed himself.

He was banged up, his arm in a sling, his leg propped up, the drain coming out of the wound in his stomach. He was as stoic as they came and hadn't complained for a minute about the pain. It was the lack of food that had him griping.

He'd had a little bit of surgery to clean things up, and was already chomping at the bit to get out. The doctors promised he'd be released by the end of the weekend, assuming he continued to improve rapidly.

"You know," he said, between gulps of broth, "you never gave me an answer."

She narrowed her eyes at him.

"About?"

"You know what about. On the mountain, when I asked you to—"

There was a soft knocking on the door.

Xander grumbled, "Damn nurses."

Sam glanced over her shoulder and saw Fletcher standing there.

"Fletch!"

She jumped up off the bed and went to him, hugging him hard.

"Glad to see you're both okay. But God, you're a mess," he said.

Sam's hand went to her throat, which was black with bruises. She knew how bad it appeared; she had looked at the mirror in her bag once, then quietly put it away. She'd gotten lucky. They'd both gotten lucky.

"What are you doing here, Fletch? Aren't you busy wrapping things up in D.C.?"

"I am, but I volunteered to come out here and bring Loa Ledbetter to her daughter. She's decided she wants to try for custody, after everything that's happened. The people who adopted the girl, her name is Miranda but Carter called her Ruth, are coming out, as well. Apparently Carter kidnapped her last year. She's been in the missing person's database this whole time."

"At least they get to have a happy ending."

"That's true. This whole case has been screwed up from the get-go. But the upside is Carter is dead, and they recovered all of his equipment from the camp, including the stores of abrin he'd managed to make. He had enough explosives to take out a small city. Who knows how many other places he was going to hit."

"Are there more injuries from the blast in Boulder?"

"Seems not. Even though the bombs were laden with abrin, the explosion neutralized it. So instead of spreading it like he'd hoped, it was destroyed. And thank goodness, because if he'd managed to make it work, we'd have casualties on our hands."

"Small blessings," said Sam.

"Yeah. So good job to both of you for figuring out where he was. And since all that's taken care of, I needed to talk to Xander for a moment. Sam, would you excuse us?"

Xander shifted with a grimace.

"Let her stay. Whatever you have to say you can say in front of Sam."

Fletcher shrugged. "All right. Don't shoot the messenger. Alexander Whitfield, you are under arrest for the manslaughter killing of Ryan Carter. You have the right to remain silent. Anything you say can and will be used against you—"

"What the hell are you doing, Fletch?" Sam felt her blood pressure spike sharply. "How dare you try to arrest him? He saved my life. He stopped a madman."

"And killed a man in the process. He's not a cop, Sam. He's a civilian, and he's got to answer for his crime. I didn't want it to be like this, but trust me, it was going to be worse. I talked Bianco down off the ledge. She was going to send in the Denver police and have them cuff him to the bed. I talked her into letting me do this so we can handle it quietly. Don't worry. I'm sure things will work out in court."

"You have got to be kidding me," Sam spit at him.

"Hon, ratchet it back for a minute," Xander interrupted wearily. "He's partially right. I did kill a man, and I do have that on my conscience. But, Fletcher, I was acting in a legal capacity when I hit Carter with that arrow."

"How can that be?" Fletcher asked.

"Call Reed McReynolds. Police chief up in Dillon. He deputized me before we went up the mountain."

Fletcher raised an eyebrow. "You've got to be kidding me. What is this, the Wild West?"

Sam watched Xander grin and couldn't help smiling herself.

"Yes, it is. Especially when you're dealing with this much terrain, and crazy people. We did it just to be safe. I was happy to take that oath. I meant it. Every word."

"You did it to cover your ass. I told you I wanted him alive."

"He was about to kill Sam, Fletch. What did you want me to do?"

Fletcher gritted his teeth and breathed deeply to try and calm down.

"Off the record, I applaud what you did. But Bianco has her sights set on getting somebody behind bars."

"Well, I'm not willing to be her sacrificial lamb. But I can help you with something."

"What's that?"

"My friend Will Crawford. Sam saved his life up on the mountain. He now owes us one. And since you might be interested in the things he's been doing over the past few years, I thought you could arrest him, instead."

"What's he been doing?"

"He's a hacker," Sam said. "Used to work for the government, then turned on them. He's been buying and selling exceptionally sensitive information to the highest bidder. Ledbetter went into the Mountain Blue and Gray because she thought he was attached to them, and she was trying to track him down for the CIA. But it was Carter who was the link back to Crawford. He was the one she was after, though she didn't know it."

"That's insane."

"Insane, yes, but true," Xander said. "He's been hurt pretty badly, but right now, I think he saw God and maybe is having a change of heart. You arrest him quietly, instead of me, and I bet you can get him to turn on his entire organization."

Fletcher scratched his eyebrow.

"All right. I'll see if I can make something happen with it. But let me ask. Why would you be willing to sell him out?"

"I'm not selling him out. He did it to himself. If he's spawning any more followers like this Ryan Carter character, he needs to be shut down. I didn't say he was my friend because I agreed with him. It's more that he's someone I've known my whole life. And if he's inciting this kind of hatred, he needs to be stopped."

Fletcher nodded. "I agree."

They were quiet for a moment, then Sam decided a change of topic was in order before Fletcher reconsidered.

"So what about the rest, Fletch?"

"Well, we're still working on how Carter managed to dose the cigarettes and the inhaler, but since the congressman's briefcase was 'missing' for a time and found at his house, we think Carter must have broken in and planted the tainted inhaler. We think that the Metro attack might have gotten Leighton worried, and in his stress he felt like he needed a shot of the inhaler. His wife told me he used it multiple times a day—apparently his lungs were totally shot."

"I saw a report that she's running for his seat in the special election."

"That's right. I went by her place last night, and she told me she was going to run. Told me a bunch of interesting things, actually. We were trying to figure out why Carter hit the reproductive center in Boulder—he had so many to choose from, why that one?"

"That did cross my mind," Xander said.

"Turns out that's where the Leightons were doing their in vitro. It's one of the best clinics in the country, really cutting-edge technology, and Gretchen Leighton only wanted the best. After their son died, she wanted another child, but Leighton said no. When she found out about Ledbetter, that he had an illegitimate daughter, she put her foot down. The procedures were supposed to happen this week. We assume, since Carter was stalking her, he was aware of their plans, and tried to completely eliminate any chance they had at having another child. A completely perverted way to show his love to Loa."

Loa. The pawn in all of this, along with her poor daughter.

"How's Ledbetter taking it all? She's lost a mother, a father and the father of her child."

Fletch shook his head. "She's incredibly pragmatic. She knew he was bad news, that he was gearing up for something. He'd been emailing and calling lately, trying to touch base. She was scared to death of him, but she had no idea that he had any of this planned to woo her with."

"What about the text? Did you ever figure out who sent it?" Sam asked.

"We are still waiting for the paperwork to clear the service provider. I am starting to think it was a hoax, just a crazy reaching out. There's no evidence of texts sent to Leighton from any of the players we've nailed down, so…

"The first funerals are tomorrow, Dr. Ledbetter and Marc Conlon, one after the other at the Washington Cathedral. Leighton's service is Monday, and there will be some typical D.C. pomp and circumstance around it."

"I don't know if we'll have Xander cleared to travel yet or not. But if we can, we'll be there."

Fletcher looked at her. "There's only one outstanding problem. Outside of me having to explain to Bianco why Xander isn't in custody and me having to go to the A.G.'s office and get sworn affidavits that you actually were deputized."

"It won't be a problem, Fletcher. I promise," Xander said.

"Good."

"What's the problem?" Sam asked.

"Remember the DNA match from the Indiana killings?"

"Yes, of course. Did the second DNA test eliminate Leighton as a suspect?"

"Not exactly."

Sam felt the shock on her face. "What? I thought you were sure it was Glenn Temple, the chief of staff, who committed the murders."

"I did, too. This is between us for now, okay? No, the new DNA came back, and it was a match to Peter Leighton."

"So Leighton was the killer?"

"Not exactly. It was a *familial* match."

Xander and Sam looked at each other. "Who was it?" Sam asked, but then realized who it was. A legitimate mistake in the lab, if two men shared the same name.

Peter Leighton, Junior.

"The DNA showed it was the congressman's son who was the killer. We think that's why they shipped him off to the Army. To curb his unnatural tastes. And of course, he died, and there hasn't been a murder on record that matches the M.O. since. We have a request in with his unit, asking about his behavior. Making sure there are no more victims. But it looks like the case is now solved."

"But what about Glenn Temple?"

"Temple's just another guy. Prickly, but outside of using a false name, innocent. We confronted him, to tell him we knew what he was up to, and found him packing for a trip. He was heading back to Indiana to start laying the groundwork with the state for the special election. Gretchen Leighton is a shoe-in. He's going to be her chief of staff."

"Wow. God, Fletch. I can't believe all of this happened in such a short period of time. Are you going to stay at the JTTF?"

"Oh, hell no. The minute the ink is dry on this case I am back to my ho-humdrum life at Metro, and I can't wait. I don't need the glory. And I certainly don't need the drama. Give me a simple, straightforward murder any day."

He glanced at his watch. "Hey, I have to go. Let me know if you get sprung and want a ride back to D.C. I've got the JTTF plane, and I can get you on it. I'll be here until tomorrow. You've got my number. Feel better, Xander."

He stood, and a look passed over his face. It hurt him to see her with Xander, but she couldn't help that. Sam got up and hugged him again, extra hard, and said, "I'll give you a call."

He just nodded and tipped his finger to his forehead, then left.

Sam watched his retreating back, then crossed her arms and looked at Xander.

"Unreal," he said.

"Completely."

"So, Sam. We were interrupted."

"Xander, let's get you mobile, first. Then we can talk. All right?"

He looked deep into her eyes, searching for some sort of sign that she wasn't rejecting him. She smiled and kissed him, and for now, that was enough.

CHAPTER FIFTY-TWO

Savage River
Dr. Samantha Owens

Xander was discharged from the hospital on Monday, and they went back to Dillon until he was cleared to travel a few days later. Despite his parents' protests, Xander was adamant. He wanted to go home.

They flew into National on a commercial flight and Sam drove them into the mountains, to the cabin in the woods. Thor was overwhelmed to see them, jumping and barking and turning in circles. Xander was gimping around on crutches, his arm wound making it difficult, but not impossible, to keep the weight off his leg.

It was hard to believe it had been less than a week since the attacks. Everything felt different. Not as innocent. Like her free time in D.C. was over, and real life was back. In another month, she'd start teaching at Georgetown, opening yet another chapter in her life.

Sam got Xander settled, and despite his protestations to the contrary, he was asleep within minutes. She walked Thor and enjoyed the feeling of freedom that came with this whole mess being behind them.

She sat on the porch and watched the sun traverse the sky. After a while, Xander woke and joined her, and they sat in a happy, contented silence, Sam swinging in the chair, Xander on his bench, petting Thor.

When the air began to cool, Sam shivered and said, "Let's get away from all of this. From the mountains, from D.C., from everything."

Xander gave her an amused look.

"You know you can't run away."

"I'm not talking running away as much as an escape. Something completely antithetical to everything. Someplace you've never been. Anywhere."

"Where do you want to go?"

"I'd say the beach, but I can't imagine you lying quietly in a chaise longue for more than a day without getting totally bored. So what about New York?"

"New York?"

"We can get lost there, Xander. Lost in the crowds, in Central Park, the museums. We can have a little vacation."

"A vacation. In New York. With millions of other people looming over our shoulders. And me on crutches."

"Consider it…desensitization."

He smiled. "Let's walk."

He grabbed her hand, and she helped him up. He used her under one arm, and the other crutch in his good hand. They started walking, slowly, around the yard. It was the best way for him to regain his strength. She couldn't believe she'd nearly lost him. She half wanted to run away, so it could never happen again, and half wanted to throw him to the ground, feel the grass under her legs and take him for her own.

After ten minutes, they started back toward the house.

"All right. I'll be able to walk without these in a day or two. Let's go to New York. Why not?"

"Why not, indeed."

"I've never been, you know."

"To New York? Seriously?"

"Just one of those things. I'd like to see Brooklyn. And the Bronx. Oh, and maybe a Yankees game?"

"Mets."

"Yankees."

"Uh-oh." Sam laughed. "This may be an insurmountable issue."

"Well, why don't we just agree on the Red Sox, and be done with it."

"Red Sox? My God, next you're going to tell me you like the Cubs."

"I do." He held his right hand to his heart, and they were both laughing now. The sun began to slip behind the trees, and Thor bounded ahead of them, racing back and forth with a stick in his mouth. The scent of jasmine and pine grew heavy on the wind, and Sam sighed, deeply, completely and totally content.

They managed to get up the steps to the porch, and Sam stopped and turned to look down the mountain. Everything was in its summer bloom, coated with the dusky sunset, and she didn't think she'd ever seen a prettier place.

"On second thought," she said, eyebrow cocked. "We could just watch the games from bed. Though you'd have to buy a television."

Xander pulled her hand to his mouth, lightly resting her skin on his lips. "You hussy. Teasing me with dreams of Yankee Stadium, then whisking them away." But he kissed the inside of her wrist and, with the dog barking joyfully behind them, they went inside.

★ ★ ★ ★ ★

ACKNOWLEDGMENTS

My village expands. I couldn't do this without them. Thanks to:

My dear agent, Scott Miller, who goes above and beyond all the time; My lovely new editor, Miranda Indrigo, whose well-placed touches made this book so much stronger and my former editor Adam Wilson, who loved this idea from the get-go; My intrepid publicist Tiffany Shiu, who earns her cookies; Everyone at Harlequin Mira, especially Valerie Gray and Margaret Marbury, who are such a joy to work with; and Sean Kapitain and Tara Scarcello in the art department, who've crafted such a gorgeous look for Sam's books. My team at Brilliance Audio, especially Sheryl Zajechowski, Natalie Fedewa and the amazing Joyce Bean, make the written word come alive.

Without regular contact with the following people I would surely go insane: Laura Benedict, Jeff Abbott, Erica Spindler, Allison Brennan, Alex Kava, Deb Carlin, Jeanne Veillette Bowerman, Jill Thompson, Del Tinsley, Paige Crutcher, Cecelia Tichi, Alethea Kontis, Jason Pinter and Andy Levy. Y'all are the best.

Sophie Littlefield, for the cello concertos and the best road trip ever.

Joan Huston who played the role of comma cop with aplomb.

Sherrie Saint, the woman whose brain is a scary, scary place, helped so much—from the abrin to Godzilla. I have never enjoyed a Starbucks date quite like our afternoon in Franklin discussing cow necropsies.

Dr. Sandra Thomas guided me through the proper terminology for Sam's scenes at the morgue. Frothy is all her fault. As always, mistakes are my own.

Two lovely young ladies gave money to charity to appear in this novel—Loa Ledbetter—Loa, I hope I got the hair, and your spirit, right. And my friend Andrea Bianco, who helped me get into a lot of fun and trouble in junior high. Thank you both for trusting me to do crazy things with your names.

Huge thanks to all the incredible librarians and independent booksellers and book reps who have been recommending my titles. Without you I would be lost. And a special shout out to the fine folks on Facebook and Twitter, who keep me honest.

A lot of research went into this novel—and several websites and books helped tremendously. I would be remiss if I didn't single out SurvivalCache.com, which ended up being a daily resource. If you're interested in "prepping" or simply some common sense precautions to take if you live in a nasty weather zone, I highly recommend getting to know Joel and the crew.

Finally, I must say thank you to my family. To my mom, who cheers me on daily, and my daddy, who takes me golfing to get away from the stress of writing. And as always, for Randy, who never seems to tire of hearing various plot points over dinner, no matter how bizarre. I love you, honey. And I like you a lot, too.

A man has been found shot dead at the side of the road.

The police believe he's a carjacking victim.

Medical examiner Dr Samantha Owens knows it's murder.

The victim is Sam's old boyfriend, ex-army Ranger Eddie Donovan, and she has evidence to support her claim—four little words written on a slip of paper delivered to Eddie before he died: DO THE RIGHT THING.